I0536478

The Libram of Fate

Mark Cole

This is a work of fiction. All characters and events portrayed in this book are fictitious, and any resemblance to real people or events is purely coincidental.

THE LIBRAM OF FATE

Copyright © 2013 Mark Cole

All rights reserved.

Edited by Janet Taylor-Perry and Lottie Brent Boggan
Cover art by GoOnWrite.com

ISBN: 0692239677

ISBN-13: 978-0692239674

First edition: December 2013

10 9 8 7 6 5 4 3 2

To Mom and Dad and Dad.
There aren't words for what I wish I could say,
so you'll just have to make do with these.
Thank you.
I love you.

Table of Contents

Prologue – The Penning

--Ninety-nine thousand years ago--

"You are sure this is the wisest course of action, Keeper?" Ureon asked, her wings in a protective shroud.

The Keeper of Fate looked about the Amphitheater of High Seats to all those assembled. "Brothers and sisters, I have seen eons come and go, stars born, burn, and die, and stared into the heart of the Void. Yes, I am sure," the ancient angel said, his powerful voice resonating in the Amphitheater of the High Seats.

The final page of the Libram of Fate lay open before the Angelic Council. Holding his sleeve back, he dipped the quill into the inkwell.

"But," Ureon protested, "she will be your daughter."

The Keeper removed the quill from the inkwell and set the feather in its holder with delicate care. He knew the doubts Ureon voiced were likely shared by many of the council.

Taking care to look each in the eye as he spoke, the Keeper said, "I am aware. There is no other conclusion to this Libram of Fate. All of the signs have pointed to this end. I do not understand why you all protest."

"You have never had children, Keeper," she said. "You do not understand the pain you will cause yourself."

The Keeper nodded and clasped his hands behind his back. "Of that, I am also aware. Concern yourself for me not. I will not allow a child to stand in the way of duty. This must be done. My daughter's death will be the catalyst that pushes him to the pinnacle he must reach before the end."

"Very well," Ureon said. "Finish the Penning, Keeper. And may this Guardian forgive what you have done."

The Keeper lifted the quill and brought it to the final page of the Libram of Fate.

On the day of Magic's triumph, the Nexus shall fall and a wrathful Guardian rise in her place to lead the Nine to balance.

--Today--

Josh cased the little electronics store in downtown Seattle. *Where's the owner?* the nineteen-year-old thought, growing agitated. He flicked his head to get some of the shaggy black hair out of his eyes.

The shops were just beginning to close and turn off lights up and down the street, but the vagrant had chosen this store because it stayed open thirty minutes longer than all the others nearby. His stomach rumbled. *I gotta get some cash.*

The homeless teenager touched the shotgun under his ragged trench coat. Josh couldn't believe his good fortune at finding the gun behind a dumpster. He had used the last of his money to buy a loaf of bread and some sandwich meat ten days ago. *I should have bought some shells for the shotgun. I was just so hungry...*

Josh saw the shop's owner walk from the back. The guy was huge, but it wasn't the first time the young man had seen him. He took his hand from the shotgun and jogged across the street. There was a jingle as he pushed open the door to the shop.

The owner had his back turned to the door. "Welcome to Max's," the big man said in a deep voice. "There something I can help you with?"

"Sure," Josh said, his voice shaking. "Just looking right now."

"Sounds good," Max said. "Let me know if you see anything you like."

"I will." Josh acted like he was browsing along the wall of computer accessories as he worked his way toward the register. The shotgun shifted against his leg, and Josh darted a hand over to it to hold it in place. He looked over to see if the owner had noticed the movement, but the big man was gone. *Where the hell did he go?*

"You don't want to do this, kid," a deep voice said from behind him. Josh spun, drawing the shotgun as he did, but a large hand caught the barrel. The young man stared into the owner's eyes and gulped.

Max ripped the shotgun from his hands and turned it over, inspecting the weapon. "You didn't even turn off the damn safety." He worked the pump a couple times, and no rounds came out. The big man narrowed his brown eyes and glared at Josh. "I don't know if you are really brave or really stupid, trying to rob a place with an unloaded weapon."

"A bit of both," Josh said. His stomach rumbled again, and the big man sighed. *Why's he sighing?*

"No," Max said. "I'm going to go with desperate. When's the last time you ate, kid?"

Josh wasn't sure. "Haven't eaten anything that's not from a garbage can in the last few days," he said. "You going to call the cops?"

"Why? Have you committed a crime?"

"I guess not," Josh admitted. *Good job, idiot. Your first heist, and you lose your meal ticket.*

3

Max muttered something under his breath about knowing better. "You have a place to sleep?"

"Yeah."

The muscular man grabbed Josh by the shoulder and sat him down behind the counter where he couldn't easily escape. Max put the confiscated shotgun beneath the counter next to an all black, much nicer looking one. "One with a roof, bathroom, and kitchen?"

Josh was silent for a moment. *Place like that takes money.* He shook his head.

Max sighed again. "You have any clothes other than the ones you have on? It sure as hell smells like you've been living in a trash can, not just eating out of one."

"I got a black shirt, but no more pants."

"You have parents?"

Josh's face went blank, and he shook his head. He had bounced from foster home to foster home until he hit sixteen and ran away. He had had a job as a dish boy for a while, but the restaurant had closed.

Max rubbed his bald head. "You have an ID and Social Security Number?"

Frowning, Josh asked, "Why's it matter?"

The man crossed his arms and glared at him. "Answer the damn question, or I *will* call the cops."

"Yeah," Josh said. Max held out his hand, and Josh pulled out his beaten-up leather wallet and handed it to him.

Max flipped open the wallet and looked at the cards. He pulled out the ID, set it on the counter, and handed Josh his wallet back. The man pushed a button on the register, and it opened with a ding. He pulled out a few bills and handed them to the young man.

"I don't accept handouts," Josh said with a frown.

The owner slammed the drawer closed, and Josh jumped. "It's not a handout; it's an advance. One half week's salary after taxes. You know the supermarket two streets down?" The younger man said he did. "Get down there and buy some clean clothes and food, and then get your ass back here. I'm keeping your ID, Joshua Hrynkiewicz, as insurance."

Josh stared at the man as if he was insane. "Why are you doing this?"

Holding up two sausage-like fingers, Max said, "Two reasons: I need some help around the shop, and I think you need help getting your shit together. Now go."

Josh stood and walked out of the store. He could have left his ID and run off with the money, but the thought never really occurred to him. It wasn't until he gone all the way to the supermarket that he realized how much money the big man had given him. *Three hundred bucks!*

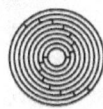

Max rubbed his eyes and stood up. *Where the hell are you, Alex?* he thought as he took the rest of the cash from the register. Max Gilroy dropped the money in a small blue banker's pouch and deposited it in his safe beneath the floor in his shop. There was another smaller safe he kept unlocked that only held a hundred dollars, just in case of break-ins and robberies that went south.

That kid's probably not coming back, he thought as he locked the hidden safe and covered it back with the carpet square. Max walked to the front door and locked it. He walked around the small shop and started shutting down computers.

"What is this world coming to?" he asked no one. "This is the second time in three months." The last time someone had broken into the shop and stolen the contents of his smaller safe. The robber would have stolen his stock too, if all the computers weren't bolted down and the new-in-box ones ordered from a warehouse with each sale. Max had been out of town trying to search out Alex, but it had been to no avail. It was as if the other man had fallen off the face of the Earth.

As far as I know, he's dead in a ditch somewhere with his girlfriend, but if he was leaving, he could of at least left a note. Door kicked in to his apartment but nothing missing. No signs of a struggle, and the cops weren't a lick of help. Whatever... I hope I did the right thing by telling the apartment complex that they should just repair the door and keep the apartment under his name as long as he kept paying for it. If he's dead, he won't need the money, and if he's alive, he'll need a place to stay when he gets back.

A knock on the glass stirred Max from his reverie. Joshua Hrynkiewicz was standing outside, holding a few very full shopping bags. *Well, I'll be damned if I stand by and let the world go to complete shit. At least I can help one person.*

Chapter One – Victory City

Terra Duval took a deep breath. The smell of rot was strongest around Ygg, the World Tree. She flaked the decaying tree bark from her hand, and touched her husband's sword that she wore on her back. She surveyed her surroundings; everywhere her eyes landed they were met with death and putrescence. It suited her mood well.

"I think this is what caused everything to die," Caitlyn Shadowpaw said, holding up a shard of obsidian. "It was jammed into one of the roots not far from here." The Changeling of the Fang's golden eyes studied Terra with concern as she walked over and handed her the stone.

Terra Duval, the Nexus, Paragon of the Realm of Magic, held the inert piece of the Obsidian Tower. Fifteen days ago, her husband destroyed the seat of power the Overlord Azreal had on Dae. When Alex razed the tower, the anti-magic shards, which were imbued with the power to block one's magical ability, stopped working. They were born from the Obsidian Tower, and with its destruction, their energy ceased.

The Nexus gave the shard a perfunctory inspection then squeezed it as hard as she could. It cracked loudly in her grip and crumbled to dust. Caitlyn gave her a curious look. "It was too small to do what we needed. There is nothing we can do here. At least we now know why the sprites never came to our aid."

"They were one with the World Tree," Caitlyn said. "Beings of pure magical energy, it's no wonder they couldn't stop the shard from corrupting Ygg."

"We should return to the capital," Terra told her. "The council will want to hear this."

The changeling nodded and let out a deep sigh.

"What is it?" Terra asked.

7

"Wait a moment," Caitlyn said. "There's something I feel I need to do." She dropped to her hands and knees, and Terra watched as her green shirt and pants turned black and changed into fur.

The changeling's bones and sinew snapped as she changed into the primal form the sprites had awoken in her when last they were here. Her fingers drew into her palms and nails lengthened into claws several inches long. She howled in pain as spikes grew from the each vertebra in her spine. Her tailbone stretched into a tail many feet long. Caitlyn's jaw cracked and formed a black muzzle, and her canine teeth elongated into prodigious fangs.

Born a panther, Caitlyn was the only changeling on Dae that could change into three forms: her birth form, her human form, and the primal form she now assumed. "When you first gave me this ability," the changeling told the specters of the past, "I treated it as something dangerous had been forced upon me. But now, I finally understand. You sprites were doing what you thought best to defend the home we all share. I thank you now, like I should have over a month ago. You will all be remembered."

Caitlyn lifted her head to the sky and issued forth a mournful howl. She faced Terra. "I'm done. Let's go."

Terra nodded and opened a portal to return them to Victory City. Caitlyn padded through the hole in space with Terra close behind. The portal closed, leaving an eerie silence in the once vibrant marsh. At the roots of Ygg, a small, green sprout pushed through the earth.

Dust filled the air around her as Terra stepped through the portal to Victory City. The racket of construction and calls of men ordering supplies was jarring after the relative quiet of the Wraith Marshes. She watched as a slab of marble was floated into position and magically mounted to the foundation of what would soon become the base of the new gateway arch. The early spring sun warmed the air enough for her to take off the black jacket she wore.

Sunlight glittered through a crystalline statue across the clearing designated for travelling magic. Terra strode to the monument. She cared not for the fine details in his sword and armor, though she had been the one to put them there when she had created the statue. Her eyes were locked on the face of the man she had immortalized in magically created diamond. The Nexus placed a shaking hand on the statue of her late husband.

The twelve-foot statue towered above her. Alex Zane stood, clad in plate from the neck down, pointing a sword to the east. Terra had ordered the main avenue run east to west along his blade so he would shine with the rising and setting sun.

Alex was the Guardian of Balance, a man from Earth who was born when the Nine Realms were thrown out of equilibrium. Terra had been captured by Azreal, a powerful Demon Lord and the Overlord of Hell, and Alex led an army to the Obsidian Tower to save her. Alex succeeded in rescuing her, killing Azreal, and destroying the demon's tower, but not before Terra and Caitlyn had sustained grave injury at the Overlord's hands.

"Be quiet so I can heal you," Alex said.
"No," I told him with a limp shake of my head. "You will die."

"I don't care about that," he said, almost yelling. "I won't just stand here and watch you die!"

"And I won't watch you die either. I would rather die with you than live without you." I waved my hand toward Caitlyn, so he would see her and understand. I was so tired, so weak. It was hard to talk.

Alex had unleashed the birthright none of them knew he had and used his powers as a half-demon, half-human hybrid to heal Caitlyn, taking the changelings wounds into him.

"Will she live?" I asked him as everything began to go dark. Alex nodded. I asked him if he would kiss me one last time, before it was all over. He dropped to his knees beside me, placed his hand on my stomach, and gently kissed me. I couldn't keep my eyes open any longer, and the looming darkness swallowed me.

Then there was light, warm, blinding, and beautiful. My eyes opened, and he had healed me.

But healing her had come at a terrible price. Alex died so she might live.

Terra let her hand slip from the statue and placed it over her womb, where their child grew inside her. *He saved us, Jessica,* she thought to her unborn child. *He gave his life to save us.* Terra kissed the tips of her fingers and touched them to the statue of the man that had given them all a second chance.

"I love you, Alex," she whispered. Terra turned to see Caitlyn talking with Brahm Ironfist a short distance away. The dwarf, used to the constant heat of Adorac Volcano, wore a heavy, blue long-sleeved shirt and thick black pants.

"How're ye holdin' up?" the dwarf asked as Terra drew near.

"I'm alive, Brahm," she said, her voice hollow. "How are you?"

The grizzled graybeard nodded. "I am well." He looked behind her at Alex's statue. "I miss him, too."

"I know," Terra said. "The council's waiting on us, I'm sure." She led them to the large tent still being used as the council chambers. Victory City stood where the Obsidian Tower had once dominated the landscape.

Victory Construction Site is a more apt name, Terra thought as she looked around. Marble and granite blocks, some more than fifty feet in length, were strewn about with no apparent coordination. Groups of four stonemasons used magical power to hew perfectly sized stones from the tremendous blocks. More masons used cushions of air to place them and infinitesimal lines of fire to fuse them in place. The housing was coming along at a steady pace. Soon, there would be room enough for people to begin settling in Victory City and start anew.

The construction groups paused as the trio walked past. Eyes stared at Caitlyn, still in her primal form.

"Did ye run into trouble while ye were in the marshes?" Terra overheard Brahm ask Caitlyn.

"No," the changeling answered. "There was nothing alive there. It's more a swamp than a marsh, now. The World Tree has died." The sharp crack of bones and hiss of pain brought Terra's head about. Caitlyn was back in her natural panther form. They continued walking, and the stares ceased.

"What do that mean fer Dae?" Brahm asked.

"I don't know," Terra said loudly enough to be heard over the construction. "That's why we need to meet with the rest of the council. We need to see if Silvia has had a vision that could be of help."

"Aye, we do." Brahm's voice dropped to a low mutter as he continued talking to Caitlyn. Terra let it go on for a few moments. She knew what they were discussing.

"Please don't talk about me like I'm not here," the Nexus said, anger seeping into her voice.

The conversation stopped, and they walked in relative silence for a time. A master stonemason shouting at his apprentice for some error or another stopped when he saw Terra pass. "I'm sorry for your loss," the older mason said as she walked by.

Terra looked at him over her shoulder and nodded acknowledgement. *Five years ago, they despised me. Now they feel sorry for me.* She felt anger begin to gnaw at her. Taking a deep breath to steady herself, she fed her anger into the void of emotion she had plunged herself into since Alex died.

I did die with him that day, Terra thought. *And only one thing can restore me to life.* They drew clear of the construction and approached the council tent. She held the flap open for her two concerned friends. *Vengeance.* The flap closed behind her as she followed them in.

Caitlyn looked from Terra to her biological sister, Silvia. The two women were locked in an argument, and the uncomfortable tension made Caitlyn sit still as stone.

"I don't think we should risk attacking again so soon," Silvia Shadowpaw, the Fanglady and leader of the Changelings of the Fang, said. "We need some time to rest, recover, and train soldiers. Not to mention we have no idea what the World Tree's death will mean for our world." Caitlyn's sister sat regally on her wooden tent chair as if it were the marble seat their mother had held when the Arcane City still stood. Her thick, black hair hung just below her shoulders, and her yellow eyes shown with conviction.

"I understand that," Terra said. "But we should strike while the iron is hot. Azreal's forces are still reeling from the blow we dealt them here. It'll be a week before the gateway arch is built and will take another ten days to imbue it with the necessary magic to create gates. Seventeen days must be enough time."

"To train an army? Terra, you know that isn't realistic. I know you only just lost him, but you are letting your grief..." Silvia stopped talking when she saw the glare leveled at her.

"Don't, Fanglady," the Nexus said, changing the tone of the conversation to one of complete formality. "We will attack as soon as the gateway arch is ready."

King Harbronn, King of the Dwarves, cleared his throat. He wore his crown of thorium and gold and spoke over steepled fingers. "Nexus, I do think the Fanglady's correct in her reasonin'. What'd happen if we marched the army to battle? Who'd defend Dae? I do no' need remind ye that Dae do no' have a global groundin' field like the other Realms do, save Earth. Azreal's forces could gate back in anywhere an' with no army to fight 'em off, we would lose all the ground we've gained."

"We don't have one, *yet*," Terra said. The five other council members, Caitlyn, and Brahm looked at her curiously. She reached down and lifted a small brown leather sack she had tied to her belt. The contents clinked like glass as she it down. She upended the sack and four midnight-black obsidian shards tumbled out onto the table. Frowns replaced curiosity as the council realized what the crystals were.

The Winglord Aeryn Steelfeather, leader of the Changelings of the Wing, pushed back the sleeves of his thin leather tunic, picked up one of the foot-long stones and held it with a delicate grip. "Anti-magic shards?" he asked.

"Yes," Terra said. "Azreal used them to nullify magic, but I think they can amplify it. With these, I can create a grounding field that will force all gateway magic through the arch."

That's why she was searching for larger shards, Caitlyn thought. *Why didn't she ask me to help her, instead of keeping me in the dark?*

"How?" Bahamut, the Scalelord, asked in his deep bass rumble.

"By imbuing them with the required magical energy, I can create a resonance field that will tremendously increase the grounding field's coverage," Terra said.

Harbronn cleared his throat. "Ye lost me on that last bit, Nexus. Wouldn't that just make it where we can no' use gateway magic at all?"

"A resonance field amplifies the power of any spell constructed of the same magical energy that the field has. The grounding field prevents the use of teleportation and planar travel inside its borders."

"Aye," King Harbronn said. "If ye made a huge groundin' field, then we'd no' be able to teleport or use gateways."

"That's right. We would be unable to use any type of instantaneous travel anywhere on Dae," Terra said. Protests erupted around the table, but she silenced them with a hand. "But if I were to invert the grounding field at the gateway arch, it would increase the total range of the field and allow travel to and from that one point to anywhere on Dae and the other planes."

Inversion? Caitlyn thought. *What moldy old tome did she dig that up in?*

"That only solves one problem, Nexus," the leader of the Changelings of the Scale noted. Bahamut's red eyes, slit with vertical pupils, stared deep into Terra's hazel. "What would prevent someone from simply opening a portal here and flooding an army through?"

"A keystone seal, like the one the angels of Bara have, would prevent anyone from coming through without the keystone in place," Terra said.

"And how do you plan on getting a keystone seal?" Chieftain Rageclaw, the Clawlord, asked. He was in his bear form and loomed above the others seated at the table. "Last we heard, Bara was still under siege by a horde of demons and undead."

"Exactly," Terra said. "The last we heard was five years ago. We need to send a scouting party to the Realm of Good and find if the angels still stand."

"Who're ye plannin' on sendin' on this insane mission?" King Harbronn asked.

"I don't plan on sending anyone," the Nexus said with grim determination. "I plan on going." Objections were shouted around the table. "Silence!" she shouted over the clamor. "I am the Paragon of the Realm of Magic, and this is my plan."

I love you, Sister, but you can't do this, Caitlyn thought. The changeling had kept silent long enough. "That's why it's a terrible idea." She rose to all four and padded to Terra. She lowered her voice so that only the Nexus could hear. "Please, adjourn this meeting so I can talk to you in private. I'm worried about you."

Terra gritted her teeth and looked to be on the verge of ignoring her. "Fine," the Nexus muttered.

She raised her voice and spoke to the five council members. "I will hold my decision in abeyance, but we will meet again this time tomorrow." The council members stood and filed from the tent. Terra put her head in her hands and let out a slow breath.

Caitlyn watched as Brahm put a hand on Terra's shoulder.

"Does it ever stop?" the Nexus asked.

"Ye know the answer to yer question as well as I, Terra," Brahm said. "Did ye ever truly stop missin' Michael after he died sendin' ye to Earth?"

Tears dripped onto the collapsible oak table. "No," she choked out, "but after a while it started to hurt less."

"Aye, that it does." The old dwarf wrapped his friend in a fatherly hug. "And this pain too shall pass."

A few moments of silence elapsed as Brahm comforted Terra. Caitlyn climbed onto the table, and she nuzzled her cheek against the crying woman's.

Terra took a few deep breaths and composed herself before leaning back. She wiped away her tears and looked at Caitlyn with red-rimmed eyes. The changeling studied her adopted sister's hazel irises. "I'm going to Bara in your stead."

"No," Terra said without hesitation. "It's my idea. Not yours."

"Why did Alex save your life?" Caitlyn asked, anger seeping into her voice.

"Caitlyn," Brahm admonished. "Don't…"

Terra's face went blank. Caitlyn waited, but there was no answer forthcoming. "Why Terra? Why, after healing me, did Alex save your life too?"

"Because of the baby," Terra said, her breathing becoming rapid. "He saved me so our child could live."

"And you would risk all of that, just on the off-chance you *might* be able to find some way to either get or make a keystone seal. He saved you so you could raise his child." Caitlyn's eyes flicked to the hilt of the Guardian's Blade sticking up above Terra's shoulder. "So you could have something of him other than that cursed sword.

"*The Guardian's Blade*," Caitlyn spat out the name as she looked into her friend's eyes. "If he hadn't died bringing us back, that damnable sword would have killed him as surely as a knife to the heart. You didn't see him as we drew near the Obsidian Tower, Terra. He wasn't sure who he was half the time. He was talking to Brahm as if they had gone on adventures across the sea together. The previous Guardians' memories were killing him. You should find some hole and bury that sword deep."

Terra shook her head, almost panting. Sweat beaded on her brow, and she trembled. "I can't do that." Her eyes unfocussed, and her head swayed. "I killed him. I gave him the blade, Caitlyn. He gave me a child, and I killed him. I... I can't... Breathe..." Terra's eyes rolled back in her sockets, and Brahm caught her before her head slammed to the table.

"Stay with her," Caitlyn shouted as she leapt from the table and flew out of the tent. "I need a healer!"

Chapter Two – Innocence Lost

"Hanna's takin' care o' Terra," Brahm said. Caitlyn nodded. She had changed into her human form. Leaning against some boxes near the council tent, she watched the setting sun make Alex's statue glow with orange light. "The girl said she'd recover, but that she's no' quite sure what happened."

"I know what happened," Caitlyn said. "I got angry and pushed her over the edge." She looked around to make sure none could overhear. "Do you know what it's like to miss someone you loved, to have a hole in your chest, and not be allowed to talk to anyone about it?"

Brahm sighed and rubbed his hand down his face and gray beard. "Come with me, Cat. It helps to talk abou' these things." He led her a short distance away to a cook pit that wasn't being used. He sat with a groan. "Me old bones're not getting any better with age."

Caitlyn snickered. "I seem to remember your 'old bones' fighting demons quite well just a few weeks ago." Brahm shrugged, and Caitlyn watched him struggle over how to begin. She turned to watch the last of the day's light leave the statue of the man she shouldn't have fallen in love with.

"When did ye first realize ye loved 'im?" Brahm asked.

"Just before I fought Rageclaw," she replied, her thoughts elsewhere. Caitlyn realized what the wizened dwarf had said and whipped her head about to stare at him.

"I'm old," the dwarf grumped, "no' stupid. I saw how ye looked at 'im. Alex did no' love you back?"

Caitlyn shook her head. "He thought of me as a little sister."

"As he should've. When did ye start havin' feelin's fer Alex?"

"From the very beginning, I guess. I felt drawn to Alex the first time I saw him. He stood there, facing down a panther with a wooden sword," she said, a sad smile on her face in the encroaching gloom. "He would have charged through the gate to Dae alone for the woman he loved. He was confused and afraid, even if he wouldn't admit it, but the determination that burned in his eyes... Alex would have gone to the gates of Hell and beyond for her. And woe unto any who stood in his way."

"Ye feel that because he ne'er returned yer love ye're more entitled to be angry about his death?"

"What? No! I don't feel that way at all."

Brahm rose to his feet and walked to her. "Then what were ye bloody thinkin' tearin' into Terra abou' the flamin' Guardian's Blade? Ye bloody well know she's barely keepin' it together."

The dwarf's brown eyes bored into hers. Brahm towered over her. When she could bear his glare no longer, Caitlyn closed her eyes and lowered her head. "I just... I hated seeing how he was near the end. He wasn't himself, Brahm. That damn sword did it to him, and I lost control of my temper. I didn't mean to say all those things. To hurt Terra like I did."

Brahm let out a sigh and knelt in front of her. He lifted her chin, and Caitlyn looked into his eyes. "I know ye didn't, Cat. Ye need to realize that Alex was no' the first person Terra's lost. She's in a deep, dark place now. Both men she's loved have died, violently, in front o' her. Ye do no' go through somethin' like that an' forget abou' it."

"I'm sorry," the changeling said.

"It's no' me ye need to be apologizin' to."

Caitlyn nodded and rose to her feet. "Let's go see if Hanna is done with Terra."

The baby seems fine.   A little small though. Something is strange about her womb, Hanna thought. The seven-year-old Changeling of the Wing rubbed her eyes.   She had been up all day tending the few still recovering from the Siege on the Obsidian Tower.

The remaining wounded were infected with the undead necrosis, but she had come up with a way to prevent the disease's spread through their body. Mistress Therese said Hanna was the most gifted healer she had ever seen, and that the men were alive because of her.   *It isn't enough though, they can't return to their families until I find a cure.*

"A penny for your thoughts," the Nexus said.

"Your baby is fine," Hanna said.   "It's hard to tell because of the protective magic and energy around her, but I'm pretty sure she's okay, Nexus."

"Thank you. Please, call me Terra."

"I'm not sure I should, Nexus. I don't think that would be proper."

Terra laughed. "I insist, but only if you let me call you Hanna."

Hanna smiled. "All right... Terra."

"Caitlyn told me you knew Alex."

"I did," she said.   "He was very nice to me. I was sad when I heard he had died. If only I had been closer then maybe I could have done something for him." Hanna stifled her tears. *This was his wife, Dummy. Don't make her feel worse.* "I'm sorry. I didn't mean to..." She didn't know what to say.

"No, Hanna, it's not your fault. His death was no one's fault. Fate conspired against us all," Terra said, but her tone belied her true feelings.

She blames herself, Hanna thought. *I can't heal her with magic, but maybe there's something I could say to make her feel better.* "Do you really believe that?" Terra hesitated a moment before nodding.

"It isn't good to lie to your healer," Hanna said.

Terra studied the little girl. "How old are you?"

"Just because I'm young doesn't mean I'm stupid," she snapped. "And I'm not letting you change the subject. Why do you blame yourself for his death?"

Terra looked more baffled at her tone than angry. The Nexus looked down. "I gave him the Guardian's Blade, Hanna. Even if he had lived through healing Caitlyn and me, he would have still died soon anyway."

"Good people die every day," the little girl said. She felt five times older than she was. "I know that better than a lot of people. It was my job to make sure they didn't. It was my job to heal them so they could go back out and get cut up, eaten up, and killed."

"I'm so sorry," Terra said.

Hanna shrugged. "I'm one of the lucky ones. I was with my father, healing people on our expedition while the rest of my family was butchered by Azreal." The girl let out a grim laugh. "My mother didn't want me to go. She thought it would be too dangerous."

"Have you always been a healer?" Terra asked.

She's trying to keep the conversation pointed at me. Fine, I'll answer her questions, but I'm not done helping her. Not yet. "I was four the first time I healed someone. It was my little brother. He fell from our nest and broke his wing. I flew down to him and healed him, while I was still in my bird form."

Terra's eyes widened in surprise. "You can use magic in your birth form?"

Hanna nodded. "I'm the only one anyone's heard of that can. I hadn't even been taught what magic was, much less how to use it. Healing him just felt right. I never told anyone what I did, and it was a year later when I tried healing a little pixie boy that had cut open his arm on his dad's knife." Terra winced in sympathy.

"Yeah," Hanna continued, "since I hadn't told anyone I had been healing all the little eaglets' hurts, no one told me you had to be the same race as the one you're healing. When the flesh of my wing split open and I started bleeding, I did what any scared five-year-old would do, I screamed. I had no idea what was happening. That was when my parents learned of my skill in healing. After that, it was constant schooling and practice at the magical arts. I hope to be the most powerful healer this world has ever seen, some day."

"That's a noble goal. One that I'll never be capable of," Terra said.

That's right, she's a half-angel. "I just wish I had been able to make it to Alex sooner. I could have healed him in my human form."

Terra shook her head. "There was nothing you could do."

Hanna squinted her eyes at the older woman. *She's hiding something else from me. Why does everyone keep secrets from the little girl? I think I've shown I can handle them...* "Terra, if you hadn't given Alex the Guardian's Blade, what do you think would've happened?"

The woman put a hand on Hanna's head and tousled her hair. "I appreciate you trying to make me feel better, but I've been through that same rationalization too many times for me to believe it anymore. I know, logically, that I had to do what I did, but in my heart, I can't help but feel like he should still be alive."

"I understand," Hanna said as she rose. "I need to check on my other patients before I sleep for the night. By your leave?" Terra nodded that she could go. *This isn't over yet, Terra,* Hanna thought as she stepped out into the night. *I've never left a person in the same or worse condition than when I found them.* The little girl began planning how best to help her new friend as she walked to the medical tents.

Terra lay on her bed in her large tent and thought. *What a poor little girl. The things she has seen to make her like that...* She brooded on Hanna and didn't notice the flap of her tent swing open. A throat clearing brought her head up. Caitlyn and Brahm stood just inside her quarters.

"I'm sorry," Caitlyn said before Terra could tell them to leave. "What I said was thoughtless and hurtful, and I didn't mean to upset you."

"But you did mean what you said," Terra said. Her friend didn't say anything. "I forgive you." Terra's gaze shifted to the Guardian's Blade. It rested across the top of her small writing desk. "I just can't let it go, not yet. Maybe not ever. The blade imprints the mind of the wielder upon it. It's like part of him is still here. The Guardian's Blade is the only thing I have of him, the only thing he touched."

"That do no' be true," Brahm said. The two women looked at him. "Alex touched our hearts, an' he'll always be there."

Terra felt a small smile touch her face as she placed a hand over her stomach. "That he did." A short moment of silence passed as everyone in the tent focused inward. "I just had an odd conversation with Hanna Steelfeather." Terra told the two of them of the little girl's visit.

"She's a smart one," Brahm said.

"Did she really say she could use magic in her bird form?" Caitlyn asked. Terra nodded. "That's extraordinary."

"What concerns me is that she is still here," Terra explained. "A girl of seven years should be off making friends, not treating the wounded."

"Hanna won't leave them," the changeling said. "I asked her a couple days ago why she was still working for the healers, and she told me that was where she belonged, helping everyone she could. She thinks she can cure the undead necrosis. So far the girl's succeeded in preventing its spread throughout the infecteds' bodies."

Terra's brows drew down. "That's impossible. Why hadn't you told me about this?"

"You've been busy jumping all over Dae looking for those anti-magic shards every chance you got. You remember, the things you didn't tell either of your closest friends about?" Caitlyn said.

I'm not sure it will work. "I didn't want to get either of your hopes up in case I didn't find enough of them." Brahm and Caitlyn both had an annoyed look on their faces. "I'm sorry. I should have let the two of you know what I was doing." *I want it to be only my fault if it doesn't.*

"Do no' worry about it any longer," Brahm said. "Ye need to be gettin' to sleep. It's no' healthy fer ye to be missin' out."

"I'll sleep after I have a chance to talk to Caitlyn for a moment," Terra said. Brahm bade them goodnight and stepped out into the dark. Terra held out her arms to Caitlyn, and the changeling fell into them with a fierce embrace.

"I'm so sorry," Caitlyn whispered in her ear. "I couldn't see past my own hurt to help you through this."

Terra shushed her friend. "It's all right," she said as she rubbed her hand down the changeling's black hair. She felt like crying, but there were no tears left in her. *There is still too much for me to do.* "I know you loved him, Caitlyn, and I should have been there for you too. We've been letting each other down, not something sisters should do."

Caitlyn laughed. "A changeling with an immortal half-human, half-angel adopted sister, we do make a strange pair."

"Do you want to sneak into Silvia's tent and have a pillow fight like the good old days?" Terra asked.

The changeling leaned back and smiled. "Aren't you a bit old for pillow fights?"

Terra hit her friend with a pillow. "That's not a nice thing to ask someone. I'll have you know that I'll be a spry fifty-six years in a couple months. That's not any real amount of time to us immortals."

"What's it like?" Caitlyn asked.

"What? Being immortal?"

"Yeah."

Terra thought it over for a moment before shrugging. "I don't know," Terra said, tucking some of her red hair behind her ear. "It's normal to me. I remember when you and Silvia were born twenty-two years ago. Your sister was born first and then you came out, like you were chasing after her. I had never seen a birthing before and was a little grossed out by the blood. But as soon as the two of you were cleaned off, you looked like the cutest little balls of fluff.

"It was very kind of your mother to take care of me after mine passed away. You, Silvia, and your mother gave me something I had never really had before. A real family. I never really felt like my mother truly loved me. She was always cold to me, like she only took care of me out of a sense of duty."

"You never told me about that. I'm sorry," Caitlyn said.

Terra patted her on the shoulder. "Don't worry about it, I have two sisters now, and I wouldn't trade them for anything."

"Good," Caitlyn said with a grin. "Because you're stuck with us."

"I wouldn't have it any other way, which is why I don't want you to go to Bara." Terra watched her sister mentally dig her heels in and prepared for an argument. *Stubborn as a stone*.

"Fine, if I can't go, then neither can you," Caitlyn said.

"If neither of us can go, then who are we going to send? We are the most powerful magic users around." Silence grew between them, neither of them willing to continue arguing or give ground.

"I'll do it," came a woman's voice. They both whipped their heads about to stare at the tent flap. Silvia stood there in her glittering silver dress. Her black hair shimmered in the lamp light.

"No," both women protested in unison. Silvia crossed her arms and stepped into the tent.

Silvia felt a pang of jealousy at seeing her sister and Terra arguing over eachother's safety. She had never been as close to either of them as they were to each other. They were so caught up in their argument that neither had seen her pull back the tent flap and were surprised at her volunteering.

"Yes, I will." She held up her hand to forestall further protests. "I may not be as powerful as either of you, but you cannot deny that I learn new spells faster than either of you. Also, I don't think we need to send a strong sorceress to Bara. If the Realm of Good is still under siege, then whoever goes will have to rely on stealth, not force, to get around. And if it isn't, then there is no need for great magical power either."

"What if you do get captured?" Caitlyn asked. "What would we do without the Fanglady that kept us together while Dae was under Azreal's thumb?"

"If I were captured and killed, then the title of Fanglady would pass to you," Silvia said. Caitlyn opened her mouth, but Silvia didn't stop speaking. "And you would do the job admirably. Besides, as soon as that gate is built and all planar magic is forced through it, this city will become a giant target. The most powerful of our warriors are needed here."

Caitlyn continued arguing, but Silvia watched Terra's face. *I knew you would see the logic of what I'm saying, older sister*, Silvia thought. Terra laid a hand on Caitlyn's arm, and she stopped talking.

"Are you certain of this?" Terra asked.

"I am."

"Are you two serious?" Caitlyn demanded.

Silvia looked at her two-minute-younger sister. "Neither of you are going to Bara. I am, and I won't be bullied about by either of you."

Caitlyn hurled the nearest thing she could lay hands on at her twin sister. Silvia caught the pillow and threw it back at her, hitting her in the face with a feathery whump. Terra snatched it away from Caitlyn's grasping hands and hit her with it again. Caitlyn glared at the two other women and stormed out of the tent muttering under her breath.

"Are you really sure?"

Silvia sighed. "It has to be someone, Terra, and I'm the one that makes sense. I went to Bara seven years ago and have a general idea of what I'm looking for. I'll do my duty."

"Very well, Silvia. Are you going to take anyone with you?"

"I'll ask Timothy if he'll accompany me, but I won't order anyone to come."

Terra nodded. "Very well. Good luck, Sister."

"Thank you. Good night, Terra." Silvia left Terra's tent and walked the short distance to hers. Lights were on. *Timothy must be inside*. She opened the flap and saw she was correct. He sat backwards in the chair facing her writing desk, his chin resting on his ebony-skinned arms. She smiled when she saw him.

"What did she say to your proposal?" the elven prince asked as he stood and spun the chair around so she could sit.

Silvia sat in the wooden chair and let out a sigh as Timothy massaged the tension from her neck and shoulders. His hands were warm on her cool skin. "Terra agreed. Caitlyn was less than thrilled about it though."

"Ah," he said. She let out a small moan as he worked on the tight muscles close to her spine. "I didn't think your sister would be with her so late. Have you told either one of them about us?"

"No, my love, I haven't. It really hasn't seemed like a good time. I was going to tell them months ago in Starfall, but I never really had an opportunity. A Fanglady falling for the captain of her guard, that's scandalous," Silvia joked.

Timothy barked a laugh. He leaned down and whispered, his warm breath tickling her ear. "I think it's less inappropriate when the captain of your guard happens to be an elven prince, but who am I to think such things."

Silvia turned her head to kiss him. "Only the most amazing elf I have ever had the good fortune to know." Timothy smiled and kissed her again. Silvia's lips parted, and she tasted the mint leaves he frequently chewed. He broke off the kiss and glanced at the small bed. "What are you thinking about doing, Timothy?" she asked with a smirk.

With strong hands on her waist, he lifted her from the chair. "Something *scandalous*," he said with a mischievous gleam in his eyes. He laid her on the bed, and with a snap of his fingers, the small lamp in her tent went out.

The next sixteen days passed, and Terra became more frustrated with every night wasted. She had been unable to create an inversion in a grounding field any larger than an orange, and she hadn't been able to even start working with the anti-magic shards.

"What's wrong?" Caitlyn asked the night of the last day before the arch was set to be functional.

Terra looked up from the book on the small desk in her tent. "I just can't get this spell to work!" she said in exasperation. "There has to be something I am missing. This should work."

Caitlyn walked to her and looked at the enormous, leather-bound tome. She didn't recognize any of the runes on the page. "What language is this?"

"Valkyrin," Terra answered.

The changeling stared at the book, but it was a look of amazed confusion. "How did you get a book written by the valkyrie of Caine? And how can you understand it?"

Terra looked up at her. "I know every language," she said absently.

"What? How?"

"One of the perks of being a half-angel," Terra explained. "Just like how half-demons get some of the abilities of full-demons, half-angels get some of the skills of the full-blooded. I can't fly or become ethereal, but I can read, write, speak, and understand every language in the Nine Realms."

"The Daemen didn't seem to have any kinds of powers, other than being stronger than their size would suggest," Caitlyn said, getting sidetracked from her original question.

Am I going to tell her the truth about Alex? Terra thought. *She deserves to know. Alex did use his powers to heal her.* "Daemen are the spawn of a minor male demon impregnating a human woman. Typically it's rape, but some women give themselves willingly for a specific boon. Half-demons are only born of a Demon Lady and a human male."

"Why only female high demons?"

"The human body can't handle the strain of carrying a true half-demon to term." *I wonder what's going to happen to me from our child...* "A half-demon has incredible strength and speed. They also gain telekinetic abilities and some of the physical aspects of a high demon when they get older."

Caitlyn's brow drew down in thought. "They were solid green," Terra heard the changeling mutter before her eyes shot open wide. "I don't know how it's possible, but I think..." She stopped talking when Terra held up a hand for her to be quiet.

"Don't say it out loud," the Nexus said. "Tent walls are thin, and I don't want anyone to know more than is absolutely necessary."

"Why haven't you told anyone?" Caitlyn whispered.

Terra lowered her voice and gave her sister a cautionary look. "Have you ever heard of an angel and demon hybrid?" She patted her slightly protruding stomach.

Caitlyn's eyes looked wide enough to roll out of her head. "No," came the choked whisper.

"Neither have I," Terra said. "And until I learn more, everyone will just continue to think my daughter is mostly human with a bit of angel blood."

Caitlyn nodded and her eyes shot up to the tent flap. Terra turned to see Silvia walking in. The observant Fanglady caught the mood in the tent and walked over with a look of concern on her face. "What's wrong?" Silvia asked, echoing her biological sister's earlier question.

"I'm not sure I can create an inversion in a large enough grounding field," Terra said, bringing the conversation back to the original problem.

Silvia tapped a finger against her lips in quiet contemplation. "Where have you been encountering the problems?" the Fanglady asked.

"I can't create the field *and* make an area of inversion without it being tiny," Terra explained.

"Why don't you have someone else do it?" Silvia asked.

"I…" Terra trailed off when she realized the thought just hadn't occurred to her. She was so used to being powerful enough to work any spell on her own that it hadn't crossed her mind to ask for help. "I don't know how to cast a spell with another person," she admitted. The two changelings stared at her. "I've never needed to!"

Caitlyn and Silvia met eyes and laughed. "It isn't hard. Children do it all the time," Caitlyn said before laughing again.

Terra rolled her eyes. "I'm glad the two of you are so amused, but we are working under a tight deadline."

The other women suppressed their giggling. Silvia said, "It really isn't difficult. But first, explain what inversion is so Caitlyn can help you with the spell."

"Why me?" Caitlyn protested.

"Weren't you just bragging the other day that you had more magical power than I did?" Silvia asked.

Caitlyn frowned. "I wasn't bragging."

Silvia raised an eyebrow at her. "The fact remains that you two are the most powerful sorceresses in the whole Realm. So, inversion."

"It works by creating an area of the spell that has the exact opposite composition from the rest of the spell," Terra said. "For it to work properly, the inversion has to be linked to the spell and created at the exact same time."

"That doesn't sound difficult," Silvia said. "Terra, make a grounding field about the size of the inside of the tent but don't finish it. Leave it almost done near the top." A few seconds passed as a complex lattice of all four elements was laced throughout the inside of the tent. A look of mental strain began to build on Terra's face as she held all of the magical energy in place without completing the spell.

"Perfect," Silvia said. "Now hold it just like that. Caitlyn, can you see the last few threads that aren't yet connected?" Caitlyn said she did. "Good, transition them through aligned elements to their opposite." They all three watched as Caitlyn changed a line of fire to air then water. "That's right. Just do that with all the loose ones and make it a small ball of the opposite elements but the same pattern."

Sweat began to bead on Terra's forehead from the strain of holding the complicated spell in place while Caitlyn finished her part. *This should work,* Terra thought. *I should have asked Silvia for help earlier. Hurry though, Sister. This isn't as easy as it looks.*

In just a few more seconds, Caitlyn finished, and the spell snapped into existence. A grounding field the size of her tent with a large inversion hovered around them. "And there we go," Silvia said.

Terra hugged her sisters. "You are a genius, Silvia," she said after she broke the embrace.

The Fanglady blushed and shrugged. "It just made sense after you explained it. Have you made any progress on the anti-magic shards?"

"No," the half-angel said. "I've been trying to get this to work the entire time. But now, I think I just need to use my power as Nexus to imbue the crystal with the same energy as the grounding field, inversion and all, and I'm pretty sure it'll work."

"That sounds like it should work," Caitlyn said. "You'll just need some way to link the shard to the spell."

Silvia's eyebrows drew down, and she shook her head. "I don't think you need to include the energy from the inversion. We want the coverage area of the field to increase, not the inversion. That spot needs to stay where it is."

"I'll try that," Terra said as she pulled out one of the shards. She opened herself to the immense ocean of power that made up the latent magical energy of Dae. It was a rush every time she accessed her powers. It made her feel as if she could do anything. *Maybe I could try bringing Alex back... HE'S DEAD! You can't change that!* she screamed at herself.

With a shake of her head, Terra focused on the task at hand. She drew the correct proportions of the four elements into the crystal. The black stone began to clear as white light eddied through its depths.

Terra pulled energy onward into the anti-magic shard until it glowed brighter than the lamp in her tent. She looked up from what she was doing to see that the borders of the grounding field had passed beyond the canvas walls, but the inverted area remained in place. "Go outside," she muttered. "Tell me if it keeps getting bigger the more energy I imbue the crystal with." Caitlyn nodded and walked outside. Terra drew more of the latent magical energy into the shard.

"It is," Caitlyn called. "It's expanding the more you put in it."

Terra stopped pumping magical power into the shard.

Caitlyn came back into the tent. "You stopped?"

Terra nodded. "Well, we just need to do this again tomorrow afternoon, and we'll have a grounding field that covers the entire planet."

"Can you push that much energy into the shards?" Silvia asked.

"That won't be a problem. Even if it takes me a few days, I'll get it done. Are you and Timothy going to be ready to go tomorrow?"

Silvia nodded. Her lips were pursed as if she were engaged in an intense internal debate. "There's something I need to tell the two of you," she said at length.

"Sure," Caitlyn said. "Is everything all right?"

Picking at her nails, Silvia avoided the two women's gazes. "I'm in love with Timothy," she blurted out. "I just wanted the two of you to know that I'm not going to be... alone if something happens while I'm on Bara."

A twang of pain and loss echoed through Terra, but she forced herself to be happy for her sister. "That's great!" she said with almost sincere enthusiasm.

"Congratulations," Caitlyn said. "I'm happy for you."

Silvia looked up. "Neither of you are disappointed?"

The two women looked at each other then back at the Fanglady. "Why would we be? We're your sisters, not Mother," Terra said.

"Well... Because I'm the Fanglady, and he's not even a changeling, much less one of the Fang."

Terra reached out and grabbed Silvia's hands. "Do what makes you happy for as long as you can," Terra said. Pain reached up and took a firm grasp of her heart. "It's an ephemeral thing that can be stolen away at any moment."

Silvia nodded and wrapped Terra in a warm embrace. Caitlyn put her arms around the two other women. "I'm so sorry," Silvia whispered. "I wish there was something I could do for you."

"There is," Terra said. Both women drew back from her and stood side by side.

"What is it?" they asked at the same time.

Terra clenched her fists; her nails dug painfully into her palms, but she ignored it. "Help me protect Dae so we can strike out from here and kill the bastard responsible for Alex's death."

Both women nodded with understanding.

Chapter Three – Eternius

The sun was almost down when the spells were in place for Silvia and Timothy's departure. Silvia, Timothy, and Caitlyn stood near the Guardian's statue while they waited for Terra to finish opening the gateway to Bara. A thousand guardsmen stood about the moonstone arch to prevent anything from crossing over from the other side. "Are you sure you don't want to take more people with you, Sister?" Caitlyn asked her older sister.

"I am," the Fanglady said with confidence. "If we are going to do this, then it needs to be swift and silent."

"Good luck, Silvia." Caitlyn wrapped her sister in a fierce embrace. "Please be careful and come back."

"Don't worry," the older changeling whispered as she returned the hug. "I'll be fine. Don't forget, I have the best swordsman on all of Dae with me." Caitlyn nodded as they separated. "Is it time?"

"A few more seconds," Terra muttered. She stood before the twenty-foot-tall moonstone arch with her hands held out in front of her as she channeled power into the arch. The Nexus was one of the few people left on Dae that had the requisite power and knowledge to make inter-planar gateways.

I am ready for this, Silvia thought as she handed her pack to Timothy. She braced herself for the pain of changing into her panther form. Unlike most other changelings, Silvia never got used to the pain of shifting forms. She stayed in her human form most of the time because of the excruciating experience.

Silvia steadied her mind and focused on the form of her birth, sensing every hair and muscle. She shook as bones cracked and tendons snapped. Her vision went white with the blinding agony of every fiber of her being shifting size and position. Silvia cried out in pain as her jaw cracked and elongated. After a transient eternity, the changes finally stopped.

The Fanglady rose from the dirt on four shaking legs. Timothy looked down on her with pursed lips. "I hate seeing you in so much pain," he said.

Silvia let out a steadying breath and sat on her hindquarters. She looked at the elf. "It's fine. This pain is my birthright, and it will be safer for me to be in this form. Who knows, I may need to outrun you."

"I would love to see you try, even in your panther form," Timothy said with a laugh. Bright, yellow light bathed the area around them as the portal to Bara opened. "Let's go," he said. The plan was for them to go through the portal, test the Eye of the Stars that would hopefully allow them to talk to Terra, and make contact with the angels, if possible.

Silvia and Timothy walked up to the gateway arch. "I'll keep it open as long as I can," Terra said. The two nodded and stepped through.

The bright light dazed Silvia for a moment. A brilliant white star hovered above the City of Spires bathing everything with warmth. Her claws clicked against the translucent golden ground. *It's like glass mixed with gold*, she thought. Silvia took a deep breath and wrinkled her nose at the smell of rotten meat.

Her eyes finished acclimating to the light, and she saw an Obsidian Tower only a few miles away on the path between the outer and inner rings of the floating island. Panic began to gnaw at her. "Get the Eye out and test it," Silvia said. "We need to be away from here before they notice the gateway."

"Already on it," Timothy said as he pulled out the orange sphere.

Alex had created the magical communication device by communing with the Cat's Eye gem in

Starfall. He had driven the Guardian's Blade deep into the crystal and caused it to create five fist-sized replicas of itself. The Guardian had also caused the Cat's Eye to open, giving it a vein of blue that ran down the center, making it resemble a giant orange eye. It had been renamed the Celestial Eye, and the smaller stones, the Eyes of the Stars.

Terra had attuned the crystal to Timothy that morning. "Nexus," the elf said. "Can you hear me?"

A second passed. "I can," Terra answered through the crystal. "I was fairly certain the Eyes would work, but I don't think they will continue to after I close the gateway. Are you safe enough to continue on?"

"We need to hurry," Silvia said. "They'll be coming for us soon."

"We are, but we need to go. There's an Obsidian Tower a few miles south of us. We're going to try circling around the outer ring to get past it," Timothy said to the Eye as they began moving away from the Baran arch. The Fanglady agreed with his plan as she padded alongside him.

"I will open another gate in twelve hours to make sure everything is going well," Terra reminded. "Good luck."

Silvia looked over her shoulder just in time to watch the gateway, gold on their end, wink shut. "The inner and outer rings wrap all the way around the City of Spires," she said. "There are bridges connecting the two in line with the seven gateways into the city. If we continue circling around to the west then we should come to the Gate of Truth, then the Gate of Justice. We should go in through the second. It'll be far enough away from the Obsidian Tower to be safe."

The two ran beside the waist-high wall that ringed the gaps between the inner and outer rings. Timothy glanced over the side of the wall down into the gap. "I don't see a bottom," he said.

"There isn't one. Angels can fly. What's a bottomless drop to them?" Silvia asked. She had been surprised when Timothy had told her he hadn't been to Bara before. "The entire plane is just this island that floats in endless nothingness. The only thing out there is the star above us."

Timothy glanced up. "Get down," he whispered, his voice harsh. He crouched against the wall, and Silvia did the same.

"What did you see?" she asked as softly as she could.

He turned about so she could see his lips. "Black wings," he mouthed.

Angel wings are white. Silvia nodded. They stayed like that for a few minutes before risking a glance over the wall. Neither saw anything, and they continued heading west along the outer ring.

Silvia and Timothy ran for about an hour before they reached the bridge that ran to the Gate of Truth. Silvia got a good look at the City of Spires's diamond wall. The hundred-foot-thick, quarter-mile high wall glittered in the white sunlight. The gate was hundreds of feet tall and made from transparent quartz. *Just as amazing as the first time I saw it.*

She had come to Bara once before when she was younger. Her mother had thought it would be good for Silvia to see the two Inner Realms that could be visited.

"Silvia," Timothy said, shaking the changeling out of her memories. "Look past the south side of the city."

The Fanglady hopped atop the short wall so she could see over it. She let out a hiss of air at the sight of a second, smaller Obsidian Tower to the city's southern side. "So there are two here." Silvia glanced over her shoulder. They were about halfway between the Gates of Truth and Justice. "We may as well keep going," she said as she jumped back down.

After another thirty minutes swift jog, they arrived at the two and a half mile long bridge that connected the inner and outer rings. There were no walls to either side of the bridge, and they were sure to be seen as soon as they started across. Silvia tamped down her paws. "Are you ready for a race, my love?"

Timothy grinned warmly. "Just try to keep up," he said with a wink.

I plan on it. If either of us are too slow then we are going to be killed... or worse. "Let's go," she said as they started running across the bridge. They only made it a few hundred yards when the alarm was raised at both Obsidian Towers. Demonic howls echoed across the emptiness.

Silvia eyed the towers and the distance they had yet to go. *It's about three miles to the gate from the outer end of the bridge. We can make it.* A group of five winged demons took flight from the southern Obsidian Tower. *Must go faster.*

Timothy pulled his longbow stave from the holder on his back and strung it in one fluid movement while he ran. He held the yew longbow in his left hand. "We have to hurry Silvia. I'm sure the angels have seen us, but I doubt they will put the city in danger to save just the two of us. We need to get to the gate far ahead of anything on the ground."

"Yeah," Silvia panted. She was already winded from their over-ten-mile jog around a third of the outer circle, and now the long run was beginning to take its toll. "Right behind you."

Almost twenty minutes passed as they ran across the bridge. Only a half-mile remained to the amethyst

Gate of Justice, but Silvia was starting to fall behind. Timothy saw she was beginning to lag and paused for her to catch up. He fired off an arrow at the approaching flying demons, but the shot fell short. A score of hellhounds raced from both the north and south sides of the inner ring.

"Hurry, Silvia," he said, trying to encourage her as she ran past. "We are almost there. Not much farther."

"I, can see, that," she gasped. The winged demons drew close enough for Timothy to shoot at, and he let fly. Five arrows loosed found five targets, and winged demons spiraled out of the air. The hellhounds ran over their corpses without slowing.

Silvia and Timothy made it to the Gate of Justice with a few minutes to spare. They pounded on the amethyst. "Open up!" Timothy roared. "We are from the Realm of Magic. We offer our assistance in exchange for information!"

The Gate of Justice didn't budge an inch.

"Why aren't they opening the gate?" Timothy asked as he drew another arrow and aimed high enough to hit the oncoming hellhounds.

"Either they don't believe us," Silvia said. "Or they plan on letting us die."

"No, there is still another half-hour before we need to check on Silvia and Timothy," Terra said. "What do you need?"

I don't know how to tell her I'm worried about the baby's growth, Hanna thought. She sat down on the bed in the Nexus's tent, her legs dangling above the canvas floor. "I just thought that I should come and check up on you and the baby. You've been using a lot of magical power recently, and I wanted to make sure it wasn't hurting the baby."

The Nexus's brows drew down in concern. "Do you think that's possible?"

Hanna shrugged. "Anything's possible. You're the first half-angel Nexus." She couldn't think of any other way to phrase her statement, so the little girl just came out and said it. "I think your baby's development is farther behind that it should be. Your child is mostly human and over four months along, but you're hardly showing."

The changeling watched Terra tense up as she talked. "I don't think it's anything to be concerned about," Hanna interjected. "I just think it would be better if we knew more."

Terra looked at her with an unreadable expression. "Very well," the older woman said after a while. "If you think it's best."

Hanna nodded and placed her hands on the Nexus's slightly swollen stomach. She sent a complex probe of all four elements into Terra to try assessing the baby's health. A bubble of force and magical energy unlike anything she had seen blocked her from reaching the child. *There it is again. It's weird, but I feel like something's actively pushing me back. I know it's not Terra doing it.*

"Why do you talk like that?" Terra asked.

"Like what?" Hanna responded, focusing more on the task at hand than the conversation. *Maybe if I try going in through the umbilical.* She maneuvered the probe around to the cord connecting mother and daughter. Her assumption was correct. The umbilical ran through a small gap in the shielding energy.

Hanna pushed the smallest probing tendril she should make toward the gap.

"Like an adult," Terra said.

Hanna shrugged. "As the eldest child, the duty of the leader of the Changelings of the Wing will likely fall to me when my father dies. It's part of my job to speak properly." The probe passed through the gap in the bubble. She shuddered at the sudden feeling of openness. *This isn't right. There's way too much room for the baby in here. She should look almost ready to deliver.*

"What's wrong?" Terra asked, her voice rose with concern.

"Nothing. Still looking." *Some sort of compression field? A pocket dimension linked to this one?* The possibilities baffled the girl. Her connection to the womb was suddenly cut off, and the backlash of the collapsing spell made her wince in pain. "Why did you sever the probe?" Hanna demanded.

Terra had an offended look on her face. "I didn't do anything."

"Then who..." Hanna muttered. Her eyes were still locked on the woman's stomach. "You don't think the baby did?"

"I don't know, Hanna," Terra said. "When I was being held in the Obsidian Tower, Azreal was using his machina to drain the energy from me. He should have bled all of the life force from me, but something Jessica did kept me feeling vital."

"How?"

Terra shook her head and shrugged. "I don't know. It's nothing I'd ever heard of. Did everything seem fine?"

"Yeah," Hanna said. "You know about the bubble of energy around your baby?" Terra said she did. "Well, it's more than some kind of protection. It's like there is more room inside the sphere than there should be. I think that's what is keeping you from getting bigger."

The Nexus chewed her lower lip with a curious look on her face. "Was there anything wrong with the baby?"

"I hadn't made it that far yet," Hanna explained. "The probe was severed before I even found her."

Terra nodded as she stood from where she had been sitting next to Hanna on the bed. "Well, it's time to open the portal to Bara. Maybe you can try again tomorrow."

"I will, Terra." Hanna thought for a moment. *Something's not right.* "Wait." The Nexus paused before she exited the tent. "I thought you said you didn't have to check on them for another thirty minutes."

Terra nodded. "That was about thirty minutes ago. I'll see you in the morning, all right?" The half-angel stepped out of the tent into the crisp morning air.

That's not possible, Hanna thought. *I was not examining her for thirty minutes. Unless...* Hanna's head spun as theories began rising. She dismissed each one as impossible. The Changeling of the Wing hopped down from the bed and left the tent.

There's something I'm missing. Some key fact that will make this all make sense…

Terra had felt her baby cut off Hanna's spell. *I've never read anything about an unborn child using magic*, she thought. *But that wasn't just magic. There was something else in that pulse of energy that cut off Hanna's probe.*

The Nexus brooded on the matter as she walked to the gateway arch. Walking past several thousand guards, she drew up to the glittering moonstone. She felt a pang of longing as she looked through the semi-circle at Alex's statue. Caitlyn stood nearby, fidgeting in her human form. Terra knew she was worried about Silvia.

"It's time?" Caitlyn asked.

"It is. Are you ready for whatever is going to come through that gateway?" Terra asked. They had talked earlier and come to the consensus that there would likely be an army of demons trying to flood through the gateway as soon as they opened it.

Caitlyn flexed her fingers and nodded. "I am." Hundreds of arrows stood before her to launch through the planar gateway as soon as things began to come through.

Brahm walked up. The old, grey-bearded dwarf was covered head to toe in his magical unrefined thorium armor. The black platemail carried some powerful enchantments. "The guardsmen're ready, Terra. We're awaitin' yer command."

"Be ready for anything," the Nexus shouted as she turned to face everyone watching. Grim faces saluted.

Weapons were drawn and bows readied. Terra turned back to the gateway arch and began channeling energy into it. In a bare handful of seconds, the gateway to the Realm of Good opened.

"Silvia, are you there?" Terra asked through the Eye she pulled from the pocket of the white dress she wore. Several seconds passed with no response.

"Do you think something happened?" Caitlyn asked.

One of the guardsmen shouted as demons began to flood through the gateway. Winged imps flew through above armored Daemen. Hellhounds dashed around and through the ranks.

"Silvia!" Terra shouted. "If you're there, you need to hurry up and answer. We're under attack!"

The back ranks of guardsmen loosed arrows at the flying demons. Screeches of otherworldly pain echoed through the spring morning. Caitlyn lifted hundreds of arrows set up at the base of the gateway arch on a bed of air and hurled them at the approaching Hellspawn. Each arrow pierced three or more of the monstrosities on the Daein side of the gateway and more on the Baran side. Shouts rose as battle was joined.

"We are here," Silvia said through the Eye. "The angels almost didn't allow us access to the city, but the Keeper let us in. Things are bad here. Close the gateway; we can talk again after I've had a chance to speak with him."

"Twelve hours," Terra said just before she cut off the flows of magic to the moonstone arch. The demons only part of the way through the gateway were cut in half as it snapped shut. Only a few enemies remained alive, and they were quickly slaughtered.

A rapid inspection of the dead revealed that none of their own had died, and only two were injured. "We were bloody lucky," Brahm said.

"No," Terra said. "We were just prepared, but now they are certain someone is opening portals to Bara. We need something to keep them from coming through." She had an idea and moved everyone back from the arch.

Terra took a deep breath and reached deep into the earth around the marble base of the gateway arch. She used her power as Nexus to raise a large dome of stone around the entire structure. Using fire and air, she compressed the stone until it was a perfect half-sphere of transparent diamond. She cast the most powerful preservation she could on the shielding wall. The diamond glittered in the morning light.

Caitlyn admired her work. "Wow," she said, "that will hold them for a while."

"It will," Terra agreed. "The preservation will take even a Demon Lord a few minutes to cut through. The diamond wall will last only a few seconds after that, but it's the hardest thing I can make for the preservation." She tweaked the spell a bit. "There we go, in addition to making the wall impenetrable while it's in place, the preservation will keep anyone from being able to cast a spell through it."

Brahm grunted. "How'd ye learn to do that?"

Terra laughed. "I read a lot. Knowledge is a weapon you hone through years of study. Azreal has decades on me, but I have a few tricks I'm certain he hasn't seen before." She studied her barricade a few seconds longer then turned to go to the council chambers. The marble building should have been finished the night before, and the Nexus was eager to fill the council in on the morning's happenings.

"I thought Azreal was dead," Caitlyn said. "Didn't Alex kill him?"

"He did," Terra answered. "But Azreal's the Overlord of Hell. Just like my Paragon power allows me access to all of Dae's magical energy, his power as Paragon of the Realm of Evil prevents his death from being permanent as long as he is away from Hell."

"Killin' a Paragon's no easy task," Brahm said.

"You know this from experience?" Terra asked.

"Aye.   I've fought alongside two different Guardians, Alex, an' Corin before him, an' yerself. Ye're as strong as those two were, Lass. Do no' doubt that fer one second."

Terra shook her head. Hardly restrained anger at Azreal seethed under the placid surface of her calm expression. *Not strong enough to save my husband's life.*

The Keeper of Fate sipped water from the golden goblet clasped delicately in his mythricite armored hands. The intricate armor looked like gold, but it was many times harder than the soft metal. The well-oiled leather beneath the enchanted plate didn't make the slightest whisper as he placed the cup on the marble table.

The Paragon of the Realm of Good had allowed the two Daein into the City of Spires and now met with them in his personal rooms in the Great Spire.

"Thank you for granting us entry, Keeper," the raven-haired woman said. "I am Silvia Shadowpaw, Fanglady of the Changelings of the Fang, and this is Timothy Eldu'vain, the third prince of the Northern Elves and captain of my guard."

The ancient angel nodded greeting.   "I am Eternius, Eldest of the Order of Archangels. May the peace of the City of Spires be upon you. I take it your Realm is free of Azreal's influence?"

"It is, Keeper," Silvia said. The changeling spoke with an air of calm authority. "We were able to push the Overlord from our home and destroy the Obsidian Tower he had erected."

"That is good. I am pained by the loss of your Paragon," Eternius said. The stalwart angel was surprised to find the words were true. *She was nothing more than a pawn*, he thought, banishing the emotion.

Silvia looked at Timothy with a confused look on her face. She looked back at him, unconsciously avoiding his hazel eyes that held untold millennia of knowledge. "The Nexus is well," Silvia said. "She was the one I spoke with a few moments ago."

The Keeper's blond brows drew down. *Something has steered Fate astray.* "What of the Guardian?"

"Alex gave his life to save my sister's and the Nexus's lives. He is the one that killed Azreal and destroyed the Obsidian Tower."

The dark-skinned elf spoke up for the first time. "He was a good man. The Nine Realms is a lesser place without him."

Eternius clenched his jaw. *It is an ill omen that Fate must be corrected when the Libram's final page is in play. I must get word to the Life Wardens.* The beginnings of a plan began to form. "All lives must end when Fate has decreed. My forces are insufficient to strike at one of the towers and still defend the city. What assistance have you come to offer?"

The changeling pulled out the stone she had been speaking through earlier and placed it on the table. Eternius held out his hand toward it, and she nodded. The angel held the spherical gemstone in his hand. *This is something of the Outside. It seems benign, though.*

"This is an Eye of the Stars," the Fanglady said. "With it, I can talk to the Nexus while the gateway to Dae is open. You said your forces are insufficient to strike out from the City of Spires. We have an army ready to flow through the gateway and help retake your Realm. If we were to keep the northern Obsidian Tower occupied, would you be able to destroy the southern one?"

Eternius steepled his fingers and thought for a moment. "We would, and then it would be a simple matter to strike the remaining tower in a pincer strike. When will your forces be prepared?"

"I will need to speak with the Nexus again to be certain, but no more than a few days, a week at most."

"Very well," the Keeper said. "And what information do you request in exchange for your assistance?"

"The Nexus was able to erect a grounding field over all of Dae," the changeling said.

I have underestimated my daughter's power.

"The only thing we now need for the plane to be free of the threat of re-invasion is a keystone seal, much like the one Bara had."

Eternius nodded. "The creation of a keystone seal is no difficult task. It will prevent anyone from traversing through a portal to your world without it in place. I will create one for your Realm myself once Bara is freed."

The angel stood and stretched his wings. "Feel free to take up temporary residence in any of the rooms on this level of the Great Spire as my personal guests. You will find a fountain in each room. The waters of Bara will slake your thirsts and sate your hunger. Be at peace until the time for battle has come."

Silvia and Timothy both stood. "Thank you for your hospitality, Keeper." The two turned and began walking from his chambers.

Curiosity overcame his judgment. "What is her name?" Eternius asked. *My daughter's name.*

The changeling and elf stopped just before the baobab wood door. "Whose name, Keeper?" Timothy asked.

"Your Nexus."

"Her name is Terra," Silvia answered. "Terra Zane."

Terra, a fitting name for an earth-bound half-angel. Eternius gave himself a mental shake. *The time for idle fancy is long past. I must consult the Libram of Fate before making any rash moves.* "Thank you." The two nodded before setting out.

The Keeper waited for the door to click closed before he shifted to his ethereal form. White light filled the room, and he saw everything through shades of gray. The angel willed himself upward through the spire that was his home. He passed through several stone floors until he reached the pinnacle of the Great Spire.

The Source shown down on him, bathing him and everything in the open roofed Amphitheater of the High Seats with white light. Lesser minds thought the Source was a star, but Eternius alone remembered when it had been much, much more. *Not since the Dawn, when the Nine Realms were created and the madness of the Void sealed away, has such power been needed. Back when the Nephilim roamed the space between the Realms and the Outside...*

The Keeper of Fate assumed his physical form and walked to the mythricite plinth. He opened the Libram of Fate and unceremoniously flipped to the last page. Eternius knew every word in the prodigious tome by heart, but he still felt the need to ensure he was not mistaken. "This is only the third time Fate has needed to be brought back in line with the Libram," he muttered. "A birth, a war, and now a death..." He felt a presence at his back.

"So, Fate must be brought back into alignment?" Ureon, the Seat of Faith, asked.

"You were in the wall listening," Eternius said without emotion. "You know this Libram's ending, Sister. The Source knows you protested against it hard enough."

She shuffled her wings in an angelic shrug. "I was curious," Ureon admitted. "I wanted to know why our visitors were here."

"And now you do. You should have had faith that I would have told you."

Ureon laughed at his jibe. "You know I do not lack in faith, Brother, only patience."

Eternius studied his sister angel. Ureon's ice blue eyes were framed with long silver hair. Her delicate chin and pouting lips made her look childish in his eyes. "Your new face suits you well," the Keeper said.

Ureon laughed again as she spun in a pirouette, the long skirt the same color as her eyes flared out. She rested a hand on her mythricite breastplate. "You don't mean that as any kind of compliment, Eternius. Ah, your ability to push the limits of our inability to lie is so refreshing. So many shades of truth with you." She dragged her fingers down the yellow stubble on his weathered jaw. "You've had this face for as long as any can remember. Why do you not change it?"

"Do you really want to know, Ureon? Or are you making a jest?" Her playful manner often pushed him to the boundaries of his tolerance, and Eternius was not in the mood for it.

"I want to know. No jokes," she said with wide-eyed innocence.

"This is the face I awoke with, those billions of years ago. I have never changed it. This aged face is part of who I am."

Ureon nodded. "I understand." Her face took on a pensive cast as she studied his writing in the Libram of Fate. "I will ask you, one final time, the question Aurius asked you when this one was Penned. Are you certain this is the wisest course of action?"

A twisting of emotion pulled at Eternius, but he ignored it. "There are no more pages, and no more room for corrections, Sister. This is the way it must be. My daughter must die so the Nine Realms can survive."

Chapter Four – On the Brink of Hope

"Nexus, allow my squad to serve as your personal guard on Bara," the one-handed man said. He knelt on the white marble floor, his right hand in a fist on the stone and the stump of his left behind his back.

Terra sat in the Nexus's chair in the council chambers and studied the human. His dark brown hair hung down to his jaw line. Wrinkles around his fatigued brown eyes hinted at horrible experiences the young man had lived through. He looked vaguely familiar. "So, you are the man that was leading the band of refugees through the deserts in the south."

A smirk began to rise at the corners of his mouth. *He's a proud one,* Terra thought.

"We're more a band of freedom fighters and undead hunters than refugees, Nexus. We would serve you well. As I have before," he said the last softer than he had the rest.

Memories clicked into place in her mind. "I *do* know you," Terra said. "You're the young guardsman that first night on the wall. And you told me the Crystal of Davinir had been destroyed. How did you make it out of the Arcane City when it fell?"

A wince of long forgotten pain crossed his face. He replaced it with a sad smile. "Guardsman Darren Wright, reporting for duty. A lot of luck and some poor fighting on my part got me out of the city a few days after it fell. I am ashamed to admit that I hid for several days in the cellar of an inn with another guardsman and a baker's daughter after it was clear the city couldn't be saved.

"We were able to strike out from there after the demons withdrew. A few undead remained. I had to cut off my own hand after I was bitten. That part's not something I care to remember. Paul and Ell are my left and right hands now; they're the two lieutenants of my little company." A deprecating laugh escaped Darren's lips. "Well, I've still got my right hand, so I guess you could say they take turns being my left."

"Stand," Terra said, "and wait a moment." Darren rose to his feet in a rustle and jangle of leather and chain armor. Terra turned to Brahm and Caitlyn, standing beside her. "What do you think?" she asked, her tone low enough to only be heard by her two friends.

"The boy's bloody young, but his people love 'im," Brahm said. "He also showed that he an' his know their way around a battle. They say he's lucky. A bit brash an' headstrong but lucky all the same."

Caitlyn looked at the guardsman turned leader, and Terra saw him preen under her gaze. The changeling turned back to her. "I don't like the look of him. He's too young."

"Bah," Brahm interjected, "Ye just do no' like him 'cause he's young an' overly brave. Like yerself." Caitlyn glared at the dwarf but didn't argue. "I say give the lad a chance. It'll no' hurt to have him around, an' his band is small enough to no' hurt the army fer bein' taken out."

Terra agreed. She turned to Darren. "Guardsman, you are now officially raised to the rank of Captain. You will lead my personal guard, to be selected at your own discretion."

"Thank you, Nexus," Captain Wright said.

"You're welcome, Captain. But don't expect to sit out of combat. We will be where the fighting is hottest to stick a blade into the belly of Azreal's forces."

The man grinned. "I wouldn't have it any other way. By your leave, Nexus?"

Terra nodded, and with a deep bow, Darren strode from the council chambers. She waited for him to finish the long walk between the marble colonnade before asking, "Are there any other matters that require the Council of the Free People of Dae's attention?"

Terra looked about the semi-circular room at the other four members of the council that were present. Aeryn, Chieftain Rageclaw, Bahamut, and King Harbronn all shook their heads. "Then let us adjourn for the day. Tomorrow we strike out to free Bara from Azreal's clutches. Rest while you can."

Aeryn Steelfeather remained behind while the other councilors departed. "What do you need, Winglord?" Terra asked.

"I have something of a personal request, Terra," he said in his soft voice. "It seems that my daughter wants to accompany you to Bara."

"And you want me to tell Hanna no," Terra finished.

Aeryn shook his head. "Quite the contrary, I think it would be wise of you to take her along."

Terra was stunned. "What? She's seven, Aeryn. She would be in grave danger the entire time."

"I am aware of the danger," the Winglord said. "As well as my own daughter's age, Nexus. There is no healer more skilled in the entire Nine Realms, and Hanna is quite capable of evading capture. She is also becoming quite proficient at combat magics, under your own tutelage, I understand.

"Hanna is a prodigy, Terra," Aeryn explained. "She picks up magical theory as easily as other children pick up stones. My girl makes intuitive connections that would take days for a master magician to come up with. It pains me to send my only surviving child into danger, but, Luna save me, if she is ever to reach her full potential, not only as a sorceress or Changeling of the Wing, but as the future Winglady, it will be out there where she can do the most good."

She's just so young, Terra thought. *The girl certainly doesn't act that way though, and he's right, she would do more good on Bara than here.* "I have been teaching her some combat magic when she comes to check on the baby, but only for her own defense. I'm not trying to turn your girl into a weapon."

Aeryn smiled. "I know, and I did not mean to infer that I was upset about you training her. Better she learn it from someone that knows what she's doing than Hanna trying to puzzle it out on her own." The Winglord stood. "I trust my daughter's judgment implicitly. If she thinks she should go with you, then she has a good reason for it."

"I'm just not certain bringing her into a warzone is the right thing to do," Terra said.

"Nexus, I know Hanna. She's been with me almost every single moment of her life since she hatched. Our entire family was killed when Azreal attacked Highwind Point; she needs to feel she's doing something to help. I leave the decision up to you, but please consider bringing Hanna with you. Have a good day." Aeryn bowed to her as he walked from the council chamber, leaving Terra alone with Caitlyn and Brahm.

What would Alex tell me to do? Terra wondered.

"He'd tell ye to do what ye thought was right," Brahm said. She realized she had voiced her question aloud.

"Alex would say, 'Everyone is needed, Terra,' but he would still feel bad about putting her in danger. We lived by those words, and I think we still should," Caitlyn said.

Terra sighed. "You're both right. I don't like it either, but Aeryn has a point." She looked at Caitlyn. "Can you find Hanna and let her know she's coming in the morning?" Her sister nodded and set off.

The Nexus and the dwarf shared a companionable silence. *I should tell Brahm about Alex,* Terra thought. *He helped Alex make it to me.* "Brahm," she said.

The dwarf placed a hand on her shoulder. "Aye? What's botherin' ye, Terra?"

"There's something you should know about Alex," she whispered.

Brahm leaned in close to her ear so he could whisper and not be overheard. "I already know he was no' human. Ye do no' need to tell me more, an' do no' talk to anyone else about this. No' even yer little nurse. Especially her. I do no' care how mature Hanna is, she's still a child."

Terra stared at the old dwarf. "When did you?"

"A week or so back. I need to keep remindin' people that I'm bloody old, no' bloody stupid," Brahm muttered. "Ye remember the story I told ye abou' the time I went to Gile?" She nodded. "Ye remember me tellin' ye abou' the man an' the pregnant *lady* I met there?"

Terra's mouth dropped open. *Brahm met Alex's parents!* "That's..." she started to say.

"Bloody unlikely," the dwarf finished. "But no' impossible. How many pregnant... ladies could there be?"

She conceded the point. "I'm scared," Terra admitted, coming to the crux of what was bothering her.

"O' what?"

"Well, that special kind of lady is the only thing strong enough to bear the kind of baby that Alex was," Terra said, taking care to skirt around anything too specific, lest an unseen ear overhear.

"And yer worried about what yer baby could be like?" Terra nodded. "Bah, ye worry too bloody much," Brahm said. "If bearin' Jessica meant ye'd die fer her to be born, would ye do anythin' different?"

"No," she said with anger in her voice at the implied suggestion.

Brahm smiled. "Good. Then live like everythin's goin' to be alrigh'. We've enough trouble on our hands without borrowin' more."

Terra took a deep breath and let it out, trying to push her worries away with her exhalation. She smiled at his tough, bearded face. A seed of hope burrowed deep into the stony soil of her heart. "You're right. Thank you, Brahm. You should get some rest. We are going to have a long day tomorrow."

The dwarf nodded. "Ye should get yerself some rest too, Lass. Tomorrow'll be the first of many long days."

"I will, Brahm. I just want to sit here and think for a while."

"As ye will," her wise friend said as he left her side.

Brahm walked down the long colonnade and closed the heavy wooden doors behind himself leaving Terra alone in the council chambers. She lifted the wooden Guardian's Blade from where it rested at the arm of her chair.

"Are you there, Alex?" she asked the blade. "I know some part of you lives on in this sword. I just wish we could talk." Terra caressed the blade with a tendril of magic, but there was no apparent reaction. *I miss you, Alex. You always seemed so sure of everything. I could use some reassurance now.* Terra closed her eyes, fell asleep in her chair, and dreamt of better days.

"But, seriously, do you have wings?" Alex asked me. We were in the room Silvia had let him use in the Fanglady's Manor in Starfall.

"I do." *But I hate them*, I left unsaid.

Alex scratched his head, looking adorably confused. "I don't want to seem unobservant, but I've seen you naked quite a few times. Where are they?"

"They aren't wings like you are thinking," I said with a fake smile on my face, trying to keep him from worrying about me. "Pure breed angels have flesh and blood wings and can fly, but half-breeds like me don't, and we can't fly. Our wings only serve to mark us, just something to set us apart from humans."

He asked the question I dreaded most. "May I see them?"

"Alex, I've never..."

"Please?" he asked.

Don't make me do this! I screamed in my head. *I can't say no to him! Not right after I told him I wouldn't keep any more secrets.* "All right." I slid from the bed and stood in front of him, doing a good job of appearing calm. "Are you ready?"

"Don't you need to take your shirt off?" Alex asked, confused.

"Are you just trying to get me to take my shirt off?" I asked with a smirk, trying to stop what was happening.

"That's not what I..." he huffed. Alex crossed his arms and leaned against the desk. "I'm ready."

Please don't hate me. It would destroy me to see you looking at me like so many others. I closed my eyes, unwilling to risk watching his reaction. I lifted my arms and spread my wings of glowing blue energy. *Why isn't he saying anything?* Every bottled up fear bubbled to the surface.

"Can I touch them?" Alex whispered. I nodded. He pushed his hand through my left wing. It was a strange feeling, knowing his hand was there but being unable to physically feel it. "Does that hurt you?"

I shook my head. *I can't believe you are showing him these things*, I thought. *He must hate me now...* My eyes started welling with tears, and only my closed lids kept them from spilling out.

A sudden sharp pain on the top of my head made my eyes shoot open. *Ow! He thumped me!* "What was that for?" I demanded.

He put his hands on my face and wiped away my tears. "I have never seen you more beautiful than you are right now," he said as he stared into my eyes.

"You don't understand," I protested for some insane reason. "These wings..."

"Are a part of you," he said in a tone that was loving but firm. "I love you, Terra. Everything about you. Never be ashamed of who you are; that's all we can be."

Terra opened her eyes. She sat in her chair, clutching the Guardian's Blade to her chest. *Are you really there, Alex?* There was still no response. *I must have fallen asleep.* Terra stood and noticed she was giving off a soft blue light. She had never released her wings while she was sleeping before. *Never be ashamed of who you are,* echoed in her mind.

The Nexus looked down at the wooden sword in her hands. "I am doing the right thing. I'll do what I can to avenge you and take care of our daughter, Alex." She sheathed the sword in the leather scabbard on her back. "I love you."

Terra strode from the council chambers with her wings still visible and her head held high.

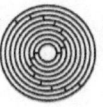

Tomorrow, we march to war once again, Mason the stonecutter thought as he worked. He found working the stone relaxing, and it would often help him work through his problems. *There has been so much death already.*

It was getting on toward nightfall, but Mason wanted to finish cutting the stone he had in front of him. He studied the grain in the white marble he was working on, found the natural pressure lines, and began to create a paper thin line of fire and earth. Mason the mason, everyone in the guild called him. *There's a reason I'm the best,* he always joked. *I was born for this job.*

Before he could direct the flows of magic, the stone turned light blue with reflected light. Mason turned and saw the Nexus walking just a few feet away. The man had sought refuge with the northmen after the Arcane City had fallen, and he had been at the Gap of Druun when the Nexus had devastated the army about to overrun them. She had her wings spread out wide now just like she had then. A throng of men and women trailed in her wake.

Mason wasn't sure if it was the determined look on her face or some unknown force of will, but he joined the ever-growing mass of humanity and followed her.

"Have you seen Terra?" Caitlyn asked Brahm. She had run into him outside of Terra's tent. It looked as if something was going on near Alex's statue, and Caitlyn was eager to see what it was.

"I was abou' to ask ye the same question," he said. "I've no' seen her since I left her at the council chambers a couple o' hours ago." Brahm's eyes drifted to the mob of people gathered around Alex's statue. "Let's go see what's goin' on."

The two of them walked along the dirt and partially cobbled street and, after a few minutes, made it to the edge of the group. "What's going on?" Caitlyn asked.

A man with large arms and a leather apron gave her a grave look. "I think she's going to start soon," he said in a deep rumble.

"Who's goin' to start what, Blacksmith?" Brahm queried.

"The Nexus."

Caitlyn felt earth magic be drawn from the air around her, and an earthen dais rose from the middle of the assembled thousands. Terra stood atop the small stage with her wings spread wide, bathing those around her in soft blue light. Her red hair glowed in the light. Caitlyn watched her cast a voice amplification spell.

"People of Dae," Terra said, her voice soft but carrying well. "Tomorrow, we strike against the forces of Hell so that we may free the Realm of Good," she started.

"Why?" a man near the front shouted. "Why should we give up our lives so that the angels can be free?" Murmurs rose from some of those assembled, and many voices were raised to quiet the man.

"Stop," Terra ordered, silencing everyone. "He has the right to speak his mind, as do you all. We have suffered much these last five years. We've lost much."

"You weren't here! Where were you when we needed you most?" another woman's anonymous voice shouted.

The Nexus squared her shoulders, but she had a sad look on her face as she scanned the crowd. "You are right. I wasn't here, but it was *not* me that we all needed most." Terra held her hand out to the Alex's statue. "It was this man, my husband and father of my unborn child. Alex Zane, the Guardian, showed us something in ourselves that Azreal thought he had stomped out. Something that we were certain was gone, never to return."

Terra pointed in the general direction of the first man that had spoken. "You asked why we should give up our lives for the angels. When I returned home after finding the Guardian, I saw a people entrenched in depression and death. A people beaten and hiding, waiting for their eventual destruction. But, when called, you all fought against impossible odds with the Guardian of Balance leading the charge. I ask you, why did you do that? What did Alex return to you that had been all but forgotten?"

Silence greeted her question. It was a young boy that had climbed on the leg of Alex's statue that answered her. His high, innocent voice projected far enough for all to hear. "He gave us hope."

Terra looked toward the boy and smiled. She turned back to the crowd. "That's right. He showed us that no matter how bad everything looked, there was always a chance. He taught me that no matter how much reason we have to be mired in despair, bereft of a reason to keep fighting on, we always hang on the brink of hope.

"And now, do we stop fighting and go back to cowering?" she asked.

"No," a few voices shouted. Caitlyn looked down at Brahm; he had his hands cupped around his mouth and winked at her.

"Do we go back to awaiting the destruction Hell will certainly try to wreak upon us again?" Terra asked, determination lending volume to her voice.

"No!" more yelled.

"Do we sit here, safe in our homes, showing the future generations of our world that we hid when everyone needed us most?" the Nexus put before them.

Caitlyn, Brahm, and all those assembled screamed at the top of their lungs a resounding, "NO!"

Terra's voice dropped to a loud whisper, but the spell ensured every word could be heard. "Or do we strike out from here and show the Nine Realms that the Daein people bring hope to all the oppressed?"

A wordless roar rose from her people, and the Nexus smiled. It was a long time before the cheering subsided, but Terra finally looked at peace. "Tomorrow," she began again as soon as it quieted enough, "we strike against the forces of Hell so that we may free the Realm of Good..."

Chapter Five – A Solid Foothold

"I know it's not my place to question your plans, Nexus," Captain Darren Wright said as he scratched the back of his head. He was standing next to one of several stacks of steel hand-sized discs not far from the gateway arch. "But are you sure this is the best plan?" The pretty changeling with the golden eyes huffed at him, and he glanced at her. *What's her problem?* the newly promoted captain wondered.

"As captain of my guard," the Nexus said, bringing his gaze back to her, "it is always your place to question anything that concerns my safety." She let out a sigh; motes of blue light floated down from her wings. "You've seen how much damage I can do, and as long as Caitlyn keeps the gateway open, I'll have access to the magical power of Dae."

Captain Wright lifted one of the thousand metal discs taking extreme care to not touch the razor sharp sides. "Will you be able to handle this many separate threads of air?" he asked. Darren had no real aptitude for magic, instead relying on the strength of his arms and his sword and shield to see him through battles.

"With ease," came her confident reply. The Nexus turned to General Ironfist. "Is everything ready, Brahm?"

"Aye, Terra. Everyone's in position. We're waitin' fer the two o' ye."

"Start opening the gateway to Bara, Caitlyn." The changeling walked off, her green dress swirling just above her ankles. Darren stared at her hips sway as she left. *Caitlyn. That's her name.* "Captain." *That's right.* "Captain Wright." *She's pretty se-* "Darren!"

Darren's gaze shot over to the Nexus. The smirk on her face and glare on General Ironfist's made him blush. "Yes?"

"Now's no' the time fer oglin' the pretty girls, Boy. Ye've work to do," the dwarf said.

"Yes, Sir." He saluted General Ironfist with a fist over his heart and turned to the Nexus. "All hundred of your guardsmen and women stand ready to serve, Nexus."

"Brahm, pass the word for everyone to stand ready. And can you let Aeryn know I'll send for Hanna as soon as we gain a secure foothold on Bara? Caitlyn should have the portal open in a few minutes." General Ironfist nodded and set off toward the main body of the army shouting orders as he went. The Nexus turned to face Darren. She had her wings tucked in tight behind her. "Captain Wright, address me as Terra, please. You will be protecting me for a very long time, so let's dispense with some of the formality."

Darren nodded. "Thank you, Terra. Feel free to do the same." His long-time friends and lieutenants, Paul and Ell, walked over. They stood to either side of him. "Nexus, my seconds in command, Paul Cavendish and Ell Nyberg."

Terra shook their hands. Paul's black hair was back in a ponytail, and Ell's shock of blue-green curls was held at bay by a white headband. "Ell, that's elven for girl."

Grinning, Ell's purple eyes sparkled. "That it is, Nexus!" She pulled back her hair to reveal a pointed ear. "I'm half-elven on my father's side. Thank you for accepting our proposal! It has been Lefty's dream of serving alongside you again."

Really, Ell? Just going to put my business right out there? Darren thought. "I'm sorry, Terra, but we never learned how to get this baker's daughter to shut her mouth."

The half-elven woman spun about and clapped Paul on his back. "Well, this lout hardly talks twenty words a day, so I have a lot of ground to cover to make sure the silence doesn't become boring."

Paul frowned at her, but he kept his characteristic silence. Darren's eyes widened when Terra started laughing. *Not exactly how I saw the introductions going...*

"Thank you, Ell. That's the first good laugh I've had in a while," the Nexus said.

Ell danced over to Darren and quickly stuck a pin in each side of his collar. "What are you doing?" he said. The captain pulled out his collar to look at it. A silver shield with slightly glowing blue wings now decorated his black shirt.

"It's our new insignia. Do you like it?" Ell asked with her head cocked to the side. Darren noticed that she had one winged shield on one side of her collar, and an unadorned shield on the other. Paul wore the same.

"I would have liked to have some input on it, since I'm your captain... You let her do this last night?" he asked Paul.

"Had to. She wouldn't leave me alone until I helped her make them," the big man said with a deep bass.

Ell turned to face the gateway arch. "It's almost time," she said, her voice suddenly serious. Her brows drew down, and she checked to make sure the two daggers on her hip were clear in their scabbards. "Everyone's in position."

"Good," Terra said. "Now stand back." The Nexus held her hands low. As she raised them, the metal discs floated into the air. Terra closed her eyes as she focused on managing all of the individual threads of air suspending the circular razors. They began to whirl in a storm of flickering steel shards.

The gateway to Bara opened.

Terra lost herself in the intricate dance of air. She closed her eyes and began emitting pulses of air and water and feeling their echo. Everything was a portrait of black and white in her mind's eye. Terra saw individual blades of grass and beads of sweat on Caitlyn's brow. She saw a soldier a quarter-mile away adjust the grip on her bow. The Nexus had complete awareness of her surroundings.

The gateway materialized, and demons began to flood through without hesitation. A hundred discs flew forward and turned them into shredded meat. Blood and gore filled the air and soaked the ground. More than one soldier lost their lunch at the sight. Terra hurled seven-hundred-fifty of the blades through the portal and charged through it herself with her personal guard in close pursuit.

Large pockets of demons and undead waited on the Baran side of the gateway. Terra cut down as many as she could without straining herself by making the threads of air too long. Swaths of her magical vision were blocked off due to the fields generated by anti-magic shards. The Daein army began to march through behind her personal guard. *I need to clear a larger area.*

Terra gathered all of the discs to her. She arrayed them in front of herself in a tight semicircle. With a pulse of fire, she vaporized the steel discs into searing plasma contained in paper thin balls of air. The Nexus launched the spheres. Everything they touched was boiled into non-existence.

The smell of burned hair and flesh assailed Terra as she opened her eyes. Nothing in front of her moved.

"Yeah," Darren said from just behind her. "That was a better plan than anything I could have come up with."

Terra smirked at him when she looked over her shoulder. Captain Wright had his large kite shield strapped to his left arm and a long sword in his right hand. He sheathed the sword into a concealed scabbard that ran the length of his shield.

"Isn't that heavy?" Terra asked. She had sensed some enchantment on his weapons and armor but hadn't analyzed them yet.

"No," Darren said. "It has a weight manipulation enchantment. My weapons weigh whatever I want them to."

I've never heard of that kind of enchantment before. Terra studied her surroundings. It had been less than a couple minutes since she walked through the gateway, but a significant portion of the army was already through. The northern Obsidian Tower was just under four miles away, just where Silvia said it would be.

"Stay here and make sure everything goes smoothly on this end," Terra ordered. "I need to check on Caitlyn. Holding a gateway to another Realm open for a long time takes considerable effort."

"Will do. Ell, go with her and make sure she stays safe."

Terra started to object, but she decided against it. *He has a point. We are in enemy territory, regardless of how secure it may seem.* The half-elf fell in step beside Terra as they walked toward the gateway.

"That was amazing, Nexus. I never knew you were so talented. I'm only skilled at enchanting and alchemy," Ell said.

"Thank you," Terra said. "I don't like alchemy. It's too time consuming, and as long as I am on Dae, I have access to enough energy to conjure anything I need."

Ell was silent for a minute. "That's a good point," she said just when Terra was starting to think she had offended the woman. "If I had that much power, I wouldn't need to use alchemy either!"

"Are you the one who enchanted Captain Wright's sword and shield?" Terra asked.

Ell beamed but waited until they had passed through the gateway before answering. "I enchanted all of Lefty's gear! It took a couple years, but now everyone in the guard has some level of enchantment on their weapons and armor."

"Wow," Terra said. "That's quite the feat."

Ell giggled. "It was something to pass the time."

They drew up to Caitlyn and halted. "How are you holding out?" Terra asked the changeling.

"I'm fine," she said through clenched teeth. Terra watched as the threads of magic for the portal began to change, but Caitlyn forced them back in place.

"When did this start happening?" Terra asked, her tone sharp.

Caitlyn grunted as she fought against another influx of magic. "Couple seconds ago. What's happening?"

"Someone's trying to open a portal to Dae," Terra said. Caitlyn groaned.

"Maybe someone is trying to come help us," Ell suggested.

Terra shook her head. "No, the only Realms not under siege by Azreal right now are Science, Chaos,

Evil, and Death, and they are all allied with him. Well… Life is free, but no one ever comes or goes from there."

"What can I do to help?" Hanna asked as she ran over.

Terra let out a sigh of relief. "I know I haven't taught you any kind of planar magic yet, but do you see what Caitlyn is doing?"

Hanna nodded.

"Do you think you can do that?"

The little girl thought it over for a moment. "It's not as complex as healing, but it takes a lot more power. I won't be able to do it for more than fifteen or twenty minutes."

"Caitlyn, I'll take over for you. Ell, go let Darren know I'm staying on this side. Hanna, you and Caitlyn are going to go through the portal and make sure the other side stays stable. I'm sure they are going to start attacking that side too."

Terra set herself to the task of taking over maintenance of the portal from Caitlyn. Once she had her spell ready, Terra tapped Caitlyn on the shoulder. The changeling removed her threads, and the Nexus took seamless control of the portal. The spell bucked and pushed against her, but Terra fought back just as hard.

The other three went through the portal to go about their tasks. *About a quarter of the army is through. I can keep this in place for a couple of hours, at most.* Terra flinched as a black arrow flew past her head close enough for the fletching to tickle her ear. *What is going on over there?*

Darren stumbled through the gateway, blocking a second arrow with his kite shield. "The demons are attacking, Nexus. They are firing arrows deep into our ranks."

"You don't say," Terra muttered.

"One of my men took one to the knee, but Hanna's healing him now."

Terra nodded. "Good. Send the guard back through, they can stay with me on this side in case anything happens."

Darren stepped back through the portal to Bara and carried out her orders. In seconds, members of her personal guard were gathering around her. Most of them wore a simple shield on one side of their collar. There were a few with a winged shield, and only Paul and Ell had both a winged shield and unadorned one. Darren was the only one with two winged shields.

"Protect the Nexus while she maintains the portal from this side," Darren said.

Finally, Brahm thought. *Took the bloody men long enough to get through the flamin' gateway.* They had taken minor losses in the demons' counter attack, but the forces of Dae had a solid foothold on the Realm of Good. "Silvia, are ye there?" the grizzled dwarf asked through the Eye.

"This is Timothy," came the reply. "Am I speaking with Brahm?"

"Ye are. How're things goin' on yer end?"

There were a few seconds of hesitation. "The angels are taking wing now to strike against the southern tower. As long as you can keep the one on your end occupied, the Keeper says there should be no problem dealing with the one here."

"Good. How long's he sayin' it's goin' to take?" Brahm asked.

"No more than a few hours."

Brahm groaned.

Timothy heard the noise and asked, "What is wrong with that?"

"Someone's tryin' to open a bloody portal to Dae. Terra's back on the other side keepin' ours open, but she's no' sure she'll be able to keep it up fer more than a couple o' hours."

"Hold on," Timothy said. A few minutes passed while the army marched forward. "The Keeper of Fate says to order your men to not look up, or they will be blinded. He says to hold their shields in the air to shadow their eyes."

"When?" the dwarf asked.

"As soon as possible. Hurry," Timothy implored.

Brahm saw a flicker of light shoot up from the Great Spire in the middle of the city. It was streaking toward the star far overhead. "Get yer shields up over yer heads!" Brahm roared. "Do no' look up!" His orders were echoed up and down the lines. Shields were raised overhead without hesitation.

Brahm saw a young archer without a shield was looking around with a confused look on his face. "If ye do no' have a bloody shield then use yer hands, ye bloody beardless recruit!" The boy clapped his hands over his eyes. Brahm was about to run over and brain the man with his upraised shield when it happened.

Everything went awash in blinding white light. A deafening roar filled the air, and the ground beneath Brahm's feet trembled. "What's bloody happenin'?"

As suddenly as the roaring light had started, it stopped. "That was the power of the Source," Timothy said in an awed voice.

"What'd it do?" Brahm asked as he blinked, trying to recover his vision.

"Eternius just destroyed the smaller Obsidian Tower, and a substantial amount of the inner ring to the south of the city."

Brahm was speechless. He regained his voice a few moments later and asked, "Why'd he no' do that earlier?"

"The other angels didn't want him to," Timothy explained. "They said it was far too dangerous using the Source's power that close to the city. He said something to them then flew up to it. Brahm... It's just... gone... The tower and everything around it."

Brahm passed the word of the unexpected victory in the south to his men. "That's one down, me boys, an' one to go."

A cheer went up around him, and the army surged forward. Streaks of light soared over the walls of the City of Spires as angels flew into battle. The demons in the remaining Obsidian Tower were caught in a pincer attack between the hammer of vengeful liberators and an anvil of their ancient foes. The Hellspawn didn't stand a chance.

Chapter Six – Hello, Father

Terra was exhausted. She wasn't sure how much longer she would be able to prevent Azreal's forces from pushing her gateway out of place. Caitlyn and Silvia walked through the gateway. "It's done," her sisters said in unison. "Bara is freed."

"The keystone seal is back in place on their side," Silvia continued. "The Seat of Faith is keeping the portal open on their side." An angel had walked through while she was talking, but Terra hadn't gotten a good look at him.

"Will you be able to maintain the gateway to my home for a few more minutes? A keystone seal will not take long to create," the angel said with a powerful voice.

Terra clenched her jaw. *I've lasted this long,* she thought. *I can last a few minutes more.*

Hanna walked through the gateway and stood next to Caitlyn with her hands in the pockets of her brown leather pants. Just on the edge of Terra's vision, she thought she saw Hanna's brows draw down and eyes widen in a look of confused alarm. The little girl's eyes darted from Terra's face to something behind her. A few moments passed, and Hanna moved out of her periphery.

"Is everything all right, Hanna?" Terra asked.

"Yeah," the changeling responded. "I think so."

Hanna must have asked Darren a question because the captain said, "Definitely the eyes and nose."

A shimmering red light covered the portal. "The keystone is in place. You can release the spell now, Nexus. Nothing will come through," the angel said.

Terra stopped funneling energy into the moonstone arch and sagged with exhaustion. A midnight black portal opened, and a huge undead malformed monstrosity slammed against the seal. *The Realm of Death. Good thing I didn't lose my concentration. We would have been overrun.*

She turned to thank the angel for his help but froze when she saw his face. Hazel eyes stared back at her.

"Hello, Father," she said with her voice quaking and fists clenched.

"Hello, Daughter." Eternius had known who she was the moment he passed onto her Realm. The observant little girl and the one-handed human were right. He and Terra did look much alike, but even if they hadn't, there could be only one person with those glowing blue wings of light.

"I am Eternius, the Keeper of Fate, and you must be Terra Zane, the Nexus." He felt confused when his daughter's eyes narrowed at him.

"We should give them some privacy," Silvia said.

"No," Terra snapped. "I have nothing to say to this person." She began to walk away, but Eternius stepped into her path.

He saw the Guardian's Blade strapped to her back between her shoulders. "Wait, there are things you need to know."

Terra looked up at him with a withering glare. "I'm sure you could have taken time to tell me whatever they are in the first fifty years of my life. You know? That's the part you were never there for. Now move," she ordered.

Eternius glared into her eyes that were so much like his own. "I will not."

A shove of air caught him unprepared and made Eternius stumble a few steps to the side. *How dare she use magic against me!* He grabbed at her arm as Terra walked past, but she snatched it away. *Fine, two can play this game, Daughter.*

Eternius reached out to bind her with tendrils of air, but the Nexus severed his spell and slammed a shield around him. He was unable to cast magic past the barrier of all four elements. Terra wove it tight around him like a second skin.

"You are in my Realm, Keeper," she said with a finger pointed at his face. "And you will do as I say. The shield around you will dissipate in a minute's time. If you move or try to cast spells against it, the spell will cause you unimaginable agony.

"I will not see or hear from you again while you remain on *my* Realm. You will stand there until the necromancers grow bored with bashing their creations against the keystone seal. You will then open a portal back to Bara and go through." Terra walked off without saying more.

Maybe if I hadn't used the Source so recently, I could have bested her, Eternius thought, but he wasn't certain. The one-handed man left with the people who wore pins on their collars. The little girl and Silvia's sister left as well, leaving Eternius alone with Silvia. "It is critically important that I speak with her, Fanglady."

Silvia sighed. "I think the time for that has come and gone, Keeper, but I will talk to her. I've only seen her so angry a few times. I would recommend doing what she said and waiting for her to see you on Bara."

The spell faded away just when Terra had said it was going to. *That was a unique spell. I've not seen the like.* Eternius nodded. "I shall do that." He pulled his wings in tight around him like a cloak and settled in for a long wait.

Terra's fists still shook with the riot of emotions roaring through her. She went to her tent to discover all of her personal effects were missing. Letting out a frustrated huff, Terra remembered that her permanent quarters had been finished that morning by the stonemasons. *They must have moved everything into it.*

She stepped back out of her tent and began walking down the unfinished streets. Small wooden markers denoted the borders of their placement. Caitlyn caught up to her before she had gone more than a hundred feet from her tent. "Don't you think that was a bit extreme? He's your father," the changeling said.

Terra spun on her sister. "That person is no father of mine! He had plenty of opportunities to see me after my mother died, but he was nowhere to be found. Fifty years, Caitlyn!"

Caitlyn wrapped her arms around her. "I know. I was there for some of them, remember? Please, don't let your anger get the best of you."

Terra took a deep breath and slowly let it out. She felt the pounding in her temples subside a little. "I'm sorry for yelling at you. I'm exhausted, and that was the last thing I expected to see today. You can let go of me; I need to lie down, and all of my things were moved to my new house."

Caitlyn released Terra and walked beside her. "It's as if the city is dead," Caitlyn said. "Almost everyone is still on Bara. We can't open a gateway back there until the one from Ignia is closed."

"After I get some rest, I can cut their gateway to shreds and force onw to Bara, even if they have one open there." Terra placed her hand over her stomach. It had been over a month since she felt nauseous from the pregnancy, but the recent emotional turmoil was beginning to wear at her resilience. She let out another slow breath and mentally pushed her emotions away, determined to deal with them later. "I just hope I don't have to. I don't want to speak with him again so soon."

Darren, Silvia, and Hanna caught up to them. Captain Wright glanced at Caitlyn before speaking. "I sent the guard to their quarters," Darren said. "With the keystone, we are safe here."

"Good," Terra said. "You should get some rest too. I'll be fine with these three." Darren nodded and set off toward her guard's barracks.

Hanna giggled as soon as the man had left earshot. "He thinks you are cute, Caitlyn. He looks at you every time you're around." Terra smirked at the little girl's astute observation. *Not much gets past her.*

Silvia laughed when Caitlyn sputtered. "Well, I can't stand the sight of him," the changeling said.

Terra saw her sister glance over her shoulder at Darren's retreating backside. "Then why are you turned around looking at him?" she asked.

Caitlyn snapped her eyes back forward. "I... just wanted to make sure he couldn't hear what we were talking about."

"Sure," Silvia said. "Whatever you say."

Caitlyn crossed her arms across her chest. The other two women laughed at her consternation, and Hanna grinned. They walked in mirthful silence the rest of the way to Terra's new home.

The single story building had a decent sized kitchen, sitting room, bedroom, and nursery that was going to serve as a guest room until the baby arrived. Terra wanted a residence identical to everyone else's, but Silvia insisted it would be inappropriate. They had argued for some time over the dimensions of her house. Silvia wanted her to have something grand, and Terra said she didn't want the stonemasons to build her a palace before others had a place to live.

Silvia relented on that point and told the stonemasons to erect a modest place on a large tract of land that would eventually hold a palatial estate. Terra resided in what would be part of the servant's quarters when the full structure was completed.

"Welcome to my humble abode," Terra said with a joking bow after she opened the door. Silvia rolled her eyes as they all walked in.

A young woman of fourteen years with short blonde hair and servant's livery walked into the sitting room from the back of the house and let out a tiny yelp. She saw Terra's wings and turned pale. "Nexus! What are you doing back? I'm Deidra Belles. If it pleases you, I'll serve as your maid and chef. It's very nice to meet you," the woman blurted out.

It took Terra a moment to sort out the unexpected outpouring of information. "It is nice to meet you too, Miss Belles. I will not be needing anything for the rest of today. I trust you have residence nearby?" she said formally. The serving woman nodded. "Good, thank you for your attention to my needs. I will see you in the morning."

"Yes, Nexus," Deidra said as she went back in the kitchen and out the back door.

Terra looked at Silvia. "Did you set this up?" she asked.

"I did," the Fanglady said. "You are the leader of our entire Realm, Terra. You should be properly attended. The girl has no parents, no special skills, and is very shy. She wouldn't have served well in the army or any of the other groups of people. It made sense to install her as a servant, and you needed one."

"I would like it if you would at least talk to me first," Terra said. Her stomach rumbled, and she realized none of them had eaten since that morning. "It's well into the afternoon. How does an early dinner sound?"

"Great," Hanna said. The girl walked into the kitchen. Hanna was pulling things out of the pantry and placing them on the counter.

"Are you cooking for us?" Caitlyn asked.

Hanna laughed. "No, we are all cooking something my mother used to make before..." She fell silent for a moment. "Just something she used to make. Terra, can you find some milk or cream? Silvia, can you heat some water to boiling." The young girl tossed a few ears of corn to Caitlyn. "Can you remove the corn from the cob?"

Under Hanna's watchful gaze, the three women prepared a hearty chicken soup with corn and egg in it. They moved to the sitting room and ate multiple bowls of the thick soup with a hot black tea. "That was delicious," Terra said after all of the food was gone.

"I'm glad you enjoyed it," Hanna said. "My mother would always make it for me when I wasn't feeling well. I saw your hand over your stomach earlier, and that made me think of it."

Terra smiled. "Thank you." *I don't know what it is but having her around makes me feel better. It's like she's here to take care of me. That's ridiculous. She's not even one fifth my age. I should be the one taking care of her.*

83

Silvia took another sip of her tea and set it down on the table. "Terra, there's something I need to speak with you about, and I don't want you to become upset and ignore me as soon as I start."

"This doesn't sound like something I'm going to enjoy," Terra said.

Silvia shook her head. "It likely won't." The woman gathered her thoughts before beginning. "Eternius believes that there is something he needs to discuss with you."

As soon as Silvia said her father's name, Terra's face became an emotionless mask. "You're right. I don't want to talk about it."

Silvia looked at her with pursed lips. "He was very explicit, Sister. His exact words were, 'It is critically important that I speak with her.' He wouldn't have said that had he not meant it."

"Angels can't lie, right?" Hanna asked with a yawn. She rested her head against Terra's shoulder.

"That's right," Terra said. "But they can be wrong. They can say things out of mistaken beliefs. The truth is relative to everyone, Hanna. What one person *knows* to be true can be wildly incorrect, but to them, that is fact." Terra drank some of her tea. It was beginning to cool, and she channeled a thread of fire into it to warm it back up. "I don't trust him. People like the Keeper of Fate always has a secondary motive for everything they do."

Caitlyn let out a sigh. "Do you not trust him, or are you angry at him for abandoning you?"

Terra glared at her sisters. "Please don't team up on me."

"We aren't teaming up on you," Silvia said. "We just happen to agree with each other. I think you're letting your emotions get in the way of your judgment.

Even if you don't want to speak with him, at least go and listen to him." Caitlyn nodded her agreement.

"Fine," Terra said, holding up her hands in surrender. "But not today. I'll visit him on Bara in a few days. We'll need some time to move the army back through and plan a coordinated strike on Caine."

Caitlyn let out a short breath. "I'm not so sure that's a good idea," she said.

"Why not?" Terra asked.

"I know it's going to sound strange," Caitlyn said, "but one of the things Alex said before he came up with the plan to rescue you from the Obsidian Tower was that we weren't going to have enough people to maintain a breeding population on Dae if we didn't win soon. We need time to rally our forces and rebuild, not only our cities, but our numbers."

"What are you suggesting?" Terra asked. "That we delay fighting Azreal for a few years while we have children and raise them to fighting age?"

Caitlyn shook her head. "No, I'm just saying that we can't invade Caine and go to straight into another war. The only reason we won this fight with so much ease is because Eternius did something with the star above the City of Spires. We need to gather more information before we strike out."

"Okay, we'll just do what we did with Bara and send someone to the Realm of Order to scout and discover what is going on," Terra said.

"I think that would be unwise," Silvia said. "We may force Azreal's hand if we strike so aggressively again."

Terra felt as if she was under attack. "You two spoke about this while you were on Bara, didn't you? Was this Eternius's idea too?"

"No," Caitlyn said. "We talked about this over a week ago, before Silvia left to go to the Realm of

Good. Terra, we aren't out to get you, but we have made great strides in the recent days. We should show some prudence."

They're right, Terra thought. *I'm overreaching.* Soft snores brought their gazes to Hanna still leaning against Terra's shoulder.

"I'll get her to bed," Caitlyn said.

"There should be a small couch in the nursery," Terra said. "She should be comfortable in there."

Caitlyn nodded as she lifted the child and carried her to the back of the house. As soon as she returned, there was a knock at the door. "I'm already up," Caitlyn said as she walked to the front door.

"Captain Wright," Terra overheard Caitlyn say. "What do you want?"

"Oh, Miss Shadowpaw," Darren said. "I apologize. I thought this was the Nexus's residence."

"It is. Do you need to speak with her?"

"I just wanted to let her know that her... that Eternius had departed back to Bara. The army is coming back through the gateway now. General Ironfist was inquiring after her," Darren said.

"I'll let her know. Goodbye," Caitlyn said as she shut the door in his face. She came back into the sitting room and sat back in her chair. Terra and Silvia both glared at her. "What?" she asked innocently.

"That was rude," Terra said. "Why would you do that?"

Caitlyn picked at her pants. "He reminds me too much of someone that I... lost," she said.

"Who's that?" Silvia asked.

"Just a man I thought I loved," Caitlyn said. "I don't want to talk about it."

He has the same color hair as Alex, but that's about it. I guess Darren acts a little like him. Not that much though. "I'm sorry," Terra said. "I won't bring it up again." *He's the captain of my guard. You'll have to get used to him eventually.*

The three women drank the rest of their tea. Caitlyn said she would let Brahm know everything was fine and left. Silvia went to let Aeryn know his daughter was sleeping at Terra's.

The half-angel got up and went to the nursery. Hanna was lying on the soft couch. Caitlyn had covered her with a light blanket. "Sleep well, Hanna," Terra whispered.

She went to the next room and lay down on the left side of the bed. The Guardian's Blade rested on the bed's right side. Terra reached out and touched the wooden sword. "Good night."

Four days passed before Terra found herself walking across the Bridge of Faith toward the City of Spires. Only Darren and Caitlyn accompanied her to the Realm of Good. Their awkwardness toward each other hampered any talking, which suited Terra's mood well.

They walked the few miles from the gateway to the pearl Gate of Faith and had no trouble entering the city from its northern side. "Who enters within the walls of the City of Spires?" a silver haired female angel asked.

"The Nexus of Magic and her two overzealous guards," Terra answered. She had wanted to come alone, but neither of the other two would hear a word of it.

"Greetings, Nexus. You may call me Ureon, the Seat of Faith. You are granted entry. May the peace of the City of Spires be upon you," she said with a smile. "Your guards may wait in the Spire of Faith. I will take you to the Amphitheater of the High Seats to meet with the Keeper."

"Thank you," Terra said. The Spire of Faith, made of pearl just like the gate, stood a half-mile before them. "I'll meet you two there," she said to them. They both started to protest, but she cut them off. "I will meet with Eternius alone. You'll just have to enjoy each other's company."

Caitlyn glared at her as she followed Darren toward the spire. *I told you I wanted to come by myself.* "Please," Terra said to the angel. "Lead the way."

"It will be much faster if we fly. Will you permit me to carry you?" Ureon asked. Terra nodded, and the angel stepped behind Terra and lifted her. With a beat of powerful wings, the two took flight. "Your wings are beautiful," the angel said as soon as they were airborne.

"Thank you," Terra said. "As are yours." The Nexus looked down on the City of Spires. She had never had the opportunity to visit this Realm. Her duties as Nexus had kept her too busy for idle travel.

"The City of Spires is a perfect circle measuring five miles wide," Ureon said. Her tone was light. "The wall is made of diamond and measures exactly a quarter-mile high all the way around. There are seven gates spaced evenly along the wall. They are named after the seven virtues.

"Each gate is five hundred feet wide and tall," she continued. "Starting to the north and going clockwise, they are: Faith, my gate, made of pearl; Intellect, Myrius's gate, made of topaz; Love, Lyriel's gate, made of ruby; Honor, Aurius's gate, made of sapphire; Hope, Tyrien's gate, made of emerald; Justice,

Emeriel's gate, made of amethyst; and Truth, Ymerion's gate, made of quartz."

The two flew over the Spire of Faith. "I've read some about your city," Terra said. "The seven spires are made of the same gemstone as the gates. There are seven roads that run through the bases of the spires, and they all meet at the base of the Great Spire. Each of the seven Seats, also called the Seven Aspects, live in the spires with one thousand other angels. The Keeper of Fate resides in the Great Spire. He is leader of your Realm."

"That's all correct," Ureon said. They reached the edge of the Great Spire and began to fly straight up. Terra knew the largest spire was five miles high and banded in all seven of the gemstones and crowned in mythricite, a gold-like substance unique to the underside of the island that the City of Spires floated upon.

"How did the angels find this island to build the City of Spires on?" Terra asked. "I mean, there's nothing out here."

"Well," Ureon said, "technically, this isn't an island. We build the city on the roots of this realm's world tree?"

"What do you mean, 'this realm's world tree.' Does each realm have one?"

"That is correct. Each realm has a tree that it's focal point for energy from the Source."

Terra's eyes widened. "What would happen if a realm's world tree was destroyed?" she asked with a trembling voice.

Terra and Ureon settled down in the center of the Amphitheater of the High Seats. There were eight chairs, seven were of the various gemstones, and one of the golden mythricite. There was a plinth with a book open to the end nearby.

"What are you saying?" Ureon asked.

"Dae's world tree is dead. It was destroyed by an anti-magic shard. There was nothing the sprites could do to stop it."

The angel's fresh face turned serious and her tone dark. "Do not tell anyone of this," she commanded. "It will cause undue concern, and there are trying times ahead for the Nine Realms."

Caught off-guard by Ureon's sudden change of demeanor, Terra nodded. "I won't tell anyone."

"Swear it, Nexus. The future of the Nine Realms hangs upon your word."

"As the Paragon of the Realm of Magic, I swear to keep this secret."

Ureon smiled and all vestiges of seriousness faded. "Please wait here. I will return with Eternius shortly."

Terra nodded, and the angel turned transparent and passed through the floor. *Turning ethereal would be handy*, Terra thought. She looked around the meeting place but didn't find anything of interest until her eyes fell upon the book at the center.

This must be the Libram of Fate. It was open to the last page. *I wonder what it says.* Terra walked to the plinth and saw it was written in angelic. She started at the top of the last page. It read, 'On the day of Magic's triumph,'

The book slammed shut before she could see more. Terra looked up and saw her father across the stand from her. He was covered from his collar down in layered mythricite platemail. "I apologize, Terra, but these words are not for the eyes of the uninitiated."

"I understand," Terra said. She suddenly wanted to yell at him, to scream every hurtful thing she had thought since she was a child, to throw every time he had never been around when she needed him in his face, but she fought against the impulse. "Silvia said you needed to speak with me."

"I see you have the Guardian's Blade with you," Eternius said. "Why do you carry it?"

He wanted to talk about Alex's sword? "It's the only thing I have that belonged to my husband."

Her father studied Terra from head to toe. His gaze lingered for a moment on her stomach, but he didn't say anything. "Is that the only reason?"

Terra nodded. "Why do you ask?"

"I needed to know the truth of something I had read," Eternius said. "I am sorry for all of the pain you have been through in your life, my daughter."

"Stop," she said. "The time for 'I'm sorry' and 'Let me give you some advice' has long passed. As far as I'm concerned, you're just the man that impregnated the woman that bore me. You're as much my father as she was my mother."

"What happened to your mother?" Eternius asked.

Terra glared at him. "She died when I was hardly more than a child, not that she seemed to want me much. Lenora Shadowpaw, Silvia's mother, adopted me and raised me as her own. Every day, I hoped that I would see you, the only living person whose blood I shared. But you never showed up. So don't play the concerned father so late in the game. Like I said, the time for that has passed."

Eternius stood perfectly still, his wings tucked around him. "I can see that. Is it your plan to liberate Caine now that your home is secure?"

"No," Terra said with a shake of her head. A few strands of red hair spilled over her face, and she tucked them behind her ear. "My friends have convinced me that it would be best to rally for a time. In a few months, we'll assess the situation on the Realm of

Order, but until then, we will rebuild and resettle the land. There is much work to do on Dae."

"Would you like the assistance of some of my people?" Eternius asked.

"It would be appreciated, Keeper." *I don't have a father,* Terra thought. *This angel is nothing more than the Paragon of his Realm.* "Some of your more skilled at water and earth magics would be of great aid getting the agriculture back in full swing."

"I will see it done." The two talked for a time on affairs of state and coordinated ways to assist each other, but there were no more personal discussions. They separated ways with a handshake. Eternius summoned Ureon back to give Terra a ride to the Spire of Faith.

The Nexus collected her two friends and departed the Realm of Good.

"You should stop eavesdropping every chance you get," Eternius said as soon as Ureon returned.

"I'm usually the last one to be told everything," she said. "I have to listen in when the opportunity presents itself."

His daughter's words had unnerved Eternius, and he was having trouble sorting out his feelings from their meeting. *I will do my duty*, he told himself.

"Did you find out what you needed to?" Ureon asked.

"I did," the Keeper of Fate said. "A part of me hoped there would be a second meaning to the words in the Libram, but I now see that was wrong."

Ureon fluttered around him. "So you are going through with it?"

"It will take some time to prepare, but it must be done."

"I hope you will be able to forgive yourself," the Seat of Faith said.

"As do I."

Chapter Seven – The Outsider

Azreal stormed down the halls of the Overlord's Temple in Hell. Demons, cultists, and necromancers all ran the other way when they saw him coming. "INCOMPETENT FOOLS!" he roared. His completely black eyes were narrowed slits of unadulterated rage. The Demon Lord had only just revived a few hours earlier, and the news of Bara's liberation had set him in an ill humor.

His only desire was to inflict endless pain upon the demons that had been in charge of holding Bara, but they had been slaughtered when the Realm had been liberated, depriving him of the pleasure of killing them slowly. An imp cringed up to him. Azreal turned to face the puny lesser demon. "What?" the Overlord asked.

"Dark Lord, you are summoned to Ignia to meet with…" The imp gurgled its last few words as Azreal crushed the life from its body with a web of telekinetic force. He walked past the ruined lump of blood, meat, and bones.

How am I going to explain this failure to the Great Lord? Azreal thought. Only one being would dare summon the Overlord anywhere. Azreal's rise to power had been precipitated by the Great Lord's arrival on the Realm of Death. The Outsider had given Azreal the power he needed to slaughter the previous Overlord and take his place.

A being from beyond the Nine Realms. I shed the leash of the previous Overlord just to don another… But this leash is not so burdensome. The Demon Lord left the halls of his temple and stepped out into the pitch black world of Hell. Azreal looked about with his heat sensing eyes. Narrow walkways, some that stopped unexpectedly in dead ends, floated over the Black Star.

The entire Realm of Evil is at my fingertips, Azreal thought. *All these warrens and covens crisscrossing this ancient malevolence. I will bring about the end. If my bastard nephew hadn't ruined my plans on Dae.* The Demon Lord seethed at the memory of Alex running him through. *If I ever see that half-breed again, I will show him why it is unwise to cross the Overlord of Hell.*

Lost in thoughts of revenge, Azreal walked the short span to the Hellgate. The wall of flesh opened wide at its master's behest. Its thousand eyes followed Azreal as he traversed the forsaken threshold to Hell.

A wave of his hand opened the black gateway to Ignia, and he stepped through. The ever present smoke burned his lungs with an acrid stench. Things unseen shambled in the obscuring darkness of the upper level of the Realm of Death. Azreal waited there for the Great Lord to arrive.

Within moments, a formless shadow descended upon the Overlord of Hell. <The Realm of Good has been liberated,> it sent into his mind with telepathy.

"Not for long," Azreal asserted. "It can be recaptured. The Guardian will be dealt with."

The shadow lingered in front of him for a moment. Azreal thought he could make out where eyes should have been. <The Guardian is already dead. He gave his life to save the Nexus. But they are both immaterial at this point. Eternius used the Source to scour an Obsidian Tower from existence.>

"Then everything is proceeding according to plan."

The Outsider swirled around him. <Almost. Events have been manipulated for an eternity to bring us to this point, Azreal. Only a few more things

remain.   First, you must strike out on Caine with a devastating blow...>

Chapter Eight – Nightmares

Where am I? Who am I?

Hanna's eyes fluttered open. *What was that noise?* she thought. The curtains of the second room in Terra's house were closed, and there was no light shining behind them. *It's still night.* Terra had taken Hanna in as an apprentice, and they had been training every chance they could while the Nexus wasn't meeting with the council. The last two months had gone by quickly for the young girl.

"Hanna, help!" Terra shouted from the next room over. The changeling leapt from the covers and ran into the older woman's bedroom. A light hovered overhead, and the comforter on the bed had been thrown back. Terra's face was pale, and her white bed sheets were red with blood.

Everything slowed as Hanna began to take in every minor detail. Her parents and teachers had said it was amazing that she was able to soak in every aspect of a situation, but when she was stressed or dealing with someone that was injured, everything froze, giving her time to assess the situation.

Terra's dress was bloody from her waist down. *Bleeding from her uterus most likely.* Her face was pale, and the spot of blood covered a large portion of the sheets. The blood immediately around where Terra lay was wet, indicating that the mattress had soaked up a lot. *She must have been bleeding for a long time before she woke up. I have to stop it, or she will go into shock.*

The observations took only a second, and the seven-year-old changeling sprang into action. She sent a probe into Terra's lower body at the same time she wove a compress of air. The probe deemed her guess accurate, and Hanna pressed the air into Terra. The woman cried out in pain, but the bleeding had to be stopped.

"I know it hurts, Terra, but you could die if I don't stop this." Hanna reached her hand across the room and pulled a cushion off of the couch with another flow of air. Using still more air, she lifted Terra's legs and floated the cushion under them to try preventing her from going into shock. Blood tried to surge past the block of air inside of Terra. The woman cried again at the painful pressure.

I have to find the source of the bleeding. Hanna sent the probe of energy into Terra's womb. The bubble of magical power and energy that surrounded the baby was much larger than normal. *The sudden change in size stretched the lining of her uterus until it began to rupture.*

Hanna sent the probe into the gap of the field around the baby. The area inside was still disproportionately large. It took the little girl a moment to find the baby within the bubble. She touched the baby with the probe and splitting pain tore through her head.

An alien feeling of curiosity flooded into Hanna's mind. *You are killing her!* the changeling screamed in her mind at the baby. *Stop!* Hanna withdrew the probe when the sphere receded in size. Terra's uterus grew smaller.

The young medic opened a small gap in the blockage of air to drain some of the blood that had pooled inside of Terra. When Hanna deemed enough had drained to not cause too much pain and pressure, she put the block back in place. The bleeding slowed. Terra let out a small moan of relief. She was still pale, and Hanna would need to monitor her for a few more hours, but it seemed the danger had passed.

"What happened?" Hanna asked as she wiped the sweat from her forehead. The room was cool, but her exertions had been taxing. *I've never maintained four different spells at the same time before.*

Terra's voice was weak. "I don't know," she said. "I had a strange dream… I was trying to escape from somewhere. Then I was being ripped apart from the inside. That was when I woke up, and it hurt so much. The blood… Is the baby all right?"

Hanna wasn't sure how to tell Terra that if she had not been there then the woman would have died. Hanna wasn't even sure what she had done to get the baby to stop expanding the bubble of force. *Did Jessica hear me?* "Your baby is fine. But…"

"What?" Terra whispered.

"Let's get you cleaned up first. We can talk about it in the morning." Terra nodded.

Hanna went to the kitchen, got a pot, and filled it with water. She grabbed a few clean cloths and went back into Terra's bedroom. Hanna had carefully maintained the air compress while she was out of the room, and she was relieved to see it was still in place. The changeling channeled fire into the water until it boiled. She put two of the three cloths in the boiling water.

Hanna watched the water roil for a few moments and then extracted the heat from the water with a thread of air and fire. She set the warm pot on the nightstand. Using a razor sharp filament of air, Hanna cut Terra's blood-soaked dress from her body and slid it out from under her. She changed the air knife into a soft bed of air and using more weaves of air, lifted the

Nexus from the bloody sheets and mattress and placed her naked body on the magical bed.

"You're getting better at handling complex bits of air," Terra said, her voice just above a whisper.

"Thank you. I'm going to clean you off now. Hold still." Hanna used the warm cloth to wipe the drying blood from Terra's body. When she was done, she sent another probe into the woman and saw the bleeding had slowed to an insignificant level. The young girl removed the compress of air and placed the dry cloth over Terra's privates to soak up the slow trickle of blood.

Holding the floating bed in place, Hanna went to Terra's closet and got another night dress. Taking care to not move her around too much, she slipped the dress over Terra's head and pulled it down to cover her completely. "I'm going to lay you down in my bed," Hanna said. "I'll sleep on the chair in there so I can be there if you need me."

"Okay," Terra said with a weak smile. The older woman let out a sigh and began to snore softly.

She must have lost more blood than I thought. Hanna took extreme care moving Terra through the house and had her hovering over the other bed in a few minutes time. The young girl watched over the woman until the curtains began to lighten with the coming dawn.

Terra yawned and stretched her arms and legs. She opened her eyes and saw she was in Hanna's bed, and the young changeling was sitting in the chair. Terra felt something between her legs. She reached down and found a small white cloth that was spotted with blood. She stood and walked over to Hanna.

"Hanna," Terra said as she touched the young girl's shoulder. "Wake up."

The girl's eyes opened, and she stared at Terra. Dark circles were under Hanna's brown eyes. "What are you doing out of bed?" Hanna demanded. "Lie back down."

"What's going on?" Terra asked, confused at the young girl's orders. She sat back down on the bed but didn't lie down.

Hanna looked at her dumbfounded. "Are you trying to tell me you don't remember anything of what happened last night?"

"The last thing I remember was laying down in my bed. Then I woke up in the wrong room, and you're in the chair," Terra looked down, "and I'm wearing a different night gown."

Hanna rubbed her eyes. "Hold still." Terra watched as a medical probe entered her abdomen. She felt a slight tingling sensation as the changeling checked her over. "That's not possible," Hanna muttered. A few more seconds passed. Terra wanted to ask the girl what wasn't possible, but she had learned it was useless to talk to Hanna while she was examining someone.

"Well," Hanna said. "I don't know how, but you are fine. There isn't even the smallest sign of any tearing at all, and it seems you aren't missing any blood."

"Missing blood? What are you talking about?"

Hanna shook her head. "You really don't remember." She slid from her chair. "Let me show you something." Hanna walked to the door and waited for Terra to get up.

Terra rose from the bed and followed Hanna to the master bedroom. Blood was everywhere. The room reeked with the smell of it. Her sheets, mattress, and shreds of her dress were covered in brown, dried blood. "What happened?" Terra asked, unable to comprehend the sight.

Hanna rubbed her face for a moment before speaking. "You were calling for me last night. I came in here, and there was blood everywhere. The bubble around the baby was expanding and was beginning to rip the lining of your uterus. I think the baby read my mind when I touched her with the probe, and she made the shield around her get smaller again. I treated you, cleaned you, and moved you to my bed so I could watch over you."

Terra's mind ground to a halt. *There's no way that can be true,* she thought, but the evidence in front of her screamed otherwise. "How can I not remember any of that?" Terra asked.

Hanna threw her arms in the air. "I don't know! How can you be perfectly healthy now when no one can heal you? You almost died last night, but now you are fine."

"How did it happen?" Terra asked.

"I don't know. But if you had been alone, you would have died, Terra. Of that, I'm certain."

Terra walked out of the room. She was having trouble focusing her gaze on anything. Terra walked into the living room and sat down on the couch. Hanna followed her.

"Are you okay?" Hanna asked.

"I almost died last night," Terra muttered as she stared at her hands clasped in her lap. *Maybe I'm not strong enough to have this child.* The thought skittered across the edges of her consciousness, and Terra did her best to ignore it.

Hanna sat down in the chair across from the coffee table. "Well... Yes, but I don't think Jessica knew what she was doing," she said. Terra looked up at her with one raised brow. "Your baby is doing things I've never heard of or read about. You're just over seven months right?"

"Seven months and a week," Terra said with a nod.

Hanna chewed on her lip while she thought over what she was going to say. "Most babies are moving around a lot when they get to that period. Maybe that's what was happening here. When the probe touched her, I felt a strong sense of curiosity."

"That's the second time you've mentioned being able to read her mind. How did you do it?" Terra asked.

"I was checking for what was causing your bleeding, and I was able to touch Jessica with the probe of magic. Now, this is all a guess, but when I did, I'm pretty sure she used it to establish a telepathic link. She sensed that I wanted her to stop what she was doing, so she did." Hanna sighed. "I have no idea if that's right, or just coincidence."

"Try again," Terra said.

"What?"

"Since I can't heal anyone, I've never tried to learn that kind of magic. It's impossible to use a medical probe on yourself anyway. I want you to try again and see if you can talk to her."

Hanna nodded. The young girl closed her eyes, and the Nexus watched as an infinitesimal line of magic wove itself from Hanna's head and reach into Terra's belly. The Nexus hadn't seen such a small probe before, and she barely felt it enter her body. Only the tiniest tingling, and Terra's ability to see the spell, belied its presence.

After a few seconds, Hanna opened her eyes with the spell still in place. "I'm touching her, but she's not doing anything. I think she may be asleep."

"Can you tell what she's thinking?" Terra asked.

Hanna shook her head. "No, but she fidgeted when you talked. I'm not sure if she's asleep or just floating there." The young girl closed her eyes again to get a better mental image of the baby. "I think her eyes are open, but it's hard to tell. Talk again."

Terra looked down at her belly as she tried to think of something to say. "What should I say?"

Hanna snapped a hand up to her forehead. She let out yelp of pain. "Stop! That hurts!" she shouted.

"I'm not doing anything," Terra started to say, until she realized the girl wasn't talking to her. The Nexus looked more closely at the medical probe connecting Jessica to Hanna and saw a filament of gray energy that shouldn't have been there. *What is going on?*

"Thank you," Hanna said as she lowered her hand. The girl opened her eyes and looked up at Terra. The gray line of energy still was encapsulated in the probe. "She's definitely awake. It felt like she was scouring my brain. It hurt, but I'm fine. I can feel her emotions, but her mind… it doesn't make sense. There isn't any language, just…" Hanna screwed up her face in thought. "I can't explain it."

"I'm just glad she's fine," Terra said. Hanna giggled. "What?"

"She thinks you sound funny," the changeling said. Terra looked at her with a curious expression. "No, that's not right. That was me trying to understand the feeling. Make a sound." Terra hummed a few notes of a lullaby she had made up for Silvia and Caitlyn when they were younger. Hanna grinned.

"She's happy to hear you. I think she may have understood that she was hurting you from what she read from me last night. No, she doesn't understand happy or hurt. That's me. You make her feel warm… No, that's not it." Hanna let out a breath of frustration. "It's hard to understand. There's no frame of reference. She's curious again. I think she felt my emotions."

Hanna's voice took on a soothing tone as she said, "I'm fine. Don't worry. I'll talk to you again." She withdrew the spell. The grey filament lingered for a split-second after the spell was gone before disappearing as if it had never been.

"That was amazing," Terra said.

"Yeah," Hanna said. "I've always wondered what babies thought about, but it's odd to experience it. There weren't thoughts like the ones I have. It's all just feelings. And curiosity, so much curiosity. She wants to know… everything. When she first reached out to me, it felt like she was ripping my memories up to the front of my mind, and it hurt. But she stopped when she felt my pain.

"She won't try doing what she did last night," Hanna continued. "At the end, it was like there was a feeling of stretching and a negative feeling."

The back door opened, and they looked to the kitchen. Deidra stepped into the sitting room. "Oh," she squeaked when she saw the two people staring at her. The young woman had lost some of her shyness, but the smallest things kept surprising her. "Good morning, Nexus, Miss Steelfeather. Would you care for some toast and eggs with tea for breakfast?"

"Yes. Thank you, Deidra," Terra said. *She will break down into tears or scream if she sees my room.* "Also, don't worry about cleaning my room or turning down my sheets. I will take care of it today."

"Yes, Ma'am," her maid said. The young woman's blonde hair had grown longer in the past two months since she entered Terra's service, and she had it back in a short ponytail. Her hair swung back and forth as she turned about and entered the kitchen. Pans clanged as she began to ready breakfast.

"We'll talk more about this later," Terra said. Hanna nodded, and they began the day's instruction.

After Deidra left for the day, Terra moved her mattress, sheets, and dress out to the expansive backyard and burned them to a cinder with a compressed block of fire and air. *I think that would raise far too many questions if it got out. I can trust Hanna not to tell anyone*, Terra thought as she walked back inside. She got an extra set of sheets from the small linen closet in the short hallway that adjoined the two bedrooms and lay down on the couch in the sitting room. *I'll get a new mattress tomorrow.*

The Nexus slowly fell asleep thinking about her baby.

Her eyes opened, and everything was awash with a pale green light. She looked to the left and saw a glass cylinder that held a woman with a long gray braid. The woman looked young, but she had dark rings under her eyes. The gray haired woman floated in a thick green gel.

It's the same dream again, Terra thought. *Please, wake up, I don't want this.* Her rational mind faded away as she was swept up in the false reality.

"Oh, good," Doctor Moore said. "You are awake. It is time to begin the operation."

Terra pulled against the manacles holding her tight to the cold metal table. She looked down at her naked body. Her belly was swollen. She was ready to give birth. Like the slam of a sledgehammer, a contraction stole her breath. Every muscle in her body tensed, and she screamed in pain.

"Ugh," the doctor said as he wiggled a finger in his ear. "That's enough of that." He put a gag in her mouth and turned his back to her. Terra heard the clink of delicate metal on metal. She felt another contraction starting to swell, and she sank her teeth deep into the gag. Her scream was muted by the ball of rubber in her mouth.

"Much better," the man who invented the extraction pods said. He turned back to her holding a small piece of metal that glowed on one end. "Now, laser scalpels are a bit old-fashioned, but I've found that a hands on approach is usually the most satisfying."

The man bent over her middle, and Terra felt searing pain as the hot blade cut through her distended stomach. She wanted to struggle, but a tremendous pressure started to push on her from the shoulders down. Black ropes of demonic power held her in place, save her head. Terra looked right and screamed in fear and anger.

Azreal's nightmare black eyes stared back at her. His blood-red lips widened in a grin.

Terra awoke gasping for breath and sat upright on the couch. The Nexus clenched her teeth, and she forced her breathing to slow. "You won't have her,"

she growled at the darkness. The woman stood and walked to the curtained window. She drew aside the white cloth enough to glance at the sky. *An hour or so until dawn*, she thought when she saw the lightening sky.

With a thought, Terra released her wings, and a soft blue light filled the room. She hid them at night while she was sleeping. Their light made it hard to drift off.

I should get ready. We've waited long enough. I'll not stand by any longer while another Realm remains under Azreal's thumb. Terra walked to her room and stopped in the middle of the room. She looked from the closet to the large double-doored wardrobe. With a resolute nod, Terra threw open her wardrobe's doors. Her refined thorium armor reflected the light of her wings.

It's time for action.

Chapter Nine – Caine

<I can make you more than you are. I can give you power.>

Terra stood before the gateway arch. The smells of dirt and cooking were strong, and birds chirped from the tops of the buildings surrounding the small park in the center of Victory City.

Brahm, Caitlyn, Darren, and Ell flanked her, two to each side. The half-elf had beaten Paul in a game of Rock-Paper-Scissors to see which of the lieutenants would stay behind with the rest of the men. Hanna was perched on Terra's shoulder in the peregrine falcon form of her birth.

Looking at ease in his unrefined thorium armor, Brahm asked her, "Are ye ready, Terra?" He stood with his black warhammer across his shoulder.

"I am," Terra said. She had needed to make some modifications to her armor for it to fit over her slightly protruding belly, but it was an easy task to accomplish. The Nexus carried a short spear with the Guardian's Blade sheathed at her hip and a shortbow slung over her back. Azreal's ability to block magic had caused her to get captured before, and she intended for it to not happen again.

Caitlyn was in her panther form, and she twitched the tip of her tail about impatiently. "Good, I could hardly believe it when you walked into the council chambers yesterday morning wearing platemail. I think you almost made Silvia's eyes roll out of her head." Darren, in his leather and chain armor, laughed at her joke. Caitlyn stopped moving her tail.

"I'm just glad we aren't sitting around anymore," Hanna said from Terra's shoulder. "We shouldn't be waiting while other people are suffering."

Ell laughed. "Me too. If we'd stayed here much longer, one of these masons would've stolen my heart. I like 'em big and brawny."

Terra shook her head and laughed. She had gone before the council the day before and said she was going to Caine with or without the blessing of the other councilors. The entire council, including the newly appointed members, had erupted in protest. Terra stood before them, her armored arms crossed beneath her breasts and just stared at them, silent and unblinking.

The protests died off, and Caitlyn and Brahm joined her. A few seconds later and she was joined by the other three members of her party. The six had stood before the council, unified in their mission. "When do you leave?" Aeryn had asked.

"Tomorrow morning," Terra answered.

The Winglord nodded, his expression grave. "Bring my daughter back to me safe."

"I will," Terra said. She turned and walked from the council chambers, taking her friends with her. A day of rushed preparations and night of fitful rest found the six people before the moonstone semicircle.

Terra took a calming breath. She closed her eyes and let it out slowly. The morning air of early summer was cool on her skin, but it wouldn't remain so for long. "It's time." Terra cast a complex weave of all four elements and delved deep into connecting the portal.

Imagine nine concentric rings. Each ring is connected to the two adjacent, her mother's voice echoed in her head. *Life, Good, Order, Magic, Balance, Science, Chaos, Evil, and Death. Close your eyes and reach through the portal and connect two rings with a thread of magic.*

Terra shut her eyes and visualized the nine circles of the Nine Realms. She made a bridge between her ring and the smaller one closer to the middle. There was some resistance, but Terra pushed through it. The portal opened, and the Nexus placed the keystone seal, a small silver disc with a lock engraved into it, on the side of the gateway arch. The barrier of force lowered.

The portal to the Realm of Order was red. Terra couldn't see anything dangerous on the other side, just a view of grass that quickly gave way to sand and the ocean. As they had discussed, Caitlyn, Brahm, and Darren went through first. Terra counted to ten and followed them through, taking care to maintain the portal as she did.

The salty smell of the ocean and the soft shush of waves made her feel at ease in the alien Realm. Terra looked left and right. They were on the point of a grassy island, and aside from themselves and the grass, there were no other signs of life. She turned around and had to crane her neck all of the way back.

The Cainen gateway arch was made from the roots of the largest tree Terra had ever seen. She had thought the World Tree on Dae was big, but the size of this tremendous ash tree was mindboggling. *It has to be at least three or four-thousand feet to the nearest branch. They stretch out so far…*

The branches of the tree Terra could see were each at least a mile in length, some much longer than that. She couldn't see how high the tree went, but she was certain it went up to the clouds. Hanna took wing from Terra's shoulder and landed atop the wooden gateway arch.

"Terra," Hanna said. "Something's wrong with my magic."

The Nexus looked at the young changeling. The look of concern on the girl's face had Terra searching for what could be bothering her. The woman closed her eyes and tried to sense any latent magical energy in the area. There wasn't any because they were away from the Realm of Magic. "There isn't any magical energy here," Terra explained. "Conserve what you have collected in your core, after it runs out you'll be using your own energy for spells."

"I'm going to fly around for a moment," Hanna said. "I have better eyes than any of you like this." Terra nodded her permission, and the Changeling of the Wing took flight, gaining altitude and working her way around the tree.

"We should begin making our way around the tree as well," Ell said. The half-elf's curly blue-green hair was back in a barely restrained pony tail that bobbed when she began walking to the left around the tree. Terra used the Eye of the Stars to tell Silvia everything seemed fine, closed the portal back home, and followed behind her.

"You grew up in the Arcane City?" Terra asked her guardswoman.

Ell nodded, making her hair bounce more. "My mother was a baker, and my father was an alchemist. They met one day when he came in to buy bread. They said it was love at first sight. I was twenty when the city fell. If it wasn't for Lefty and Paul, I would have died with my parents."

Terra was in the Arcane City when it had fallen, and she wanted to know how others had survived to make it out of the city. She put the question to Ell. The normally talkative half-elf didn't speak. "If the memories are too painful, you don't have to tell me," Terra said.

"No," Ell said with a shake of her head. "I was just thinking of how to start. It was absolute chaos. I was back at the bakery trying to get the last of our things together for the evacuation. Another portal to Starfall was going to be opened in an hour. My parents were both helping the guards hold the wall when I felt the explosion.

"I don't know how, but I knew both of my parents had just died," Ell continued. "I collapsed in the doorway of the bakery holding a cutting block I was carrying to the small cart we owned. I could hear the screams…" The woman shuddered. She was silent for a few moments before continuing.

"A small winged demon landed next to me and tried to stab me with a black knife. I came out of my daze in time to pull one of the big cleavers from the block. When it was over, I was kneeling over a chopped up pile of blood, flesh, and bones. I grabbed the demon's knife and a knife from our cart and stood there in the middle of the road to await my death. 'I won't make it through this,' I thought, 'but I'm going to take as many of them as I can with me.'

"So there I was, standing in the middle of the street with my two knives, when Darren and Paul came charging around the corner. 'What are you doing?' Darren shouted at me." Ell laughed. "I realized how silly I must have looked. He reached me and grabbed my shoulders. 'We have to get out of here, but the city's surrounded. Do you have a place we can hide?' he asked me. I nodded and led them back into the shop."

Terra was so engrossed in the tale that she tripped over a small offshoot of a much larger tree root. She stumbled a few steps but caught herself. Ell, also lost in the retelling, didn't notice the woman lose her balance.

"There was a trapdoor that's hard to see in the cellar of the shop. We hid in there for a few days until the smell of our waste drove us out of the space. The city was completely empty, demons, undead, and all. There weren't any bodies left, only smears of blood where people had fallen. Darren led us south.

"We made it out of the city, but we were stopped by a small group of undead. Darren wouldn't let us attack them, we tried to outrun the group, but they kept catching up. Finally, when it came to fighting them or dying, we did what we had to. Darren was," Ell stopped talking mid-sentence.

"What?" Terra asked.

"I was bitten on my left hand by a zombie," Darren said from in front of Ell, his tone was grim and angry. The half-elf had seen him and stopped talking. "It was my brother's reanimated corpse, that was why I didn't want to fight him. As soon as his teeth sank into my flesh, I drew the sword from his belt and cut off my hand at the wrist. I was not going to become like him. While he was eating my hand, I cut off his head. This is his sword and shield. Caitlyn and Brahm are just ahead. Hurry."

The two women sped to a jog and followed Darren to where the dwarf and changeling waited. "What's the problem?" Terra asked. They were in a small grove in the space between two roots. Caitlyn and Brahm were crouched against the root as if they were hiding.

"That's the bloody problem," Brahm said as he pointed over the root.

Sealing away her wings so she would not be spotted, Terra walked to him and lifted herself so she could see over the prodigious root. An Obsidian

Tower stood a few miles past the end of a bridge that connected the island they were on to the mainland. All of the vegetation on the mainland was dead and brown. The tower had drained the life from everything as far as Terra could see.

The Nexus lowered herself back down and looked at the others. Hanna fluttered down and alighted atop Caitlyn's back. "There's another tower around the other side of the tree," the younger changeling said. "We are on an island in a small inlet with bridges to the east and west connecting it to the rest of the land. It's pretty far away, but there is a fortress straight north. We'd have to swim across the water, though. There isn't a bridge on that side. There are mountains past that. Everything here is dead; I didn't see anything living."

Terra let out sigh. *Are we too late?* She lowered her hand and gripped the Guardian's Blade. *Alex would come up with something. We need to find out if there are any survivors.* "We'll wait here until nightfall," Terra said as she glanced at the sky. She wasn't sure how long the days and nights on Caine were, but the sun was near its zenith. "As soon as it's full dark, we'll start across the water. Are those leaves big enough to work as boats?" Terra asked Hanna.

The girl ruffled her feathers in thought. "They are big, but they would only fit two at the most," she said.

"Good. Can you fly up and cut four down?" Hanna nodded and with a beat of her small wings, she took flight. Terra laid out the bones of her plan while they waited on their impromptu boats to come floating down.

Caitlyn sniffed.   Once they left the island, everything in the Realm had taken on a washed out feel to it, even the smell of decay. She was on a leaf with Ell. The half-elf used a paddle made from the fourth leaf. The sliver of moonlight gave them just enough light to see, but too little to give them away.

Looking to her left, Caitlyn saw Darren paddling Terra, and Brahm paddling himself across. Hanna flew high overhead, keeping a watchful eye over them. There wasn't much of a current in the inlet, and they made the other beach in an hour. Caitlyn hopped from the improvised canoe, planted her legs, and bit into the side of the leaf, holding it in place of Ell to get out.

The half-elf climbed out and nodded in thanks. Caitlyn released the leaf, and it floated away. Brahm, Ell, and Darren crouched around Terra. "Demons have excellent heat vision," Terra whispered. Although she was a fair distance away, Caitlyn's keen ears caught the conversation. She kept watch on their perimeter with her sharp eyes. "But they won't be able to see us if we are more than a half-mile or so away. So stay low and quiet."

The five of them began to run through the tall dead grass, doing their best to disturb as little as possible. The three taller people moved in a high crouch, but Brahm and Caitlyn were low enough to not stand above the five-foot-tall grass. A few hours passed, and they paused to gather their breath. A couple of minutes later, Hanna landed on Brahm's head. The dwarf pursed his lips in consternation, but he kept silent.

"If we can keep up this pace, then we will make it to the fortress in two or three more hours," Hanna said. She looked at Terra with sharp eyes. "How are you doing?"

"I'm fine," the Nexus said. She took a few sips of water, then poured some water into a tin cup for Hanna to drink. "Have you seen anyone but us?"

The Changeling of the Wing flitted to the cup and dipped her beak in to drink. "There are a few patrols out, but they are following a fairly predictable path. I can see where they've beaten down the grass; they don't stray from that area. They are acting like they expect something to jump out of the overgrowth at them."

"Good," Terra said. "Hopefully that means there is some kind of resistance." She looked about taking in the washed out look of her surroundings. "There needs to be. This Realm is on the edge of death. The Obsidian Towers are draining the essence of this place."

"What would happen if a Realm died?" Darren asked as he took a bite of dried meat. Caitlyn almost snorted in derision at his question, but she held it in. *He just wants to know. I'm going to be stuck with him for a while. I don't need to take things out on him, just because he looks like Alex.*

"I don't know, but what do you think would happen if the Realm of Order stopped existing?" Terra asked.

Darren gulped. "Chaos would reign."

"If everythin' didn't bloody stop existin' all together," Brahm added.

"I'm going back up," Hanna said. "If I see anything in your way, I'll let you know."

Terra nodded. Everyone rose back to their feet and set off to the north. They ran for about another hour before the scream of a hunting bird made them freeze in their tracks. The party drew their weapons and crouched lower in the tall grass. Caitlyn worked her claws into the soft earth. She heard the heavy footfalls of something large coming their way.

The light breeze shifted in directions, and the smell of ash and brimstone assailed her nose. Caitlyn's sharp eyes saw a soft, red glow approaching from the south-west. *What is that?* A grinding sound, like stone blocks rubbing against one another, grew as the light came closer. The Changeling of the Claw saw a smirk appear on Brahm's face. Caitlyn looked at him with a curious look on her face.

Gargoyle, he mouthed.

A type of stone golem, gargoyles were imbued with fire magic that allowed them to fly. Caitlyn wasn't sure why he was smiling, until Brahm hefted his warhammer. *Of course,* she thought, *a dwarf would be able to turn a stone golem to rubble in no time. Especially if they had the Hammer of Dwarven Kings.*

The ground shook under the gargoyle's heavy steps as it walked past them. Only a few feet separated the group of crouching people and the twelve-foot mass of stone and heat. The red glow came from fiery fissures along the stone golem's humanoid body. It didn't seem to have noticed them as it continued on its way north-east.

Ell let out a slow breath and stood. Caitlyn thought the half-elf looked nervous. *She's probably never seen a gargoyle before. I've only read about them...* Hanna let out two short calls from overhead, the all-clear signal, and they started north again.

"That thing was huge," Ell whispered. "Why didn't Azreal attack Dae with those?"

"Golem are easy to destroy with magic," Terra whispered back. "Just channel a little bit of earth into their head, and they go inert. You don't even have to do a specific spell, just a thread." Ell nodded, and they kept running.

The fortress city rose up above the grass. Caitlyn could make out a five tiered structure inside of the high walls. The farther the buildings were from the gate, they higher they rose. *So archers have a clear line of sight at anything coming in through the gate,* Caitlyn thought. There weren't any lights visible in the city.

Another cry of alarm from above brought them to a halt. Hanna landed on Darren's shoulder. "We are surrounded," she said. "There was nothing there, then golem began to rise out of the ground. I think they've known we were here for a while. The city isn't safe. It's empty, and the gates are wide open. We have to run."

As soon as the Changeling of the Wing had stopped talking, a stone golem rose up a few feet in front of them and began to crash toward them. Terra channeled the barest line of earth magic into its head, and it shuddered then stilled. "That's all we have to do for these. We need to get to the mountains. If the city is overrun, and there is a resistance, then maybe we can find them there."

"What about going back to the portal?" Caitlyn asked.

Terra shook her head. "They will expect that and have it cut off completely. And Silvia has orders to not open a portal for another six hours. It would open and close, and we would be nowhere near. They would capture us, and... You don't want them to capture you." Terra had been in an extraction pod before, but she had never told Caitlyn about it. "We need to get out of here. North-west, away from the direction that gargoyle was going."

Terra released a pulse of unfocused earth magic, disabling all of the golems within a few hundred yards, and they ran.

Chapter Ten – Hunted

At what cost?

The sun rose and set before they had a chance to rest. The dogged pursuit had kept Terra, Caitlyn, Brahm, Darren, Hanna, and Ell running at full tilt. Gargoyles and efreet, the elemental denizens of the Realm of Chaos, filled the air, keeping Hanna from scouting ahead for them. Fortunately for the pursued, their enemies were easily dealt with. A thread of earth magic would disable a golem or gargoyle. Efreet were a bit more difficult to kill, but a pulse of energy the opposite of an efreet's alignment would stun it for a time.

They had made it to the mountains, and Terra had caused a landslide to collapse the path behind them, blocking off pursuit. Seizing the opportunity to rest, the women and Hanna set up a watch rotation so the others could rest. Caitlyn had changed back into her human form so she could help protect them with magical energy, and she was on the first hour's watch. Darren and Brahm made a hurried dinner. The dwarf went to sleep, leaving Darren on watch with Caitlyn.

Maybe I can finally have a chance to talk to her, the human thought. The crescent moon was slightly larger tonight, and he found his way to the stone Caitlyn was sitting on. "Hey," Darren said.

"What do you need?" Caitlyn asked him, her tone bordering on hostility.

Darren ground his teeth. "Have I done something to make you angry?"

With a sigh, Caitlyn shook her head. "No, you haven't. I'm sorry."

Might as well get to the heart of the problem. "Why don't you like me?"

There was a moment of hesitation before Caitlyn answered. "I'm not sure."

"You're lying to me," Darren said. "You know why you don't like me, but you don't want to tell me." Caitlyn started to protest. "No, it's all right. If I didn't like someone, I wouldn't want to tell them why if it was something they couldn't help. I guess I remind you of someone you lost?"

Caitlyn stared at him with a slack-jawed expression. "Who told you?"

Darren smiled softly. "You just did. I'll leave you alone, then. It would have been nice to have someone to talk to on watch, though. Be safe." He turned and walked away from her.

"You too," Caitlyn said.

Darren glanced over his shoulder at her and smiled again. "Don't worry. I can defend myself well enough." A look of painful shock crossed the changeling's face. "What's wrong?"

"Why would you say that?" she whispered. For a moment, Darren thought she was angry, but he was surprised to see tears begin to well in her eyes. He walked to Caitlyn and put his leather armored arms around her. She was tense in his embrace.

"I'm sorry," Darren said, not quite sure what he was apologizing for.

Caitlyn shook her head. "No, you don't need to be sorry. That was one of the first things he told me. I was just thinking about when he and I met before you came over here. You just caught me off guard." The changeling slid over, making room on the stone outcropping. "I don't feel like talking about it, but you can sit here with me if you want."

Well, it's something. I guess. Darren sat next to her, and they watched the night together.

Terra awoke when it came time for her to stand watch. She had taken the second shift, one of the worst, since it disrupted sleep the most. Looking about for Caitlyn, she saw the changeling and Darren sitting on a stone outcrop not far away. Terra drew her cloak tighter around herself; the mountain air was cooler than it was on the plains.

The Nexus walked over to her friend and the guardsman. "You can go to sleep, Caitlyn. I have it from here." The changeling nodded and slid down from the rock. Without speaking to either of them, Caitlyn went and lay down. Terra climbed up the rock and sat next to Darren. "Is everything all right?" she asked.

"Yeah," Darren said. "We were just sitting here."

"Did you tell her you like her?"

Darren blushed and stared out into the night. "No."

"That's good. I don't know how she would react." Pain at the memory of Alex's death gripped Terra's heart. "Caitlyn is still upset over the loss of someone she loved when she was fighting Azreal's army. She just needs some time."

"What about you?" Darren asked.

Terra laughed softly to keep from waking anyone up. "Are you going to tell me you love me?"

"Uh, what? No! I mean, yes, but not like that. I love you like, um, as a leader not romantically," the captain rambled.

Terra shook her head and smiled. "I'm joking, Darren. I knew what you meant. I'll be fine. It hurts a little less every day, and I have Alex's baby to care for. Don't worry about me."

Darren nodded. A few minutes passed, and Brahm walked over. "Get yerself to bed, Boy."

"You're early," Darren protested.

"Aye, an' I'm also yer general givin' ye an order. There's somethin' I need to talk to Terra abou'."

"As you command, General Ironfist," Darren said, his tone stiff and formal. "Good night, Terra." The guardsman went and lay down.

Rather than scramble up the stone, Brahm leaned against it. "How're ye doin'?" he asked.

"I'm fine, Brahm. What did you need to talk about?"

The dwarf was silent for a time while he thought over what he was going to say. "Terra, I do no' think we'll be makin' it out o' this one."

Terra drew her brows down. She slid from the rock and stood next to Brahm. "What do you mean?"

"I've been thinkin' abou' it," he said, "an' it seems like the golems're herdin' us deeper an' deeper into the mountains. As long as we keep goin' this way, they're satisfied an' do no' harry us. As soon as we try to turn away from this path, they're on us like flies on a boar carcass."

Biting her lower lip, Terra thought about their experiences of the previous day. *It does seem that way, but if they are leading us into a trap why let us rest at all?* She posed the question to Brahm.

"I do no' know," he said after thinking it over for a moment. "If yer quarry can no' escape, then ye may as well run 'em ragged. Maybe Azreal wants us to be somewhere before he captures us. Maybe he wants us to see something. I have no idea. The Overlord's one to play with his food before he eats it."

Terra shook her head. "I don't think Azreal knows we're here yet. He would have come to personally gloat."

Brahm shrugged. "All I know is that another day o' bloody runnin' round like we've just had, an' we'll all be dead on our feet. If no' just flat out dead."

"I just wish we had heard something from Silvia. That's two check-ins she's missed. Something's wrong back home, and I'm not there to help," Terra said.

"Do no' second guess yerself. Ye're where ye need to be, an' there's nothin' that can change that now."

Terra nodded but didn't say anything else.

It was the early hours of the morning when Timothy put his hand on Silvia's shoulder. He found her standing in front of the gateway arch again, just staring at the black portal to Ignia, the Realm of Death. The keystone seal had done its job of keeping the undead on their side of the portal. "Please, Silvia, you have to rest," Timothy implored. "You can't just stand here waiting for the portal to close."

"I have to," she said. "None of the magic users left here on Dae are strong enough to force a portal past this one, but even the necromancers of Ignia will grow tired. When that happens, there will be a short break, and I will open a portal to Caine and let Terra know what's happening."

Kissing her on the top of her head, Timothy nodded into her hair. "I understand your feelings. Both of your sisters are out there, and you don't know what's going on and can't tell them everything is fine here. Post someone here to tell you when the portal goes down. You won't be any good to anyone if you pass out and can't be woken up to open a portal or use the Eye of the Stars. Please, get some sleep. I can stand here until morning."

Silvia nodded numbly. "Let me know-"

"If anything changes," Timothy finished. "I will. I love you. Sleep."

She nodded again and walked toward her home.

Be all right, Nexus. Timothy stared into the inky depths of Ignia.

The dawn came too early for anyone's liking. They quickly gathered their things and began to move again. Brahm's observation of them being herded began to seem more likely as the day of running went on. As long as the party continued in a north-westerly direction, they were left alone, but as soon as a junction appeared or another mountain pass came up, they were attacked with relentless ferocity until they went the desired direction.

"They are definitely forcing us somewhere," Terra said. "Do we fight our way along a different path, or do we let them spring the trap and fight our way out of it?"

Caitlyn, loping alongside Terra in her panther form, said, "I'll see if I can scout ahead a little." She bounded off.

"I'm fer fightin' our way through. I do no' like havin' me path chosen fer me," Brahm said. The others all agreed.

A few more minutes of running and Caitlyn returned from her short expedition. "There's a pass just ahead. It goes almost straight east, toward the center of the mountain range."

"Then east we go," Terra said as she vaulted over a waist-high stone. "This will likely deplete the last of our magical energy. Once you run out, don't keep casting, we'll need our stamina. Destroy the head and a golem is destroyed."

Brahm scrambled over the same stone Terra had jumped over with a smile on face. "Finally, a good fight." He said the power word for his amulet, and the armor of the first Brahm began expanding from the unrefined thorium necklace. The dwarf gained a look of unstoppable power as the magical armor worked its way down his arms and legs. The strength amplifying properties of unrefined thorium armor could only be safely used by a dwarf, and Brahm was already exceptionally strong.

"It's a blind right turn," Caitlyn said. "I didn't see it the first time, but when I was coming back I saw it. The opening is a cleft rock only wide enough for one person at a time, but it opens up once you get through. It's coming up." A snapping of bones and sinew announced the arrival of Caitlyn's primal form. Foot-long incisors and long, razor-sharp bone spines protruded from the back of the now six-foot-tall panther.

Brahm charged up to the front of their line and drew his warhammer from the hanger on his back. As soon as Caitlyn said, "Now," Brahm hooked his right hand into the cliff face and swung onto the pass. As expected, a mass of golems, gargoyles, and efreet blocked the path.

Bellowing, the Grand General of Dae crashed into them. Terra had never seen the dwarf leap into a fight with such wild abandon. Every mighty blow of his warhammer shattered a golem. Every strike caused a gargoyle to explode in a geyser of flame. Every hit caused an efreet to turn to dust.

Efreet began to land behind the ferocious dwarf, but Terra, Hanna, and Ell blasted them with magic, stunning most of them and killing a few. Seeing an opening, Darren and Caitlyn rushed forward to help the dwarf. Only three people could stand side by side in the pass, and they used the tightness to their advantage. Brahm shattered golems whole, while Darren and Caitlyn tag teamed them. Caitlyn used her tremendous weight and powerful muscles to knock the golems off balance, and Darren sliced off their heads.

The tight fighting and slow advance went on for some time until the left side of the pass opened in a sharp thousand-foot drop. "Be careful," Terra shouted.

Brahm laughed at the statement. "No," he yelled as he knocked three golem over the drop, "I'm goin' to bloody jump right off."

Terra shook her head at the dwarf and glanced over her shoulder. Golems pulled themselves free of the stone around them. *Looks like they aren't trying to herd us anymore.* The Nexus used the last of her magical power to cast a pulse of pure earth magic. All of the golems and gargoyles went inert. Terra drew her shortbow and loosed a few silvery refined thorium tipped arrows at any efreet she could see. They fizzled as the enchanted arrowheads absorbed the elemental energy in their bodies.

"Push!" Terra yelled. The party blasted through the frozen golems, and the pass began to descend slowly. A few hundred yards down the slope, golems began to shake free of the mountainside again.

"Is something summoning them?" Ell shouted. The woman had her two knives out and waited for one of the golems to come close enough before she struck.

Terra tried sensing any magic being used, but she couldn't feel anything. "I'm not sure. They could be using something other than magic to bring them to life."

A stone golem crashed through the wall to Terra's right and knocked her over the long drop to her left. Hanna screamed, and a rope of air wrapped itself around Terra, pulling her back to the pass. Terra panted heavily at her brush with death. "That was close," she muttered. "Thank you, Hanna."

The little girl nodded and lashed out at the golem. Hanna had fashioned two whip like coils of pure earth energy and was using them to devastating effect. *I used way too much magical power making that landslide last night,* Terra thought. *I should have been more conservative.*

"If magic isn't summoning them," Hanna asked, "then what is?"

"Demonic power could," Terra said.

<Up,> echoed in Terra's mind. Her gaze rose, and she saw a winged speck flying far overhead.

"Probably from that," the Nexus said, pointing at the sky. A flash of brown passed her as Ell dove under Terra's upraised arm. The half-elf spun into the group of golems that had been rising from the pass while Terra's attention was elsewhere.

Ell climbed atop the back of the closest golem and drove an enchanted knife deep into its skull. She back flipped off of it and landed on the shoulders of another and dispatched it as well. She rode the collapsing behemoth to the ground and rolled back to her feet. Terra had seen some graceful fighters in her life, but never one that struck with such precision.

The group finally broke through the bulk of the enemy forces and charged down the pass. *It looks like we might make it*, Terra thought.

Seamus let out a sigh as he checked the battery on his laser rifle. He had managed to scavenge a working rifle from a Fyrian soldier he had killed with his bow. The rifle recharged in direct sunlight, but they hadn't been to the surface in a while. He finished cleaning the rifle and began reassembling it in the weak light of the glow ball.

The young man was an einherijar, a warrior that had fallen in battle and had his soul recovered by a valkyrie. His valkyrie, Brunhilde, had died when Valgarde had fallen. The ruined southern city was only occupied by ghosts now. He was fortunate that Kara, the valkyrie he was bound to now, had been near enough to save him from fading away after Brunhilde's death.

How long have I been on this world? Seamus wondered. *Over a year, I know.* Seamus had awoken in a bed in Valgarde while the city was still under siege with no memories of his previous life other than his name. They had thrust a bow and arrow into his hand and told him to repel invaders. Though he couldn't remember anything of what he was before he died, he was certain he had never used a bow and arrow before.

Somehow he knew how to hold the bow, how far to draw, and how to aim it like a master.

The marshal knowledge of the valkyrie is passed on to her einherijar, Seamus remembered. Brunhilde was a strong valkyrie, and she was familiar with many different kinds of weapons, but Kara was a master of every kind of weapon.

The white haired valkyrie knew how to kill with every weapon ever produced. She was the leader of the Valkyrie. *Now she's the only one,* the boy thought. All the other valkyrie had died when Valgarde fell. Only Kara and her two einherijar had made it out of the city alive. Seamus had been near the gates of the city when Brunhilde died, and Kara had sensed him fading away. She bound him to her and became the only valkyrie with three einherijar.

Seamus finished assembling his rifle and looked at the other person in the cave with him. Naru was an Asian woman with short black hair. She was cleaning the hilts of two phaseblades. The weak white light glittered off of the red scale mail she wore. *That woman has a thing for red,* Seamus thought. *Red armor, red beams on her phaseblades... I guess it's to go with all the blood she spills...*

<You need to do a better job guarding your thoughts,> Naru said in his head. <I can hear you.>

Seamus swore under his breath. Einherijar were telepathically linked to their valkyrie and each other. "Sorry."

"Don't worry about it," she said. "You weren't wrong."

Kara's authoritative voice filled Seamus's head. <There is something going on topside. Are you two ready for a fight?>

<Always,> they responded in unison.

<Good,> Kara sent. <Get up here. It looks like they need help.>

"A box canyon," Darren said. "That damnable pass led us to a box canyon." Vertical cliff faces thousands of feet tall blocked off three sides of the trap they had forced themselves into. The six members of the scouting party put their backs to the far wall and faced the way they had come.

"I didn't know where it went," Caitlyn snapped at him.

Darren let out a slow breath. "I wasn't blaming you. I'm just... less than thrilled at how we've ended up."

An innumerable amount of stone golems formed a wall a few hundred yards away. They weren't advancing, but they weren't falling back either. "Looks like we have a standoff," Darren said.

Terra shook her head. "No, they were given instructions to hold us here. I think someone is coming to collect us."

"What should we do?" Hanna asked, her young voice composed despite the circumstances.

Caitlyn growled. "Fight tooth and claw when they show up." Yips and barks echoed through the mountains, and she hissed. "Hellhounds. Inbred dogs, I'll rip them apart."

"Calm down, Caitlyn," Terra said. "I have a plan."

"You've had a plan this entire time?" Ell asked.

"One I'm making up as we go," Terra said. "I'll think of something. Just follow my lead."

The calls of hellhounds grew louder as the minutes slowly dragged by. Terra had collected a little bit of air and earth magic from what Caitlyn and Hanna had been creating, but it wasn't enough for anything flashy. *Maybe I could create a wall of fire, but I don't have any of that kind of magic in my core... I'd be exhausted, and if it didn't work then I would be a weight dragging everyone down.*

Terra scanned through her options while they waited. *If we could kill the demon controlling all of the golems, then we would have a chance, but I don't even see it flying about anymore. We are going to die here. NO!* she shouted in her mind. *Don't think like that. You'll figure something out.*

A few more minutes of frantic thinking passed, and the golems began to step aside. The golden effigy of a hellhound atop some kind of floating barge came around the curve that led into the canyon. The golems cleared the path, and Terra could see the barge was drawn by a team of a hundred red-furred hellions. A male demon stood atop the obsidian and gold barge, and a nude succubus with black, leathery bat wings sprawled out beside him. The smell of sulfur filled the air with the hellhounds' acrid breath.

The demon wore black plate armor with spikes and sharp protrusions. His milky white skin made him look almost human, but his solid red eyes belied the demon's ancestry. The demon caught sight of Terra's wings and smiled. "Nexus," he said in High Demonic, "what a pleasure it is to see you this fine day. I am Lord Raziel, the Houndmaster. How might I be of assistance to one of your... sought after power?"

Terra glared at the Demon Lord. "I just thought I would go for a walk," she replied in Daein Common. "But it seems I've lost my way. I would appreciate it if you could direct me back to this Realm's gateway arch."

Raziel burst into derisive laughter. "What is he saying?" Caitlyn asked.

"He's just playing with his food," Terra said. "Don't do anything until I do." A high pitched squeal made the Nexus wince, and she saw double for a moment. When her vision cleared, Raziel was studying her curiously, and Terra saw a black tendril of energy connecting each of the golems to the succubus. *There you are.* The black tendrils faded away along with the ringing in her ears.

"You are indeed lost, Nexus," Raziel said. "This Realm has fallen. There are none here that would fight your good fight. I will gladly escort you to my Obsidian Tower so I can more properly receive you. I have even come unarmed as a gesture of goodwill."

"How polite of you," Terra responded. "But, I feel that I must decline your invitation. The hospitality of demons is something I've come to look at sideways."

Raziel shrugged and turned his back to Terra. He knelt next to the succubus and stroked her jaw. Terra saw her opportunity and scooped a few pebbles from the ground and launched them with a powerful blast of air. The stones hit an invisible barrier that encapsulated the floating barge and bounced off. A shimmer of light pulsed along the barge.

Raziel looked over his shoulder at Terra. "Isn't Fyrian technology amazing, Nexus? I think so. This is called a force field or some such drivel. It repulses anything that attempts to cross at too high a speed. It also unravels any magic that pierces the barrier. I am unarmed, but I am also invincible as far as you are concerned."

Brahm shifted his weight as if he was going to leap at the Demon Lord, but Terra held him back with a hand. "It's all just talk right now."

"Oh, does your dwarf want to try his hand against me, Nexus?" Raziel chided. "I have been drinking deep from the extraction chamber here on Caine, and I am certain I could rip him limb from limb, even with his magical armor."

"He's as strong as Azreal was on Dae. Don't try anything," Terra said to Brahm. Terra looked back at Raziel. She wasn't sure, but it looked like a small shadow shifted behind the Demon Lord on his barge. A blue beam of light turned on, bathing the barge's occupants in a pale glow. Everything erupted in absolute chaos.

Raziel's right arm was severed at the shoulder at the same time the succubus let out a shriek of terror. A huge man wearing silvery armor leapt out of the crowd of golems and silenced the succubus's scream with the swing of a greatsword. Her head sailed into the air and all of the golems slumped.

Hellhounds strained against their leads, and with a snap, the leather tore from its connection to the barge. Caitlyn, Brahm, and Darren dove into the mass of hellspawn and began cutting the dogs down.

Terra's eyes never left the woman fighting the Demon Lord on the barge. The blue sword blocked one of black light that Raziel had created. She kicked the demon in his midsection, and he stumbled back a step. The Demon Lord threw up a barrier of midnight black energy, and she cut through it with her sword of glowing blue light.

A high pitched whine came from Terra's left. There was the sound of something popping, and a bright flash traced a line of white across her vision. The Demon Lord's black sword disappeared, and he clamped his hand over a wound in his side. Before the woman on the barge could strike again, the Demon Lord vanished in a crackle of electricity.

The woman screamed in rage at Raziel's retreat. She looked at the large man on the barge and hopped down. A young, auburn-haired man wearing camouflage and carrying what looked like an Earth rifle jogged over with a woman with black hair. The two of them began picking through the contents on the barge while the two on the barge walked toward Terra.

The Nexus studied the two as they drew closer. Wearing blue, white, and black platemail that covered her from shoulders to feet, the woman stood five-feet nine-inches. Her arms were bare, save for a bandage on her left upper arm and gauntlets that covered her hands. Her open faced helmet revealed a young face with gray eyes, and long gray braid went down her back and ran all the way down to her knees.

The man was also in plate armor, but it covered every inch of his six-and-a-half feet. The mask of his helmet was a bear, and it only left his ice-blue eyes exposed. He sheathed the greatsword on his back and stood like a silent centurion when the woman drew up to Terra.

The gray-haired woman looked Terra up and down, and her gaze darkened. "Nexus," the woman said. "What are you doing here?"

Terra frowned at her. "My friends and I are trying to assess the situation here on Caine. I am the Nexus; who are you?"

"I am Kara, the last free valkyrie. All the others of my kind have either been killed or captured and taken to one of the Obsidian Towers." Kara studied the skies. "We need to get back underground. I'll fill you in on the details as we walk." The valkyrie began to walk away from Terra in the direction the young man with the rifle had come from. The large bear-helmeted man fell in step on Kara's right side, so Terra walked to the woman's left.

"What happened here?" Terra asked. She noticed the washed out colors had taken on a more normal shade when the valkyrie was about.

"Five years ago," Kara started, "when Azreal first attacked, he blocked us off from Yggdrasil and the gateway arch. The souls of fallen warriors go through the ash tree and are collected by the valkyrie. Without access to it, we were unable to collect the souls and bind them to us, making them einherijar. Over the last five years, he ground us down.

"Four months ago, Valgarde, the city you passed to get in the mountains, fell. Thousands of my sisters and their einherijar were captured and taken to the Obsidian Towers. That was when Caine started to die. I don't know if any of the other valkyrie are still alive, but I think not. How long has the Realm of Magic been free?" Kara asked as they stopped before a rock face, her tone as unyielding as stone.

The man stepped through solid-seeming stone, and Terra's eyes widened. "About four months now," she said.

Kara spun on her. "What!" she shouted. "You mean you have been rid of Azreal's forces the entire time my world has been dying!"

Terra matched the woman glare for glare. "Do you think I would have just stood by if I had been able to help? We came as soon as we could. With the angels, we destroyed the Obsidian Towers on Bara, and now we are here to help you."

"With what?" Kara snapped. "The six of you? What luck. Except two of you aren't real warriors, Nexus. Unless you expect me to believe you can fight without magical power. Even if you really were a master of the bow you carry, which I can tell you aren't from the way you carry your quiver, you can't expect me to honestly think that little girl is really some ferocious fighter. So, grand, I've doubled my forces and gotten six more mouths to feed."

Caitlyn stepped between the two women and growled at the valkyrie. Her fangs still dripped red with hellhound blood. "You should be happy there's any help, valkyrie."

The woman shook with rage. "Happy?" Her face turned red. "I'VE WATCHED MY ENTIRE PEOPLE DIE AROUND ME, CHANGELING!" Her voice dropped to a deadly whisper. "I'm many things, but happy is not among them." She pointed at the cliff face. "The path through is clear. It's an illusion. Just step through."

Brahm stepped through the illusion first. "Terra," he called, his tone one of alarmed caution.

Terra stepped through the wall behind him and froze. The man had taken off his helmet when he entered the tunnel. His face was one Terra had not seen in years. It had been over five years since her first husband had died, but she could still close her eyes and remember his blond hair and blue eyes. "Michael?" she choked out.

Chapter Eleven – What it Means to be Paragon

<You must cast aside the part of you that makes you weak.>

Michael studied the red-haired woman in the cave mouth's light. Her hazel eyes were wide, and her breathing bordered on panic. She would likely pass out soon if she didn't get it under control. "Did you know me before I died?" he asked. *The first time I've met anyone that knew me from before.*

The half-angel wrapped her glowing wings tight around herself. They were his favorite shade of light-blue, like the cloudless sky, and he thought they were beautiful. The woman herself was pleasant to look upon, but he felt nothing for her. Kara was his life now.

"I did," she said, her voice unsteady. The dwarf looked ready to catch her should she faint. "We were married."

"Oh," Michael said. *What in Hell am I supposed to say to that! Not, 'Oh.'* "It's nice to meet you." *She already knows you!* "What's your name?" *You are just going to say every wrong thing you can think of aren't you!* Michael heard Seamus laughing in his head. <Shut up, Boy.> The laughter stopped abruptly.

"My name is Terra Zane," she said.

"What's the hold up?" Kara shouted from outside the cave.

<You didn't tell me I was married to the Nexus in my previous life,> Michael sent to her.

A moment of silence. <I didn't know, and it doesn't matter; that life is gone. Get a move on before someone sees this entrance.>

Terra stared at him with a confused jumble of emotions on her face while he talked to Kara across the valkyrie bond. "We need to move deeper down the tunnel. I'll lead you to our camp," Michael said. She nodded and followed behind him without speaking. Michael picked up a glow ball and held it aloft as he walked down the sloping tunnel.

It took an hour for them to arrive at the large cave they used as a camp. There was a small lake with cave mushrooms growing on an island in the center. Michael checked the snares and other traps to ensure no one had discovered the hideout while they were gone. Everything checked out, and he walked to the growing group of people.

Conversation among the Daein people stopped when he drew up to them. "I can't believe it," the older changeling with black hair and golden eyes said. *She must have been the big cat,* Michael thought. *The eyes are the same.* "It really is the Bear."

Seamus snorted a laugh. "That's a damn good nickname for him. Big as a bear, and about as smart as one." The boy let out a yelp when Naru thumped him.

<You talk too much,> Naru sent. <Now shut up and come help me inventory the supplies we seized. Let them be for now.>

Michael thanked her with a nod that she returned. "You'll have to excuse Seamus," Michael said to the Daein. "He hasn't been with us long and hasn't learned civility. Did I know all of you?"

Terra's eyes locked on his. "Some of us. It's safe to say that everyone has at least heard of you."

Michael drew his brows down. "Why's that?"

The girl with the sea-foam green hair said, "You were pretty famous before you died. You were Champion of the Grand Arena. You were the last defender of the Arcane City before it fell to Azreal. Everyone's heard of you."

Frowning, Michael asked, "How did I die?"

Tears welled in the Nexus's eyes. "I'm sorry. I can't," she said before she walked away from the cluster of glow balls they had been gathered around. Terra walked to the edge of the small lake and stared out over the calm waters.

Michael looked at the others with a questioning look on his face. "Yer no' the only person she's lost," the dwarf said. "Me name's Brahm Ironfist, an' I met ye once in the Arcane City after ye took the title o' Champion. I'm no' sure how long it's been fer ye, but to all o' us, ye died just over five years ago. Ye were linked to Terra as her shield, an' ye died sendin' her to the Realm o' Balance to find Alex Zane, the Guardian."

"I thought she said her name was Terra Zane," Michael said.

"That's right. My name's Caitlyn Shadowpaw, and I'm Terra's sister. Through adoption," she quickly added at his raised eyebrow. "It took her four years to find Alex, and another year before they could come back to Dae. She fell in love with him, and they were married. He died four months ago when Dae was freed. She's pregnant with his child."

It makes sense now. Kind of. "So she's lost two husbands, just to rediscover one of them exists but doesn't remember her."

Everyone around him nodded. Kara walked up to his side, and he looked down at her. The recent battle had his blood running hot, but he couldn't do the things he wanted to in present company. "Did you know any of this?"

<No. I told you I didn't, my love,> Kara sent. Her tone was even, but her body language screamed that she was feeling jealous.

<It is rude to talk so others cannot hear,> Michael said with a frown. <And you don't need to feel jealous. I feel nothing for that woman.>

Kara glared at him. "No, I didn't know any of this. I only knew that you were a Daein warrior that had died. I'll be out scouting for our next attack when you're done with your one-sided reunion." The valkyrie stalked off, sweeping up Naru and Seamus in her wake.

"What's her problem?" Caitlyn asked.

Michael's tone was soft, but firm. "Kara was a different person before Valgarde fell. She loved battle, but the thrill of it did not consume her as it does now. The five-year siege wore on her, and the city's fall caused something in her to snap. Kara's smile would light up the room," Michael said, smiling at the memory, "and her laughter would make even the most dire situations seem better."

"You love her," Terra said from behind him. He hadn't heard her approaching.

Michael turned to her and nodded. "I do. I'm sorry, Terra, I truly am, but what we had between us died when I did. Death severs all bonds."

The Nexus looked like the weight of the Nine Realms had just come crashing down on her. "I just... I understand."

She blinked, and a pair of tears ran down her cheeks. Michael fought against the urge to console the woman. *She would get the wrong idea,* he told himself. "What does it mean to be Paragon?" Michael asked.

Terra brushed away her tears with the back of a gauntleted hand. "Why do you ask?"

"I need to know." Her eyes took on an iron hard cast as she met his. Terra's entire posture changed to one of determined authority. *Is this the same woman from just a second ago?*

"It means you are the protector and judge of your Realm," The Nexus said, her tears forgotten. "It means that in everything you do, you must strive to advance the causes of your Realm and be the living embodiment of its virtues. It means your words are the law of your Realm, and you are given powers to enforce them."

"Where do those powers come from?" Michael asked.

The Nexus pondered the question for a moment. "I don't know. I was born with the ability to control all of the latent magical energy of Dae, but away from the Realm of Magic, I am the same as anyone else. The Overlord can't be permanently killed while he's away from Hell. If he does die, he resurrects there. I'm not sure what the other Paragons' powers are, other than the Guardian having the Guardian's Blade."

Michael nodded. His decision was made.

Kara looked out over a forested valley a few hundred feet below. A large troop of undead searched the valley floor for signs of their meager resistance. *About seven thousand undead with a few hundred of the malformed.* Her hand was inches from the lever that would trigger a devastating landslide.

When she wasn't actively fighting, Kara and her einherijar rigged traps throughout the mountain range. Valkyrie and einherijar didn't sleep, so they had plenty of time to prepare for battle. Most of the undead were in the kill zone, and she pulled the lever. A rippling explosion knocked dust from the top of the cave. A few small stones trickled past the mouth of the cave, and then, with a deafening roar, most of the higher peak crashed into the valley, destroying the force of undead.

She searched for some sense of satisfaction, but she found only the hollow knowledge that it would never be enough, that she would never slaughter enough of the monsters to bring her sisters back.

<Are you still angry with me?> Michael sent.

<Yes.>

<Why?> he asked. <I haven't slighted you in any way.>

Kara sighed. He was right. She shouldn't be angry with him, but the valkyrie couldn't help her feelings. Kara logically understood that her emotions were quickly spiraling out of control, but she couldn't bring herself to care enough to bring them under rein. <I know you haven't,> she sent to him with a tender tone. <I'm sorry. There was a large patrol of undead. I crushed them with the landslide we engineered last week.>

<I felt it. We need to use less explosives next time. We are running low.>

<I know,> Kara said. <They are being much more careful about what they bring into the mountains. Seamus told me there wasn't anything useful on that barge.> Kara's rage flared at Raziel's retreat. It wasn't the first time she had fought him, but it was the first time she had almost killed him.

Seamus and Naru were on the opposite side of the valley, cleaning up the remaining undead. <Only a few of the undead weren't caught in the landslide,> Seamus reported. <Naru and I took care of them.>

<Good,> Kara told him. <Return to base.>

<I've made up my mind,> Michael said.

Kara felt a trill of expectation. <And?>

<I'll do it. I'll become the Paragon of Caine.>

Kara would have kissed the man had he been in front of her.

Terra walked to Caitlyn. The changeling was in her human form, and she was eyeing the roof of the cave as if it were going to collapse down on them at any moment. Michael had told them the rumbling a few minutes ago was from an engineered landslide and that they were in no danger, but Terra was certain Caitlyn didn't believe that last part.

"How are you?" Terra asked her sister.

"I'm fine," Caitlyn lied. "How are you?"

"I'm fine too," Terra lied back.

Frowning at Terra, Caitlyn said, "You're a terrible liar. Tell me the truth."

Terra sat down on a crate near the water. "Where am I supposed to start, Caitlyn? I was just starting to really come to terms with Alex's death, then I find out Michael is alive. But instead of the husband I lost, he's some man who's never even heard of me and is in love with a valkyrie. Not to mention Kara isn't sure whether she wants to accept our help or strangle us for taking so long to get here."

"She'll most likely do both," Caitlyn said. She had taken Michael's explanation for the valkyrie's behavior to heart. "Now, is this really about Michael, or are you searching for something to fill the gap Alex's death left?"

Chewing on her bottom lip in thought, Terra considered the question. "I don't know. I thought I had gotten over Michael's death, but seeing him is bringing back feelings and memories I thought I'd buried before I married Alex. Maybe I could have done things differently when we were leaving the Arcane City, and Michael would have lived…"

"But then you wouldn't have fallen in love with Alex," Caitlyn said.

"And maybe he would still be alive too. Maybe it would have been better that way. I would have had Michael, and you…" Terra shook her head. "What am I thinking? I'm sorry, Caitlyn."

The changeling smiled at her. "It's all right. We have to play the cards that fate deals for us."

Terra studied Caitlyn's golden eyes. "Are you sure this is what fate has laid out for us? I just wish it was different."

Caitlyn chuckled. "You're the one whose father is the Keeper of Fate. I'm pretty sure this is right where we should be right now."

Biting back the comment about Eternius being no kind of father to her, Terra said, "Do you think there is some wiggle room, though? Some way to change fate?"

"I don't know," Caitlyn said. "But if you could, should you?"

Terra considered the question, but before she could answer, Kara entered the cave and made a beeline to Michael. Jealousy rocketed through Terra as Michael wrapped his arms around the gray-haired valkyrie and kissed her.

"So," Ell said from behind the two women, making them both jump, "if your husband died, then you married someone else, and you find your first husband alive on another Realm, but he doesn't remember you and is in a relationship with another woman, does that make him your ex-husband, late-husband, or something else?"

Terra snorted a laugh at the absurd convolution of it all. "Good question," the Nexus said. "I'm not sure. I'll let you know when I wrap my head around it."

The auburn-haired man, Seamus, she remembered, waved the three women over. The Daein gathered around the valkyrie and her three einherijar. The raven-headed woman with the slanted black eyes glared at Terra, but she didn't say anything.

"You helped me make up my mind, Terra," Michael said with his arm across Kara's shoulders. "I'm going to become the Paragon of Order, the Justicar."

Hanna looked confused. "How do you become a Paragon?" the little girl asked. "I thought people were born that way."

Terra looked at changeling and shook her head. "No, every Realm is different," she explained. "The Nexus is born as the Paragon, the Guardian's Blade chooses its wielder, and the title of Overlord is passed on to the one that kills the previous Overlord." Terra lifted her gaze to Kara. "How is the Justicar chosen?"

"There is a process," Kara said. "It requires the one attempting to become the Paragon to complete three trials. One of intelligence, one of will, and one of strength."

"What are the trials?" Terra asked.

"The prospective Paragon must climb the storm peak, Leiptrfell, and receive the Thunder Stone from the summit," Kara explained. "The climb is treacherous, and the einherijar must rely on his wits to see him through it. The climb must be unaided, and any interference will mean the trial must begin again."

"Interference..." Darren said. "If Azreal's forces attack does that count as interference? Does that mean we will have to protect him while he tries to climb?"

Kara nodded. "That's right, but we can't be on the mountain. We will have to block the three passes that lead onto Leiptrfell and prevent them from gaining access to the mountain. After he takes the Thunder Stone, he must climb back down the mountain. That concludes the first trial.

"Second," she continued, "Michael will need to travel to Yggdrasil and commune with the tree by passing underneath it and reaching the spirit within the tree."

"That doesn't sound hard," Seamus said. He looked just as interested in the requirements as the Daein.

"No, it doesn't," Kara agreed. "But the test of will comes from the spirit of Yggdrasil, and it is unique to each potential Paragon. Upon successful completion of the trial of will, Yggdrasil will give the einherijar a perfect shaft of ash. The Thunder Stone and the ash pole must be joined together to create the spear, Gungnir, and start the third trial, the trial of strength.

"To complete the third trial," the valkyrie said, looking up at Michael. "You must strike a blow against Jormungandr. It is a red sea serpent that is too big to comprehend. The stories say it wraps completely around the ocean of Caine, and that a single drop of its poison will leave you in eternal screaming torment. You have to take the bloodied spear to the temple and drive it into the Justicar's Altar. Then you will ascend from being an einherijar, to Justicar."

"Terra!" a muted voice shouted from the Nexus's waist. "Can you hear me?"

"That's Silvia!" Terra and Caitlyn yelled at the same time. Terra tore off her glove she wore under her gauntlet and pulled the Eye of the Stars from the pouch opposite the Guardian's Blade on her belt. "I'm here. Is everything all right?"

"Yes," Silvia said, sounding relieved. "Don't know how long I will have you. Everything here is fine. Ignia has been maintaining a portal here to keep us from opening one. None of us are strong enough to force a portal through theirs. The keystone seal is holding. How are things on your end?"

Terra looked up at Kara. The valkyrie nodded. "Bad, Silvia. This Realm is almost lost. There is only one valkyrie alive that we know of. Her name is Kara. We have a plan to try fighting back, but it sounds like a long shot." Michael and Kara both frowned at her. "Sorry."

"Don't be," Silvia said, not realizing Terra wasn't speaking to her. "I don't know how much help we can offer. If your situation there is anything like it was here on Dae when there was an Obsidian Tower, then you can't use planar travel magic from Caine. The Realm of Death is starting to—" her voice was beginning to break up, "—ortal open—" The Eye of the Stars fell silent.

"Silvia, can you hear me?" Terra asked. There was no reply. Terra placed the Eye back in her belt pouch and rubbed her face. "I don't think we can expect any help from them until we deal with the Obsidian Towers here."

"The ten of us?" Naru asked, her tone teetering on the brink of unrestrained rage. "How?"

"I'd no' worry too much, lass," Brahm said. "If four o' us could destroy one Obsidian Tower, I do no' see why ten canno' take care o' two."

"But we had Alex with us," Caitlyn said.

The dwarf nodded. "Aye, an' we'll have the Justicar with us this time 'round. We'll find a way."

Darren cleared his throat. "What great power does the Justicar gain that would allow us to attack an Obsidian Tower? I know the Guardian was the one that destroyed the tower, but we also had an army last time, and there was only one of them."

"That's what we'll have," Michael said. The einherijar walked to a canvas bag and pulled out an ivory horn with a gold mouthpiece and bell. "This is the Gjallerhorn. Anyone can sound this warhorn, but only the Justicar can invoke its power. With this horn's call, all of the previous Justicar are summoned from beyond the grave to Ragnarok, the Final Judgment."

"Why didn't you do all of this years ago?" Caitlyn asked.

Kara glared at the changeling. "The warhorn was lost. We only found it recently. Without it, the Justicar is about as useful as the Guardian without his blade."

Ell, after having displayed an uncharacteristic silence, asked, "Where was it?"

Seamus pointed at the small island in the middle of the lake. "It was in the middle of that damn lake, along with all these glow balls."

"Why was it there?" the half-elf asked.

"No idea," Kara said. "It's been missing for centuries. The other valkyrie thought summoning Jormungandr was more dangerous than dealing with Azreal's army without the Justicar."

"Is it really that dangerous?" Hanna asked.

"It is," Kara said. "'And the skies will turn red with the summoning, and the seas red with the blood of the World Serpent's enemies.' and 'Feasting upon Yggdrasil, Jormungandr waits to strike down those foolish enough to challenge him.' That's what the songs say about Jormungandr. I've never seen it before, but some of the older valkyrie spoke of the serpent with more hatred than they did Azreal."

"Are you sure this is the only way to make Michael the Justicar?" Terra asked.

Kara looked down her nose at her. "I am unless you are keeping an army in your swollen stomach, Nexus."

Terra's hand twitched. She wanted to slap the valkyrie as hard as she could. Kara's eyes narrowed. She had read the gesture and lifted her chin, daring Terra to strike her. Michael stepped between the two women.

"You should all get some sleep," he said to the Daein people. "If we are going to strike out for the Leiptrfell soon then you will need to be well rested. Don't concern yourselves with your safety, we shall stand guard."

Chapter Twelve – Failure Will Not be Tolerated

No.

Doctor Sigma Moore began attaching the terminals on the prosthetic arm to the nerve endings on Raziel's shoulder. *Demon physiology is so similar to ours, but so alien at the same time,* the Fyrian doctor and scientist observed. *The nerves control the muscles, but they do not seem to convey pain like ours do. I wonder how their brain processes damaged tissues. Is this convergent or divergent evolution? A shared ancestor, perhaps.*

"How stands Fyr on the most recent events?" Raziel asked, interrupting Doctor Moore's thoughts.

"The majority of the Corporations want to join in the efforts to eradicate the remaining resistance, but the *Architect*," Doctor Moore spat the title, "is forcing them to wait. Thelonius is requiring the vote to join with Azreal to be unanimous, as is his right as Paragon." The renegade scientist's eyes narrowed. *It should have been me as Paragon. He only won the vote because Atlas Labs threw their support behind him.*

Raziel hissed. "Pay attention to what you are doing!" the Demon Lord shouted.

The doctor's laser scalpel had burned a small hole in the demon's shoulder. "Apologies, I'll repair that injury when we are finished." Sigma Moore turned his attention back to the surgery.

The pale green light of the extraction pods cast the only light in the large room, aside from the surgical lamp Doctor Moore had brought in. The extraction pods were the doctor's own design. They allowed the siphoning and transference of the life energy of anything placed inside them. The green biostatic gel was toxic if it entered the bloodstream, but he had circumvented that problem by engineering life support tubes that kept the occupant alive longer and actively pumped anti-toxins into the subject's body.

Adapting the extraction pods to work on non-human beings had been an endeavor that yielded many tidbits of information Doctor Moore found interesting. He had discovered subjects with the ability to control magic had many times the baseline amount of life energy, but his real breakthrough had come when he drained life from valkyrie with einherijar bonded to them.

The valkyrie could survive an indefinite amount of extraction as long as the einherijar they were linked to were cared for. Somehow they valkyrie shared some of their essence with their warriors and could not die until their einherijar were slain. This had the extraction chambers running at full capacity in both Obsidian Towers with still a couple valkyrie available for experimentation.

If I could discover how the bonding process between the loose soul of the einherijar and the grounded soul of the valkyrie worked, then I could use that information to suspend aging in both subjects. The cause of science could be advanced many years. Doctor Moore ground his teeth but didn't lose concentration on the surgery. *That is why I should be Architect, not that bleeding heart Theodore Thelonius! I am advancing science. I am working to make the world a more enlightened place, not that visionless hack!*

"What is this?" a silky smooth voice asked. Doctor Moore removed his fingers from the safety buttons on the scalpel and looked up into the nightmare black eyes of the Overlord of Hell

"Dark Lord Azreal, I am attaching a prosthetic arm to Lord Raziel," Sigma Moore said.

Azreal nodded. "I can see that," he said with a sneer as he looked down at his subordinate Demon Lord. "What happened to it?" Azreal demanded in a voice that would not accept a half-answer.

The demon's pointed teeth gritted. "The bitch cut it off," Raziel said. "Kara... I'll have her head."

"What happened to Verbek?" Azreal asked. The succubus had been the Dark Lord's favorite pet.

"One of her einherijar cut off the succubus's head."

Azreal glared at Raziel. "Her ability to create and control golem was extremely valuable, Raziel. How did the valkyrie lure you into the open?"

"She didn't," Raziel said, his voice getting softer with each word.

"Who did?" Azreal asked with a glare that promised a slow death if he was lied to.

Raziel's next two words were so soft the doctor almost missed them. "The Nexus."

Azreal's eyes flew wide open, and his right hand clamped down on Raziel's throat. "You let the Nexus escape?" he roared. "She was here, in a Realm you have completely under your control, AND YOU LET HER EVADE YOU?"

Raziel made a choking sound and nodded. Azreal lifted the other Demon Lord by his neck and slammed him into the surgical table. The steel legs buckled under the weight of the blow. Azreal reached over and tore the half-attached prosthetic off. Black blood spurted anew from Raziel's stump.

The stunned demon began to feebly fight back, but Azreal subdued him with black bonds of telekinetic force. Raziel floated into the air above the passive doctor. Azreal looked at the empty extraction pod behind Doctor Moore. "Why is that one empty?" the Overlord asked.

"The valkyrie became conscious while she was still in the gel. She tore the tubes from her body and died from toxic shock after approximately thirty minutes of submersion. It appears that they are partially immortal, but if they sustain too much damage, they are killed. I have since increased the anesthetics in all the other patients to keep them from awakening," Sigma Moore explained.

"Was it a painful death?" Azreal asked as he stared at Raziel's red eyes.

"I wasn't there at the time of her death, but it is safe to assume it was excruciating," the doctor said. He watched as Azreal floated Raziel over the extraction pod. The Demon Lord seemed to be struggling against the crackling bonds of demonic energy, but he was overpowered.

Azreal lowered him into the extraction pod slowly. Seeing that he would have the opportunity to collect some more data, Doctor Moore quickly punched a few commands into the control console. He began to get vital readings on Raziel just before the open scar of his shoulder was plunged into the glowing green gel.

Doctor Moore watched as the subject's body was slowly overcome by the insidious gel. *Fascinating, it seems the gel is extracting a tremendous amount of energy from the Demon Lord. I haven't seen figures this high since I had the Nexus in the older model of the extraction pods.* The bars on the screen began to plummet when the toxins reached the subject's brain. *Pity,* Doctor Moore thought, *I could have learned so much more…*

"Failure will not be tolerated," Azreal said.

Doctor Moore looked up at him. "Of course, my lord."

Chapter Thirteen – Leiptrfell, The Lightning Mountain

<Are you certain? The offer will only be made once.>

Michael studied Leiptrfell as if he had never seen it before. The tall mountain stood in a deep bowl and soared up to the clouds. The peak scraped the dark grey cumulus clouds that always hung overhead near the mountain. A bridge of stone wide enough for two people to stand side by side spanned the chasm between the other mountains and Leiptrfell. Brahm, Terra, and Kara stood behind him.

"Once I start, is it going to be obvious someone is attempting the trials?" Michael asked.

Kara nodded.

Michael grunted and resumed his surveillance of the mountain. *There don't seem to be any easy paths of ascent. I'll take that path...* He brooded on his planned climb.

<Are you ready?> Kara asked. He looked over his shoulder at her. She looked both impatient and nervous.

Michael nodded and started toward the soaring heights of Leiptrfell. "Good luck," Terra called.

"Thanks," Michael shouted back. He jogged across the stone bridge. A few minutes and he set foot on the slopes of the stormy mountain. A foreign voice boomed through his mind, <Trespasser, do you attempt the Trial of the Justicar?>

"I do," Michael said.

<Very well. May the wits of the First Ones be with you,> the deep voice boomed again.

"Who are the First Ones?" Michael asked. His voice was drowned out by a rippling ring of lightning emanating from the peak of the Leiptrfell. The rippling ring of light drew clouds from all across the Realm. They began to spin centered on the mountain. "Yeah, it's pretty obvious someone started the trial," he muttered.

A path rose to the left and another to the right. Michael couldn't see any discernible benefit to either one, so he took the one to his right. "Here we go."

Hanna ruffled her feathers and sought a more comfortable position on the weathered mountain pine. The rolling lightning and accompanying thunder had surprised her. *Looks like it won't be good flying weather after all,* she thought as the wind began to pick up. She flitted from the branch and landed next to Ell.

The changeling focused on her human form she had only discovered a year ago. Her father had been proud of her learning to change forms at such a young age. Most other changelings didn't experience their human forms until they were nine or ten, but Hanna had made that change when she was six. The pain was excruciating.

Hanna steeled herself for the torment, but it seemed no matter what she did, it always overwhelmed her. Bones began to crack, join, and grow heavier. Feathers flattened over her skin and became clothing. Sinews and muscles snapped and shifted into new positions. Hanna's body lengthened. Nerves screamed in blazing agony as they dragged through her flesh. Her beak shortened, and flesh and muscle slowly covered it.

The changes took only a few seconds, but the agony made it feel like an eternity. On all fours, Hanna trembled with the receding pain, and tears fell onto the stone beneath her. Ell crouched next to her with a hand on her shoulder. "It's alright, Hanna. Come on, stand up. It'll pass soon."

The half-elf helped Hanna rise to her feet. Naru, the einherijar with them, looked at her. "How bad does it hurt?" she asked.

Fighting to control her shaking muscles, Hanna gave a jerky nod. "Imagine you are on fire, and someone is breaking every bone in your body while they stretch you out on a rack, then you have an idea of what it feels like when the changes start. It hurts more in the middle."

Hanna wasn't sure how she felt about the einherijar. The woman had been glaring at Terra every time they were together, and Hanna couldn't figure out why. On the other hand, Naru had been considerate of what Seamus wanted and had volunteered to go with Hanna and Ell to the western bridge where the fighting would likely be lighter. *Maybe she doesn't like Terra because she has a past with Michael, and Kara loves Michael.*

"Did you see anything while you were up there?" Ell asked.

"No," Hanna said. Lightning flashed overhead through the clouds and thunder made everything around them shudder. *Definitely bad weather for flying.* "I don't think we'll see anyth—" she was cut off as an arrow clattered to the ground ahead of them.

An animated skeleton danced around the bend in the path. Hanna stood frozen. She had never seen a skeleton, and her pulse quickened and eyes widened. Everything slowed. Hanna watched as Naru swung a laser rifle from her back in slow motion and sighted in on the skeleton. She studied the woman's stance and how she operated the rifle. Naru let out a short breath and squeezed the trigger. There was a flash of light, and the skeleton's skull exploded in a puff of bone dust. The immediate danger past, everything crashed back in around Hanna.

"May I see your rifle?" Hanna asked. The word was still a little foreign to her, but she said it like she had grown up hearing the word. Naru frowned at her but handed Hanna the Fyrian laser rifle.

It was a bit long for her, but the light weight surprised the changeling. Two bobbing skulls appeared around the bend about a tenth of a mile away. Hanna matched her stance to what Naru's had been, and with a short breath out, she squeezed the trigger twice. Twin puffs of bone dust filled the air, and Naru stared at her with wide eyes.

"How did you do that?" the woman asked.

"I saw you do it," Hanna said. She kept the dangerous end of the rifle pointed down the path as the young girl looked over her shoulder to talk. "It's pretty simple. It shoots an amplified beam of light out of the open end?"

"That's right," Naru said with a guarded tone. "The open end is called the muzzle. There are a series of lenses and mirrors inside the barrel and the housing of the rifle. It's recharged by sunlight through the black panel on top." The einherijar crossed her arms over the red platemail that covered her chest. "You have more skeletons to deal with."

Hanna looked back down the path and saw Naru was right. The path was filling up with a milling surge of fifty or so undead. *I wonder if I can use a disc of air and fire to amplify the strength of the beam.* Hanna wove a small disc, convex on the side facing the skeletons, just in front of the muzzle and pulled the trigger. The laser rifle hit the disc, and Hanna was blinded by the light.

"What did you do?" Naru shouted. "I can't see!"

Hanna blinked repeatedly to clear her eyes. When she finally regained her vision, her jaw hung open. The beam had destroyed the undead, but it had also vaporized a large swath of the path and anything else within a wide two hundred-foot-long cone. *Shortens the range, but increases the strength. I bet a bigger one would have a larger effect.*

"What did you do?" Naru echoed, her tone astonished.

"I made a magic lens like the ones in the rifle, but it was outside the muzzle."

"That's amazing," Ell said. She patted Hanna on the head. "It's too bad we don't have more of those rifles." Naru and Hanna agreed.

"You stay right there," Naru said. "The rifle's charge is going to run out if we shoot at every little thing that comes along, but if we start getting pushed back, be ready."

Hanna nodded and tightened her grip on the laser rifle.

Michael pulled out another piton, and with delicate precision, he tapped it into the cliff face. He lifted himself higher, but the next natural handhold was just out of his reach. He swore under his breath and pulled another piton from the bundle of them in his pack. *I'm going to run out soon.*

He tapped the new piton in and lifted himself up. A bolt of lightning struck the mountainside far above him. Michael felt a rumbling deep in the mountain and looked up. Boulders slammed into and bounced off of the stone cliffs above him. The big man dug his hands into the hold above him and hoisted himself onto a small overhang that had a dark cave.

Michael leapt into the cave just as the rockslide hit the stone platform he had been on seconds before. The overhang broke off and crashed down the mountain with the rest of the slide. "That was close," he muttered and looked around the cave.

It seemed to be natural, and it curved about ten feet back. The ground had an upward grade. Michael went to where the cave turned, but he couldn't see anything in the darkness. He pulled a glow ball from his pack and held it high.

The remains of a man rested by his feet. A white skull smiled at him above tarnished chainmail and a wooden buckler. A sheathed sword lay beside the unlucky soul. Michael reached down to pick it up. The leather scabbard crumbled to dust under his hand, and the steel was pitted with rust. *I wonder what killed him.*

Michael shrugged. The cave appeared to be a tunnel that ran through the heart of the mountain with a rising slope. *Might as well see where this leads.*

The skeleton's bones snapped when Caitlyn slammed into it. In her primal form, she used her bulk to knock down and crush the never ending tide of the grinning undead. Darren stood off to the side, separating heads from shoulders with Seamus between them wielding a gun.

When Caitlyn had asked what it was, he had said, "It's an adaptive ammunition, fully automatic, assault rifle/shotgun hybrid." He looked up at her with a smirk. "I call her Sally." The young einherijar oozed excitement about using it, but when he had tried to explain what it did to Caitlyn, she felt her eyes begin to gloss over.

The gun made a metallic clattering sound, and a column of skeletons collapsed. Seamus slid what looked like a brick of iron into the bottom of the gun. He cackled maniacally and shouted, "Gotta feed ol' Sally! I love this gun!"

This kid's insane, Caitlyn thought. She swiped at another skeleton and shattered its ribs and spine. *I wonder how far up Michael has gone?* Caitlyn slammed another skeleton against the cliff face to her right. The tide of undead slackened, and the changeling looked about for a cause. There was a bend in the trail not far ahead that prevented her from seeing what was coming from more than a few hundred feet away.

Caitlyn looked at Darren. He looked bored as he fought the two skeletons that were on either side of him. Darren blocked a blow from the skeleton to his left with his large kite shield and shattered the skull of the one to his right with his longsword. The threat to his open side dealt with, the captain made short work of the last skeleton. Even though they had been fighting for over an hour, Darren did not look winded in the slightest.

"*Skeletons,*" Darren sneered. "Brainless weaklings. Is everyone all right?"

"I'm fine," Caitlyn said.

Seamus grinned. "Me and Sally're doin' just fine," he said as he stroked his gun like it was his lover.

Caitlyn's eyes narrowed when she noticed Darren's sword had begun to glow with a white light. Darren had also seen the sword light up, and his face darkened. With her acute feline ears, Caitlyn heard the guardsman's fist tighten on the leather wrapped hilt.

"What is it?" she asked.

Darren's breathing grew heavier, and his jaw clenched. "Malformed," he said through gritted teeth. The wind whipped the smell of rot toward the three defenders of the eastern bridge.

"Ugh," Seamus said. "They smell terrible. Why's your sword glowing?"

"It's enchanted to when the Malformed draw near," Darren said absently, his focus down the path absolute. "I would destroy all of them myself if I could," Caitlyn heard him mutter.

Shambling zombies came around the bend in the path. The odor of decaying flesh assaulted them, drowning out every other smell. Caitlyn wished she could change into her human form so she wouldn't have to endure it, but she had completely depleted her reserves of magical energy. It would be far too dangerous to continue casting spells and risk becoming too exhausted to fight.

"Remember," Darren said. "You have to destroy the brain. Even a loose head can still infect you with the undead necrosis if it bites your foot. Caitlyn, don't bite them."

Caitlyn glared at him and was about to say something sarcastic in response, but the look on his face made her hold her tongue. There was a fire in his brown eyes that reminded Caitlyn of Alex. She shook her head to clear thought. *Alex is dead. Darren isn't... Maybe...* A zombie shuffled into her striking range, and Caitlyn swiped at its head with a paw. The muscles in its neck were decayed, and the head came loose and slammed into the wall next to her, popping open like an overripe melon.

Two more of the undead took the place of the one she had just killed. Caitlyn was unsure of how best to attack them. She batted their grasping arms aside while she considered the problem. *If I attack one, the other could bite me. Maybe being in this form isn't the best for this.*

"Caitlyn, get down!" Seamus shouted. Caitlyn ducked, and Sally clacked loudly. The two zombies' upper bodies were reduced to shreds as a large burst of iron shards tore through them. They collapsed in front of her, but more still took their places. "I recommend we fall back onto the bridge so you two can knock them over the sides," the red-headed einherijar said.

Darren and Caitlyn agreed, and they began a measured retreat. Once they were a few hundred feet down the narrow stone bridge, the three stopped backing up. The hungering monsters were pushing each other off the edges of the two-person wide bridge as they surged to get them.

"Good call," Darren said.

"Thanks," Seamus said. Few zombies actually made it to the defenders, and they were easily knocked from the bridge into the chasm. The bottom of the long fall was cloaked in shadow and wasn't visible, giving it the illusion of a bottomless pit.

At the mouth of the bridge, a slew of zombies went sailing over the edge as a ten-foot-tall Malformed crashed through them. The atrocity was cobbled together from at least five men. It had five arms and two thick legs. White, foul-smelling pus issued from the seams between the different bodies. It had a large cleaver in one hand and charged across the bridge at them.

Darren roared at the undead monstrosity and ran to meet it. He slammed his kite shield into the bridge and ducked behind it. Caitlyn felt the stone tremble under the weight of his shield. Terra had mentioned to her that he had some kind of unique enchantment on his shield, but Caitlyn had forgotten the specifics until this moment. *Weight manipulation.*

The Malformed slammed its cleaver against his shield and a shower of sparks shot into the air. Darren used the opening to lop off two of the monster's five arms. Whenever his sword bit into the undead's flesh, there was a sound of hissing and a smell of seared skin. The Malformed howled in rage and tried to grab Darren with one of its hands, but the captain lopped off the hand at the wrist.

The huge undead monster lifted its cleaver back to swing at him again. Darren slammed his shield into the bridge again. Caitlyn heard a popping sound as the stone began to crack beneath them.

"Darren!" she shouted, but it was too late. The Malformed's blow was too much for the weakened structure to handle. Darren, the Malformed, and the few zombies that had crowded in behind the larger undead fell into the abyss as the bridge crumbled.

Caitlyn jumped forward, but she couldn't catch the edge of his cloak before it went over. "No!" She looked over the edge and saw Darren grinning up at her. He had driven his sword into the jagged remnants of their side of the bridge and had a death grip on the hilt with his hand.

"It's nice to know you care," he said. "I could really use some help, though, or else you really will need to be screaming."

Caitlyn quickly assumed her human form, ignoring the pain that accompanied changing. Both she and Seamus lay down on their stomachs and reached down to Darren. Caitlyn caught his truncated left arm and got a good grip on the vambrace that covered his forearm. Seamus grabbed his other arm, and they pulled Darren up.

After they had him safely on the bridge, Darren leaned over and grabbed the hilt of his sword. The razor sharp blade had cut through the stone like a hot knife through butter, and he didn't have to work at it long before he had his weapon back. Darren sighed as he looked down the drop.

"Ell is going to kill me," he said. "It took her forever to get that enchantment right."

Caitlyn hit him on the chest. "Forget your stupid shield," she said. "You almost died!"

Darren smirked at her. "Nah, I realized what was happening when you shouted my name. Gave me just enough time to catch myself." He poked her nose. "You saved my life. Looks like I owe you one."

Caitlyn felt her face grow hot. She crossed her arms beneath her breasts and glared at him. "I'm just glad you're safe."

His smile widened. "Aw, it almost sounds like you would've missed me. What was all of that 'No!' business anyway?"

She blushed deeper and narrowed her eyes at him more. "Shut up, before I throw you over myself."

"Umm… Guys?" Seamus said.

The two looked at him as if they had forgotten he was there. "What?" Caitlyn and Darren asked in unison. She glared at Darren, and he grinned again.

Seamus pointed at the far end of the bridge. The zombies were still trying to make it to them and were falling into the gap between the other mountains and Leiptrfell. "The bridge is gone. What are we supposed to do now?"

Darren laughed at the undead falling into the bottomless pit. "Stupid," he muttered at the monsters. "Well, we can't go that way, and we can't go over Leiptrfell to help Terra or Ell, so I guess we have to wait for Michael to get finished. Use your link to Kara to let her know what happened and keep a sharp eye on the sky for anything stupid enough to try flying in this weather."

Seamus nodded and was silent for a few minutes. "Kara says you're right, and we should stay put." The einherijar shrugged. "Well, at least it isn't raining."

"Don't," Darren started to say. A boom of thunder drowned out his words, and it began to downpour. The captain glared at the young einherijar. "Just perfect," he said as he pulled up the hood of his cloak.

Caitlyn laughed and changed back into her primal form. She was confident their part in this battle was done, but it paid to be prepared. *What was all of that 'No!' business?* echoed in her head. She looked up at the high peak of Leiptrfell and wondered if Michael was getting close to the top.

Michael looked out over the northern approach to the mountain. As he surmised, the cave was a tunnel that ran straight through Leiptrfell, gaining altitude as it went. There was no bridge on the northern side, and if it had not been for the rain, Michael was sure he would have been able to see the Hall of the Fallen and the ocean in the distance.

He leaned out into the deluge and looked for another path up the mountain, but there wasn't one. *Looks like it's back to climbing.* He swung out onto a short ledge and sought out handholds. They were slick in the rain, and the wind pulled at him as if it was trying to fling him from the mountain.

Don't rush, he thought. *Don't lose your wits. If I try to hurry now, I'll fall.*

Kara sneered at the daemen as they tried to overwhelm them. She met them head on with her buckler and phaseblade. The crackling sword of blue energy cut through their black plate armor as if it were tissue. "Half-breed spawn of lesser demons," she shouted at them, "come and get me!"

There was a loud crack as Brahm shattered a daemon's breastplate. The dwarf had earned her respect in the last four hours since the battle had begun. He had the legendary endurance of his kind. His strikes never slowed or lost their strength, and his magical armor turned his already crushing hits into killing blows. Kara was unsure whether the hellspawn were more afraid of him or her.

Even the Nexus had shown herself to be a good warrior with her thorium tipped spear. The half-angel moved with a dancer's grace, spinning into and out of a deadly routine. Every time she paused, the spear found a weak point in armor, gouging out eyes and slicing arteries at the joints. *I may not like her, but I respect her prowess,* Kara thought. *Even without magic, she's doing well. But she's tiring; her attacks are slower.*

Kara cut down another daemon, slicing him in half from shoulder to waist. A mist of black blood filled into the air and was washed away by the rain. The forces of Hell surged over an ever growing wall of the slain to attack the three defenders, and they had almost been pushed back to the bridge.

The valkyrie did not want to fight over the pit in the rain, and Kara was glad she had decided to hold a hundred or so yards in front of it. It had given them room to fall back without putting them in extra danger. There was still about another hundred feet before they were forced out onto the bridge.

Kara took her attention from the fighting for a split second to ask Michael, <How close are you to the top?>

<Closer than the last time you asked me,> he sent back with a curt tone.

"Get yer bloody heads down!" Brahm shouted.

Kara ducked out of reflex and felt the ground shudder beneath her. She lifted her head and saw an enormous gargoyle to either side of them. The golems of stone and fire were three times taller than Kara. The rain hissed off of them.

A pale crimson-haired man walked from behind the gargoyle in front of them. His pure black eyes stared at them.

"Azreal," Kara hissed.

The Overlord sighed. He waved his hand above them, and a dark canopy diverted the rain. "Why does everyone say it like they aren't happy to see me?" he said. "Kill a few million or billion people, and everyone brands you as a 'bad guy'. By the way, how many valkyrie are left alive?"

Kara's vision turned red. She could feel blood pounding in her head. Before she could charge the Overlord, a mailed hand caught her wrist. "Do no' do that," Brahm said. "He's no' sure he can take the three o' us, that's why he's no' attacked yet."

"Oh ho!" Azreal laughed. "Is that what you really think, Brahm Ironfist? What was it like watching your friend, the Guardian, die? Oh, that's right, you weren't there!"

Brahm shook his head at the Demon Lord. "Ye'll no' goad me into a fight, Azreal. I've come to term with me friend's death. My question fer ye is, what did it feel like when Alex ran ye through?"

<Michael,> Kara sent, <how much longer?>

Azreal glared at the dwarf. "Well, my nephew is dead, and I am here, so I think we all see the ultimate outcome."

<Almost there. What's wrong?>

<It's Azreal. He's here, but he isn't attacking us. He can't kill all three of us without being banished back to Hell again. We are at a standoff.>

<I'll hurry,> Michael responded.

"Are you done?" Azreal asked. "It's rude to use telepathy while someone is talking."

"What do you want, demon? Come to bore us to death?" Terra said.

Azreal smiled at her. "Oh, Nexus, always creative with the insults. Haven't you already said that I bore you once before? Bah, don't worry about it, I'm sure you'll come up with something better to say eventually. No, I am here to tell you that you and your Daein friends are free to leave *my* Realm."

Kara risked a glance back at Terra. The Nexus frowned at the Overlord. "What game are you playing?" Terra asked.

Azreal held his hands up and feigned a hurt expression. "Your words wound me, Nexus. No game. You get to leave with your pet dwarf and other guards, and I get the valkyrie."

"No deal," Terra said. "If you want her so bad, then try taking her. I watched Kara dismember your lieutenant with ease. I think she could do the same to you without any help."

Kara grinned. *Please try something*, she begged. *I have thousands of my sisters' lives to avenge.*

Holding his hands out by his sides, Azreal said, "I came here in good will, Nexus. I am unarmed—"

"Come a bit closer, and I'll show you what it means to be unarmed," Kara interrupted.

Azreal clenched his fists. "I really don't like it when people interrupt, valkyrie. Don't do it again."

Kara laughed at him. "Or what, Azreal? Brahm's right; you would have attacked already if you thought you would come through it unscathed. Tuck your tail between your legs and run, demon. I've heard enough of your worthless drivel to last an eternity."

Azreal snarled and lashed out at her with a whip of black demonic energy. Kara snapped her sword through the whip, and it vanished into nothingness. Kara heard the creak of a bow behind her, and an arrow flew over her shoulder straight at Azreal's astonished face. The Overlord threw up a barrier of energy, but the enchanted thorium arrowhead pierced it. Azreal caught the arrow just before it punched through his eye.

Kara held her sword up before her. "I take it you aren't familiar with who I really am," she said. "I am the Shield Maiden, leader of the valkyrie and last of my people, and I stand in the gap between you and *my* Realm. You will not have it." Kara pointed the sword at him. "This is Gram, and with it, I can sever anything you throw at me, demon."

There was a deafening crack of thunder as a bolt of lightning struck the ground between Kara and Azreal. The rain fell on them again as the canopy Azreal created was shattered by the blast. Michael stood between them, pointing the Thunder Stone at the Overlord like a knife.

"You have no power here, Overlord," Michael said. "You are outnumbered." Michael pointed the Thunder Stone at the gargoyle blocking their path to Leiptrfell. A crackling bolt shot from the spear point and made the golem explode. "And you are out gunned."

<Everyone get onto the bridges! Get as close to Leiptrfell as you can!> Michael screamed through his bond to Kara.

<Already on it,> Seamus said.

<We are too,> Naru said.

<Be careful,> Kara said as she motioned Brahm and Terra back. Azreal glared at them as they backed out onto the bridge.

Michael smiled at Azreal. "Do you know what your problem is, Overlord?"

"I'm sure you are about to tell me," the Demon Lord said.

"You think you can just walk around, doing what you want, and there will be no repercussions," the einherijar explained as he backed toward the bridge, keeping the Thunder Stone pointed at Azreal. He stopped when he had both feet on the stone bridge.

"Now, I know you're fast, but are you faster than a bolt of lightning?"

Michael slammed the point of the Thunder Stone into the ground. In a perfect circle around Leiptrfell, lightning fell and spread outward, engulfing everything in the destructive wake. Azreal crushed a small metal ball in his hand and vanished between two flashes of lightning. Michael stood. As soon as the stone broke contact with the ground, the pounding lightning stopped.

<We're safe,> Michael said. <He's gone.> The sky cleared, and the howling winds and rain stopped. <Regroup at the southern bridge. Let's head back to camp.>

Chapter Fourteen – Fenris, The Wolf

I won't give up what makes me who I am. I don't care what I'll gain.

Everyone sat around the pile of glow balls in the middle of the rebel's cave as Michael filled them in on the details of his climb. "The peak was flat, as if someone had chopped off the last fifty feet of the mountain. So there I stood," he said, "being pelted by rain and pulled at by fingers of freezing wind. Lightning was striking all around me, keeping me from moving toward the stone in the middle.

"But there was an order to the strikes. I was just beginning to get a feel for the pattern when *someone* interrupted me," Michael said staring at Kara.

She grinned at him. "We were in mortal danger at the time," the valkyrie said.

Michael rolled his eyes. "It's always the same excuse with you." He threw up his hands in feigned distress. "Aaaa, help me, Michael, I'm being overwhelmed. Save me, Michael, there's too many. Protect me, Michael, the Overlord of Hell is here."

Kara threw a bone from the last of the salted boar ribs at him. Naru had made a tangy sauce from a few herbs she had gathered on their way back, and had transformed the over salted ribs into a delectable dish. The bone hit Michael in the chest, and he laughed. Terra felt a bittersweet blend of emotions at the sound.

"Anyway," Michael said, "before I was so rudely interrupted, I had to start over counting the strikes, when I finally decided to just trust my instincts. I almost got cooked, but I think I have a lot more luck than any normal man should. I made it to the Thunder Stone, and as soon as I touched it, I had a strange awareness with everything around Leiptrfell.

"After that, I used its power to travel along a bolt of lightning, threaten the most powerful being in the Nine Realms, and clear us a path out of there." Michael said the last part like it was of no real importance, but Terra recognized the smug smile on his face.

"What took you so long?" Terra asked.

Michael's eyes widened, and his mouth dropped open. Terra started laughing, and everyone else joined in. "What's so funny?" he huffed when they were all done.

Seamus patted Michael on the back. "She sure took you down a peg, big guy," he said with another laugh.

Kara stood and held her hand out for Terra to take. "Will you come with me for a moment? We have something we need to discuss."

Raising an eyebrow, Terra took the proffered hand and let Kara pull her up. They walked away from everyone to the entrance to the cavern.

"What did Azreal mean by his nephew being dead?" the valkyrie asked, still facing away from Terra.

The normally composed half-angel stammered as she scrambled for an answer.

"I'll tell you what it sounded like to me," Kara continued as she slowly turned to face Terra. "It sounded like Azreal said the Guardian was a half-demon. The same Guardian that Caitlyn told Michael you were married to." The valkyrie looked pointedly at Terra's swollen midsection. "The same Guardian whose child you carry."

"You're correct," Terra said. She thought Kara looked too relaxed, her hands too close to her sword hilt. "Why should that concern you?"

"You've lain with the enemy!" Kara hissed. "You are a traitor to all the Nine Realms."

Chills ran down Terra's spine as her blood boiled. "Frankly, I don't care what you think about me, but if you ever speak of Alex that way again, I will kill you.

"You don't know the smallest thing about half-breeds, *Valkyrie*. How dare you assume his lineage has any bearing on his actions!" Terra's voice softened with each word, until she was growling at Kara in a furious whisper. "What you know will never pass your lips."

Kara's face turned red, and her fists tightened. "You have no power to enfor-"

Terra snapped her wings out wide, and her glare darkened. Motes of blue light cast varying shadows across the half-angel's face. "I am the Paragon of the Realm of Magic. I will bring this entire mountain range down on your head if you do the slightest thing to put my child in any more danger than she already is. You will *not* utter a word on this. Am. I. Clear?"

Kara returned Terra's glare for a moment before nodding agreement.

"I'm glad we understand each other," Terra said as she turned to walk back to the rest of the group.

Ell had a frown on her face, and she glared at Darren. "Where's your shield?" she asked.

"Uh," Darren stammered. "Well, we were on the bridge, and, you see, there was a Malformed, and I was blocking its attacks, and you know how heavy I make the shield when I'm fighting something that big. The bridge kind of collapsed under me, and I almost fell to my death. I would have had Caitlyn not shouted at me, but the shield fell."

Ell's face darkened. "It fell."

Darren scratched the back of his head. "Uh, yeah."

"Do you even remember how long it took me to get that enchantment right, Lefty?" Ell scolded.

"Six months," Darren muttered.

"Six months!" Ell shouted. "You just don't care about how long it takes to enchant something!"

"That's not—" Darren tried to say, but she wasn't listening.

"And that's not even the first shield you've lost! Why, I'm half a mind to…" The half-elf shot to her feet. "ARG, I'm just so angry at you right now!" She stormed off and stared out at the lake.

The eight other people looked from Darren to Ell. "Aren't ye goin' to say somethin' to her?" Brahm asked.

Darren shook his head. "Ell's no good to talk to when she's angry. She'll just throw everything you try to say back in your face. She has to cool down first."

"I heard that, Darren Leopold Wright!" Ell shouted.

Darren winced. "Yeah, she only uses my full name when she's really mad at me. Maybe I should go talk to her." He put a hand to his knee and tried to stand. Darren lost his balance and fell back to the floor. Caitlyn hopped to her feet and offered him a hand up. The captain took it, and the two of them went over to confront Ell.

Terra looked at Caitlyn walking beside Darren with a raised eyebrow. Brahm caught Terra's eye and winked. The two shared a private smile. Terra looked back at Kara and Michael. *They really do look good together.* "So," she said, "what's the plan now?"

"The next test is the Trial of Will," Kara said. "We will travel through the tunnels to Yggdrasil where Michael will commune with the spirit of the tree.

There are many stories about Fenris, the wolf, and most of them aren't good. They say that he is from before the creation of the Nine Realms, and he is there to tempt the souls of the einherijar into going astray from their path to become Justicar. That's all I know about the Trial of Will."

"But tonight," Michael said. "We rest. We can set out in the morning."

Caitlyn walked down the dim tunnel beside Darren. The changeling wasn't sure how she felt about the man, but she was growing more comfortable around him. Terra walked in front of them with Ell in front of her. Darren's mouth was slightly open, and his brows were drawn together. When they had gone to talk to Ell earlier, she had torn into him and ignored any attempts at peacemaking. He stared past Terra and the half-elf's bouncing blue-green locks.

"Do you love her?" Caitlyn whispered.

"What? Who, Ell?" Darren whispered back with a shocked tone.

"Yeah."

Darren snorted a laugh. "Like a little sister who sometimes thinks she's the big sister. I just wish she wasn't angry with me. I didn't mean to lose the shield."

"I'll talk to her again for you," Caitlyn said.

"I don't think it'll help, but thank you."

Caitlyn walked up to Terra and tapped her on the shoulder. "Hey," her sister said.

"Hey," Caitlyn whispered back. "Playing the mediator." She raised her voice a little. "Ell, can I talk to you for a minute?"

The half-elf looked over her shoulder and nodded. She shot Darren a glare, and Caitlyn heard him pause for a few seconds then resume walking farther back. "Is everything all right?" Ell asked.

"Everything's fine," Caitlyn said. "Darren says that he's sorry for losing the shield."

Ell sighed. "I don't care about the stupid shield," she said. "Well, I do care about it. The thing was hard to enchant. Working steel is like trying to cut leather with a cheese knife; you can do it, but it takes a really long time."

"Then why are you still angry with him?" Caitlyn asked.

The half-elf shrugged. "When we were together in the band, we always looked out for each other, and I was upset that he almost died when I wasn't there to protect him."

"Do you love him?" Caitlyn asked. The changeling saw Terra's eyes widen as she looked over at her.

"Ugh, Lefty? Not in the way I think you're thinking. Like a little brother that sometimes thinks he's the big brother," Ell said. Caitlyn laughed. Hanna looked back over her shoulder at the three women, but she kept her distance when Terra shook her head. The young changeling had a gun that looked similar to the one Seamus had used the day before strapped to her back. "Why's that funny?" Ell asked.

They may as well be brother and sister, Caitlyn thought. "Darren said the same thing."

Ell looked at Caitlyn with an upraised eyebrow. "He said he loved me like a brother? That's weird." Caitlyn opened her mouth to explain, but Ell laughed.

"I had you going for a second. I knew what you meant."

Terra smirked at the exchange. They walked without speaking for a few minutes until Ell broke the silence. "What about you, Caitlyn? How do you feel about him?"

Caitlyn felt her face heat and was glad for the gloom. "I don't *not* like him."

Ell grinned at her. "Well, that's good. Please go let the man you don't not like know that I'm not mad at him anymore."

Slowing down to fall back to Darren, Caitlyn thought over her answer to Ell's question. *It's true. I don't* not *like him, but I'm not sure if I like him like that.*

Darren caught up to her and held the glow ball near her face. "Your face is red," he said, making her face blush again. *Stop doing that!* "Is she still mad?"

"No," Caitlyn said, wishing she could drain some of the extra blood in her face. *I should have changed into my birth form*, she lamented. "She just thinks you should be more careful."

Darren nodded. "Thank you. You didn't have to do that."

Caitlyn shrugged. "No problem."

Hanna looked back at Terra with a questioning look on her face. The Nexus nodded this time, and Hanna slowed to let her catch up. "How are you feeling?"

Terra looked at her with an upraised eyebrow. "I'm fine."

I need to talk to her alone. Hanna looked at Ell. "Could I talk to Terra alone for a moment?"

Ell nodded and took a few quick steps forward. The half-elf seemed put off by Hanna's speech not matching her age, but she never said anything about it. "Is something wrong?" Terra asked.

Hanna stared at Terra's face and said, "I don't like being lied to." *And there it is*, the little girl thought when a split-second flash of panic flickered through Terra's eyes. She had been taking a gamble being so blunt about her observation, but it had paid off.

"I don't know..." Terra started. "I'm sorry. I should have told my doctor earlier. When did you figure it out?"

"I had never seen demonic energy before," Hanna explained. "It's a lot like magic. I can sense when it's being used like magic. I can see it being woven like magic." She glared at the woman. "How am I supposed to properly take care of you when you are holding things back from me?"

Terra looked torn between snapping at her and apologizing. "You can't," the Nexus said, taking a middle road.

"You're bloody right I can't," Hanna said. She had never sworn before, and the word felt odd, but she knew it was the correct place to use it. Terra looked down at her in shock. "Alex was a good man," the little girl whispered. She felt tears well up in her eyes. "How could you do that to him? With one of *their* kind no less."

Staring at her without comprehension, Terra asked a dumbfounded, "What?"

Hanna's whisper grew harsh. "How could you cheat on Alex with a demon?"

"Is that what you're actually upset about?" Terra asked. Hanna nodded and blinked away tears. The half-angel leaned in close and whispered in Hanna's ear, "Alex was a half-demon."

Hanna's mind ground to a stop, but there were no brilliant flashes of insight, no ideas rushing forward. She stood still and stared straight ahead, trying to make sense of what Terra had told her. The Nexus put a hand to her back and urged Hanna along. Her feet began to move mechanically.

"But," Hanna said, "he was so nice."

Terra placed a hand on her head. "I know he was," she whispered. "I've come to realize that not everyone and everything is as it seems. Not all demons are bad, just like not all angels are good. They are just trying to get along in the Nine Realms like the rest of us."

"You've met a bad angel?" Hanna asked with a dubious look.

"Not precisely, just one that wasn't good. He would give up his own daughter to do what he thought was right," Terra whispered. Her tone turned serious, and she put a hand on Hanna's shoulder. "You can't tell anyone about Alex. If they found out what he was… found out what Jessica is, then it would be very bad for me. You know she is capable of things we've never heard of. I just want to keep her safe."

Hanna nodded. *That's why she didn't tell me.* "Can you keep her safe?" she asked without thinking. *Good job, dummy! Stress her out, great for a pregnant woman. Well, we are in constant danger and could die at any time, so I guess if she isn't stressed out already then there's something wrong with her…*

Terra had said something while Hanna was berating herself, and she had missed it. "What did you say?"

"I said I can try. That's all any of us can do," Terra repeated.

"I'm sorry for getting angry at you and thinking what I did."

Terra ruffled her hair. "Don't worry about it. I should have told you sooner." Hanna felt Terra grab the butt of the laser rifle and wiggle it a little. "Why do you have this?" she asked.

Hanna grinned. "Naru said it was more useful to me than her, and that I could keep it."

Frowning at the changeling, Terra opened her mouth to say something, but she was interrupted by Kara announcing, "We're here."

Michael stood in the middle of the earthen bubble. A bundle of roots hanging down from the ceiling glowed with bright white light. "What should I expect when I step into them?" Michael asked.

Kara shook her head. "I have no idea. Every story is different. Be ready for anything."

Michael nodded and kissed her on the lips. She smelled like her blue steel armor with a faint bit of sweat. Her soft lips tasted salty. "I love you," he said.

She smiled at him. "I love you too. Be careful."

<I'll keep both eyes open,> he sent with a wink.

Michael walked into the hanging roots, but nothing happened. He pulled the Thunder Stone from his pocket and touched one of the roots. Everything went white.

<Trespasser, do you attempt the Trial of the Justicar?> a voice whispered in his mind.

"I do."

<Very well. May the will of the First Ones be with you,> the voice whispered again.

That's twice the First Ones have been mentioned. Who are they? Michael wondered. He looked around the empty white space. Spinning in a circle, Michael saw there was no point of reference anywhere.

"Do you really want to know?" a powerful voice asked from behind him. The essence of the place inside of Yggdrasil resonated with the voice.

Michael turned to see an enormous male wolf looming over him. "Fenris," he said.

The wolf nodded. "That is one of my names. I've had so many over the eons. It grows lonely here. So, do you desire to know about the First Ones?"

Unsure of what the trial was supposed to entail, Michael nodded. The white blankness was replaced with a black canvas. Michael and Fenris stood upon a white wooden disc that floated in the emptiness. Shards of earth and other elements sailed past them.

"Where are we?" Michael asked.

The wolf let out a canine chuckle. "So eager! I love humans! They always want to KNOW. Now, now, now! I'm sorry, pup. This is a story that takes some time, but your new question is at the root of your first. We are in what will become both the Nine Realms and the Outside. This is a time before the Dawn."

"The Dawn? Of creation?" Michael asked.

"I give you points for trying," Fenris said, "but it is at one time yes, and at the same instant, a resounding no. If the Dawn was the point at which all was created, then where are we now?"

Michael thought the question over and shrugged. "Ah, good, I see you are not full of useless pride, needing to always be right. Remember that and hold it dear, for many more times in your life, you will be wrong," Fenris said. The statement carried an air of command.

"I will," Michael said.

"Good," the wolf said. "As I was saying, this is a time before the Dawn." Distant flashes of light pierced through the darkness. "Ah!" Fenris said with fake curiosity, "What is going on over there?" The disc of white wood soared through the darkness drawing nearer the lights.

As they drew closer, Michael was able to discern that they were explosions of a massive aerial battle. "You are close," Fenris chided, reading Michael's mind again, "but how can you have an aerial battle with no air?"

"Then what are we breathing?" Michael asked.

A large wolfish grin engulfed Fenris's head. Teeth as long as Michael's arms glistened with saliva. "Are you breathing?"

Michael froze for a second when he realized he hadn't drawn a breath since he entered the space inside Yggdrasil. He snapped a hand up to his throat and felt no pulse. *Am I dead?* Fenris laughed again.

"No, little human, you aren't dead. This is a place of the soul and the mind, not the flesh. Do not fret, your body is safe at the roots of my tree."

Michael nodded and looked back at the ships firing at one another. One group was of a sharp angular design, red and white in color, the other bent into shapes he had never seen. It hurt his eyes to look at their warping green and black colors. A solid beam of crackling black and white energy lanced out from one of the angular ships and punctured a gaping hole in one of the darker ones. A burst of white light, and the strangely shaped ship puffed into non-existence.

"This is the First War," Fenris said. "The Eternal War." Fenris motioned to the red and white ships. "On one side, the First Ones, on the other, the Outsiders, though they aren't known as that yet. There wasn't an Outside yet, or an Inside. Everything simply was." The wolf leaned down and put his left eye inches from Michael's face. "Do you want to see what a First One looks like?"

Sensing that Fenris was trying to test his mettle, Michael stood his ground and nodded, doing his best to ignore the unblinking brown eye that was larger than his body. The disc zoomed down toward one of the First Ones' ships. Michael clenched his teeth when he saw they were going to crash into the ship. The disc and its occupants passed through the crystalline walls of the ship.

"It is good to be brave," Fenris said, his voice different again, "but prudence is also a virtue. Don't let your bravery overcome your caution too often, or it could have deadly consequences, not only for you, but those you care for also. The brave too often live and suffer while the ones they love fade away."

"I'll remember that," Michael said.

"Good." The disc drew to a halt before a humanoid crystalline creature. The being had two legs and two arms connected to a torso with a head on top, but it was transparent and red like a ruby. "These are the First Ones. They had a true name, but it is lost to time."

A name Michael had never heard before bubbled up in his mind. "Life Wardens?"

Fenris laughed. "And now you are reading my mind! Will the wonders never cease? The First Ones became the Life Wardens of Aria, the Realm of Life, in millions of years and in the blink of a wolf's eye."

A pearlescent First One ran past them and stood next to a panel. It pushed a hand into the panel, and a viewport opened. There was a feeling of something trembling, and the black and white beam fired again.

The red First One stood beside the milky white one. It placed a red hand on a white shoulder.

"What are they saying?" Michael asked.

"This is a place of the mind, pup. How about you use yours?" Fenris chided.

Michael closed his eyes and tried to cast his mind toward the two First Ones.

<We haven't enough time, Luna,> the red one sent.

Luna, made of moonstone, she will give her life to bring about the birth of the Changelings and magic itself. They will always remember her, but forget what she really was. Michael wasn't sure where the thought came from, but he was certain it was true. <The Source is almost ready, Mars. Can the Nephilim guard us?>

<The angels and the demons were not happy, but he is, my love,> Mars sent. *Mars, made of ruby, he is the scientist. He still exists to this day, in a form.*

<Is the blade ready? He can hardly be our guardian without it,> Luna said.

<It is, and he already has it.>

There was a moment of hesitation. <Does he know he will be unable to follow us? That he will be left here, without the sword? It is a creation of the other place and will vanish when we transition.>

<He said that fate fits the last of his kind. The Nephilim said he would forever roam the place between the one we create and this one, guarding it from the others,> Mars sent.

Michael's link to the two First One's was cut off, and he opened his eyes. He and Fenris were back in the white space. "Wait," Michael said. "All that gave me was so many more questions. Who is the Nephilim?"

"He is but a man. A rather unique man," Fenris conceded, "but still just a man. I'm sorry, pup, but that information is not for you."

"What is the Source?" Michael asked.

"Ah, a question I can answer. The Source was created by the First Ones to act as a catalyst in the creation of the Nine Realms. Using its unfathomable power, they created the universe as we now know it. They gave definition to the Outside, the Void, the Nether Realm, the Spirit World, by giving it something to be distinguished from. The Nine Realms, the Inside, the Nine Realms, the Scales of Balance, they are here to give all of us a place to exist in relative safety."

"The Scales of Balance," Michael said. "What happens if a Realm collapses?"

Fenris shook his head. "Can't happen. Not from the Inside or the Outside."

"Can't happen?" Michael said. "Do you have any idea of what is happening outside of your tree? Kara is the *last* valkyrie. She is the only thing preventing this world from being destroyed."

Fenris grinned at him. "Is she? Always hold true to your convictions, but be willing to change them when you get more information on a subject. Being intractable can get you killed as easily as a sword through the heart. And sometimes the sword will not be one of steel."

Michael nodded. "Then what else is holding back Caine's destruction?"

Laughing again, Fenris poked Michael with a claw. "So modest... That's why you're here, isn't it, pup? You believe in this Realm! Just by existing in this place with your valkyrie, you are preventing the end. You are stopping the scales from swinging too far out of balance, and the Outside from swallowing us whole."

Fenris paced around Michael in a circle. "Did you know there are two different kinds of memories, pup?"

"No, I didn't. What are they?" Michael asked.

"Well, you have memories of the flesh," the wolf explained. "Those exist in the mind and are accumulated over the course of a life and lost when you die."

Michael got a feeling that he knew the answer, but he asked anyway. "What are the other kind?"

Fenris darted around to the front of Michael and crouched, staring at him with those huge eyes. "Memories of the soul! The memories that make up all of the lifetimes you've ever lived! The important parts of every life, at least. Every decision that defines who and what you are! I'm going to ask you a question, and you get two chances to tell me the truth. Get it right the first time, and you get the shaft of Gungnir, and you can go snake hunting right away."

"And if I get it wrong?" Michael asked.

Fenris grinned, and his eyes glowed with an inner light. "Get it wrong, and I open your eyes to all of the memories buried within your soul. Then you get your second chance."

"What if I guess incorrectly again?"

Fenris raised an eyebrow and shrugged his front shoulders. "Some do refuse the truth, even when it's staring them in the face. If you get it wrong a second time then I have to eat you. Believe me, I don't really look forward to that part. Most einherijar souls I have tasted have a rather bitter taste, but I have a feeling yours would be a... shock to my pallet. So, einherijar, what is your name?"

Michael thought it over for a moment, but no ideas came to mind, so he told the truth. "Michael Stormbringer."

Fenris leapt to his paws and laughed until he started wheezing. "Oh, you were so close! Stormbringer, that's rich. But wrong." Faster than Michael could react, Fenris swiped a paw at him. Claws ripped into his body that wasn't a real body, and Michael felt something come loose. Memories began to pound through him. He was swept away in the inundating flow.

Michael Stormbringer looked down at Terra and smiled. *I love you,* he thought as he slammed his warhammer onto the gateway arch, shattering it with his wife on the other side.

Michael Stormbringer had known Terra on sight, when he had saved her in the mountains, but she wanted to play coy and act like someone else. *I'll protect this woman with my life,* he thought as he placed his warhammer on his belt.

Marcus Leiptr lifted his warhammer high as he charged the Hellgate. The eyes all swiveled toward him as he slammed his weapon against them.

Marcus Leiptr's warhammer soared through the air and crushed the demon's head. "I'll kill all of you for taking her from me!" he screamed.

Marcus Leiptr kissed his bride. He had saved her from a bandit attack, and it had been love at first sight.

Thunder roared over the corpse of his dead wife. He charged into the waiting mass of demons and was slain, but not before he killed all of the demons.

Thunder broke the arm of a man that was trying to rob the woman in the alley. She thanked him with a kiss and a smile.

Thunder was an orphan. He got the name from the other street rats by the way his feet boomed so loud they could hear him from a mile away. A man offered to train him as a gladiator.

Past memories of a thousand lives flashed through him. They were always the same, but each was different. Raised from the common masses, he is given a warhammer, uses it to rescue a woman, and they fall in love. He dies avenging or protecting her again. He reached the last of his memories.

Thor drew back Mjolnir and hurled it with all his might. The Hellgate burst open under the weight of the blow. "OVERLORD!" he roared. "Come and face justice, you traitorous bastard!"

Thor cradled his wife's dead body. He and the Overlord had fallen in love with the same woman, but she had loved Thor. The Overlord flew into a rage and killed his Freya then fled to Hell. *I will chase you to the ends of the Nine Realms or the Outside itself for this betrayal.*

Thor blocked what would have been a killing blow to the woman on her knees. She was one of the first of the new race the First Ones had created. She was a valkyrie, and her platinum gray hair was the most beautiful thing he had ever seen. Thor pushed the Outsider's vorpal blade back and decimated the being of shadow under one of Mjolnir's charged strikes. "Thank you," she said. "The Nine Realms are almost complete. We'll be safe soon."

The man gasped. A purple thing stood over him. <I am Jupiter,> he heard in his mind. <You are Thor. You are the first Justicar. And this is Mjolnir, your weapon.>

The flood of memories stopped, and Thor rose to his feet. Fenris stood before him.

The wolf grinned at him. "I ask you a second time. What is your name?"

"I was Thor, the first Justicar, but I am still Michael," he said.

Fenris winked at him. "That you are."

He blinked, and he stood in the earthen cave beneath Yggdrasil. Already, the memories of his soul were fading. Before he could take a second breath and regain his bearings, all the memories of his past lives save those of Michael Stormbringer and Thor had blown away like wisps of smoke in the wind.

He pocketed the Thunder Stone, walked over to Terra, and knelt before her. "I truly am sorry for the pain you've had to live with these last five years, Terra. That night I saved you in the mountains, I thought I would protect you with my life. I'm glad I lived up to that oath."

"You remember," Terra said.

He nodded. "Some." He stood and took Kara's hand. He looked at the valkyrie's long gray braid and shook his head with a laugh. *Some things never change.* The Nexus had a hurt look on her face. "As I said before, death severs all bonds, Terra. It is true that I loved you once, but that had its time, and that time is gone. Do you understand?"

Terra looked down at the ground. "I do, Michael."

A small piece of wood fell from the roots of Yggdrasil. Michael walked to the wooden shaft and picked it up. He brushed one of the glowing roots, and Fenris's voice echoed in his mind.

<I thought you would rather face Jormungandr with an old friend at your hip.>

The piece of white ash was harder than steel, but it was only two feet long, far too short to be the shaft of a spear. *You wily old wolf,* he thought. Michael pulled the stone from his pocket. Letting out a mighty roar, he slammed the ash handle into the stone. With a resonating boom, the two pieces fused into one and changed shape.

The Thunder Stone was a shimmering piece of silvery metal, and the ash haft had become engraved with intricate lines. Mjolnir felt comfortable in his hands. He felt strength like he hadn't known in a thousand lifetimes flow through his veins. *Some things never change,* he thought again.

"So," the dwarf said, "I do no' mean to say the obvious, but that's no' a spear."

"Right you are, Brahm. This is Mjolnir, the warhammer of the first Justicar." Michael grinned at him. "My warhammer." A vertical circle of light appeared near the glowing roots, and a breeze scented with salt air filled the cave. "Let's go, we have a wyrm to summon."

Chapter Fifteen – Jormungandr, The World Serpent

<It seems some part of you remains. Good.>

Terra stood on the slight rise that overlooked the ocean; two steep paths ran past either side of the rise down toward the beach. The wet, salty air pulled at her hair, making it ripple behind her like a torn, red flag announcing their arrival. There was a wooden and granite hall a half-mile to her left, and a granite cliff that hung out over the ocean not far to her right. She looked back at the portal Hanna and Ell were walking through and shook her head. *That shouldn't be possible. The Obsidian Towers block all attempts at teleportation.*

"It's not teleportation," Michael said as if he read her mind.

"What is it then? It took us from one place to another," she said without looking over her shoulder at him.

"What is the portal touching?" he asked.

A tree grew adjacent to the portal. *An ash tree.* "So that tree is part of Yggdrasil, and you used it to move us here through the tree. Clever."

Michael laughed. "Very, but it wasn't me. It was Fenris, the wolf that lives inside the tree. He did this."

"Why would Fenris help us?" Kara asked. "All of the stories say he is a capricious beast that would sooner devour you than help you."

Terra turned about and looked at the valkyrie and her einherijar. *His eyes look different,* she thought. *My Michael really is gone.* Terra studied the man that had been her husband in what felt like another life. She felt nothing for him, no tugging pull on her heartstrings, no desire or nostalgia, nothing.

"Oh, Fenris is capricious. He certainly does whatever whim strikes him, but I think he wants to help, just in his own way." Terra heard the portal close behind her with a pop. "Good, we're all here," Michael said. "It is time for the last Trial of the Justicar. Kara, Seamus, Naru, and I will go to that cliff and summon Jormungandr.

"When he comes, the sky will literally turn red," he continued. "I don't have to kill it, only draw blood with Mjolnir. It... won't be easy. The serpent's body is covered in scales that are thicker than I am tall. I'll have to climb onto his head and strike him where his scales are thinnest. You six will have to fight off any of Azreal's forces until I can go to The Hall of the Fallen," he pointed at the wood and stone hall, "and place a drop of blood from Jormungandr on the Justicar's Altar. When that is done, Jormungandr will go back out into the ocean."

"What if the bloody Overlord shows up again?" Brahm said.

Michael smiled. "Jormungandr can't be killed, and only weapons wielded by valkyrie or einherijar can harm it. If Azreal comes, then we all flee and let him die fighting something he can't defeat." It was late morning, and the sun was nearing its apex. "It is almost time. One more thing, if I haven't completed the ritual before the sun touches the horizon, then get underground."

"Why?" Darren asked.

"If the sun drops behind the horizon, then Jormungandr will rain poison down on us all. It doesn't matter where it touches you. If the slightest fleck of it touches you, you will drop dead on the spot. It will feel like an eternity in your mind, but it will be too late for anyone to help you. Do you all understand that? I won't sacrifice my friends if I can't do this." He looked each of them in the eye and waited for them to nod before he looked to the next.

"Stand ready," Michael said. "These two paths are the only way down to the beach for a hundred miles. Hold them, and the Hall of the Fallen and the cliff will be secure."

Kara looked at Terra. "Our lives are in your hands," the valkyrie said.

Terra nodded. "We won't let you down."

Kara and her einherijar jogged down the eastern slope toward the stone cliff. Terra could hear the waves slam against the cliff from her distant perch. She walked to the ash tree and placed her left hand against it. The Nexus surveyed their surroundings, trying to see if there were any natural choke points other than the two paths.

There was a sharp pain in her belly, and Terra put her right hand over her thorium plated middle. A few seconds passed, and the pain faded away. She resumed her survey but didn't see anything helpful. *Looks like I'll have to make something to funnel them our way.*

Terra took a deep breath and cleared her mind of all thought. She focused on the core of her being, sensing the magical energy at her center. *It was good to bring Caitlyn and Hanna with us,* she thought. Normally, when she was on Dae, Terra absorbed an equal mix of all four elements, but since she was away from her home, there was no latent energy to absorb, except what Caitlyn and Hanna created as changelings.

Ever since their frenzied run through the mountains, Terra had not cast a single spell, and over the course of the last two and a half days, she had absorbed a considerable store of earth and air magic. She reached tendrils of earth deep into the ground around her. Clenching her fists and pulling upward, Terra raised thick sections of stone from the surrounding granite cliffs. Beginning to feel lightheaded, she released the spell.

Terra dropped to a knee and shook her head. *I think I overdid it a little.* Caitlyn helped her stand. A wall ran several hundred feet in either direction, with a gap in the middle just over thirty feet wide. Terra didn't have to look over to see that it ran straight from the cliff wall on both sides, giving the forces of Hell no easy approach to the beach save through the Daein people.

Brahm let out a low whistle. The wall of stone was ten feet thick and five times that in height. "This'll make things a bit more simple. I was tryin' to think o' who should split up into each group."

"Just doing what I can," Terra said. She shook her head again to clear the last bit of lightheadedness.

"You didn't have to do that all on your own," Caitlyn admonished. "We could have helped you."

"It's fine," the Nexus said. "Earth is too unwieldy to cast it in a battle against anything other than golems." She looked at the distant figures running up the beach cliff.

Michael stood close to the edge of the cliff. He looked back at his companions and smiled. <Are you

all ready?> he asked. Seamus and Naru nodded in unison.

<We are, my love,> Kara sent. <Let's begin.>

Thrusting his warhammer into the air, Michael shouted, "Jormungandr, I summon you!" A peal of thunder from Mjolnir rippled across the water.

<Tresspasssser, do you attempt the Trial of the Jussticar?> a voice hissed in his mind.

"I do."

<Very well. May the sstrength of the Firsst Onesss be with you,> the voice whispered again.

The dark blue water began to roil and shudder as Jormungandr awoke. As far as Michael could see, the water turned a brownish-gray as hundreds of years of sand and silt were shaken from the sea serpent's body. The red-scaled body began to rise to the surface. Water sluiced off of the scales; Jormungandr's body covered the entire bottom of the ocean. The sea level fell several feet, and Michael was unable to see any of the dirtied water save what was at the bottom of the cliff. Everything was a seething mass of red scales. The sky turned red with the reflected light from Jormungandr's body.

"How big is this thing?" Seamus muttered.

"It's called the World Serpent for a reason," Michael said. The broad body began to lift into the air, and wind buffeted the four when the serpent's head finally whipped into the air. Jormungandr opened its mouth, bared its fangs, and hissed at them. The beast's teeth were a hundred feet long, and its head was five times that.

"Who ssummonsss Jormungandr?" it said with a deafening roar.

Michael stepped to the edge of the cliff. "I, Michael Stormbringer, called you here!"

"Prepare yourssself for the end," the serpent hissed. Jormungandr darted in to bite the four people on the cliff, moving so fast it appeared to be a bright red blur. Michael set his feet and met the Jormungandr's attack with a blow of his own. He struck the beast just below its left nostril, knocking its head up into the air.

There was a loud cracking noise, and Michael saw there were flakes of red scale on Mjolnir but no blood. "Feel the might of the First Ones, snake!" Michael roared as he hurled Mjolnir at the World Serpent.

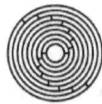

The sky seemed as if it had been drenched in blood. Darren stared at the battle happening in the distance. *They look like ants fighting... well, fighting a snake.* A loud crack came from behind Darren, and he turned to see a red-headed man walk through a small black portal a few hundred yards away. "Who's that?" he asked.

The black portal closed behind the man. He lifted his hands into the air, and an enormous portal fifty feet wide opened behind him. "Azreal," Terra said through gritted teeth.

"Should we run like Michael said?" Hanna asked.

Terra shook her head. "No, he could have teleported in on the beach, but he doesn't want Jormungandr to attack him. I don't think he'll come closer until we've been overrun. We just have to deal with whatever he throws at us."

Hanna nodded. Darren watched as the little girl unslung the rifle from her back and pulled a lever on it. The gun emitted a high pitched whine, and she pointed it at Azreal. Hanna did something, and the rifle shot a thin line of light at Azreal. The beam was devoured by a bubble of black energy that rippled into existence and disappeared when it hit. She fired the gun again, but it was stopped by the black shield again.

"I'll get you one day," the seven-year-old girl promised.

Darren patted her on the shoulder. "We all have reason for revenge, little one," he said. "We'll have it but not today." Hanna nodded in grim determination.

The howling of dogs echoed across the distance. Hundreds of red-furred hellhounds charged through the portal toward them. "When it's not bloody zombies and skeletons, it's bloody hellhounds," Brahm said. Caitlyn dropped to all four and changed into her primal form.

Hanna looked up at Darren. "Help me into that tree, so I'll have a good spot to shoot from." Darren nodded and boosted the changeling up to the lowest branch before he took his place between Terra and Caitlyn. He glanced over his shoulder to see Hanna scramble around the tree and braced where a branch and the trunk met. *Smart kid.*

Streaks of light lanced out from overhead as Hanna fired at the hellhounds. Each shot had a demonic dog going down in a tumble of legs, but there were far too many for her to kill all before they closed the distance. Caitlyn, Darren, Terra, Ell, and Brahm stood almost shoulder to shoulder in the thirty-foot gap between the two walls. The forces of Dae and Hell joined battle.

Seamus squeezed Sally's trigger, and she clattered a few rounds at the huge snake's head. He was beginning to run low on the blocks of steel he had brought for ammunition. Sally was an adaptive ammunition rail gun. The metal blocks were subjected to magnetic fields strong enough to rip a precisely sized round from the block, and then divert the magnetic field toward the muzzle, launching the round with an extremely high velocity.

The young einherijar sighed. The bullets were doing nothing to Jormungandr. The massive snake seemed to have forgotten Seamus was even there. He gritted his teeth in anger. *Fine, see how ignoring me works for you.*

Seamus pulled an extended barrel with a large scope and a bipod on it from where it hung on his back. He pressed an ejection button on Sally's side, and the barrel popped off and clattered to the ground. He snapped the longer barrel into position and flipped down the legs of the bipod. He dialed up the round size and magnetic gain as high as they could go. Sally whistled an out of parameters alarm at him, but Seamus pushed the bypass and looked down the scope.

Jormungandr's left eye was enormous, easily fifty feet tall, and Seamus was less than three hundred yards away. There was no way he could miss that shot. *Ignore this,* the einherijar thought as he squeezed the trigger. With a loud hum and clack, a round the size of a fist was launched from the end of Sally's barrel at a speed close to one-tenth the speed of light.

Sally exploded in his hands, and a piece of shrapnel from the detonation shredded Seamus's neck. Blood gushed from his jugular vein, but he was aware enough to smile when Jormungandr roared in pain. The World Serpent's left eye deflated in a torrent of white and grey ichors. It clamped the lid over the ruined mass and glared in Seamus's direction with its remaining eye.

<That'll teach him to ignore me, huh?> Seamus whispered to his friends as he lost consciousness.

Hanna fired shot after shot into the mass of Daemen that was pushing against the line of Daein. She had killed every single one that tried to scale the wall with a precise shot through the head. The Changeling of the Wing was happy the laser rifle's solar panel was still recharging the gun even though the sky was red.

A woman's scream came from below, and Hanna saw Terra had fallen backwards. "Hanna," Ell shouted. "Help her!"

The changeling didn't see any blood, and Terra was holding both hands over the distended plate of thorium that covered her middle. *Oh no,* Hanna thought. She slung the laser rifle across her back and hung from the branch she was on. She dropped to the ground and scrambled over to Terra.

The Nexus's breathing was rapid when Hanna made it to her, but the pregnant woman was getting it under control. Without explaining anything, Hanna sent a medical probe into Terra's belly. *Good,* she thought, *her water hasn't broken.* Hanna knew she would run out of magical power soon, and having a probe to monitor Terra would drain her of energy in the blink of an eye.

Hanna saw through the probe that Terra was just coming off of a contraction. "Terra, you are going into labor. Your water hasn't broken. I'm going to try stopping it."

Terra snapped a hand onto Hanna's arm. "How? You can't use healing magic on me."

"And your pregnancy isn't a normal one," the young healer said. "Let me see what I can do." Hanna closed her eyes and moved the probe down the umbilical cord and touched Jessica's head with it. Her ears rang, but it wasn't as painful as it had been the first time she connected to the baby.

<Hanna,> a small voice sent. <Time. It's time.>

The changeling was momentarily confused by the unborn child's use of language. The last time she had been telepathically linked to Jessica, the baby had communicated through emotions.

<No, Jessica,> Hanna sent with a feeling of warning. <It's not safe. You and Terra would be in danger.>

A feeling of confusion bubbled along the bridging spell and energy. <Terra. Terra. Terra. That's a new name. Who is Terra? I am Jessica. Is the other me, the one I hear when she dreams, the one that always thinks I, Terra?>

"Hurry if ye can, Hanna!" Brahm shouted. "We can no' hold fer long!"

Hanna didn't understand, but she didn't have time to argue or think about her response. <Yes. It will not be safe for you now. You and Terra will be hurt, maybe killed, maybe worse.>

A scream of fear and alarm made Hanna cringe in pain. <YOU CAN'T LET HIM TAKE ME!>

"Hurry, kid!" Darren shouted.

<I'M TRYING TO SAVE YOU NOW!> Hanna screamed back at the unborn child. <Can you wait? Can you not come yet?>

<Don't want to be alone... Yes, I can wait,> came a quiet response. Hanna felt a sense of emotional hurt thrumming across the telepathic bond.

<Then wait. I will talk to you again soon, I promise.> As soon as Hanna stopped talking, Jessica severed the probe, and Hanna winced under the backlash of the spell collapsing. "I'm sorry for yelling at you," Hanna said.

"What?" Terra asked over the din of battle.

"Not you. It's fine. She'll wait. Get up," Hanna said as she offered Terra her hand. The Nexus accepted it, and they turned to face the line. The four remaining defenders were hard pressed to hold the gap. Black plated Daemen pressed each of the four fighters hard. Caitlyn was bleeding from a number of wounds.

Hanna drew her laser rifle and made a small magical lens of air and fire at the end of the barrel identical to the one she had made when they were defending Leiptrfell. *If a little one makes it that big...* "Terra," Hanna yelled. "Make a big lens of air and fire just like the one I have here, but as tall as Ell and just behind her."

Terra followed Hanna's orders without asking why. As soon as the larger lens was in place, Hanna shouted, "Ell, it's just like Leiptrfell. Move!"

Everything slowed in the young changeling's mind. She took a slow, deliberate breath. She could see the beads of sweat on Ell's cheek as the half-elf glanced over her shoulder wide-eyed. Hanna's finger began to squeeze the trigger as Ell tumbled out of the way. The three daemen she had been fending off all grinned the same wicked smile. Their expressions had only begun to change to one of stupid confusion when they saw the little girl standing in front of them. Ell cleared the firing angle, and Hanna's trigger finger finished its journey.

Hanna clamped her eyes closed to protect them from the flash, but she hadn't been expecting how much Terra's larger lens had amplified the power of the laser. A deafening roar tore through the air, and Hanna screamed against the pressure on her ears.

She wasn't sure how long she held down the trigger, but it was long enough to drain the battery completely, something Naru had said to not let happen. "If that happens," the einherjar had said, "then you are stuck with the Realms' most delicate club until the battery fully recharges."

Her eyes fluttered open, and Hanna observed the destruction she had wrought. Terra's larger lens had widened the beam to almost match where the line was being held. The Daein were all panting in the sudden reprieve. A twenty-foot-deep trench stood before the gap. The remaining Daemen stared at Hanna in fear.

The laser rifle chirped at her. She looked down at the battery indicator and saw that it was already full. Hanna glanced up at the sun and saw it had traversed about half the distance from its peak to the horizon. *Have we been fighting that long?* She shrugged. *Doesn't matter,* she thought, *we aren't done yet.* The Changeling of the Wing shouldered her rifled and fired into the mass of Daemen.

Kara lay on the ground breathless; her sword, Gram, clutched in her fist. Jormungandr had slammed against the base of the cliff making the part Kara had been standing on collapse into the sea. A shadow loomed over her, and the valkyrie heard an angry hiss.

Regaining her wits in time to roll aside from the fang, Kara scrambled to her feet. Naru stood between her and the World Serpent. Jormungandr drew in a deep breath. "Watch out!" Kara said as she ducked behind her buckler. The valkyrie knew she was too far away from the serpent's mouth to roll away from the blast of acidic poison, and her buckler didn't cover enough of her body to protect her.

If Michael can complete the ritual before he fades away, he'll survive, Kara thought just as Jormungandr hissed. Red metal slammed into the valkyrie and knocked her onto the flat of her back.

<Thank y—> Naru started to say before the droplets of acidic poison touched the einherijar's skin. Kara felt another rush of strength and vitality return when the first einherijar she had ever bonded died.

'Valkyrie give a measure of their own strength to their einherijar to bond them and keep them from fading away,' Frigga, her teacher had told her after she had been born from Yggdrasil. 'While your einherijar live, you are weaker but immortal. With their deaths, we are strengthened but can be slain.'

Kara rolled her friend's dead body from on top of her. "No, Naru, thank you." Michael stood on the edge of the cliff and battled Jormungandr alone. The valkyrie looked down at her armor. The acidic poison had eaten away at some of the plates. There were holes on a few, and Kara counted herself lucky that it had kept her safe, but it was a useless, riddled mess now.

I can lose the weight, she thought. Kara let go of her shield and tugged at her breastplate. The leather straps snapped under her amplified strength. She kicked her legs, and her lower armor came free. The valkyrie ripped off the vambraces covering her forearms and lifted the blue and silver helm from her head. She dropped the helmet next to a mass of ruined gray hair.

Her now jaw-length hair swayed in the breeze. Her white sleeveless undershirt and shorts rippled. Kara dug her toes into the dirt. The sun was beginning to near the horizon. *Seamus died making you half-blind. Naru died protecting me.* Kara smiled. *Let's see if I can have a death half as worthy as theirs.*

The last free valkyrie charged the serpent barefoot, screaming as she closed the gap with lightning speed. She shot past Michael and launched herself into the air. Jormungandr turned its right eye toward her so it could see her, just as she hoped it would. Kara threw Gram as hard as she could at the World Serpent's eye.

<Now!> she screamed across her bond to her surviving einherijar.

Jormungandr closed its good eye and pulled away from the flying sword. Kara looked back and up and saw Michael slam Mjolnir into Jormungandr's snout again. Great gouts of blood, hard to distinguish from the red sky, filled the air, and Kara smiled. She looked down at the rapidly approaching rocks. <This was a good death,> she sent to Michael.

A bolt of lightning etched across her vision and crashed into the ground below her. Michael stood below Kara with arms outstretched to catch her. She landed in his arms, and he grinned at her. "You don't look dead yet," he said.

An outraged roar came from far above when Jormungandr located the two of them. "RUN!" Michael and Kara shouted at the same time.

The two kicked dirt and rocks into the air as they sprinted toward Valhalla.

Terra glanced to the west, and she saw the sun touch the horizon. She drove her spear through the visor of a Daemon's helm. Her arms burned, and every muscle in her body begged to rest, but she refused to stop. She risked a glance over her shoulder to see if Kara and her einherijar were still fighting Jormungandr.

The World Serpent was no longer hovering over the cliff. It chased something across the beach. "They did it!" Terra shouted as she turned back forward. The ditch Hanna's rifle had dug was filled in with the corpses of Hellspawn, but they kept on coming, balancing on the dead bodies as they charged. "They only need a little more time."

"We're almost out o' bloody time!" Brahm yelled.

A heavy thud made the earth tremble. Terra looked past the Daemen and saw a Battlesuit as tall as the wall she had created step through the black portal. The bi-pedal Fyrian war machine looked like the one Alex had fought in Adorac Volcano, but this one had a large box on either shoulder and one arm was a hollow tube. The other arm had a large sword clasped in it, and the entire machina was covered from head to toe in reflective armor. The Daemen began to retreat from the gap between the two walls.

"What in Hell is that thing?" Darren shouted.

"A Battlesuit," Terra said. "It's Fyrian machina." The Nexus squinted when the front side of the two boxes revealed themselves to be a collection of little doors. A flash of fire issued forth from the boxes, and the contents came flying through the air at them. Terra cast a super-dense wall of air, and the things the Battlesuit had launched at them slammed against them and exploded.

Hanna shot a few flashes of light at the machina, but the beams bounced off of its reflective armor. The hollow tube where its left arm should have been glowed green. After a few second passed, the machina shuddered, and a ball of green light blasted from the tube. The green ball hit the wall of air and was deflected to the side. It took out the top half of a section of the stone wall, leaving a gap twenty-five feet off the ground to the west.

The sun was more than half-way down, but Terra couldn't risk a look over her shoulder to see if Jormungandr had returned to the ocean. Flames shot from the back of the Battlesuit as it soared into the air. It slammed into the ground just a few feet from the gap.

"You've a big bounty on your head, Nexus," the pilot said. Terra could see him through the cockpit that appeared to be made of glass. "Worth more alive, but I guess I can't have everything in my life the way I want it." The arm-gun began to glow again. Terra tried to summon another wall of air to block the attack, but she didn't have enough energy left to make one strong enough.

"Throw me over it!" Darren shouted.

Terra used her remaining shreds of air magic to hurl Darren at the top of the Battlesuit. The pilot's eyes followed the captain's ascent while Caitlyn changed back into her human form in the blink of an eye. The changeling tore a chunk of stone from the wall and slammed deep into the barrel of the glowing gun.

Darren landed atop the glass-looking canopy and held his sword on the top of it point down. Cracks spread all throughout the transparent material as he pushed the limits of his sword's weight manipulation enchantment. The thick material shattered, and the sword impaled the pilot just as the gun backfired, blowing the left arm from the Battlesuit. Darren fell from his perch atop the machina, but Hanna caught him on a bed of air.

There was a crack of thunder behind them, and Michael stood with Kara at his side. He put Mjolnir at his waist and reached behind his back for his warhorn. The Justicar blew the Gjallerhorn and spectral men and women flickered into existence all around them. He blew the horn again, and the previous Justicars gained definition. A third time, and they were firmly in the realm of the living for as long as the Paragon of the Realm of Order needed to invoke the Final Judgment of the Justicar.

"Thor!" a one-eyed man wearing glittering armor and a holding a long spear said from atop an eight-legged horse. "It has been too long since one of the first einherijar was Justicar!"

Michael shook his head and smiled. "There will be time for a feast later, Odin." The Justicar pointed through the gap in the wall at Azreal. "We have an overreaching Demon Lord to kill."

Azreal stepped through the black portal, and it closed behind him. "Coward," Odin said.

Michael nodded. He touched the ash tree, and a portal to Yggdrasil opened. "He has two strongholds on our home, old friend. We must topple them both." The Justicar looked at everyone gathered. "To War! The Battle for Caine has been joined!"

Chapter Sixteen – Awake And Alive

If some part of me remains, then why don't I remember anything? Who am I? he thought.

<You are Alex Zane, the Guardian of Balance. And it is time to awaken.>

Alex's eyes shot open with a gasp. The stone bed he lay on was warm under his naked body. He tried to prop himself up on his arms, but he couldn't get his muscles to respond to his commands.

<No,> the voice chimed in his head. Other than being masculine in nature, the voice carried no real identifying characteristics. <Your mind will need some time to relearn your body. Don't push yourself too hard.>

Alex concentrated on working his jaw and tongue. "Whe—re am... I?" he choked out.

<Good, you can speak.> A green crystal as long as Alex's forearm floated above him. It spun in the air and flickered with green light as it communicated with him. <You are on Aria, the Realm of Life. Fate had been led astray, and you were brought back to life to return everything to equilibrium.>

"No idea—" Alex started coughing violently. He turned his head to the side and spit out a globule of red slime. "What you're talking about," he finished.

The green crystal zipped around his head and chimed as if it was disappointed. <Complete memory loss. That's unfortunate, but there is someone here that can fill you in on some of the things you are missing. I will bring her to you the day after tomorrow as soon as you are able to move about on your own. Do you have any questions?>

"Who are you?" Alex asked, his voice growing steadier.

<I am the Progenitor, the Paragon of Aria,> it sent into his mind. Alex realized the chiming was coming from the little floating stone. The Progenitor made the sound while it was communicating with him. <I am a Life Warden. We operate the Soul Foundry which collects and creates souls for every living thing in the Nine Realms. I apologize for your memory loss; it happens with half-demons.>

"Is that what I am? A half-demon?" Alex asked.

<Yes,> the Life Warden said. <All of a demon's memories are imprinted upon its soul, that way, when they are reincarnated, they have all the memories of their previous lives. That's why demons are inherently evil. They are constantly inundated with all of their previous misdeeds and the cycle continues.

<Humans, however> it continued, <only have a few memories which become imprinted upon their souls. It takes an extraordinary amount of force to make the soul's memories transfer over to the brain, but the two are connected, or else none of the memories of the flesh would become memories of the soul. Half-demons have a disconnect between the two. I have long pondered the cause, but I can only postulate that there must be a reason for the detachment.>

Alex's head began to throb. He closed his eyes and winced. "I don't understand," he said.

<Do not worry,> the Progenitor sent. <You need to rest. It is taxing for a body to reconnect to a soul, and there has not been one of your kind since before the Dawn. Sleep now, Alex Zane.>

Alex opened his eyes a crack and watched as the crystal floated through a small hole in the wall. His eyelids grew heavy, and he let them slide closed. The Guardian's breathing slowed, and in moments he was breathing the deep, even breaths of sleep.

A woman stood in the distance. She was looking down at her feet. *Who is that?* Alex thought. He was adrift in a black space with no definition. Alex looked down but didn't see his body. Propelling himself forward with a thought, he stopped in front of her and studied her.

Her eyes were clamped closed and tears ran from the corners of her eyes. The full-breasted woman wore a white shirt with long sleeves over a swollen stomach and denim pants. Her red hair was lit from behind by glowing blue wings coming from her back. *She looks so sad.*

Alex had a feeling of wholeness and looked down. He stood before the winged woman in clothing similar to hers. Alex tried to touch her left wing, but his hand passed through it. A tingling feeling from the gentle pulses of light that ran through her wings tickled his palm. He pulled his hand back and used it to lift her chin.

The woman opened her hazel eyes and smiled at him. Her cheeks dimpled, and the tears stopped. "Don't be sad, Beautiful," Alex said.

Alex opened his eyes and looked around the small room. The walls were some kind of rainbow-hued crystalline compound that he didn't have a word for. There were not doors or windows; the only break in the walls was the small hole the Progenitor had gone through the last time he had been awake. He tried to lift himself up, and succeeded this time.

Scooting back to lean against the crystalline wall behind him, Alex tried to move his legs. The most he could get from them was an uncontrolled twitching. His stomach rumbled, and Alex realized he was hungry. He didn't see any food and decided to wait for someone to come to him. If they took too long, he was certain they would attend to him if he called out, but the half-demon wanted some time alone.

The woman from his dreams lingered in his mind's eye. She had looked crushed when he first saw her, but as soon as she opened her eyes, it was as if she knew everything would be all right. *Maybe if I can find her, she can help me remember who I am.*

A white Life Warden the size of his fist zipped into the room. <Oh, you are awake and able to move. Can you stand?> it asked him in a woman's voice. Alex shook his head. <Do not concern yourself, Alex Zane. You will be moving around in no time. The Progenitor is very busy, and I will be caring for you for as long as you require it. I am,> the crystal made a complex sequence of chimes that produced a haunting melody.

Alex laughed. "I don't think I can pronounce that. May I call you Melody?"

The Life Warden chimed a high pitched tone a few times before Alex realized she was also laughing. <You may, Guardian. I am sure you are hungry. I will bring you something your kind is capable of consuming. Please wait.>

"I'm not going anywhere," Alex said. Melody chimed a laugh again and flew back through the hole in the wall. Alex thought about the red-haired woman until the Life Warden returned in a few minutes with a small crystalline plate floating before it. A table of the rainbow colored crystal extended from the wall next to him, and Melody put the plate on it.

The plate had small cubes of a white meat on it with broccoli on the side. There weren't any utensils, so Alex picked up one of the pieces of meat and popped it into his mouth. The meat bounced off of his upper lip and landed back on the plate.

<You can move, but your coordination will still be a long time in coming, Guardian. It helps to do things with your hands that require an amount of precision. After you have finished eating, would you like something to carve or any other kind of activity?>

The woman's face still lingered in his mind, but Alex was afraid he may forget it. "Do you have something I could draw with?" he asked before he carefully put a piece of meat in his mouth. He bit into it, and the taste of chicken filled his mouth.

<Certainly. Would you like graphite and paper?> Alex nodded as he chewed the meat. <I shall return.> He finished the meal while he waited for Melody to return. The chicken was warm, and while he held no particular love for the tree-looking vegetable, Alex ate all of the broccoli in an attempt to quell his rumbling stomach.

In about the same amount of time that it took the Life Warden to get his food and return, it floated back into the room with a bundle of papers of various sizes. Alex's plate floated up into the air and the stack of paper took its place. Long pieces of graphite were in a small wooden box in the middle of the bundle of papers. "Thank you," Alex said. He slid the lid off of the wooden box and picked up one of the dark sticks.

<You are welcome. Please try to work on this until you sleep again. It will help your soul attach to your body more quickly,> Melody said with her kind, matronly voice.

"How?" Alex asked. The white Life Warden paused just before it reached the hole in the wall.

<A living being is composed of three main elements:> Melody explained, <the body, the mind, and the soul. The body gives you your physical form. Strong or weak, short or tall, thin or large, your body is these things. The soul gives you your essence. Kind

or mean, loving or hurtful, good or evil, these are a few of the aspects of the soul. The mind works as a bridge between the two and regulates the support systems in your body to ensure your soul resides within your body for as long as possible.>

"But the Progenitor said the mind and soul of a half-demon like me was disconnected," Alex protested.

Melody chimed a laugh. The Life Warden grew silent, and a few moments passed before she spoke to him again. <I apologize for laughing. It was impolite to laugh at your statement as it stems from misunderstanding. The Paragon meant that there was a disconnect only between memories of the flesh and memories of the soul. The mind and soul interact in an innumerable amount of small ways, but the primary function is for the soul to generate the desires that drive you, and your mind to interpret them and judge how best to carry them out using the body as a tool to carry out the will of the soul.>

Alex nodded. "I think I'm beginning to understand it now. So essentially, the soul is the motor that drives the body through the brain."

<It is a vast oversimplification, but that is the gist of it.>

A question bubbled up in his mind. "What if one of the three is damaged in some way?" Alex asked.

Melody spun slowly in the air, and the plate revolved around her. <What do you think would happen?>

Alex scratched the back of his head. Some of his brown hair had fallen in front of his nose, and he tucked it behind his ear. "If there was some damage to the body, then obviously the mind would die and the soul leave. If there was damage to the brain, then the body wouldn't be able to carry out the will of the soul, and if the soul was damaged—"

<Souls cannot be damaged,> Melody interrupted. <They can be destroyed or removed but not damaged. Any damage to a soul would destroy it. They are incredibly complex things that can be very resilient, but if any part of it fails, the entire soul collapses. Now, begin drawing. I have other tasks that need be taken care of.>

Alex nodded and bent over the pages of paper. He tried to make a straight line on the paper, but his hand jerked back and forth. The more he tried to focus on holding his hand steady, the more it trembled. Growing frustrated with his inability to even make a simple line, Alex gripped the piece of graphite in his hands to snap it.

Stop it, man, he thought. *Breaking this won't make you recover any faster. Relax. Stop trying so hard, and just do it.* Alex placed his left hand back on the paper and lowered the graphite to the page. He closed his eyes and took a slow breath. As Alex let it out, he traced his hand across the page at a measured pace. He opened his eyes and saw a straight line bisecting the page.

Alex grinned at his accomplishment then laughed at himself. "It's a long way from a line to a portrait," he told himself. The Guardian cracked his knuckles and set himself to the task.

The demoness Odessa stood before the white Life Warden. <He calls me Melody,> it chimed to her. <It is odd having a name of words,> Melody whispered into her mind.

Odessa finished brushing her blood-red hair and slipped the white dress over her head. She looked in the full-length mirror the Life Wardens had materialized for her. *I wonder whose eyes and hair he has.* She looked at her solid, bright-green eyes that marked her as a demon. "Is he well?" Odessa asked.

<Alex is. He has no memories of his previous life, and the Progenitor insists that we keep his being a half-demon secret from any beings not personally involved in his recovery, though he will not explain his reasons.>

Because it would put Alex in danger from the ones that should be helping him, Odessa thought. She had been on the run for a long time before she was able to travel to Aria, and being a benevolent demon had earned her little more than attempts on her life. *Until I met Tom, then it earned me a child. If only Azreal had not gone mad with power... I wonder if I could have convinced him to see a better way.*

"Can he move around?" Odessa asked.

<He will be able to move about in a few hours. He had fallen asleep when I brought him clothing earlier.> A feeling of confusion Odessa knew came from the Life Warden pervaded her mind. <He is drawing a woman with wings. It's the only thing he has drawn, and he repeats the same drawing on every piece of paper I've given him.>

The Demon Lady frowned. "I wonder who it is," the demoness said.

The floating crystal spun in the air with an idle grace. <He says he doesn't know who she is, only that he doesn't want to forget her. I asked him where he had seen her, and he said in his dreams.>

"Will you take me to him?" Odessa asked. "I think it's about time I meet my son."

Alex looked at the finished drawing in his hands. *Almost perfect,* he thought. *Her eyelashes were a little longer...* He pushed the portrait from the edge of his table and reached for another blank piece of paper, but his clean left hand found none. Alex glanced over at where the pile of papers Melody had brought him had been but saw only an empty shelf of the multi-colored crystal.

Did I use them all? He leaned over the edge of the bed and looked at the floor. It was covered in half-done drawings of varying levels of skill. Alex found the one he had just completed and hopped off of the warm bed. It wasn't until he scooped the drawing of the winged woman off of the floor with his left hand that Alex realized he was standing.

Spying a basin full of liquid with a piece of cloth hanging off the side, Alex placed the drawing back on his desk and began washing the graphite from his right hand. A chiming came from behind him, and Alex assumed Melody was back to get on to him about all of the pieces of paper littering the floor again. He picked up the towel and said, "I'll clean them up in just a bit. I just finished the one on the table and ran out of paper."

Alex finished cleaning his hand off and set the towel down. "Do you like it?" he asked as he turned. A moment of shock roared through Alex when he saw a woman with long, dark-red hair holding the finished drawing. For a split-second he thought she was the woman from his dreams, but he realized her hair was a bit longer and a darker shade of red. *She doesn't have glowing wings either.*

"It is a very nice drawing," the woman said. "She looks happy. And very beautiful." The woman set the drawing back onto the table with a deliberate grace. She placed her left hand over her right and pressed them against her stomach as she turned to look at him. Alex saw the white dress bunch up under her hands as she took a fistful of the cloth. She slowly raised her head and looked at him.

A sad smile grew on her face below her emerald green eyes that had neither a pupil or white. "Oh, you are handsome," she said. "You look so much like your father. Good, you have human eyes, too."

Alex scratched the back of his head. "Umm… Thank you. My name is Alex Zane," he said as he took a step forward and proffered his hand.

She laughed a single soft laugh. "I saw this going differently in my head," she said. "I know who you are Alex." The woman unclasped her hands and wrapped him in a warm hug. Unsure of what to do with his hands and baffled at the sudden embrace, Alex patted the woman on the back; she felt much warmer than he did.

Releasing him, she put her hands on his upper arms and looked into Alex's eyes. He could see by the tiny movements in her emerald orbs which eye she was looking at. "I'm your mother, Odessa."

"Oh," Alex said. *What should I to say to her?* "It's nice to see you again."

His mother let out a short sigh. "This is the first time you've seen me since the day you were born."

"Why's that?" Alex asked.

Odessa let go of his arms. "It's a very long story. Would you like to walk around Aria while I tell it?"

Alex nodded. "I would, but I don't have any shoes." His mother lifted the hem of her dress to reveal bare feet. He chuckled. "I guess I don't need any." She turned and walked toward the door, but Alex hesitated before following her.

"What is it?" Odessa asked when she reached the door and looked back.

Alex grabbed the drawing of the winged woman from his table and walked over to his mother. He held the picture out to her. "Do you know who this is? She has red-hair like yours but a few shades lighter, and her wings glow and your hand can go through them."

Odessa shook her head. "I'm sorry, Alex, but I've never seen her before. But it sounds like you are describing a half-angel."

As soon as the words left his mother's lips, Alex knew she was right. *She's a half-angel just like I'm a half-demon.* Alex folded the drawing a few times until it was small enough to fit in the denim jean's back pocket. He had asked Melody for clothes like the ones in his drawing, and she had brought them to him while he slept. A long-sleeved white shirt and blue-jeans were neatly folded and waiting for him to don when he had awoken.

Alex followed his mother through the doorway, and he looked around. A beam of red light emanated from a wide pit a few yards from him. Bits of red crystal floated in the light.

"This is the heart of the Soul Foundry," Odessa said. "Every soul whose body dies returns here to be implanted into a new body." She looked at Alex. "Or their old one, in certain, extraordinary circumstances."

"What are those little pieces of red in the light?" Alex asked.

"Those are pieces of Mars, one of the First Ones," Odessa said as she turned to the left and started walking. "They created the Nine Realms almost ten billion years ago so all of the sentient races could have a place to live in relative safety. They also created a few of the races to help protect the realm, the Valkyrie, the Life Wardens, and the Changelings are the ones I remember being created."

Alex raised an eyebrow at her. She didn't look much older than he did. "You look awfully young for a ten-billion-year-old. Have you really been alive for that long?"

Odessa laughed. "No. Demons remember everything that happened in any of their past lives. Most of it blurs together or fades away, but there are some things you never forget, no matter how much time passes."

"Like what?" Alex asked.

"The first person I killed is one I'll never forget," she said. "I didn't want to do it, but it was him or me. It was an angel named Tyrius. He had me under the point of his sword, but I was able to knock him off balance and run a spear up under the seam in his armor between his chest plate and his groin. It shredded his bowels, heart, and lungs. He died instantly."

They exited the Soul Foundry through an opening that appeared in the wall similar to the one in his room. It slid into the wall above them and disappeared. The outside was a sphere that was no more than two miles from one side to the other. *We're inside a ball,* Alex thought.

"This is the entirety of the Realm of Life," Odessa said. "There are only eight Life Wardens that reside here."

Alex looked up and saw the Soul Foundry stretched all of the way to the top of Aria. The foundry was wider at the bases than it was in the middle, giving it the impression of two pyramids that touched at the tips. Odessa turned left again and led him toward an area that glowed with orange light.

"I would have to say the first person I ever truly loved is another thing I'll never forget," Odessa continued, "but it happened so recently that only time will tell. Your father, Thomas Zane, was an amazing man. He was your height and had muscles like yours." She looked him over and smiled. "His hair was the same color as yours too, but he kept his longer and back in a pony tail. He was Daein, from the Realm of Magic."

"How did the two of you meet?" Alex asked. He realized the area they were walking toward was a lake of roiling fire.

"I started running from Azreal as soon as I realized he was planning to kill the Overlord of Hell," his mother said. "I knew that once that happened, my twin would begin killing off the other Demon Lords and Ladies and raise others to their positions if he kept any. As far back as I could remember, Azreal was always a cruel and ambitious soul, but we were twin souls, always born together.

"A few thousand years ago, I began to realize that the war between the angels and demons was pointless. We rail against one another to the benefit of none. I grew tired of an eternity of looking over my shoulder, waiting for a dagger in my back, so I left Hell. A few hundred years ago, I left and ran as hard as I could, hiding in the shadows, darting from one to the next."

They drew up to the lake of fire, and Odessa held her hands out to it. She seemed to welcome the heat while Alex edged away from it. His mother looked at him. "Hell is a complex maze of floating walkways above a dead star. The Black Sun may be dead and not give off any light, but it is still extremely hot. I'm never warm anymore," she whispered.

Although he had known his mother for less than an hour, Alex felt drawn to comfort her. He put his arms around Odessa, and she hugged him back. The son released his mother, and she gave him another sad smile.

"Thank you," Odessa said. "Where was I?"

"You were darting from one shadow to another," Alex said.

The demoness nodded. "Almost thirty years ago now, I found myself inside the Adorac Volcano on Dae. I snuck in and squatted in the high caves, sleeping in a different one every night. My time inside the volcano was not a bad one, but it was very lonesome. One day, I felt drawn to the Adorac Falls, a lava flow that looks like a waterfall crashing into a lake of molten stone.

"There was a bridge that spanned the falls, and I recognized it as part of an old First One ship. When I stepped on the bridge, I was taken to a pocket dimension that existed in that exact space. A Life Warden that called itself The One Who Waits said I was supposed to change my fate. It told me I would meet a human named Thomas Zane, and I would bring his child into the world."

"So my birth was arranged by a Life Warden? Why?" Alex asked.

Odessa shrugged. "It didn't say, but everyone's birth is arranged by something. Are you any less alive because your birth was planned instead of just happening by a set of random circumstances?"

That makes sense. "No," Alex said.

"I met your father as soon as I left that little bubble in space. He was just standing at the end of the bridge as if he was waiting on me." Odessa laughed. "He held out his hand for me to shake it, and he looked so bashful. Tom's face was almost as red as my hair. I

225

guess he was thinking about what we were going to be doing later.

"He said, 'Hi, I'm Thomas Zane.' and he smiled at me." Alex's mother lips curled in the first truly happy smile he had seen on her face. "He was so handsome. I shook his hand and told him that I was Odessa, and Tom said that he knew. I have never seen a man so devoted to someone than the way he looked at me..."

"Where is he now?" Alex asked. *Maybe he'll know more about my past.*

Odessa shook her head. "I don't know, but I'm getting there. He said he had a gift for me that had belonged to his grandmother as a token of his hope that our love would grow." The demoness lifted a thin golden chain around her neck and held out an alabaster amulet. It had nine interconnected circles engraved upon it. "This is the Traveler's Pendant, and with it, I can open a gateway to any point on any Realm, regardless of whether it has a grounding field to prevent teleportation. There's only one restriction."

Alex looked at her curiously as he reached out to look at the amulet more closely. She reached behind her neck, undid the clasp, and placed it in his hand. The pale amulet was cool on his palm, but he could feel a strange power sealed deep within it. "You can only go to places you've been before," Alex guessed.

"That's correct," his mother said. "How did you know?"

Shrugging, Alex said, "I'm not sure. It just felt right." He handed the necklace back to her, and Odessa replaced it around her neck and dropped the Traveler's Pendant down the collar of her dress.

Odessa locked eyes with her son. "Alex, there is something you need to know about being a half-demon."

"What?" he asked.

"If people find out who you are… what you are, they will hunt you down. Everything and everyone from Hell is feared by all the Nine Realms. Don't trust anyone with the secret of what you really are. There is nothing that can distinguish you from a normal human as long as you keep firm control of your emotions."

Alex's brows drew down. "I don't understand."

Odessa put her hands on his shoulders. "If anyone finds out that you are a half-demon, that you have any links to Hell at all, then they will try to hunt you down and kill you, Alex. Every person that knows the truth of your heritage holds your life in their hands. The only time it will be obvious that you have demonic blood will be when you are experiencing an emotional extreme. Get too angry or scared and your demonic powers will awaken to help you protect yourself or those you care about.

"A half-demon's powers work differently than a full demon's, so I only know what I remember. You will become powerful, Alex. Unstoppable by almost anything that doesn't possess strength of titanic proportions." Odessa paused and squeezed his shoulders.

"But you are also the Guardian, and as soon as you get it back, you will be able to use the Guardian's Blade. I have known a number of Guardians, and they were only human. You must exercise the utmost caution if your demonic powers trigger while you are using the blade. Alex, there aren't words to describe how much damage you could do if that happened. You could unravel the universe…"

The Guardian gulped. "If I'm so angry that I trigger these powers, then how am I supposed to remain calm enough to hold them in check?"

"I don't know. You just have to try."

Well, that's the opposite of what I wanted to hear. "Why are you telling me all of this?"

Odessa's hands fell from his shoulders, and she looked at the multi-hued ground. "Because the time has come for you to continue your fight against the imbalance my brother has caused. The Keeper of Fate is an angel named Eternius. He is on Bara, the Realm of Good. He is the reason the Progenitor brought you back to life. Eternius will know how to find the Guardian's Blade. Your death wasn't supposed to happen; it ran counter to what he had written in the Libram of Fate, so it had to be reversed. That is the only time any of us get a second chance at life."

She pulled out the Traveler's Pendant and held it loosely in her fist. There was a thump Alex felt in his chest, and a yellow hole in the air appeared next to them. "Another thing I'll always remember is the day you were born," Odessa said with tears in her eyes. She let out a bitter laugh. "It seems that I traded in one bad fate for another. I saw you take your first breaths then gave you away…"

Alex wrapped his mother in a warm embrace. "Thank you for everything." *Give her this.* "I love you, Mother," Alex whispered in her ear.

"I love you too, Son," Odessa whispered back. His mother kissed his cheek, and Alex dropped his arms. "Go," she said. "The Nine Realms need you."

Alex nodded and stepped through the yellow portal.

Chapter Seventeen – Lost and Found

Alex winced in the harsh light of the brilliant white star above him. The glassy yellow ground was warm under his bare feet, and the air was comfortable. He saw a grouping of high towers surrounded by a wall that glittered like gold. *I guess that's where I'll find Eternius,* he thought as he started the long walk toward the city.

His bare feet slapped against the ground as he walked. Alex started crossing a bridge and glanced over the side. He immediately took a step away from the short wall that was all that prevented him from tumbling over the side down an endless fall. "That doesn't seem too safe," he muttered.

After nearly two hours of walking, Alex finally reached a tremendous gate that looked as if it was made out of pearl. *This place is huge. It looked a lot closer when I thought the wall was half as high.* He knocked on the gate, and a woman's voice called out to him.

"Who begs entry into the City of Spires?" a woman shouted from atop the wall.

"Alex Zane," he called back. "The Guardian, and I'm more asking than begging. I'm supposed to meet with Eternius." He almost mentioned that Odessa sent him there, but decided against it. *I don't think a demon's name is going to carry much weight with angels.*

The gate swung inward, and a woman with silver hair and ice-blue eyes stared at him. She wore shimmering golden armor and had wings of the purest white. Alex walked to her.

"Guardian," she said cordially as she offered her hand. "It is nice to meet you. You may call me Ureon. I sit on the Seat of Faith when the Angelic Council

229

meets. It will be my pleasure to take you to meet the Keeper."

"Thank you. It's nice to meet you as well." *She has an honest face,* Alex thought, *if a bit childish.*

Ureon stepped behind Alex and wrapped her arms around him. "It will be much faster if we fly. Do you mind?" she asked.

"Whatever's easiest for you," Alex said. As soon as he finished speaking, Ureon beat her wings and took off with two powerful strokes. She told him about the Tower of Faith, the geography of Bara, and the Angelic Council while she flew him to the top of the tower in the center of the City of Spires.

"There's an Angelic Council?" Alex asked.

"That's right," Ureon said.

The beat of her wings made Alex's hair ripple in the wind as they approached the largest tower. "What is the council's purpose?"

"The same as councils in the other Realms," she explained. "But we are also charged with the duty of ensuring the lights of Faith, Intellect, Love, Honor, Hope, Justice, and Truth do not go dim in the Nine Realms." She laughed softly. "Some people really do have guardian angels."

"And this is the Amphitheater of the High Seats," Ureon said as they settled down atop the Great Spire. "As you can see, the seven bands along the spire continue up to the very top, and each Seat sits in the chair that is of the same gemstone as their spire and gate."

Alex looked about the open-roofed amphitheater. There was a pedestal in the center of the room, and a thick book was open on it. "What's that?" he asked, pointing at the prodigious tome.

Ureon walked to the book and beckoned him over. "This is the Libram of Fate, Guardian. Within it is penned the fate of the Nine Realms for the last ninety nine thousand and nine hundred years, almost to the day."

"Everything that's happened in the last hundred thousand years is written in that book?" Alex asked. He looked at the Libram of Fate and judged it to be thick, but it couldn't possibly hold all of that information.

"Oh, no!" Ureon said. "Only the most major things. For the most part, every person's fate is for them to decide. But a number have their fates chosen for them. Anyone whose existence would affect that balance of the Nine Realms is written in this book."

Alex looked at the page the Libram was open to. It was the final page in the book, but the tome was written in a language he couldn't read. "Am I in it?" he asked.

"How modest!" Ureon said as she placed her hand over her heart.

Chagrinned at his unintentionally self-centered comment, Alex said, "Sorry, I didn't mean to seem so..." He trailed off when Ureon started speaking.

"The only place that mentions you says this, 'And a wrathful Guardian rise in her place to lead the Nine to balance.'" She winked at him. "It turns out that you're kind of important after all. I shall get Eternius. Please wait here."

Ureon turned into a glowing, transparent apparition and sank through the floor. *Hmm... So this is why I was brought back to life. I wonder who 'she' is from the passage Ureon read.*

"Guardian," a powerful voice said from behind him. The tone carried the unmistakable air of authority. Alex turned around and saw an older looking, hazel-eyed angel with blond hair and stubble.

"You must be Eternius," Alex said. The angel stood about ten feet away from him and made no moves to approach. Alex had an immediate impression of dislike for the angel. *Well, I'm not going to go over there to shake your hand,* the Guardian thought.

The angel nodded. "I am the Keeper of Fate," Eternius said. "I had you brought back to life because you must finish the job you started before you died."

Alex crossed his arms. "And what was that?"

"You were supposed to be returning the Nine Realms to equilibrium. That is the Guardian's task. I thought the Progenitor was going to tell you this before you came here."

My mother told me that, Alex thought. *I don't think he knows that she was on Aria.* "That's right," the Guardian lied. "Sorry, I've been out of sorts since I was brought back. I guess memory loss has a way of doing that to you."

Eternius narrowed his eyes and frowned at Alex. The angel looked over his shoulder and said, "Ureon, I have put up with enough of your eavesdropping already. Leave us."

A glowing apparition rose from the floor behind Eternius and materialized into Ureon. She gave Alex a mischievous wink and took flight back toward her gate. Alex watched her go, and when he turned back to face Eternius, the angel had crossed his arms too.

"Do you think this is a game, human?" Eternius snarled.

Well, that's no way to talk to someone. I was willing to work with you up until you started talking down to me. Which was before the conversation started... "Do *I* think this is a game?" Alex asked. "You're the one with the fancy book and the lives you have decided to move around like pieces on a board."

The Keeper of Fate snapped his wings out wide and drew himself up. *Trying to intimidate me?* Alex leaned against the plinth that the Libram of Fate was resting on and put on his best bored face. "I was given authority to carry out my duties as Keeper of Fate by the First Ones themselves," Eternius said. "And that includes bringing back those that fail to uphold what I've written."

Alex shrugged. "What do you need from me so I can get on with it?" He watched with amusement as Eternius flexed his fists. *Am I getting under your skin?*

"I find your attitude distasteful, human. I need you to go to Dae and retrieve the Guardian's Blade."

Yeah, well I find your attitude distasteful too. "Sounds like a ball of fun. How am I supposed to find it?" Alex asked, still leaning against the plinth. He realized Eternius had called him a human twice. *You don't know I'm a half-demon, either.*

"Find a woman whose name was Terra Duval. Wherever she is, your blade will be with her. I will summon Ureon, and she will take you back to the gateway arch." Eternius turned and took a step away from him.

Alex stopped leaning on the plinth and heard the drawing crinkle in his back pocket. "Wait," he said. Eternius stopped and turned back around. Alex pulled the paper from his pocket and unfolded it. "Do you know who this is?" he asked, holding it out to Eternius.

The angel drew closer and looked at the graphite sketch. He took it from Alex's hand and frowned, first at the drawing then at Alex. "Where did you get this?" Eternius asked.

"I drew it. You *do* know who it is," Alex said.

"This is the Nexus," Eternius said. The angel handed the paper back to Alex. "The Nexus is the Paragon of the Realm of Magic. I'm sure if you ask around that you will be able to find wherever she is if you wish to meet her." Alex nodded and placed the paper back in his back pocket. Eternius stepped away from Alex and faded through the floor the same way Ureon had.

Alex turned back to the Libram of Fate while he waited on Ureon. He tried to turn the page, but no matter how hard he tried, he couldn't make the page to move in the slightest. Alex put his hand under the back cover and tried to close the book, but he might as well have been trying to lift a mountain.

He heard the beat of wings behind him and a woman's laughter. "I've not seen Eternius that angry in a very long time." Ureon saw what he was trying to do and said, "It takes more than strength to move that old book." She walked around to the other side of the pedestal and flipped the Libram of Fate closed with just one finger. "It takes a special touch," she said with another wink.

"How did you do that?" Alex asked with a smirk. *I like her. Why couldn't she have been the one telling me what to do?*

Ureon stepped behind him and lifted Alex from the ground. "It takes the power of an immortal to affect the Libram, Guardian. Something a mere human isn't capable of." They flew up into the air and began a long glide toward a ring far past the Gate of Faith that Alex hadn't noticed when he arrived.

"Any immortal? Even a demon?" Alex asked.

"That's right." Ureon put her mouth next to his ear and whispered, "Or even a half-demon."

Alex tensed in her arms.

"Don't worry, Guardian, I alone among the angels know your secret, and you are in no danger from me." Her voice grew so quiet Alex almost couldn't hear it. "There are forces at work here that you wouldn't understand. The Nine Realms grow weak, and they need a strong Guardian to protect them."

Alex nodded. "I'll do my best," he said.

"We know you'll try," Ureon said.

They flew the rest of the way to the arch that was made of out the same yellowed glass as the ground in silence. The Seat of Faith set him down gently and touched the side of the arch. "This is a gateway arch," she explained. "It is the only way on to or off of Bara. Hmm... How strange, it doesn't appear to have been used recently."

"What can I say? I'm a bit of a rebel..." Alex scratched the back of his head and added, "I guess."

"You'll have to let me in on that secret some day," Ureon said. She closed her eyes for a moment, and a red hued portal to another world opened in the middle of the arch. Ureon placed a small stone in a slot on the gateway. Something shimmered in the portal, but Alex was unsure of what she had done. "On the other side is Dae, the Realm of Magic. We will need to wait for a few minutes for them to replace their keystone seal so you can travel through. They recently freed themselves from Azreal's armies and are not keen to leave an open path to their home."

"That's understandable," Alex said. "You have to defend your home and attack from a position of strength." The statement seemed so obvious to him that he had to think for a few minutes before he realized just what he had said.

"What is it?" Ureon asked about the confused look on Alex's face.

Alex sighed. "It's just... How do I know things when I lost all of my memory? How to speak, draw, and apparently wage war."

The angel smiled at him to allay his confusion. "Anyone can know a fact. The reason you were brought back to life a few days ago instead of a few months ago is because the Progenitor was implanting knowledge into your mind. That takes time.

"Knowledge is universal, Alex, but memories... they are for the individual. I suppose you could have had someone else's memories implanted into your mind, but that could have driven you mad if they didn't line up with the virtues of your soul."

The gateway's red glow disappeared, and it turned a golden color. "It is time now, Guardian," the angel said. "Remember, find The Guardian's Blade."

"I will, Ureon. Thank you." Alex stepped through the gateway onto the Realm of Magic.

The bustle of a loud city was the first thing Alex noticed about Dae. The Realm of Good had been quiet, almost to the point of being uncomfortably so, but the Realm of Magic seemed deafening by comparison. Not far to his left, a hawker tried to sell mementoes from someone he just kept referring to as 'her' and 'our beloved', and ahead of him a group of children played in front of two statues that glittered in the sun.

A woman with unruly blue-green hair and brown leather armor stepped up to him and blinked as if she had something in her eye. "Welcome to Dae," she said as she studied his face. "I am Lieutenant Ell Nyberg of the Victory City Guard. What brings you to the Realm of Magic?"

"I'm looking for something a friend of mine is keeping for me," Alex lied. He wasn't sure why he didn't want to ask the guardswoman for help, but he felt like he needed to remain as forgettable as possible.

"You are familiar with the area?" the lieutenant asked. Alex nodded. "Very well. Carry on."

Alex walked away from her and stepped down the marble platform onto the soft grass. It was early afternoon. *Feels like summer*, Alex thought as he pushed up his long sleeves. The grass tickled his toes as he walked toward the two statues. He drew closer to them and froze.

The left statue was one of Alex himself standing resolutely and pointing a sword at the milky white arch he had walked through. The right statue was the woman he had dreamed about, the Nexus. She wore armor and faced the same way as the other statue. Her hands were open, and she held them low to either side, but she stood like she was facing something down.

Wow, Alex thought. *No wonder the lieutenant was looking at me so hard. She sees my statue every day.* Alex turned to the children; they had stopped playing and all stared at him.

"Yeah, it kind of looks like me, huh?" Alex said with a smile. The four boys all nodded and didn't speak. "Do you know where I can find the Nexus?"

Three of the boys looked at each other in confusion. "I can take you to where she lived," one of them said. Alex realized the one that had spoken was a little girl with short hair and dirt all over her face.

"I would appreciate it," Alex said.

"Follow me," she said as she led the way.

"What's your name?" he asked.

The little girl glanced over her shoulder at him to make sure he was following. She saw he was and stepped out onto the cobblestone road. "My full name is Alexandra Fitzpatrick, but everyone calls me Alex."

Alex snorted a laugh, and the girl looked at him with a scowl. "I'm not making fun of your name," he said. "My name is Alex too." As soon as the words left his mouth, he knew he had made a mistake.

Alexandra froze in the middle of the street and started at him with wide eyes. "You really are him, aren't you? The G—"

"I'm no one," Alex interrupted. "Don't tell anyone, please. My being here is a secret."

She nodded enthusiastically. "I won't tell anyone. I promise!" The little girl grabbed him by the hand and pulled him along at a trot. "We're almost there."

A couple minutes of light jogging and Alex found himself standing a few feet from the front door of a small house on a huge tract of land. "They were going to build a palace on the empty spot, but they decided not to now," Alexandra said as she let go of his hand.

"Why'd they do that?" Alex asked.

Alexandra looked at him with bunched together brows. "She died a few days ago," the little girl explained. Alex felt his hopes of meeting the woman he had dreamed about crash down around him. "Her funeral is tomorrow. I thought that was why you were here."

"Thank you for bringing me here, Miss Fitzpatrick," Alex said, his tone as numb as he felt. "I'll knock on the door and see if anyone is here that I can speak with."

"Okay, Guar- Mister," she called as she ran off.

He wasn't sure how long he stood on the side of the road staring at the modest home. Alex felt as if he had been crushed by a heavy weight, and he wasn't sure why. *I don't even know if I knew this woman,* he thought as he mounted the steps to knock on the door. *She could have been someone I just randomly dreamed of that looked like the Nexus.*

Alex knocked on the door a single time. It wasn't latched and swung open. "Hello?" he called. He stepped inside. "Is anyone here?" Alex closed the door behind him. *What are you doing? You can't just go walking into dead people's houses!*

Alex ignored the voice in the back of his head and looked around the foyer. The walls were painted a light brown color, and the floor was made of a darker hardwood that was cool on his feet. *Seems like a nice place,* he thought. Alex walked through the room and found himself in a sitting room with a small couch and two seats around a low table.

The couch and chairs were a light-brown, slightly darker than the walls, and the table looked to be made of the same wood as the floor. A red rug covered most of the floor in the sitting room. Alex glanced in a couple of the other rooms and saw a dining room and a kitchen. It didn't look like either had been used in some time.

A short hallway had three doors on it. The first door revealed a bedroom with a large bed, and Alex closed it right after he opened it. *It's one thing to be in a dead person's house. Another to be in a dead person's bedroom.* The second door was across the hall from the other two and opened into a washroom.

Alex stood before the last of the three doors, and an overwhelming sense of foreboding gripped him. He turned the knob and pushed the door open. The walls were a soft pink color, and unlike the other rooms, this one had a thick carpet on the floor. A couch large enough for two people to sit side-by-side was against the far wall beneath a window, and a small white wicker dresser was adjacent to it.

Stepping into the room, Alex saw that there was a crib against the wall with the door on it. The sheets were the same pink color as the walls, and a mobile hung above it. There were five plush emblems that hung down from the mobile: a puff of cloud, a little ball of fire, a drop of water, a brown rock, and in the center, nine circles that were all connected to each other. Everything in the nursery looked like it had never been used.

He reached down into the crib and picked up a pair of small pink boots that he had the feeling had been recently knitted. Everything seemed to float in his vision, and Alex reached up to touch his face. *Why am I crying?* He wiped his face and put the baby shoes back in the crib. *I should get out of here.*

Alex closed the nursery door behind him and walked to the front of the house. He was standing in the middle of the sitting room when the door opened, and a black-haired woman walked in with a man in leather armor behind her. "-for helping me with this, Darren," the woman said, looking over her shoulder at the armored man.

Darren's hand shot to his sword when he saw Alex standing in the house. Alex's put his hands in the air to show he was unarmed and said, "I'm sorry. I know I probably shouldn't be in here."

The woman's head darted about to look forward, and her golden eyes widened in disbelief. "Alex?"

Caitlyn climbed up the steps to Terra's house. "I was her captain," Darren said. "I should have protected her better."

The changeling got to the top of the stairs and turned. "There was nothing you could have done," she said. Caitlyn kissed Darren softly on the lips. "You've been here for me when I needed you most." She faced to the door and twisted the knob. "Thank you for helping me with this, Darren," Caitlyn said, looking over her shoulder at him.

She knew something was wrong the instant the door swung open. Darren's face shifted from one of seriousness to alarm. "I'm sorry. I know I probably shouldn't be in here," a voice Caitlyn could never forget said. She snapped her head back forward, and her heart stopped. Alex stood in the middle of the sitting room with his hands above his head.

"Alex?" Caitlyn said, unwilling to trust her eyes.

"You know me?" Alex asked at the same time Darren said, "Wait, *the* Alex?"

"Yeah," Alex answered Darren while Caitlyn said, "Of course I know you." and Darren said, "But you're dead."

Caitlyn shook her head. "Both of you, shut up!" She walked to Alex and hugged him as tight as she could. "How is this possible?"

"The Life Wardens brought me back," Alex said with her arms still around him. "How do you know me?"

What? Caitlyn let go of him and took a step back. "It's me, Caitlyn. I brought you through the portal to Dae to rescue Terra from the halfmen that had kidnapped her. We fought battles together." She glanced at Darren that had come to stand beside her. "You were like a brother to me."

Alex shook his head. "I don't remember any of that. When they brought me back to life, the Progenitor, Aria's Paragon," he explained in response to the increased confusion on her face, "wasn't able to restore my memories. The only thing that I think I remember is this." Alex reached into his back pocket and pulled out a folded piece of paper..

"What is this?" Caitlyn asked as she took it from his outstretched hand.

She unfolded it as Alex said, "I dreamed of her the first time I slept after they brought me back."

Caitlyn turned the paper over and let out a tearful gasp. Alex had captured the beauty and joy of the woman he had loved in perfect detail. Terra looked straight ahead with a smile on her face and hands over her swollen stomach. Her wings were down by her sides, and she wore clothes identical to the ones Alex had on now. "You drew Terra perfectly," Caitlyn said.

Alex blinked and cocked his head to the side. "Eternius said that was the Nexus I drew."

"Sit down for a minute, man," Darren said. *Good idea. He won't like this.* Alex sat down on the middle of the couch, and the other two sat in the two chairs and faced him over the table.

"Terra was the Nexus," Caitlyn said. Alex's eyes narrowed. *Eternius must have said something that made him think otherwise.* "Alex, Terra…" *Come on, Caitlyn, you can do this.* "Terra was your wife."

Alex's eyes shot wide open. "What?" he whispered.

"You two were married a couple of months before you died. She linked you to her as her Shield. I was there… When you died, she was crushed and didn't know what to do, except keep on fighting."

"How did she die?" Alex asked.

Darren looked down at his hands. "It's my fault, Guardian."

"No! There was nothing you could have done," Caitlyn protested.

The captain put his right hand on Caitlyn's knee. "Yes, Caitlyn, it was my fault. I was her guard. It just happened so fast; I felt like there was nothing I could have done, but every time I think about it, I realize I could have been closer to her. I could have taken the shot that killed her if I had been but a few feet to the left."

The three sat in silence for a few moments before Alex asked, "Did we love each other?"

"You loved Terra with every inch of your being," Caitlyn said. "It made me wish I would find something as beautiful one day." Darren squeezed her leg, and she looked at him. Caitlyn thought she could care for Darren as much as the captain cared for her, but it was too early for her to know for sure. She looked back at Alex and saw that his eyes were closed with tears running from the corners.

"So the baby?" he choked out.

"She didn't survive," Caitlyn said. "You died before the two of you could pick a name, so Terra decided to call her Jessica Lenora Zane."

Alex opened his red-rimmed eyes and looked at her. A tumultuous blend of confusion, sadness, and anger blazed in his green eyes. "And Eternius knew all of this?"

"Of course he did. The *angel* won't even come to his own daughter's funeral," Darren said before Caitlyn could think of a more diplomatic answer.

Alex clenched his fists so hard his knuckles cracked. Caitlyn watched as the green of his iris enveloped the entirety of his eye. *Oh no,* she thought.

"He knew this entire time, and let me come here thinking I would find her alive and well," Alex growled. He lifted his fists and slammed them into the solid coffee table. It cracked and fell in two under the weight of his blow. Unseen force pulsed out from Alex, and couch's leather covering began to shred. "A wife and child I didn't know I had, and this is how he wanted me to find out? He wanted a wrathful Guardian and now he has one."

Caitlyn had no idea what Alex was talking about. The half-demon rose to his feet and walked to the door. The door exploded outward in a shower of splinters. "What in Hell is going on? He's a demon!" Darren shouted as he ran to the front of the house. The captain had drawn his sword, and Caitlyn chased after him.

The changeling darted in front of him and put her hands on Darren's chest. "Stop," she said. "He killed Azreal when he was like this. He'll kill you. Find Brahm and bring him to the gateway arch." Caitlyn turned and started running down the stairs.

"Why there?" Darren called. "Where are you going?"

"Because that's where he's going, and to stop the man I loved from doing something he'll regret," Caitlyn shouted as she ran. She looked around and was relieved to see that Alex wasn't leaving a trail of blood in his wake. The changeling shifted into her panther form and flew toward the gateway arch. *He hasn't killed anyone yet.*

Caitlyn blew past people and carts. As soon as she reached the square she cut across it and reached the gateway arch just ahead of Alex. Ell was the guard on duty. She was holding both of her knives in her fists and staring at Alex as he stalked toward the gateway arch. Ell could have seen Alex's solid green eyes, the half-elf's vision was sharper than a human's, but there was an unmistakable demeanor to the way he was walking. It was the resolute stride of a man on a mission that would result in blood.

Changing back into her human form so Alex would recognize her, Caitlyn stood beside the lieutenant. "Ell," she panted, "that is the Guardian, and he just found out his wife and child were killed. Eternius must have said something to manipulate or trick Alex, and he is going to try to kill the Keeper of Fate."

"What!" Ell shouted. "We have to stop him."

Caitlyn shook her head. "He will kill you, and me, and anyone else that tries to stop him. He doesn't remember anything from when he was alive except Terra. Just do what he says, and we may make it through this alive." Ell looked at Caitlyn then back at the rapidly approaching Alex.

"Okay," Ell said. Caitlyn looked back at Alex and saw the grass was being pushed away from him as if he stood in the eye of a tornado. He mounted the steps onto the marble platform and glared at Ell.

"Open a gateway to Bara," he ordered. Ell nodded and closed her eyes. A few seconds passed, and the gateway spiraled open. "Remove the shield." Ell put the keystone into the slot on the side of the arch, and the seal on the Daein side winked out, but the Baran side was still shielded.

Alex slammed his right fist against the Baran keystone seal. "Here I am Eternius!" Alex roared at the gateway. He punched the shield with his left hand. "Come and face me, you lying bastard!" Caitlyn watched as Alex railed against the red force keeping him from carrying out his vengeance.

Blood from his knuckles dripped onto the white marble when Alex finally stopped trying to batter down the keystone seal. The half-demon sank to his knees in front of the portal and cried. "I don't even remember her," Alex sobbed. "They've taken everything from me."

Caitlyn knelt beside Alex and put her arms around him. "Everything will be alright," she whispered in his ear as she stroked his hair. "You don't have to do this. There are better ways. Eternius isn't responsible for her death."

Alex nodded and rose to his feet. Ell had closed the gateway and backed away. "I know what I have to do," he said.

"Good," Brahm called from the bottom of the steps. Caitlyn and Alex looked at the dwarf. She saw that Brahm had taken the Guardian's Blade from the vault the dwarf had been keeping it in. "Ye'll most likely be needin' this fer it," Brahm said as he tossed the wooden sword to Alex.

The Guardian caught his sword and stared at it with wide eyes. He stopped breathing and stood as still as his statue.

"Alex?" Caitlyn said. "What's wrong?"

Chapter Eighteen – Pain

"Well, this is awkward," a man said in Alex's own voice. Alex looked around, but he didn't see anyone. He was on the marble platform that the Daein gateway arch stood upon. The wooden sword Alex had caught was nowhere to be found either.

"Now," Alex's voice said. It seemed to be coming from everywhere at once. "I thought I was dead."

"Who are you?" Alex asked. "How are you doing this, and why do you sound like me?"

"Geez," the voice said, "so many questions. OH! I lost my memory. Well that sucks…"

"WHO ARE YOU!" Alex shouted.

"I'm you," the voice said from behind him.

Alex spun around, and looked at the man that sounded so much like him. His own green eyes stared back. The man had Alex's face, but his hair was shorter, and he wore silver platemail with nine interconnected rings engraved on it and no helmet. He held the wooden sword. "This isn't…" Alex muttered.

"Possible?" the other man said. "I know! Spooky, right?" The man turned and began to pace around Alex. Unwilling to put his back to his doppelganger, Alex kept turning to face him. The man eyed Alex up and down while he played with the wooden sword. The man flipped the sword backwards one-half turn, caught it by the tip, and flipped it forward for a revolution and a half before snatching it out of the air.

"So," the doppelganger said, "I can see you're me, but how is that possible?" He kept pacing around Alex and repeating his half-flip, catch, spin with the sword as he did.

"I was brought back to life," Alex said. "Eternius told the Life Wardens to bring me back."

"Ugh, I can't stand that guy. Eternius was less than fatherly to our late-wife when they finally met," the man said.

"You knew him?"

The doppelganger nodded. "Not personally. Terra kept the blade with her all of the time after I..." The man closed one eye and looked up while he searched for the correct term. "We?... You?... Aw Hell, it's confusing enough without getting into a who's who, I'll just stick with you being the "real" Alex. Anyway, she kept the blade with her after you died. The Guardian's Blade, well the Blade of Balance anyway, has a kind of awareness of its surroundings. It's wasn't perfect, but it let me keep an eye on her."

"But your wife just died," Alex said. "How are you so calm about this?"

"No," the other man said pointing at Alex with his left hand while he flipped the sword with his right, "your wife just died. I'm a sword, and the Voice of Balance to boot. I have to remain calm, cool, and collected. How else can I give you advice, and point out things you may miss if I don't?"

Alex shook his head and rubbed his hand down his face. *This doesn't make any sense.* "What do you mean you're a sword?"

The doppelganger laughed. "It does too make sense," he said. "You just don't understand. There's a difference. When a Guardian dies, his entire being is imprinted upon the Guardian's Blade, and he, or she, becomes the Voice of Balance, the Voice of Balance becomes the Voice of Regret, and so on, and so on, all the way down the line to the Voice of Empathy. Oh, to cut down on the confusion, how about you call me the Voice of Balance?"

"Sure. So what actually happened to her?" Alex asked.

"Battlesuit. A big robot," the Voice of Balance explained. "This one was equipped with a magical nullification crystal that removed her ability to access magical power. It shot a laser about the size of a basketball through her stomach, instantly killing her and the baby."

Alex took a deep breath and let it out slowly. "So there's nothing anyone could have done."

"There's nothing anyone was there could have done," the Voice of Balance said.

"What you mean?"

The man shrugged. "Just what I said. I can't spoon feed you *all* the information. You don't learn anything that way."

"So someone that wasn't there could have done something?" Alex asked. The doppelganger nodded. "Who?"

The Voice of Balance caught the sword again and stopped pacing around him. The man pointed the tip of the sword at Alex's chest.

"How could I have done anything?" Alex demanded. "I just left Aria today. I just came back to life two days ago!"

"And she died two days ago! If you had been there, then you could have done something!" the Voice of Balance shouted at him.

Alex glared at the man holding the Guardian's Blade. "What happened to calm, cool, and collected?" he asked as he walked over to the Voice of Balance. "You sound pretty pissed off to me. You were there. Why didn't you do something?" Alex asked, his face inches from the doppelganger's.

"Because there was no one born on Earth there to wield me!" the man roared in Alex's face. "She died because YOU couldn't get there in time. You dragged your feet, and Terra and Jessica paid the ultimate price for it!"

The hot blood of rage pounded through Alex's body. He could feel his pulse in his temples. The Guardian wanted to throttle the other man, but he knew it would get him nowhere. Alex closed his eyes, took a calming breath, and set his anger aside. When he opened his eyes, the Voice of Balance was smiling at him.

"Very good, Alex," the man with his face said. "The Guardian must be able to control his emotions, not be controlled by them." The Voice of Balance let out a sigh and took a step back from Alex.

"You see," the Voice of Balance said, "what we've got here is a little problem. Technically, you aren't supposed to be the Guardian because you died. And if the other Voices of the sword had a choice, then they would say that you can't wield the Guardian's Blade, probably because you can't remember anything." The man smirked. "But you have something going for you."

"What's that?" Alex asked.

"They don't have a choice," the Voice of Balance said with a laugh. "Now I happen to like you... Me... Us?" The man put his hand on his chin and thought for a moment. "Is that narcissistic?"

Alex shook his head at the doppelganger's antics. "I'm not sure," Alex said.

The Voice of Balance shrugged. "Who knows? We still have the issue with your memory, though. I can restore it with what was imprinted upon the Guardian's Blade. It's a complete record of your entire memory up until the moment you died. It's up to you if you want to know what I saw while you were dead."

Alex pondered the statement. "If I've lost her, then I would like to know what Terra went through up until she died."

"As you will, Wielder," the Voice of Balance said. "Now, hold very still. This'll only hurt... more than anything we've ever experienced before in our life."

"What?" Alex started to ask. The Voice of Balance darted forward and ran the Guardian's Blade through Alex's head.

For a few seconds, the only things in the universe were Alex and the pain threatening to rip him apart. It slowly faded, and memories flooded through Alex's mind at a blinding pace. Bits and snatches of his life on Earth floated up over the others. When his father was shot and killed. Enlisting in the Marine Corps. Private Seamus Kurt dying in his arms. Punching the Intelligence Officer that had given them the intelligence brief before sending them into Bogotá in the mouth. Being told by his Commanding Officer that he could either accept an early honorable discharge for his heroics, or go to a court marshal and face jail time for assaulting an officer.

Meeting Terra by beating a bunch of drunken thugs up in an alley. Falling in love with her. Moving with her to Seattle. Seeing her getting kidnapped by a halfman. Chasing after her with Caitlyn. Seeing Terra again in Starfall. Meeting Brahm. Marrying and becoming bonded to Terra.

Unleashing his demonic powers for the first time and trying to bring the infant back to life at Highwind Point. The funeral pyre. Crashing in the Silverwing.

Caitlyn defeating Chieftain Rageclaw. Terra getting kidnapped by Azreal. Killing millions of demons, efreet, and undead. Crashing in a Silverwing's escape glider after saving Caitlyn. Infiltrating the Obsidian Tower and killing Azreal, but not before the Overlord fatally injured Terra and Caitlyn. Healing Caitlyn. Almost dying before realizing the baby would die with Terra and giving the last of his strength to save the woman he loved.

Everything took on a blurred cast as Alex viewed the Voice of Balance's memories. The only person with any definition was Terra. Alex watched as she reeled with sadness after his death, freed Bara, taught Hanna, almost died when Jessica began expanding her bubble of force. He saw her journey to Caine, find out Michael was still alive, perform reckless feats of heroics, face down Azreal with the valkyrie and Brahm.

He watched as the woman he loved was vaporized by the blast of a laser. The battle ended, and Brahm found the Guardian's Blade. The next two days were the darkness of a vault until Brahm grabbed it, found Alex, and gave it to him.

The memories stopped bombarding him. Alex opened his eyes, and found that he was standing on the marble by himself. He was holding the wooden Guardian's Blade loosely in his hand. "Thank you," Alex said.

<There you go, man,> the Voice of Balance sent into his mind. <Welcome back to your life.>

"What's wrong?" Caitlyn asked.

Grief tried to roll him under, but Alex remembered his training and shut down that side of him. *My friends need me right now. I can grieve in private,* the Guardian thought as he took a deep breath and wrapped his friend in a warm embrace. "I'm sorry I didn't get to tell you goodbye, little sister," he said.

"Alex." Caitlyn wrapped her arms around him and began to sob. "I missed you," she choked out.

"Hey, now," Alex said, "none of that. I'm here now." He held the changeling at arm's length. He remembered when Caitlyn and Terra talked about the changeling loving him.

Alex looked around and saw Darren standing beside Brahm. The captain had done everything he could to protect Terra, and Alex knew he cared intensely for Caitlyn. The man had his hand on the hilt of his sword and seemed ready to charge up the steps. Alex looked at Caitlyn and said, "Go to the man that loves you the way you wanted me to."

"When did you…" Caitlyn started. Alex patted the Guardian's Blade. She let out a soft laugh. "Thank you… for understanding."

Alex nodded and watched her walk down the steps. The Guardian looked down on the few people that had gathered. "Captain Darren Wright," he said.

Caitlyn stood beside the guardsman. Darren took his hand from his sword and put it around her waist. "Yes, Guardian?" he asked cautiously.

"There was nothing you could have done to save my wife," he said. "I absolve you of any wrongdoing you have placed upon yourself and hope that you feel no more grief on the matter. I don't need you living in the past for the task I have for you."

Darren looked at Caitlyn with confusion. "I don't take orders from you," he said at length.

Alex laughed. "I know, but you do take orders from him," the Guardian said, pointing at Brahm. "General Ironfist, it is my recommendation as Guardian of Balance that this man be put on detail to protect Miss Caitlyn Shadowpaw. As one of your Realm's most powerful magic users, her safety is of the utmost importance."

Nodding, Brahm looked at Darren. "Ye heard the Guardian, boy. I'll expect ye to be at Caitlyn's side at all times."

"By your command, General," the captain said with a smile. "Thank you, Guardian."

Alex nodded at him. "Go carry out your duties. I do ask that you not move any of my wife's things from her home until I have a chance to go through them for any keepsakes." Sadness threatened to overwhelm him. *Come on, Alex, keep it together for just a little longer. You're almost done here.*

Caitlyn looked at him with drawn together brows. "Don't worry," Alex said. "I'll see you again in the morning." She nodded and walked with Darren toward her home.

Brahm stepped onto the gateway platform. "Ye did a good thing there, Alex," he said.

"Everyone deserves to be happy," Alex said. The dwarf looked up at Alex's face and recognized the inner turmoil his friend grappled with.

"Come with me. I'll take ye somewhere ye can rest, an' I'll bandage yer hands."

People stared at Alex as Brahm led him back toward the house where Terra had lived. He heard whispers of, "Guardian," and "Demon," as he walked past. Someone had already cleaned up the splinters of wood from the door Alex had destroyed and installed a new one. Brahm opened it and followed Alex inside. The broken table had been removed.

"Terra's really gone, isn't she?" Alex asked, cracks beginning to appear in his emotional armor.

Brahm led Alex to the kitchen and pulled out a few strips of white cloth from a cabinet. "Aye, Alex. She is."

Alex nodded as he set the Guardian's Blade on the island countertop. The dwarf pushed a few times on a small water pump over the sink. Alex stuck his hands under the cold water and washed the blood from his hands and fingers. The Guardian watched as Brahm wove the fabric over his knuckles. "Thank you, Brahm," Alex said.

"Yer welcome. Is there anythin' I can get fer ye?"

Alex shook his head. "No, I just want to be alone."

Studying his face, Brahm said, "Ye do no' have to stay here. I can find ye another place."

"No, here's fine. It's like I was closer to her."

"Alrigh'," Brahm said. "I'll be by in the mornin' to help ye get ready."

For the funeral. Alex nodded, and the dwarf left. He pulled open a few cabinets and closed them. He went through the entire kitchen before he found what he was looking for. The bottle was full of an amber liquid and stoppered with a cork. Alex pulled the cork out with his teeth, and he took a deep draught from the glass bottle. The alcohol was sweet but burned like whiskey.

He stood by the sink and looked out the small window into the empty field behind the house. *Drowning your sorrows?* Alex took another drink from the bottle. Warmth was spreading from his stomach. *Like you did after you told Kurt's mother that he had died?* A third drink from the bottle, and more than a third of it was gone. *I think I'm going to finish this one and need another.* Alex thought about the last time he had tried to drink himself into oblivion.

The sound of boots thumping on the wooden floor of his apartment roused a haggard and hungover Sergeant Alex Zane of the United States Marine Corps. Alex lifted himself from the floor next to his bed and looked at the clock. *Four-forty in the afternoon. Guess I missed muster,* he thought.

Alex looked at the three bottles of Tennessee's finest whiskey on the ground around him. One of the bottles had a little less than half in it. *Fuck it,* Alex thought as he slapped a hand against the bottle and poured the contents down his throat.

His bedroom door swung open, and Alex lifted his head to look at the intruder. "Damn, Sarge," Lance Corporal Max "Tiny" Gilroy said. The huge man ducked and turned sideways to fit through the narrow doorframe. The heavy gunner looked at the three empty bottles and whistled softly. "You drank all three of these last night after you punched out the Lieutenant Colonel at the bar?"

"No," Alex croaked. "I drank that one before I went to the bar, that one after I got back," he held up the one he had just downed, "and this one just now."

"How have you not shit and puked all over the place?"

Alex put a hand on the side of his bed and pulled himself up to a sitting position. "That would be conduct unbecoming a non-commissioned officer," he muttered. Max snorted a laugh and held his hand out to help Alex stand. The sergeant accepted the help but couldn't seem to find his feet. He looked down to make sure they were still there.

Max helped him get to the door. *There's no way in Hell we are both fitting through here at the same time.* "Hang on a sec, Tiny," Alex said. He stood unsteadily for a moment and shook his head to try clearing is vision. "Where's my dresser? Ah, there it is."

He stumbled over to the four drawer dresser and grabbed either side of it. Leaning back to make sure he had enough speed, Alex slammed his forehead against the wooden top as hard as he could.

Max was looking at Alex on the floor. The sergeant lifted himself from the floor and walked on steady feet to the kitchen. "Never seen a drunk cure quite like that one," Max said.

Alex rubbed his sore forehead. "Yeah, it seemed like a better idea at the time. I punched out Lieutenant Colonel Lake when I was at the bar?"

Laughing, Max nodded. "Sorry, I probably shouldn't laugh since you unleashed a shit storm on yourself. You called him... something, then hit him in the jaw. You dislocated it and knocked out a few teeth from what I heard."

Alex reached into the fridge and pulled out a beer. He used the bottle opener built into the outside of the appliance and took drink. "What did I call him?"

"I think your exact words were, 'This is from Kurt, Gunny, and the LT, you moronic fucktard.' Then you hit him so hard he went through the bar's drywall and landed on a shitter."

"Damn," Alex said.

"Yeah," Max said. "Apparently the 'moronic fucktard' has some friends in Washington, and they're after you hardcore. The Colonel went to bat for you. He's trying to play it up as PTSD, but you know that shit's not going to fly."

Alex grunted and drained the beer. He tossed the bottle in the trash and went to grab another. Max followed him into the kitchen, and the big man snatched the beer from his hand. "Are you fuckin' serious right now, Sarge?" Max asked.

Alex looked at the beer Max was holding far out of his reach. He opened the fridge and pulled out another. "Fairly."

Max snatched that one away too. "Look, I know Kurt's death got to you, man, but this isn't the way to deal with this shit. You're going to get yourself killed or kill yourself," he said.

"It's my damn job to protect people!" Alex shouted at the lance corporal. "That ass hat Intelligence Officer didn't do his cushy job as a fucking desk jockey and got my man killed!"

"I know, Zane," Max said. "I was there." The bigger man pushed Alex out of the way and opened the fridge. He pulled the twenty-four pack of beer out and put the two he was holding in it. He opened the freezer and pulled out a bottle of whiskey and a bottle of vodka and set them next to the big box of beer on the floor.

Max looked at the alcohol in disgust. "The Colonel wants to see you in the morning," he said as he met Alex's eyes. "You need to get your shit together." The Lance Corporal bent down and scooped up all of the booze. "I'm taking all this with me."

Alex leaned over the sink and looked out the small window as the door to his apartment slammed shut. Sailboats out on the bay went by far below. He vomited noisily into the sink. *What the hell am I doing?*

Alex looked at the half-empty bottle in his hand as if it was a poisonous viper. He smashed the bottle into the sink. Amber liquid ran down the grated drain. *I'll clean it up later.*

Snatching the Guardian's Blade from the counter, Alex walked to the bedroom door. He put his hand on the knob and stared at the blank door for a time. The tears began to flow, and Alex rested his head against the wood. He beat his empty left hand against the door. The Guardian's Blade clattered to the dark brown floor, and Alex fell against the wall behind him.

He slid to the floor and wrapped his arms around his knees. Alex put his head against them and cried until he couldn't anymore.

Caitlyn climbed out of her bed and slipped a dress on. It was the middle of the night, but she had grown accustomed to her new home and was comfortable walking around with little light. She made it three creeping steps before Darren asked, "So, it's like that is it?"

She turned to look at him. He was propped up on an elbow in the bed. The sheets were clumped around his navel, and Caitlyn could see the curly brown hair on his chest. "I'm going to check on Alex," she said. The silence that greeted her statement was answer enough on what Darren thought of that idea. "He just found out his wife, who was like a sister to me, died with their unborn child. My friend needs me, and if he's asleep, I'll leave."

"And if he's not asleep?" Darren asked.

"Then I will stay with him as long as he needs me to."

Darren was quiet for a moment. "You said he was the man you loved," he said after an uncomfortable silence.

He should know the truth. Especially now... "That's right. I did love him, but he was married to my sister. It would have never worked between us anyway. He was absolutely devoted to Terra."

"Caitlyn, he's a de—"

"Stop," she interrupted. "You don't know him. Alex is one of the kindest people I have ever met in my life. I am going to check on him now. You can come with me if you like."

Darren thought it over for a moment. "No," he said, "I don't think I should. I'll see you in the morning, Caitlyn."

"I'll see you in the morning," she said. Caitlyn left the house and looked up and down the street. It was late, and there was no one about. She changed into her panther form and padded to the house Alex and Terra would have shared. Alex hadn't locked the front door, and she opened it with a paw.

She was surprised to find him sitting on the floor in the hall. *His breath smells like that bottle of honey liquor.* Alex shivered. Remembering there was a blanket on the back of the small couch, Caitlyn went and retrieved it. She dragged it over his shoulders and lay down on Alex's bare feet to keep them warm. *I'm here for you, if you need me.*

Brahm arrived at Terra's house just after sunrise. He opened the front door and stepped inside. The dwarf walked to the hallway and saw Alex sleeping on the floor with a panther laying beside him. Brahm tapped his foot, and Caitlyn's golden eyes shot open. He nodded toward the kitchen and went that way.

"Smells like bloody honey brandy in here," Brahm muttered. The smell was strongest near the sink. Brahm looked in it and saw the shards of glass. *I wonder how much o' the stuff he drank.*

Caitlyn padded into the kitchen, and Brahm greeted her with an upraised brow. "Where's yer guard?" he asked in a soft whisper.

"I left him at my house last night," she whispered back.

Brahm opened the pantry and pulled out a few eggs. He pumped some water into a deep bowl and dropped the eggs into it. None of them floated, and only one stood on its end. *At least the food's no' spoiled. I'll need to thank Deidra.* "Yer house only has one bed an' no bloody places to sit if I remember right."

A snapping of bones came from behind him as Caitlyn changed back into her human form. Flames sprang from the top of the oven as she channeled some fire into it. "Thank ye," Brahm said as he started cracking eggs into a skillet.

Caitlyn leaned against the counter next to him while he cooked enough eggs for three people. "Darren was there for me when I needed him," she said. "I feel better when he's around. I think I love him."

"I'm happy for you," Alex said from the kitchen doorway.

"Good mornin'," Brahm said. "Breakfast's almost done. Grab some plates."

Alex walked to the correct cabinet and pulled down a plate. He stood there looking at it for a few seconds without moving. "What's wrong?" Caitlyn asked.

"Nothing," Alex said as he grabbed two more. "Terra just arranged her kitchen here the same way ours was at the apartment in Seattle." He set the plates down on the island countertop. "Except this is new." Alex looked up at Caitlyn. "Thank you for coming to check on me last night. I needed that blanket."

"I was worried about you," she said. "How did you know I came last night?"

"I woke up and saw you. I lay down on my side and went back to sleep."

Brahm lifted the skillet, and the fire guttered and went out as Caitlyn stopped maintaining it. He put equal portions on each of their plates. "I'm not hungry," Alex said.

I'll have none o' that. "Ye've had nothing go into yer body in the last half a day except however much o' that disgustin' honey brandy ye drank. Ye need food. Eat," Brahm ordered.

Alex shrugged and began to shovel food into his mouth. The Guardian finished first and watched impassively while the other two ate the rest of their food. "Yer armor's in the bedroom. Let's get ye ready," Brahm said. "It's gettin' close to time."

"If I don't come back from this," Terra had told Silvia before she left for Caine, "I want you to speak at my funeral."

"That won't happen." Terra had stared at Silvia until the Fanglady asked, "What do you want me to say?"

Terra let out a short breath. "I want you to tell them the truth."

Silvia stood on top of the gateway platform. The sun had been up for two hours, and the time to begin the funeral had come. Fluffy white clouds floated across the sky. One drifted in front of the sun and covered the crowds filling the green in shade. Birds called from the trees scattered around the park. Ell and Paul flanked Terra's sealed glass casket at the base of the platform.

The Fanglady looked down at the front of the crowd and saw Alex standing beside Caitlyn, Brahm, and Darren. None of the others in the throng of people were willing to be within Alex's striking distance except for Hanna and the council members. *The rumors have spread like wildfire,* Silvia thought. She cast a voice amplification spell so all could hear and began.

"Terra was a child of two worlds," Silvia said. "Born Terra Duval to the Grand Sorceress of the Arcane City, she was not sure where she belonged. It wasn't until her mother died that Terra realized she was more than she seemed. She was the Nexus of Magic.

"With complete devotion to her home, Terra diligently carried out the duties of Nexus without ever a single word of complaint. She saw the best in everyone and tried to help others see it too." A few heads in the audience nodded. "Terra cared for everyone that her Paragonship had placed under her care, but she had to care for them from afar because while she tried to forget she was a half-angel, we did not."

Unmoving silence met Silvia's pause as she let the words sink in for a moment. "Six years ago, a man rescued Terra from a band of outlaws that had come to extract vengeance for her sentencing their leader to death at trial. They fell in love and married, with Terra bonding Michael Stormbringer to her as her Shield. But their marriage was a short lived one.

"Only a month were they married before the forces of Hell struck against the Arcane City. They helped hold the city for a week and saved hundreds of thousands of lives. When the city finally fell, Michael gave his life so that Terra could go to Earth and find the Guardian. It took her five years to find him and bring Alex to us." Feet shifted uncomfortably at the mention of Alex's name.

"The impossible happened a second time when Terra fell in love with the Guardian, and they were married. Together, they freed our home of Azreal and the demons of Hell, but Terra was gravely wounded while fighting Azreal. Alex gave his life to bring his dying pregnant wife back from the cusp of death, and for a second time, the Nexus watched the man she loved die."

Silvia scanned the crowd to gauge their reaction. Some nodded, and others looked confused. "I tell you with complete honesty that such a thing would destroy me, but Terra was a singularly strong woman. She channeled her grief toward freeing the two besieged Inner Realms from Azreal's influence. Without her direct intervention, the Bara and Caine would still be occupied today.

"But their freedom came at a price, a price the Nexus paid for with the lives of herself and her unborn child. Terra gave her life so that our allies could be safe, transcending her duties as the Nexus of Magic. That day she became not only Dae's Paragon but the Paragon for all the Inner Realms. We should all strive to live by her example by giving succor those that cannot get it, helping others even when you are crying out, and protecting those who cannot defend themselves."

Silvia heard a few people crying in the assembled masses. She nodded to the crowd and stepped down from the platform.

Alex listened to Terra's eulogy with numb attentiveness. He felt hollow inside and couldn't tear his eyes from his wife's coffin. The glass box was a dark grey except for the area that covered her head. Alex could see her red hair glow like fire when the clouds moved from in front of the sun.

Silvia finished speaking and stepped down from the gateway platform. Brahm pressed gently on Alex's back so the man could say goodbye to his wife. The Guardian took the infinitely-long nine steps to gaze upon his wife. The two guards that flanked her coffin stared ahead at attention.

I love you, Terra, Alex said in his mind. *I'm sorry I couldn't get there in time to save you.* He placed his right hand on the glass coffin above where her stomach would be. *I'm sorry I couldn't save our child.* A tear splashed down onto the glass, and Terra's face swam in his vision. Alex angrily wiped away the tears so he could see his wife this last time. He leaned down and kissed the glass casket.

"Goodbye, my love," he whispered. Alex turned and walked away from his dead wife. It would take hours for all of the people to have a chance to pay their respects, and the interment was not scheduled to occur until sundown.

Why did I have to be so slow getting better? Alex screamed in his mind as he walked down the road alone. *Why couldn't I be faster?* Alex stumbled on a rock he didn't see and fell forward. He landed on his right shoulder, and the Guardian's Blade somehow fell from its scabbard and clattered against the cobblestone.

"Are you all right?" Caitlyn asked as she caught up to him.

"That's a stupid question," Alex snapped.

The changeling helped Alex to his feet. "I'm sorry," she said. She picked up the wooden sword by its blunt blade and held it out to Alex hilt first. The Guardian reached out for it.

As soon as his hand touched the hilt, a brilliant flash of silver light stole his vision.

Chapter Nineteen – Click

Alex blinked away the glare and looked at the silver stopwatch in his hands. There were nine hands that spun in one direction, and nine rings that spun in the other. <I am Regret,> Maegan's voice whispered in his mind.

"Alex, what's the sword doing?" Caitlyn asked.

What is this, Maegan? Alex thought.

<Wielder, I am the Voice of Regret now,> Maegan, the previous Guardian and Voice of Balance before him sent. <You hold the power of time itself in your hands.>

"I think it's a time machine," Alex said.

Caitlyn frowned at him. "A what?"

<There are restrictions, Wielder.>

What are they?

<One, time is a fragile thing. To protect it, you can only travel back in time to a period you were alive in. Two, your mind and soul are the only things that go back, not your body. You will arrive in whatever condition you were in at that time. And there is one more.>

"I can save Terra," Alex gasped.

<Once you succeed in the task you have assigned yourself,> the Voice of Regret said, <you can never use this form of the Guardian's Blade again.>

"You can what!" Caitlyn demanded.

What if it takes me more than one try? Alex asked.

<Time will continue to loop until you are successful, or you give up. Either way, once you begin this process, you may never use it again.>

Alex held the stopwatch out in front of him. "I can use this to go back in time and save Terra," he explained with wild-eyed frenzy.

"Alex," Caitlyn said with outstretched hands, "think about this for a second. She died for a reason. Who are you to change it?"

How far back can I go?

<Your situation is… unique. You may only return to the time when you awoke on Aria.>

That will give me hardly any time.

<I am sorry, Wielder, but I cannot change the way the process works,> Maegan said.

Do it.

The watch's hands and rings spun about for a second and stopped. There was a ratcheting noise and a small button rose from the top of the silver device. He put his thumb over the button.

"Alex, wait! You aren't thinking clearly!" Caitlyn shouted.

"I'll bring her back."

<Are you certain this is what you want to do, Wielder? It is dangerous to interfere with time.>

I am.

Caitlyn tried to reach out and take the watch from him. Alex pushed his thumb down.

"Click."

--0:00.00--

Alex's eyes shot open with a gasp. The stone bed he lay on was warm under his naked body. He leapt from the bed. <This isn't possible,> the Progenitor sent. <The mind and soul take time to join to one another.>

"I can't explain," Alex shouted. "Where is my mother?"

<You shouldn't be about,> the Life Warden protested.

"WHERE IS SHE?" the Guardian roared.

<Follow me,> the Progenitor chimed with indignation.

The doorway opened, and the Progenitor floated along ahead of him. "Hurry!" Alex yelled. The green Life Warden began to zip along at a sprint. Alex chased after him. The Progenitor opened the external wall of the Soul Foundry and turned left. Alex could see his mother standing beside the lake of fire and pushed himself to run faster.

The Guardian outpaced the Progenitor and stood before Odessa, panting to catch his breath. "Mother," he gasped.

"Alex!" she exclaimed. "Why are you naked?" She looked at him more closely. "How do you know who I am?"

"Later. Caine. Have you been there?" Alex said as he caught his breath.

"I'm sorry, but I haven't." She turned to the Progenitor. "Could you please get him some clothes?"

<I'll have another bring them,> the Paragon chimed indignantly.

Alex ran his hands through his hair. "I need to get there," he said as he paced like a wild animal. "Are there any other pendants like yours?"

"How do you- Yes, there's one other that I know of," Odessa said.

Alex grabbed his mother's arms. "Where is it?"

"The Keeper of Fate has it. That's how he came to Aria to ask the Life Wardens to bring you back to life," she said.

The Guardian took a step back and started pacing like a wild animal in a cage. "Of course he does," Alex snapped. "The top of Grand Spire on Bara. Can you open a portal there?"

His mother's eyes grew wide, and she shook her head. "Alex, they told me you wouldn't remember anything. What happened?"

"I have to save Terra's life. I need you to open a portal to Bara. I have to see Eternius."

"Who is Terra?" Odessa asked.

Alex wrung his hands. "Mother, I'll explain everything later. I promise, but right now, I need you to open a portal to Bara so I can save my wife's life."

Odessa nodded and pulled out the Traveler's Pendant. There was a thump in the air, and the portal to Bara opened. "Thank you," Alex said as he jumped through the hole in reality.

--0:17.43--

The City of Spires lay miles before him. The Guardian ran as fast as he could to the massive wall. In less than an hour since he awoke, Alex was beating his fists against the Gate of Faith. Bloody footprints trailed behind him. "Ureon! Open up! The Guardian needs to see The Keeper!" The gate swung open, and Alex ran to the young-faced Ureon.

The angel stared at him slack-jawed. "How are you here?" she asked. "You were only supposed to have awakened today. And why are you naked?"

"Ureon, I don't have time to explain. I need to see Eternius, now!" Alex said.

The Seat of Faith picked up on his urgency and scooped Alex up in her arms. She carried him like a babe as she soared through the air. "Hurry," he said.

"I can't go any faster, Guardian," she protested.

They covered the distance between the Gate of Faith and the Amphitheater of the High Seats in less than half the time it had taken the last time. Ureon deposited Alex on the floor of the room and immediately vanished through the floor.

In seconds, she returned with Eternius. "Guardian," the Keeper said with a suspicious tone, "how are you here?" The angel looked at him from head to toe.

"I know I'm naked!" Alex shouted. "Eternius, I need to get to Caine."

The Keeper raised a blond eyebrow. "Where on that Realm?"

The question set Alex back for a moment. "I don't know! Just get me there, and I'll find her."

Eternius reached under his armor and produced a pendant identical to Odessa's. There was another thump in the air, and a red portal floated in the air. Alex jumped through the gateway, and it closed behind him.

--1:08.22--

He stood at the foot of a bridge and saw an Obsidian Tower in the distance. "Almost there," he said as he ran toward it. "I'm coming Terra." The pain in Alex's feet grew as he ran. He stepped on a stone that was concealed in the tall grass and slit the sole of his left foot wide open. Alex did his best to ignore it as he kept running.

A few more hours passed before Alex could hear the sounds of a battle winding down. There was an explosion that sounded like the crack of lightning, and the Obsidian Tower he was running towards toppled. He pushed himself to run faster, but his injured left foot made him limp.

A stone statue of a one-eyed man holding a spear with an eagle on his shoulder began to draw nearer. Alex saw an army of people wearing armor gathered around it. He reached the edge of the army and weapons were bared.

--4:31.00--

"Who are you?" a man wearing furs and holding a five foot long sledgehammer demanded.

"I'm, Alex," he gasped out between breaths. "Looking, for, Nexus. Her husband," he finished poking himself in the chest.

"What's going on over there?" a man's voice called.

--4:32.00--

"A naked man says he's the Nexus's wife," the furred man shouted back.

Alex watched as Caitlyn pushed her way through the army in her primal form. She reached the edge of the group and saw him. The Guardian winced as he listened to her bones crack as she changed into her human form.

--4:33.00--

"How?" was all she said.

"I didn't make it," the Guardian said. He knew from the look on Caitlyn's face that he was too late. "Take me to her." The changeling turned, and the Guardian followed her through the ranks of the army. A few of the faces and their arms and armor were familiar to Alex, but he couldn't focus enough to try figuring out why they seemed that way.

--4:34.00--

"How is this possible?" Caitlyn asked.

"The Life Wardens brought me back. I'll explain the rest later."

There was a clear pocket in the center of the army around the base of the one-eyed man's statue. Alex saw a black plated Brahm kneeling next to some feet. The rest of the dwarf's body blocked his view. Alex and Caitlyn pushed through the last few people and stepped into the gap.

--4:35.00--

Alex stood beside Brahm and looked down at his wife's ruined form. Someone had covered her from the shoulders down with a horse blanket, but Alex could see where the laser had vaporized her stomach. The blanket sagged from the middle of her ribs to just above her hips. The Guardian dropped to his knees in the bloody mud.

Brahm looked over at him and gasped. The dwarf held the Guardian's Blade in his lap. Brahm's cheeks were damp with tears. He wrapped his hands around the wooden sword and held it out to Alex.

The Guardian touched his sword, and it immediately changed into the silver stopwatch. None of the hands or dials moved. The ratcheting noise came, and the button rose on the top.

<Again?>

"Click."

--0:00.00--

Alex's eyes shot open with a gasp. The stone bed he lay on was warm under his naked body. He leapt from the bed. <This isn't possible,> the Progenitor sent. <The mind and soul take time to join to one another.>

"I do not have time to explain. I need you to listen and do what I say as fast as possible. I need you to open this door and the one to leave the Soul Foundry and get Melody to bring me some clothes and shoes I can run in," Alex said. "Have her bring them to me at the lake of fire."

The door slid open. <Who is Melody?> the Progenitor asked.

"The white Life Warden. Please hurry," Alex said as he ran out of the room. He saw the door ahead of him already sliding up. He caught the edge of the opening with his hand and spun to the left. He sprinted to his mother at the fiery lake.

"Mother, I have no time to explain," he said. "My wife's life is in danger, and I need to get to Bara so I can save her." Odessa stared at him wide-eyed for a second before she pulled out the Traveler's Pendant and opened the gateway to Bara.

"Alex, I wanted to tell you that I'm sorry for letting you go, but it's something I had to do," she said.

"I know, Mother. You did it to protect me." The Guardian looked up at the Traveler's Amulet Odessa held in her hand. "Can I use that to open a portal?" Alex asked.

His mother shook her head. "No, Alex. It has to be attuned to the person using it, and that takes hours."

Alex nodded and saw Melody leaving a trail of white light behind her as she zipped toward him. <Here, Guardian,> she said as she deposited the clothes and sturdy running shoes at his side.

The Guardian threw the clothes on. "Thank you both," he said as he tied the shoes. Alex ran through the portal onto Bara.

--0:14.12--

He ran toward the City of Spires as fast as he could. In less than a half-hour's time, Alex was beating on the Gate of Faith. "Ureon, open up! I have to see Eternius!" The gate swung open, and Alex saw the female angel looking at him curiously. "Before you ask," he said before she could say anything, "I don't have time to explain. I need to get to Eternius at the top of the Grand Spire, now."

Ureon didn't hesitate or ask questions. She lifted him from the ground and flew toward the Amphitheater of the High Seats as fast as she could. The angel set him down next to the Libram of Fate and faded into the floor. She was back with Eternius in seconds.

The Keeper looked at Alex with a narrowed eyes. "Yes, Guardian?" he asked.

"Your daughter's life is in danger," Alex said. Eternius's eyes widened, but Alex couldn't tell if it was alarm or surprise that caused it. "I need you to use your Traveler's Amulet to take me to Caine."

"Where on that Realm?" Eternius asked him again.

Alex put his fingers to his temples. *Where on the damn Realm?* He scoured his memories of the last time he tried for some landmark. "A statue!" he said when it came to him. "A statue of a one-eyed man holding a spear with a bird on his shoulder. Can you take me there?"

Eternius nodded. "I have been to Odin's statue before." The red portal opened, and Alex dove through it.

--0:59.31--

Screams of pain and explosions came from all around him. For a few seconds, Alex thought he was in the middle of a battlefield on Earth until he saw a man run past with a broadsword. He looked about for a Battlesuit and saw three.

--1:00.00--

The nearest fired a laser into a group of people. A man screamed, "No!" and charged the Battlesuit. The blond man flew into the air and destroyed the cockpit of the machine with a single blow of his warhammer. Alex ran to the group that had been fired upon.

--1:03.38--

As soon as Alex drew near, he knew he had found Terra. Her red hair was splayed out around her, and she had a smoking hole where her stomach should be. Darren was on his knees next to her. "No, no, no," the captain said.

Alex slammed his fist against his leg. "Damn it!" the Guardian shouted. His sword lay on the ground not far away, and Alex picked it up. It changed into the stopwatch.

<Again?>

"Click."

--0:00.00--

Alex's eyes shot open with a gasp. The stone bed he lay on was warm under his naked body. He leaped from the bed. <This isn't possible,> the Progenitor sent. <The mind and soul take time to join to one another.>

"I do not have time to explain. I need you to listen and do what I say as fast as possible. I need you to open this door and the one to leave the Soul Foundry and get the white Life Warden to bring me some clothes and shoes I can run in," Alex said. "Have her bring them to me at the lake of fire."

--0:56.17--

Alex stood before Eternius. The angel glared at him. "I need you to open a portal to Odin's statue on Caine so I can save Terra's life."

The red portal opened, and Alex ran through it.

--0:56.34--

The Guardian didn't hesitate. As soon as his feet hit Cainen soil, he flew across the battlefield as fast as his legs would propel him. He drew near the group Terra was in and shouted as loud as he could. She couldn't hear him over the sound of a rippling explosion. Alex sprinted past Darren.

--1:00.00--

The laser fired a few seconds before Alex reached Terra. He slid to a stop just before Michael yelled, "No!" and rushed at the Battlesuit. Alex roared in rage. *I only need to be a few seconds faster next time.* He picked up the Guardian's Blade from where it lay.

"Click."

--0:56.17--

"I need you to open a portal to Odin's statue on Caine so I can save Terra," Alex told the Keeper. Eternius stared at him with wide eyes and pursed lips.

--0:56.30--

Alex sprinted a bee line toward Terra. He screamed in his mind to go faster as he closed the distance.

--1:00.00--

The laser tore through Terra at the exact same instant Alex slammed into her. His wife's legs lay beneath him, but her torso had torn free and was several feet away. The Guardian dry heaved next to half of his wife's corpse.

He lurched to his feet and stumbled over to the Guardian's Blade. *Only a second faster.*

"Click."

--0:56.16--

"I need a portal to Odin's statue on Caine to save Terra," Alex said. Eternius had a glare fixed on the Guardian's face and his fists were clenched.

--0:56.29--

I can make it, he thought as he ran.

--0:59.59--

Alex tackled Terra to the ground just before the laser fired.

--1:00.00--

It was so close that the beam seared the flesh on his back. The Guardian laughed victoriously. He looked down at his wife.

Her head was twisted around at an impossible angle, and she didn't move. Alex jumped back from her dead body. His hands wouldn't stop shaking as he looked for the Guardian's Blade. *I killed her,* ran through his mind without stopping.

<Again?>

"Click."

--0:59.58--

Alex pulled Terra back. The Guardian smiled at his triumph. Terra looked at him in complete bafflement.

"Alex?" she said.

--1:00.00--

Bits of brain and bone spattered Alex's face as the sniper's round tore through his wife's skull. Alex let go of her body in shock.

<Again?>

"Click."

--0:56.15--

"I need a portal to Odin's statue to save Terra," Alex said as fast as he could.

Eternius's look of anger turned to one of confusion. "The statue to Odin on Earth or Caine?"

"Caine!" Alex roared.

--1:00.00--

The laser fired just before Alex could get to his wife.

"Click."

--0:59.58--

Alex grabbed his wife and kept running. Terra stumbled a few steps, but he helped her steady herself.

--1:00.00--

An explosion blew them apart. The stump of Alex's right arm spurted blood. He looked around for Terra, but he could only find her armor plated leg.

"Click."

--0:59.58--

Alex pulled her away from the explosion but was careful to keep his balance. He ran back the way he had come with Terra in tow. Alex glanced back at her; she stared at him in wide-eyed shock. He turned his eyes back forward just as two daemen attacked.

--1:00.00--

A black sword bit deep into Alex's stomach as he was run through. Terra was unarmed and surprised, and the other daemon's sword separated the top third of her skull from her head. The daemon pulled its sword from Alex's stomach and beheaded him.

"Click."

--0:00.00--

Alex's slowly opened his eyes and drew in a deep breath. He lifted his head and slammed it back against the warm stone of the bed. *I just died... There has to be something I'm missing. Why can't I use my demonic powers?*

Alex knew he had already wasted too much time to save Terra. He let out a slow breath and swung his legs over the edge of the bed. "I need this open," Alex said. "The one to the outside, too."

The Progenitor argued with him and told Alex to get back on the bed lest he injure himself. Alex stood in front of where the door was and didn't move or speak. Eventually, the Life Warden gave up, and the doorway opened. "Could you have the white Life Warden bring me some clothes and shoes at the lake of fire? I need to speak with my mother."

<As you wish, Guardian,> the Progenitor chimed. Alex walked through the Soul Foundry at a snail's pace.

It's too late. She may as well have already died... The white Life Warden caught up to him at the same time he reached Odessa. The demoness looked at him with a ponderous blend of sadness, hope, and confusion as he dressed. Alex tied the Earth-style running shoes and stood. "Hello, Mother," he said.

"Hello, Son," Odessa answered. The Life Warden that Alex had once called Melody floated away from them.

Terra's dead, and I can't save her. Alex shook his head. *No! I'm not going to give up yet.* "Why can't I use my demonic powers?" he asked his mother.

Her brows drew down over her solid green eyes. "You only just came back to life. They will take some time to build within you. The process is similar to how a sorcerer gathers magical energy, except we convert that energy to demonic power. Also, while we are in good health, our own body supplies a measure of power that also accumulates over time."

It all comes down to needing more time. It's always time. He rubbed his hand down his face, and it came away wet. Alex looked at the hand for a moment before he realized he was crying.

Odessa stepped over to him and wrapped him in a comforting embrace. "Oh, my son," she whispered. "What's wrong?"

Alex put his arms around his mother and placed his forehead on her shoulder. "I'm trying to save her, Mother, but I can't. There just isn't enough time."

"Who are you trying to save?" she asked.

"My wife, Terra Zane," he explained. Alex lifted his head, and Odessa released him.

His mother sat on the ground with her legs tucked beneath her. She patted the ground across from her, and Alex joined her. "How are you trying to save her?"

She won't remember any of this after I start over again, but she may know something. "I used the Guardian's Blade to create a time loop. I start it back over every time I fail to save her, or if I die it starts over on its own. But I don't have enough time to get to her and save her. Every time I do get to her before the laser kills her, she's killed by something else."

Odessa stared at him with wide eyes. "How many times have you tried?"

"This is my tenth time I've reawakened here," Alex said. He felt dead inside. "I've watched Terra die nine times. I tried a few different ways to try getting to her faster, but every time I try to shave off a second here, or a second there, it still doesn't work."

"I'm sorry, Alex. I wish there was something I could do to help you, but I can't leave here. Any Realm I end up on would be a death sentence for me."

Alex nodded as he stood. "It's all right. Don't worry about it. I'm too late now anyway." He looked at the lake of roiling fire. "This really is hot," he said.

"That it is," Odessa said as she rose to her feet. "Underneath the outer flames is what is called elemental fire. It's the purest essence of flame. The Life Wardens use it to create new souls, but anything else that touches it would be destroyed."

"Good," Alex said. He dove into the flames. The pain only lasted for an instant.

"Click."

Chapter Twenty – Light and Dark

Alex lost track of how many times he tried to save Terra somewhere around one hundred and seventeen. No matter what he did or tried, Terra died an hour after he awoke on Aria. He convinced his mother to try attuning the Traveler's Pendant to him, but the process took far too long, and there was no way to make it faster. He had discovered that if he waited for three days the loop would start back over from the beginning.

That's how long it took me to use the stopwatch the first time around. Alex spent a few weeks lying on the bed in Aria, trying to come up with some way to save his wife. The Guardian had tried every possible thing he could think of. He had tried to get the Guardian's Blade from Terra and use it to protect her, but the only form he could unleash was Regret.

<All other forms of the Guardian's Blade are sealed when using Regret,> Maegan told him.

Alex knew there was no way he could rescue Terra and their child from this, but he knew as soon as he stopped the time loop they would be forever lost to him. The Guardian lay on the warm bed of stone and stared at the rainbow-hued ceiling.

How many months have I been lying here? Alex wondered. The three days played out the same so many times that he had grown accustomed to ignoring whatever was going on around him. *Or has it been years?* His mother slept in a chair the Progenitor had raised from the floor. *I don't know, but this one is almost over.*

"Click."

Alex opened his eyes and stared at the ceiling. The Paragon of the Realm of Life was droning on, but Alex turned him down to a buzz in his mind. The buzzing's tone shifted to concern then the Progenitor zipped through the hole in the wall and disappeared.

There was a thump in the air, and a yellow light suffused the room. *What?* Alex lifted his head and saw a portal to Bara at the foot of the bed. Eternius stepped through the portal, and it shut behind him. "Why are you here?" the Guardian asked. "And how?"

"I have lived through your last three days more times that I care to think about, Alex Zane," Eternius snapped. "I predate the Guardian's Blade and the Source that was used to create it. I am the only one that does, and I am the only one that knows what you are doing. It is not your place to interfere with Fate."

Alex balled up his fist and punched the Keeper of Fate in his jaw. The angel wasn't expecting the sudden attack and was set back a step. "You've known this entire time and done nothing?" Alex shouted. "You could have been helping me, and you've done nothing!"

Eternius wiped the corner of his mouth, and his fingers came away bloody. "I could take you to her right now," the Keeper said, "then I could take you to the safest place you can imagine, and Terra will still die in an hour's time. Except this time, she would just drop dead with no provocation."

"Why?" Alex yelled.

"Because it is written in the Libram of Fate."

The Guardian's fists quaked with barely restrained rage. "That's why you didn't want Terra to read it when she was on Bara," he said. "Wait. You wrote that damn book, didn't you? That's your responsibility as Keeper, isn't it?"

Eternius nodded. "I did."

"Terra's your daughter!" Alex roared as he launched himself at the angel. Invisible bonds wrapped around Alex's wrists and pinned him to the wall.

The Progenitor flew into the room through the hole in the wall. <I heard yell—Eternius, what brings you here?>

"An unruly Paragon," the angel said. "Bring him some clothes."

<At once.> The green Life Warden left.

Eternius took a few steps toward him but stopped outside of Alex's kicking range. The Guardian strained against the bonds that held him to the wall. The Keeper pointed at Alex's face. "Do you think for one moment that I enjoy this? Do you think I want Terra to die?"

Alex glared at Eternius. "I think you don't care what happens as long as your job is done. Tell me the truth, Angel, and don't bandy words with me. Yes or no, do you care what happens to you daughter?"

The angel was silent while he seemed to wage an internal battle. "Yes," he whispered at length.

"THEN HELP ME!"

Eternius shook his head. "I can't," he said. "It's my duty to ensure the Libram is secure."

"Is your *duty* really more important that your daughter's and granddaughter's lives?" Alex asked, growing desperate.

"I... I don't know." Alex felt his bonds fade away and rubbed his wrists.

The Progenitor flew into the room at the same time the doorway opened, and Odessa walked in with a concerned look on her face. Eternius saw her pale skin and solid green eyes. Odessa saw the his mythricite armor and white wings. "Demon!" the Keeper shouted the same time she hissed, "Angel!"

Eternius went for his sword as Odessa dove at him. She hung motionless in mid-air, and the Keeper froze with his sword half out of his scabbard. <There will be no fighting here,> the Progenitor said to both of them. <Aria is a place of peace for all. I do not care about your status or what enmity you may share. Continue this folly, and I will rip the souls from your bodies.>

The Life Warden released his hold on Alex's mother and father-in-law. The two glared at each other with ancient hatred burning in their eyes. "As you will, Progenitor," Odessa said.

Eternius did looked at Alex and ignored the demoness. "I'm am sorry, Alex, but I cannot help you, even if she is my daughter."

"What's going on?" Odessa asked, looking between Alex and Eternius through squinted eyes.

Alex let out a sharp breath. "Eternius can help me save my wife's life, but he refuses because it's his *duty*." The Progenitor placed the clothes next to Alex, and the Guardian began dressing.

"Ah, Eternius," she said as she recognized the angel. "It's been a few million years. I assume this has something to do with your infernal tome."

The Keeper of Fate narrowed his eyes at Alex's mother. "The Libram of Fate has helped keep the Nine Realms safe for the last ten billion years. You don't know what you are talking about."

Odessa crossed her arms. "And neither do you. That book is an atrocity. It forces an eternal conflict that has killed an uncountable number of people."

"How dare you?" Eternius said. "Just like a demon to blame someone else for their evil."

"Just like an angel to refuse to intractably cling to the rules," Odessa hissed.

Alex had had enough. "Both of you, shut up!" He turned to Eternius. The nuts and bolts of a plan began to form in Alex's mind. *I still have about forty minutes.* He remembered what Ureon had said about

285

the Libram of Fate. "Take me to Dae." Alex said. "We need to go to Victory City, somewhere people probably won't see us."

"I can't help you in this," Eternius said.

<The Guardian is the leader of all other Paragons,> the Progenitor chimed. <You must obey him if he is not violating the duties assigned to you. Thus is the will of the First Ones.>

Eternius scowled at the Life Warden. The angel touched the amulet hanging outside of his armor and there was a hollow thump and a golden portal hung in the air. "I'll come back to speak with you again later," Alex told his mother.

She nodded. "Go." The Guardian followed Eternius through the portal.

Alex and Eternius were in an alley between two buildings. He heard the loud bustling city, but the sounds were muted by the thick stone walls to either side. "Wait here for me," Alex said as he jogged down the alley. "I'll be back in no more than thirty minutes."

"Where are you going?" Eternius called after him, but Alex turned the corner without answering. It took Alex a moment to get his bearings when he made it to the road. He turned east and starting running. *I hope I'm here long enough. This is going to be close...* The portal had deposited them near where Alex needed to go, and in just a minute, Alex ran up the stairs of Terra's house.

He opened the door and charged in. Terra's serving woman, Miss Deidra Belles, was in a simple tan dress squeaked and looked as if she may swoon.

"Listen, I need your help," Alex said. "Look at my face, do you recognize me?" The woman fanned herself and took a deep breath. She took one look at him and nodded.

"Yes, Guardian. I go look at your statue every day. What do you need me to do?"

Alex darted to the woman and ushered her to the bedroom. "Terra is in grave danger," he said. He threw open the closet door and pulled open a few drawers. The smaller pieces of his armor were laid out with delicate precision. His helmet, chest plate, and the larger pieces of his leg armor were strapped to an armor dummy. "I need my armor. Take these pieces off of the dummy while I put on the smaller ones."

The woman started stripping the dummy while Alex belted and clamped the masterpiece of dwarven armorsmithing onto his body. It took twenty minutes for the two of them to get Alex covered from scalp to toe in the light platemail. "Thank you," Alex said. He turned and ran out of the room.

Deep down in your core is a sphere, Alex remembered Terra teaching him, *and it pulses with light. With every breath in, it pulses with light. With every breath out, push farther into your core.* He reached the alley where Eternius waited and paused before he went down it.

Alex closed his eyes and focused on the meditation for a moment. He pushed his mind's eye deep into the core of his being. The half-demon took a deep breath, and he saw the black ball that he assumed made up his demonic power. *I hope that's enough. I'm running out of time.* Alex opened his eyes and turned down the alley.

"We rushed here so you could get your armor?" Eternius asked.

I guarantee he won't like what I'm going to do. "And something else. We only have a few minutes left before…"

Eternius nodded and opened the red portal to Caine. "What else did you get?"

"I have it with me," The Guardian said as he went through the portal. Lasers shot all around him, and a man had his arm blown off just in front of them. The Guardian ignored the carnage and ran to where Terra died all of those times. He was about five minutes early, and she wasn't there yet. "Where is she?"

Eternius flew a few yards into the air. He pointed at a small group of people. "There she is." Alex ran toward his wife as fast as he could.

"Terra!" Alex shouted, waving his arm as he ran. Darren and Ell flanked her as they moved across the battlefield.

As soon as Terra saw Alex, she froze. "Alex?" she gasped.

He took a split second to appreciate his wife's beauty. Even with the astounded look on her face, she was the most radiant thing he had ever laid eyes upon with her glowing wings and fiery red hair. "Listen, we don't have much time. You have to come with me now. You aren't safe here and are about to die," Alex blurted out.

Eternius landed next to them, and Alex saw his wife's whole demeanor change. "What is going on?" she demanded.

Alex grabbed his wife's shoulders. "Terra. I love you. Do you trust me?"

Her hazel eyes looked into his green. "Of course I do."

The Guardian spun to Eternius and said, "The Amphitheater of the High Seats, quick."

"What are you planning?" the Keeper demanded as he opened the portal.

Alex pulled Terra through, and Eternius followed. Ell and Darren tried to come through also, but Alex pushed them back. "Sorry, not you two. Find Brahm and let him know I have Terra and that she's safe." Darren nodded, and the portal closed as soon as Alex pulled his hand back through.

The Libram of Fate was open to the last page on the mythricite plinth. The Guardian looked at Terra. *About three minutes left.* Alex pointed at Eternius. "Bind him. He can't interfere, or you will die." The angel's eyes grew wide as Terra wrapped him up in the same field she had used when he was on Dae.

"What is the meaning of this?" the Keeper demanded.

Alex grabbed the hilt of his sword on Terra's belt. As soon as his hand wrapped around the hilt, it changed into the silver stopwatch.

<Again?>

No, I'm done. There was another flash of light, and Alex held the wooden form of the Guardian's Blade.

<Are you sure about this, Alex?> the Voice of Balance asked him. <If you do it, they'll live, but you have no idea what you're doing.>

I don't care. I can finally save them.

Alex called upon the Wrathblade, and it appeared in a burst of heat and fire. The blade gleamed in the harsh white sunlight, and the leather creaked under Alex's grip. *Two minutes*, he thought. The Wrathblade drew Alex's anger to the forefront of his mind.

"I watched you die hundreds of times," Alex said, his voice shaking with rage. "I tried everything I could think of to save your life." The Guardian's pulse pounded through his head as his blood heated. "But I couldn't because of that damn book." Alex pointed at the Libram of Fate with the point of his sword.

"What are you going to do?" Terra asked.

Strength flooded through his arms as his demonic powers stormed through his body. Eternius's eyes widened when he saw Alex's eyes turn solid green with no pupil or white. "I'm going to destroy it," the Guardian said. The flames licking the sides of the Wrathblade turned from red to black as Alex focused his demonic power into it. *Less than a minute.*

"Do you have the faintest inkling of the consequences, Half-Demon?" Eternius shouted.

"I do," Alex said. He walked to the Libram of Fate with the Wrathblade by his side. "It will save their lives." The Guardian roared as he lifted the black-flamed blade and brought it down on the angelic tome.

A bubble of light protected the Libram of Fate, and the Guardian bore down with all his might. The demonic energy ripped through the shield, and the pages curled as the black flames fed on them. The mythricite plinth shattered as the Wrathblade slammed into it.

There was a shudder in the air, and Eternius ripped through the spell Terra had wove around him. "You fool! You have doomed us all!"

Alex let out a breath. The Guardian's Blade returned to its wooden form. He walked to Terra and put his arm around her waist. "I love you," he said.

Tears ran down Terra's face. "I love you too," she whispered. She spun in his arm and wrapped her arms around him with her wings spread wide.

"You," Eternius said. Terra broke away from Alex and looked at her father. The angel was pointing at her with a shaking finger. "You are pregnant." His finger shifted to Alex. "With his child."

"Yes, I am," Terra said. "What of it?"

Alex had seen many different expressions on the Keeper's face, but fear was a new one. "Do you even know what kind of abomination you are carrying?"

Other angels began landing around them. In seconds, the couple was surrounded. Alex didn't recognize any of the newcomers. The Guardian unleashed the Wrathblade again and fed everything he had into it. The black flames roared; they devoured the light from the surroundings.

"Half-demon," one of the angels said.

"What has he done to the Libram?" another asked.

Alex glanced around. *There're twenty-three of them.* "Eternius, I did what had to be done. My mother was right, and I just didn't see it before. The Libram had to be destroyed."

"The Libram was the only thing keeping the forces of Hell from casting us all into oblivion," Eternius said. "You destroyed the page where you killed Azreal and saved the Nine Realms. Anything could happen now."

"That's how it should be!" Alex roared. "How can there be balance when one Realm decides the fates of all others?"

Eternius glared at Alex. "You are an ignorant fool. You don't know what you've done. You don't even know what kind of monster grows in your wife's womb!"

A gasp rose from the on-looking angels. "Nephilim," rippled around Alex.

"I don't care. Terra is my wife, and Jessica is my daughter, and if any of you try to place a hand on either one, that is a hand you will lose. Open a portal to Caine. There is a battle to finish. Join us and help forge a new path for the Nine Realms free of Fate's interference."

"No," several of the angels said. Alex moved Terra behind him with a hand. The Nexus spread her wings wide, and a spear of white light appeared in her hands. All of the surrounding angels except Eternius drew swords. Back to back, the half-demon and the half-angel stood ready to defend themselves.

They are going to go after her. I'll have to be fast. Alex shifted his feet so he could be ready to dart in any direction.

There was a thump in the air, and a red portal hovered a few feet in front of Alex. "Go," Eternius said. "You will come to regret what you've done this day."

Alex guided Terra through the portal. He waited for her to pass all of the way through before he said, "I doubt that." The Guardian stepped through the portal, and it closed behind them.

Chapter Twenty-one – A Battle Won

Alex and Terra looked at the battlefield with Odin's statue behind them. The Obsidian Tower stood a couple of miles away. The Guardian looked at his wife and smiled. *I finally did it. She's really here.* The Wrathblade's black flames turned red then went out as Alex's anger diminished, but he had mastered that form of the Guardian's Blade, forcing the sword to stay in its more dangerous form no longer required him to feel the inundating rage.

Tears ran down Terra's face still. "I can't believe it," she said as she looked at him. "How is this possible? You died!"

Alex's smile split into a large grin. "I've always wanted to say this: 'Rumors of my demise have been greatly exaggerated.'" A nearby explosion as a Battlesuit was destroyed made the two of them duck. Alex grabbed Terra's hand. "We have a battle to finish," he said and pulled her along.

"I don't understand," Terra said as she snatched up a discarded sword from the ground. The point was broken off, but she was running low on magical energy and needed a weapon that wouldn't drain it. Terra let go of her husband and transferred the sword to her main hand. "I watched you die and your body fade away."

A fifteen-foot-tall demon slammed into the ground before the two of them. It held a large spiked mace in either hand. Alex darted around the demon and hamstrung it with the Wrathblade. "You thought you finally got rid of me, didn't you?" Alex joked as the demon fell to its knees.

Terra channeled magical power into her own body and leapt impossibly high into the air. She flipped in mid air and brought the sword down on the demon's skull. With a loud crack, her broken blade sank deep into the Hellspawn's brain. Her momentum carried Terra over the demon, and the sword was ripped from her hands. She landed next to Alex and looked at him with pursed lips and narrowed eyes. "Do you ever take anything seriously?"

Alex laughed. "I'm trying to cut down, actually." Terra rolled her eyes at him. "Sorry, I'm busy being the happiest man alive right now. I'll explain everything later. Promise." His wife nodded, and Alex saw a few familiar faces running over.

"It's bloody abou' time ye showed up, boy," the dwarf said with a smile. Alex shook with mirth.

Caitlyn padded over to him in her primal form. She touched her wet nose to his forehead. "Darren said you had taken Terra somewhere."

"Yeah," Alex said. "I had to go destroy the Libram of Fate real quick. I would have stopped to say hi if I'd had time, but I was in a bit of a rush."

"You WHAT?" Caitlyn and Brahm both shouted at the same time.

Alex held his left hand out in a soothing gesture. "It's a long story that I don't want to think about too much right now. What's the status of the battle?"

Michael, Kara, and the one-eyed einherijar Alex recognized as Odin walked over. "We already destroyed the Obsidian Tower to the west," the Justicar explained. "Azreal had all but abandoned it, choosing instead to mass all of his forces here. We have killed most of his army, but there is still some resistance. It's heavier around the tower, but he can't hold under the might of Ragnarok."

Alex held out his hand to Michael. "It's nice to meet you in the flesh. I'm the Guardian, Alex Zane."

The Justicar shook his hand. "Same here. It is good to see that you are not dead." The sound of steel being torn apart came from near the Obsidian Tower. "We will need to finish this later. There is an Overlord in that tower that will know what it means to incur the Justicar's ire."

The group cut their way across the battlefield and made it to the bottom of the Obsidian Tower. Demons and undead flooded through the four openings at the base like a black tide of death. Einherijar that had been summoned by the Gjallerhorn formed a perimeter of blood and steel and held the forces of Hell and Ignia at bay.

Michael lifted the warhorn and blew it twice, giving the signal to press the attack forward. The united strength of the three Paragons helped the Cainen army surge ahead. They were able to advance as far as the large black openings but could not gain a foothold in the tower itself. Alex saw that the enormous gateway arch in the center of the tower shown with a muddy brown color and reinforcements from Hell were pouring through.

We have to push through this, Alex thought. The Guardian tried to call on his demonic powers once more, but he had exhausted what little he had been able to collect destroying the Libram. The flames on the Wrathblade were guttering low. Alex was reaching the limits of his strength. Looking at his wife, he saw Terra had acquired a bow and arrows from an einherijar and was firing into the mass of hellspawn.

"Terra," Alex shouted over the roars of pain and screams of death.

She looked over at him. "What?"

"Link me as your Shield!"

Terra looked at him like he was crazy. She fired a few more arrows into the mass. "Right now?"

"Yes, right now!" the Guardian yelled. "I'll be able to get us inside."

She shook her head. "Alex, I don't have much magical power left. If I use it for that, I won't have any left if we run into Azreal."

"I'll deal with the Overlord," Kara sneered as she cut down a Daemon. "I'll kill him with my bare hands if I must." She lifted her arm into the air and blocked a blow with a blue vambrace. *Looks like she had a second set of armor...*

"Protect us while we do this," Terra said. Alex fell out of the front line and stood in front of her. She placed her hands on his head, and those closest formed a ring of steel around them. "Why do you do this every time there's a big battle?" she asked as a beam of light shot into the air.

"I've only done this once before," he protested. "And that was a special circumstance." Alex began to become aware of Terra's emotions and condition across the link. He could close his eyes and feel her love for him shining like a light through the darkness. "I just found out you were pregnant, and that I was dying."

"Mhmm," she hummed with a smirk. She laughed and gave her head a gentle shake, and Terra's smile widened as the link spread to her. "Now kiss me, you big oaf," she said as she pulled his head down to her.

Alex closed his eyes and kissed his wife. Terra's soft lips were warm against his, and her finger's curled in his brown hair. The bond regained its familiar feeling of permanence, and the pillar of light exploded from around them with a boom. They separated, and Alex rested his forehead against hers.

"Love you, beautiful," he said.

"I love you too, handsome."

"If you two are done," Caitlyn shouted, "then we could use some help here!"

Alex started to turn to leap into the fray, but Terra didn't release his head. "Alex," she said, "I'm almost out of magical power. You will only have a few seconds."

Alex winked at her. "That's all I need." Terra released him, and Alex felt strength and energy flow through his veins. He took a deep breath and drew on the rage of the Wrathblade. The magical flames rekindled, and The Guardian launched himself over the front line into the mass of demons and undead.

With a roar, Alex swung the Wrathblade, willing the flames to burn higher. A razor thin line of fire shot out of the tip of the sword and cleaved the monsters in two in a large semi-circle before him. The Cainen einherijar charged past him, cutting down any Alex had missed. Michael smashed his way to the obsidian gateway arch and brought Mjolnir down on it.

With a crack like thunder, the gateway shattered into thousands of shards. The energy from the link faded, and Terra walked over to where Alex stood. The base of the tower was secure.

"Thank you, Guardian," Michael said.

Alex shook his head. "No need. Let's go get Azreal."

"No," Michael said. "Kara, Odin, and I will deal with him. You and Terra are dead on your feet. Go back to Hanna and wait for us there."

"Are you sure?" Terra asked.

The Justicar nodded. "We will be more than a match for him, if he's even still here. Please, you were

only just reunited; it would pain me to see something happen to you."

"What are you doing?" Doctor Sigma Moore demanded.

Azreal glared at him. "You will watch your tone with me, Human." The Demon Lord was slicing the umbilical cables suspending the all of the valkyrie in their extraction pods. "This tower is about to fall, but I will not allow them to rebuild their forces." The Overlord sliced through another bunch of the black cables with his telekinetic powers. The brown haired valkyrie began to thrash as her air ran out.

There was an explosion as the door to the extraction chamber blew open. The metal door slammed into the closest pod, and the glass cylinder shattered. "Another one," a man's voice said. A moment passed before the man spoke again, "These valkyrie are alive!"

Doctor Moore spun about to see that Azreal had vanished. The scientist ran over to his desk and rifled about for the recall device that would teleport him back to his compound on Fyr. *Where is the blasted thing! I left it right here.*

"You!" a woman shouted at him. "Stop right there."

"Not likely," he said. Sigma Moore turned to run up the stairs to the throne room, but a one-eyed man holding a spear blocked his path.

A valkyrie in blue armor drew up to him. She was holding a phaseblade that lit up the surrounding area. "I am Kara, the Shield Maiden. You are in league with the Overlord." Kara put the tip of the blue phaseblade at the base of his throat. His skin sizzled as the sword of force burned him.

"Prepare to face justice," Kara said.

"And then we made it here," Alex said, as he finished telling the story of what him went through since he awoke on Aria. All of the Daein had returned to the camp with he and Terra and were all gathered around a fire pit as Alex told the story. He looked at Terra. "I'm sorry it took me so long to save you."

Terra wasn't sure how she felt about his story. *Alex saw me die hundreds of times,* she thought. "So I should be dead."

Her husband slammed his fist down on his armored thigh. "No!" he said. "You shouldn't. The only thing that said you should, the only thing that was forcing it to happen, was the Libram of Fate. Eternius made the damn thing, but that doesn't mean he's infallible, and it doesn't mean he's right."

"But you heard what Eternius told us," Terra said. "You destroyed the page where you kill Azreal. His forces could win."

"You did what?" Caitlyn demanded.

Alex glared at the changeling. Darren sat beside her, but the two were unusually distant compared to how they behaved when he had first seen them together. "I couldn't read the Libram," Alex said, "and even if I could, it wouldn't have mattered. I was *not* going to let Terra die."

Caitlyn nodded. "I agree," she said with a placating gesture. "We just have to be careful to not do anything too rash and make sure Azreal doesn't win."

"Alex, you saw…a lot," Hanna said. "Are you sure you are all right?" Terra saw a shadow pass over Alex's face, but it disappeared as fast as it had come.

Alex smiled at the girl. "I will be." Hanna nodded. Her laser rifle had broken near the beginning of the fighting, and Terra had sent her back here with a group of einherijar to treat any wounded.

There was a crack of thunder, and a cheer went up from the einherijar standing guard. The Daein all stood and looked in the direction from which the thunder had come. The Obsidian Tower had exploded in a column of light just like the one on Dae had. Lights settled all around them, and the wounded Realm came back to life.

Terra let out a sigh of relief. *At last, the Inner Realms are free.* "It's done. The last Obsidian Tower has fallen."

"No, it's not," Alex said. "It's not over until Azreal is dead."

"That'll no' be as easy a task as ye think," Brahm said. Everyone looked at the aged dwarf. "First, ye'll have to kill him on another Realm or catch him while he's on Hell. Then, dependin' on which ye do, ye'll have to deal with the biggest problem o' fightin' on Hell."

Alex nodded. "The darkness," he said. "I know. I just haven't come up with anything yet."

"Aye, that's a big one, but that's no' what I'm referrin' to." The Guardian looked at the dwarf in confusion. "The Hellgate," Brahm said.

Alex rubbed his head. Back on Dae, he had had the previous Guardians' memories flooding into his brain, one of them was of a Guardian assaulting the Hellgate, but they hadn't returned when he got his memories back.

<You're welcome for that, by the way,> the Voice of Balance sent.

"What do you mean, 'You're welcome.'?" Alex asked.

The aspect of the Guardian's Blade that was Alex replied, <I didn't want you to have to deal with that again. Maegan was pushing all of the information held within the Guardian's Blade into your mind. There was nothing she could do to stop it.

<It seems the mind imprinted on the Voice of Balance must be in sync with the mind of the wielder to prevent information overload. The process takes a very long time. Years. The Guardian dies before the synchronization takes place. It looks like we were meant for each other all this time,> the Voice of Balance finished.

The Guardian laughed. "You're so conceited. And thank you." He looked around, and everyone was staring at him with shocked and confused expressions.

"It... It's happening already?" Terra said. "You're hearing the voices aren't you."

Alex put his hand over Terra's. "There's nothing to worry about this time. The memories won't overwhelm me. I'm in the blade to keep that from happening."

Brahm swore. "He just got the bloody thing back, an' he's already loosin' his mind."

Laughing, Alex shook his head. "Okay, I can see how that would sound crazy. The minds of the previous Guardians are imprinted on the blade when they die. They teach the Guardian how to use the sword. I died using it, so my mind is imprinted on it. That's how I remember everything that happened while you were on Caine, my mind was there to collect the information and pass it to me when I got the Guardian's Blade back."

They all stared at him and didn't say anything. "None of you believe me?" Alex asked.

"It's not that we don't believe you," Caitlyn said. "It's just, how could you possibly know what was going on while you were dead?"

Alex held his hands out. "Because the Guardian's Blade was with Terra the entire time," he repeated. No one spoke, and Alex crossed his arms. *Fine*, he thought. "Caitlyn, it was very nice of you to play peacemaker between Darren and Ell when they were arguing. Terra, if you were having stomach pains before the fight where you summoned those two walls, then you should have said something. Hanna, thank you for taking care of my wife and daughter in that same battle; there's no way I can ever repay you."

The little girl grinned, but the other two looked at him with wide eyes. "Do me next!" Ell said as she waved her arm in the air.

Alex laughed at the half-elf's easy-going manner. "Your humor really helped Terra through a tough time, Ell. Thank you for that, and your skill with knives is amazing. Those are something I struggle with, and I'd like it if you could show me how you fight with them some time."

Ell grinned at him. "Any time, Guardian. That's amazing. So you really saw everything that Terra went through while you were dead?"

Alex nodded. "I did." He looked at his wife. "I just wish I could have been there." He felt Terra's happiness and love thrum across the link.

"I know," she said. "But you're here now, and that's what's important."

A feeling of confusion and worry flowed across the link, and Alex frowned. "What's wrong?" he asked.

"It's just what Eternius said about Jessica. Why would he say that?" Terra asked.

Alex shrugged. "I don't know. What was it the other angels called her?"

"Nephilim," Terra said.

"What did you say?" Michael asked as he strode into the camp. Kara was dragging a man in white coat by the collar. Terra repeated the word. "I've heard that before."

The valkyrie threw the man to the ground before them. He lifted his head, and Alex saw the man's ratty face and roach black eyes. Terra's temper flared across the link, and the Guardian held out a restraining hand before she could attack the man. "Moore," she said.

"Who is this?" Alex asked.

Terra glared at the groveling lab-coated man. "He's the one that made the extraction pods. He's the one that put me in one of them! That man volunteered to help Azreal so he would have a chance to use his machine on people!"

"That's enough evidence for me," Kara said. The blue beam of her phaseblade flicked on, and she lifted it above the man in both hands, point down.

Kara had just begun her downward strike and hesitated when Alex shouted, "Wait!"

"Why?" Terra and Kara asked at the same time.

Alex leaned in close to Terra and whispered in her ear. "So far, the only ones from Fyr that have attacked us have been mercenaries. If we kill this man, they could take it as a declaration of war and join with Azreal."

303

"Alex," she whispered back with a harsh tone, "this man has done more to help Azreal than any other. He's the reason Azreal is so powerful and deserves to die."

The Guardian nodded. "I understand and agree with you, Terra. But not like this. I'm not asking you to forgive him or to not kill him. Just to not do it like this." Alex was silent while Terra wrestled with her anger.

"Fine," she said after some time. Terra beckoned Kara and Michael over. Odin took the valkyrie's place over the doctor, pressing the butt of his spear into the man's back to keep him in place. Moore moaned in pain.

"What is it, Terra?" Michael asked.

"We think you shouldn't kill him yet. He should stand a proper trial on his home Realm," Terra said with a grimace.

"Are you mad?" Kara snapped. "The Fyrians are in the palm of Azreal's hand. He'll walk free."

"Not all of the people of the Realm of Science think as Doctor Moore does. The Architect is sympathetic to our cause," Terra said. "The trial will be fair, and by that I mean he will certainly be executed. It just sends the wrong message to Fyr if we kill him."

Kara crossed her arms. Michael looked at his valkyrie while they had a discussion across their bond. Kara huffed loudly and stormed away. "Moore will be your prisoner until he can be transferred to Fyrian custody," Michael said.

"Brahm," Alex said. The dwarf walked over. "Could you take custody of the good doctor?" the Guardian asked. "Make sure he remains silent."

The dwarf nodded and lifted Doctor Moore by his upper arms. Brahm slammed his forehead into the

Fyrian scientist's, and the man's eyes crossed before he went limp. "This'll do fer ye?" he asked.

Alex smiled. "Perfect." *I'll need to ensure we interrogate him before we give him up, though.* "Darren, you and Ell help Brahm keep an eye on the man. I don't want him to get a hold of a knife and think he's a hero."

Odin appeared by Michael's side. "Our time here has come to an end, old friend. We must return from whence we came."

The Justicar clasped forearms with the einherijar. "Thank you, Odin."

"There is no need to thank us," Odin said as he began to fade away. "It is why we exist. Call us, when you need us." The transparent apparition smiled. "But make sure there's a feast next time!"

Michael laughed. "I will." Odin and the other einherijar summoned by the Gjallerhorn faded away.

A large group of women Alex had not seen through all of the summoned einherijar stood not far away with only scraps of cloth covering them. Every one of them had a haggard and exhausted look. Kara was talking to a small cluster of them.

"Those are all that remain of the ten thousand valkyrie. A mere five hundred." Michael shook his head. "Azreal began executing einherijar and valkyrie alike as soon as it was clear he was not going to be able to hold Caine. It will take time for more to be birthed from Yggdrasil." The women Kara was speaking with began to move north to the ruined fortress city of Valgarde. Kara looked at Michael for a few moments before going with them.

"Are you going with her?" Alex asked.

Shaking his head again, Michael said, "No. There's something I must show you two first, and the city is secure. Kara will have no problem getting them there. I told her what I needed to do."

Telepathy would be nice, the Guardian said.

<Yeah, it's pretty great,> the Voice of Balance sent into his mind.

Ha... ha... ha... Alex thought. The Voice of Balance howled in laughter then fell silent, leaving the Guardian in peace.

"You both need to come with me," the Justicar said. Caitlyn and Hanna stood to go with them. "Fenris told me something, but it will be only for the two of them, I think. I'm sorry, but you two will need to wait here."

"It's all right," Alex said. "I'll be back soon. You aren't losing me all over again." The changelings nodded in unison and sat back down. Alex took Terra's hand in his and followed Michael to the southwest. "Where are we going?"

Michael looked over at them. "Beneath Yggdrasil."

It took almost six hours to walk to the gateway arch. There was a large wooden cave on the other side of the wooden semicircle. "This leads to the roots of Yggdrasil," Michael said. "Follow me." The Justicar held Mjolnir high in the air and the hammer began to glow with white light.

Alex and Terra followed behind him. The tunnel floor was smooth and went downward in a slow spiral. "What is this all about?" Alex asked.

"When I was undergoing the Trial of Will, Fenris showed me a war between two very powerful forms of life. It's hard to describe in words... I was able to overhear a conversation between two First Ones, and they were talking about 'the Nephilim'. I asked the wolf about it, but he said it was not for me to hear. I think he knew one or both of you would be coming by to find out about it."

"How is that possible?" Terra asked. "How could a spirit that lives inside a tree know that Alex would be coming here? He was dead."

"I think we are being played like pieces on a board," Alex said. "My mother knew of Eternius, but he had never seen her before. At least, he didn't act like he had. Plus, when I was on Bara, an angel named Ureon told me that there were forces at work that I wouldn't understand, and that the Nine Realms was growing weak."

Terra looked at him in the gloom. "Are you really suggesting that a tree knew you were going to go back in time and rescue me?"

Alex shook his head. "No, I'm suggesting that a tree knew I was going to rescue you. It's irrelevant how I did it... as far as the tree cares," he said as he glanced at the ancient roots that made up the ceiling of the tunnel.

The walkway ended in a circular cave with dirt walls, floor, and ceiling. The roots hanging down from above glowed white. *Bioluminescent tree roots. That's something you don't see every day,* Alex thought. "What do we do to talk to the wolf?" he asked.

"Touch the glowing roots," Michael said. "Fenris should do the rest."

Alex nodded. He walked to the roots and took Terra's hand again. "Are you ready?" he asked.

"I am," she said. Each grabbed a root and looked around in confusion. Terra looked at Michael. "Is something supposed to happen?"

"Uh, yeah. Maybe I was wrong," he said, abashed.

<Alex,> the Voice of Balance sent, <both of you hold me and touch the root with the tip of the blade.> The Guardian drew his sword and had Terra place the hand he wasn't holding above his on the hilt of the sword. They touched the thickest root with the tip of the Guardian's Blade. Everything went white, and the Guardian's Blade disappeared from their grasp.

"Hello?" Alex called. His voice sounded flat in the emptiness, and he held Terra's hand tighter.

"Is anyone there?" Terra said.

A colossal wolf with shaggy hair and large brown eyes appeared before them. Seeing the wolf made Alex remember why everything seemed so familiar. "Wait a second," Alex said. "This is all from Norse mythology. Odin, Fenris, Yggdrasil, this entire place is from my freshman English class!"

The wolf threw back his head and laughed. "I can say with complete honesty that that's the first time I've ever gotten that reaction from someone seeing me," Fenris said. "What are they saying about me on Earth these days?"

Alex wracked his brain trying to remember. "That you bit off a guy's hand and were tied up somewhere until the end of the world."

Fenris snorted derisively. "That's slander! It was a thumb, not a hand, and he started it! I'm not tied up, I'm caged in a jail of wood to help you humans keep existing."

"Sorry," Alex said. "I didn't mean to offend you."

The wolf shook his head. "Don't worry yourself about it, Guardian. Stay out of current affairs for a few billion years, and you're lucky if they remember you at all."

"A few billion years?" Alex asked. "How is that possible when humans didn't even evolve until... what, two-hundred thousand years ago?"

Fenris barked a laugh. "There are so many things you don't know, Guardian. Too many things for you to be swing-ing around that sword without knowing the consequences.

"The Nine Realms have existed in their current form for the last ten billion years. One of the several functions of the Libram of Fate is to ensure the resolution of any major conflicts prior to the Celestial Culmination."

"What's that?" Terra asked.

"Every hundred thousand years," Fenris explained, "the Source returns the Nine Realms to the same state it was in when they were first created. Every world, person, animal, even blade of grass is reset. For the most part, only the angels and demons know what is happening. For the last ten billion years, the same hundred thousand have been repeated."

Alex put his hand on his chin in thought. "So now that the Libram is destroyed, will these Celestial Culminations stop?"

Fenris shook his head. "They will continue to occur, but now that you destroyed one of the most important artifacts in existence, the Nine Realms are in grave danger. If this war isn't resolved before the Source peaks in energy, then the angels will be at a vast disadvantage. They are outnumbered by the demons, and all of their allies will have forgotten the conflict was even happening. Azreal must be defeated soon."

Alex grimaced. *I had no idea something like that was happening.* He looked at his wife. *I don't care though. I made the right decision.* "How long do we have?"

"A hundred years," Fenris said.

Terra and Alex sagged with relief.

"Give or take a hundred years," the wolf added.

Alex frowned at Fenris. "So it could happen very soon or not soon at all."

Shrugging his front shoulders, Fenris said, "Well, soon is a relative term, but I don't think we came to talk about semantics. So, what does bring two Paragons to honor me with their presence?"

"I think you know," Terra said. "We want to know about Nephilim."

Fenris sat down on his haunches and looked down on her. "I can see why you come seeking this information. Very well, free of charge, since I happen to like half-breeds. What do you want to know?"

"What is a Nephilim?" Alex asked.

A person appeared in the space space between Fenris, Alex, and Terra, facing the latter two. The man had tan skin with short white hair and was tall, topping seven feet, but that wasn't his most striking feature. He had the feathered wings of an angel, but they were black, and his human eyes glowed with red light.

"This is a Nephilim," Fenris asked. "This is what is created when a half-angel and a half-demon have a child. The Nephilim were the only thing the angels and demons agreed upon in the time before the Dawn."

Terra tore her eyes from the imposing figure. "What do you mean?"

The Nephilim disappeared. Everything turned black, and the three of them floated on a white wooden disc. "I'll show you," Fenris said.

Chapter Twenty-two – The Purge

The white disc rocketed past islands that floated in the Void. Some were barren, but others held various forms of life, some animal, some verdant. The disc stopped above a large crater on a barren rock and descended. Their wooden transportation landed, and Alex saw a natural tunnel in the crater wall.

"We walk from here," Fenris said, his voice thick with emotion. Alex and Terra looked at each other with confused expressions.

I wonder what's wrong? Alex thought. *He was joking around before...* He felt Terra's curiosity on the link, and they followed behind the wolf. The tunnel was far too small for Fenris's bulk, and the mythological creature shrank to the size of an arctic wolf and padded through the tunnel.

It turned ahead, and there was no source of illumination. Alex couldn't see. He felt Terra's sense of alarm grow when she tried to create a magical light and couldn't. "Fenris," she called, "we can't see where we are going."

"Hold on to my tail. Guardian, hold your wife. I'll lead you through this darkness. We'll be through it soon."

Alex held Terra's hand as they were led through the passage. The tunnel turned many more times before there was a glow ahead. The wolf and two Paragons stood in a lush underground cave with eight stone huts, a grove of trees, and a waterfall. The light came from a luminous globe hanging from the top of the thirty foot ceiling. A pair of small wolf pups wrestled not far away.

Fenris glanced at the two pups and kept walking. In the middle of the cluster of low roofed homes stood a large cauldron on a pile of red stones. A yellow substance in the cauldron bubbled. Alex heard what sounded like chickens from behind one of the huts. A half-angel with glowing pink wings and black hair stepped from the largest hut, and a she-wolf the same size as Fenris padded beside her.

"Before you ask," Fenris said, "no, they can't see or hear us."

"Why did you bring us here?" Alex asked.

The wolf looked back at him. "Be silent, and you will answer that question yourself."

"So," the she-wolf said, "Xorn got you pregnant again, did he?"

The half-angel laughed. "How did you know that Kirin?"

Kirin snorted like she was sneezing, "You reek of pregnancy. I can smell it around you like a cloud."

"Aw, do you miss smelling like that?" the half-angel asked as she lifted a large wooden stick that rested over the bubbling cauldron. She stuck the stirring rod into the yellow concoction and mixed it. "It's only been, what, three months since you had your little ones."

The she-wolf looked at the two pups, still play wrestling. "That's how long it's been. I just wish my mate would return with your husband and oldest. They go hunting for far too long at a time, Emorial."

The pink-winged half-angel shook her head and laughed again. "You know they come back as fast as they can." A little boy with white hair and black wings ran out of the house Kirin and Emorial had come from. He wore brown breeches and no shirt, giggling as he charged at the two wolf pups. "You be careful with Lupus and Fen, do you hear me, Rius?"

"Yes, Mom," the little Nephilim called back. He dove into the rolling ball of fur that was the two wolves at play and joined in the wrestling.

"Food's almost ready," Emorial called. Five more Nephilim boys, none of them appearing to be older than a teenager, walked out of two of the other huts. "You boys go wash up," she said, "then we can eat."

"All right, Mom," the youngest of them grumped. The five of them spread wings and flew over to the waterfall.

Something's not right here, Alex thought.

"Why aren't there any girl Nephilim?" Terra asked, putting her finger on the oddness of the situation.

"Perceptive," Fenris said. "Wait." The wolf had been watching the two women talk and was growing more agitated as the conversation went on.

"We're hoping it's a girl this time," the half-angel said. "I've always wanted a girl."

"I've told you time and again how rare girl Nephilim are, Em," Kirin said. "It would be a miracle if you had one after only seven boys."

Emorial sighed. "I know... It would be nice though."

"That it would," Kirin said with a wolven grin. "Then we would be a little less outnumbered with all these men about."

The half-angel laughed, a kind, lilting sound that echoed in the cave. "That it would. I was hoping there would be another girl when we found out you were pregnant."

There was a deep rumbling in the air that neither Emorial or Kirin noticed, and it took Alex a moment to figure out that Fenris was growling. *What's going on?* he wondered. There was a yelp from the entrance to the cave. Alex and Terra both turned to look, but Fenris kept his eyes locked on Kirin.

A pair of monsters that looked like a cross between a spider and a man were devouring the two wolf pups.

A demon was holding the smallest Nephilim in his arms, one across the boy's chest, another wrapped around his head. With a wrenching crackle, the demon snapped the child's neck, and he collapsed to the ground.

Emorial screamed. Kirin grew to many times her original size and lunged at the demons. An angel with golden armor came from the mouth of the tunnel and hurled a glowing trident at the she-wolf. The polearm struck her in the eye, and Kirin collapsed dead on the spot, shrinking back to her original size as she fell.

The five boys had heard their mother scream and came running. A brutal fight ensued with the unarmed Nephilim killing many times their number of demons and angels. The boys were able to wrest away weapons and held their ground for a time, but in the end, the invaders' superior numbers overwhelmed them. The five Nephilim had their heads cut off by the demons, and they were tossed about like they were gruesome toys.

Emorial had collapsed to her knees, still holding the four-foot-long wooden stirring rod. Three angels stood around her, and a fourth approached from the entrance of the cave. The demons gave the angel a wide berth and scrambled from the cave as soon as they could. Drawing a large two-handed claymore made from the same golden material as his armor, the angel stopped before the sobbing woman.

"Look at me," the angel said, shaking with rage. Tear stained cheeks and red rimmed eyes rose. "Emorial, you are charged with giving birth to Nephilim. How do you plead?"

"Why would you do this, Father?" she asked.

Emorial's father spread his wings wide. "You are no daughter of mine!" he roared.

A sudden fire rose in the half-angel. She sprang to her feet and slammed the thick stirring rod against the side of her father's face. The other three angels wrestled the wooden stick away from her and pushed her back to her knees. Her father had been knocked a few steps to the right. He spat, and blood spattered the ground.

"What is it, Father? Do your grandchildren displease you? Well, you've killed them all," she lied. "I hope you are pleased with yourself."

"Emorial," her father said after he spat more blood from his mouth again, "you have admitted guilt to the commission of a crime for which the sentence is death. As your accuser and the highest angel present, I shall carry out your sentence by means of beheading." The angel looked at the other three. "Hold her down."

Two of the angels bent her forward, but she turned her head to look up into her father's eyes. "If only you could see..." Emorial said. "I forgive you for the senseless murder you are about to commit, but not for those that were carried out at your order. My children did nothing wrong."

Her father gazed upon his daughter. "Their existence was wrong." The angel lifted the claymore high.

"I love you, Father," she said.

The blade slammed down, and Emorial's head fell to the ground. Blood spurted from her neck, and the angels let go of her body. Her father cleaned his sword on a piece of cloth. "Tainted filth," he said as he tossed the cloth away. The four angels strode from the cave.

"Why would they do that?" Alex demanded. He looked over at where Fenris had been standing, but the wolf was gone. Casting about for him, Alex found the wolf sitting beside Kirin's body. Fenris lifted his head and let out a mournful howl. *Oh, no.*

Alex and Terra walked to the wolf. They each knelt beside him. "I'm so sorry," Terra said. "She was your mate."

Fenris nodded. "And those were my pups. The last time I saw them, they couldn't even walk... I never did see them walk..." He took a deep breath and rose to all four feet. "This is how we found them. I don't know what really happened this day, but this is the most likely thing. Emorial was always talking about how she wanted a daughter, and my mate was ever the practical wolf."

"But why?" Alex asked. "Why would they do this?"

Fenris sighed. "Nephilim men are very strong, terrifyingly so. When Emorial told her youngest to be careful with my pups, she was being serious. He could have accidentally snapped one of their spines if he hugged one too hard."

"That doesn't explain why the angels *and* the demons would want them dead," Terra said. "Or why there were only male Nephilim."

"Male Nephilim aren't... compatible with other races. If one tried copulating with a weaker being, then the woman would be killed by the childbearing process. For a female Nephilim to be born is rare," Fenris explained. "One in a thousand, if that low. Nephilim have the ability to conceal their nature. The process is similar to how a changeling changes forms, but they are born with the ability." The wolf looked up into Terra's eyes. "Female Nephilim are only a little stronger than a large man, but their real power lies within.

"Female Nephilim can use both magic and demonic power simultaneously and are capable of intellectual leaps that make the most brilliant of any race seem a bit dim," he continued. "This makes them capable of things we can't even dream of."

"I still don't understand why they would do this," Alex said. "What would provoke such hatred that two races at each other's throats would join forces?"

Fenris began walking to the waterfall, and they followed him. "The floating islands in the Void can be much larger than the ones you saw. Some are as big as planets, just out there, hurtling through the emptiness. One of those was called Warren, and it was home to both angels and demons. The angels thrived on the lush surface of the planet, and the demons eked out a harsh living in the hot bowels."

The wolf sat down at the edge of the lake the waterfall cascaded into and continued. "The angels had a peaceful life, while the demons fought for every inch of their war-torn existence. After a time, a demon exploring for food stumbled upon a labyrinthine network of tunnels that led to the surface. The angels welcomed him with open arms and shared their food and homes with the curious outsider. He returned home with fantastical tales of abundance and an offer of friendship, but the other demons only saw another opportunity to strike.

"War enveloped the planet as the demons surged from their holes to attack the angels. It raged for hundreds of years while Warren soared through the Void. Eventually, it collided with another planet that contained an interesting race, a race unknown to both angels and demons."

"Humanity," Alex said.

Fenris nodded. "That's right, Guardian. The two planets exploded, scattering humans, angels, and demons across the emptiness. That was when something new happened. For the first time since time began, half-breeds began to walk the void. It was only a matter of time, a very long time, that a half-angel and a half-demon met and fell in love. Their child was the first Nephilim, a woman named Eve."

"I thought female Nephilim were rare," Terra said.

"They are!" Fenris said with wonder in his voice. "Oh, she was beautiful and so intelligent, and her birth was a miracle to behold."

"You were there?" Alex asked.

Fenris barked a soft, sad laugh. "I was. Eve was the only female Nephilim I have ever met in my eternal life," he said. "The island she lived upon was neutral in the conflict between angels and demons. We only wanted to live in peace. It was only her parents, Eve, and me." Fenris laughed again. "A girl and her wolf." He seemed lost in thought for a time before he continued his story.

"The island flew through the Void at an astounding speed, and we ended up crashing into a larger one that the angels and demons were fighting over. Neither side knew who we were, and both attacked. Eve killed them all, by herself. She would just look from one to the next, and they would keel over dead. One or two of them must have escaped to spread the story, and after that, there was a bounty on her head.

"A long time passed, and we thought we were safe. One day, we heard a boy Nephilim had been born to a half-angel we had met years before. We searched her out, but it was too late. An army of angels and demons had descended upon them and left none alive. We arrived just in time for the army to turn and attack us. Eve died, but Mariel, her mother, used her magical power to teleport me to safety. After that, I found Kirin.

"Together, we decided to try protecting the Nephilim, that's when we sniffed out Emorial and

Xorn and their two children, living in this rock. It was pure luck that we found them. We were leaping from island to island, and I managed to land right in the mouth of the tunnel." Fenris laughed. "Years of searching, and it all came down to pure blind luck. It was safe here, or so we thought. Their bodies were still warm when we found them."

A man's shout drew Alex and Terra's attention back to the front of the cave. A bald demon with red eyes had dropped to his knees and cradled the corpse of his youngest son. The other Fenris howled in anguish over his pups.

A male Nephilim stood, staring at the massacre. His fists trembled with rage, and the red light from his eyes burned brighter. "That's the same Nephilim that you showed us," Terra said. It took a moment, but Alex realized she was right.

"His name is William, after Xorn's human father, but he was simply known as the Nephilim," Fenris said.

Terra looked over at the wolf. "Why's that?"

"He's the last one," the wolf said. "Your child is the first Nephilim to be born in the last eleven billion years. In the war between the First Ones and the Outsiders, William held off the extra-planar beings while the First Ones finished creating the Nine Realms. We are all alive because he served as the first Guardian."

"Whoa, he used the Guardian's Blade?" Alex asked.

Fenris let out a wheezing laugh. "That's right. The angels and demons hated the idea of the most powerful weapon ever made being given to the most power being in existence, but they had no options. William was the only one who could do it, and he paid dearly for it. He was locked out when the Nine Realms were created, but the Guardian's Blade had been made with the Source and was ripped across space and time to go with it when the Nine Realms were created around it."

"So," Alex said, "the angels and demons had to rely on someone they had been hunting and almost killed."

Fenris shook his head. "No. Not almost killed," he said with acid in his voice, "if we had been here, then everyone would still be alive. The three of us would have turned the tide."

"How could you possibly know that?" Terra asked. "You weren't here. You were guessing on what actually happened. What if there had been ten times this number, or a hundred, or a thousand?"

The ancient wolf bared his teeth. "Then I would have died with my mate like I was supposed to."

"And none of us would exist, and all life would have been wiped out from what it sounded like," Alex said. "It's one thing to hope for a different outcome, but it's quite another to believe it would make everything better."

Fenris turned and stared at Alex with a blank expression. "Hi, Pot, I'm the Kettle. Wait, you're telling me I'm black?"

Alex crossed his arms and glared at the wolf. Terra felt confused. "What are you talking about?" she asked.

"It's a saying on his world. It means don't accuse someone of something you are guilty of," Fenris explained.

The Guardian's face flushed, and his heart began to pound. "It's not the same thing. I saved her life! You are wishing you were dead!"

Fenris shook his head. "You don't even know what you really did by destroying the Libram of Fate.

You saved your wife and child, but you threw a rock at a beehive. Brace yourself for the swarm."

Alex's anger immediately cooled, and his brows drew down. "What are you talking about?"

"Take what I told Ureon to tell you to heart, Guardian," Fenris said.

"What, about the Nine Realms growing weak and needing a strong Guardian?" he asked.

The wolf nodded. "That's right. It is time for you two to leave," Fenris said. "I have answered all of your questions, and now I must ask one of my own, and make a demand."

"What's the question?" Terra asked at the same time Alex said, "What do you need?"

The scene of death disappeared, and the three of them stood back in the empty, white landscape. "When you give birth, do it on Earth," Fenris said. "It is imperative that you do this."

"Why?" they both asked at the same time.

"There's not enough time to answer that. Second," Fenris's eyes softened, "what are you going to name him?"

Alex and Terra shared a look. Alex motioned for her to answer. "We are going to name her Jessica."

"A girl!" Fenris shouted, hurting their ears.

"Yes," Terra said, but they had already been forced from Fenris's presence. She removed her hand from the Guardian's Blade and looked at Alex. She couldn't read the tumultuous flow of emotions coming across the link from him, and his face was blank. "What are you thinking about?"

Alex sheathed the Guardian's blade and ran his hand through his hair. "I'll tell you about it later. I'm just trying to figure something out," her husband said.

She nodded and looked around. "Michael, are you there?"

A few second passed, and the Justicar entered the room through the same way they had arrived. "Done already?" he asked.

"Why?" Terra asked. "How long were we here?"

"A few minutes," the einherijar responded. "Time doesn't flow the same when you are inside the tree. I shouldn't be surprised. Did you find answers to your questions?"

"We did," she said. A pulsing feeling of confusion came across the link from Alex. "But I think someone wishes we had enough time for more."

"I can sympathize. I think I left Fenris with more questions than I had when I first saw him." Michael cocked his head to the side for a moment as if he was listening to a faraway voice. "Kara says that the remaining valkyrie are safe in Valgarde. Would you like me to take you there, or are you ready to return home?"

"What about Caitlyn and the others?," Terra said. She grabbed hold of Alex's hand and pulled him along as they walked from the cave beneath Yggdrasil. Her husband was still deep in thought and was paying no attention to anything around him. *What is he thinking so hard about?*

A few minutes of walking, and they were standing before the Cainen gateway arch. "I can use Mjolnir to open a gateway to their campsite."

Terra let out a sigh and suddenly felt exhausted. "I'm ready to go home."

"Very well, Terra," Michael said with a smile. "It's past time you got some rest." The Justicar touched his warhammer to the side of the arch, and a red portal opened. Caitlyn walked to the opening and looked in. She saw Terra and waved.

The Nexus stuck her head through the portal. "We're going home. Come on."

"I'll pack our things," Caitlyn said with a grin.

A few minutes passed, and all of the Daein people walked through the portal and waited on the side with Alex, Terra, and Michael. "What's wrong with Alex?" Ell asked.

"Nothing," Terra's husband muttered. She glanced at him, but he just stood there with his hand on his chin.

Michael closed the portal and tried opening a new one to Dae. He frowned and tried again. "Something is blocking my attempts to open a portal to your Realm," he said with a confused look on his face.

Terra shook her head. "It's the necromancers," she said. "They've been keeping a gateway open to Dae to prevent them from helping here." Terra was silent for a moment while she sensed how much magical energy she still held. *Nowhere near enough to open a portal, much less force one open...*

"Hanna, Ell, Caitlyn, one of you is going to have to open the portal to Dae. I don't have anything left," she said.

The two women and young girl nodded. "Together?" Hanna asked.

Ell smiled. "Together."

"Definitely. I don't think I have enough to force a gateway by myself," Caitlyn said.

The three sorceresses placed hands on the wooden arch and closed their eyes. Terra pulled the Eye of the Stars out of the pouch where she had left it. The portal snapped open, but the keystone seal prevented them from passing through.

"Silvia," Terra said, "we have the portal open. We need to get through."

"Words are insufficient, but I wanted to say thank you for helping me free my world," Michael said with a gentle smile.

Terra gave him a warm embrace. "I'm just glad we're finally safe," she said as she let him go. A few seconds passed, and the portal changed in color from red to gold. The seven people and one prisoner stepped through.

Eternius stood in the center of the Amphitheater of the High Seats. Every one of the angels was in place except for Ureon. *Where are you?* the Keeper wondered. The Seat of Faith had not been seen nor heard from since the Libram of Fate had been destroyed by Alex two days ago.

"A new Libram of Fate must be written immediately," Aurius, the Seat of Honor, said. "The Nine Realms are all in danger because of this false *Guardian*."

Eternius shook his head. "That is not possible," he said. "The necessary energy will not accumulate in the Source for some time. A few years at the soonest."

The Seat of Justice shot to his feet. "The Nexus and the Guardian have broken the most ancient of laws. They must be dealt with." A chorus of shouts agreed with Emiriel.

Are they mad? "No! They are our best chance at defeating Azreal once and for all. Just because the Libram was destroyed does not mean that we should cast what it said aside," Eternius protested.

"The Nephilim are dangerous, Keeper," Ymirion, the Seat of Truth, said. "You yourself said the Nexus was having a female child. Only two have come before, and both killed thousands before they were dealt with." Conversations sprang up around him as the Seats and the angels that had come to watch the meeting talked among themselves.

Why won't they see what's right in front of their faces? Eternius thought. He growled when he realized that was very close to the essence of what the demoness had told him on Aria. "Silence!" he shouted. A hush fell over the place. "I will not condone any action against the Guardian OR the Nexus."

Myrius, the Seat of Intellect, rose to his feet. "I think your vision is being clouded by the fact that your daughter is the one carrying the abomination," he said as he looked down on him. Myrius looked at the other Seats. "Her death was already foretold in the Libram, and I move that we strike against the Nexus as soon as possible."

"What? No!" Eternius shouted. "This is pure folly! The Guardian will not abide the murder of his wife and daughter!"

Aurius, the Seat of Hope and their newest member, rose to her feet. "I support the movement," she said. "If the Guardian stands in our way, then we will cut him down. I recommend an immediate vote on the matter. All in favor?" Every Seat in attendance spoke out in favor of the plan, rendering Eternius's opinion invalid.

Ureon, if only you had been here, I know you could have made them see sense. "Then you fools have doomed us all," Eternius snapped. In a fit of rage, he tore the mythricite armor from his body that was the mark of his station. Every piece of armor that crashed to the ground sounded like the blow of a hammer.

Eternius stood before the Angelic Council in his white shirt, leggings, and boots he wore beneath his armor. The Traveler's Pendant hung outside his shirt. The Keeper of Faith lifted his chin high, and fanned his wings out behind him.

"What is the meaning of this?" Lyriel, the Seat of Love, whispered. The acoustics of the amphitheater made her soft words carry well enough for all to hear.

Eternius squared his shoulders and said the irrevocable. "I, Eternius the First, abdicate my position as Keeper of Fate and all duties associated with the post. May the Source illuminate the path for those who follow in my steps." The angel took a liberating breath.

"I hope the First Ones have mercy on your souls, because the Guardian won't." There was a thump in the air, and Eternius stepped through the gray portal.

Azreal stood on Ignia and waited for Great Lord to appear. The Overlord knew he wouldn't survive the encounter with the Outsider, but that there was no point in running. The only reason he had come to meet with the phantasmal being was to try for a fast death. *If I attack it with everything I have, then it will be forced to kill me.*

<Overlord,> the Outsider sent, <you have served me well on Caine.>

Azreal looked around, but he could not see the Outsider's shadowy form in the shifting fog. "I don't understand," he said. "The Realm was liberated."

There was a hissing sound behind him, and Azreal spun. The Great Lord hovered, it's shape seeming to fluctuate as he stared at it. <You were never meant to keep the Realms you had captured. The Nine Realms cannot be destroyed from the inside or the outside.>

"Then why did I invade the other Realms at all?" Azreal demanded.

<It would do you well to show more care in the way you address me, Fleshling. The only reason you have not been replaced is because events are in motion that hinge upon swift execution. Domination or destruction of any Realm was not our goal.>

Something is happening here. "I thought we were bringing about the end of all things. You told me the Nine Realms will be bathed in purging fire."

<I told you what you needed to hear,> the Outsider snapped. <I have led you by the hand, and you have served me well, but now the time has come for a new initiative, a reward of sorts I know you will enjoy. We must strike in the unlikeliest place to keep the Inner Realms off balance. To keep them from discovering our true play.>

Azreal's brows drew down in confusion. "What are you suggesting?"

<There is one place that demons have never roamed free. One place the goodly races will be forced to save to preserve their precious balance.>

"But a strike against Aria is impossible. Portals can't be opened there."

A rippling rift appeared in the air. It shimmered in variegated hues. <You think far too small, Azreal. The impossible becomes possible with the correct application of force.>

A second Outsider floated through the rift in space and time. The hole closed behind him. <It is time,> the newcomer sent into Azreal's mind.

Epilogue – Mommy

Terra screeched as the pain radiated from her stomach to encompass the whole of her being. She needed to push; her body screamed for it; she had to push. The half-angel started to bear down, but Alex's crushing grip on her hand vaulted her back from the urge.

"Not yet, Babe. It isn't time yet. We're almost there," he said. "Where the hell is Hanna?"

"She's coming," Ell said. "Darren went to get her. Caitlyn help me open this."

The contraction slowly passed, and Terra let out a shaking breath. "Alex," she rasped, "you're hurting my hand."

"I know," he said.

HE KNOWS HE'S HURTING MY HAND! "Let go," she growled. Alex eased his grip but didn't release her.

"No," the man responsible for her pain said. "I'm not letting you go through this alone."

Terra glared at him and started to pant faster when she felt her muscles tightening again. She clamped her eyes closed and whimpered. *Oh, no, not again, I'm not ready.* Terra gritted her teeth together in an attempt to quell the scream rising through her.

"I know it hurts, Terra. It's almost over. Only a little longer," Alex said.

"You do NOT know what this feels like," she snapped. Opening her mouth to answer him turned into a mistake when she couldn't contain the howl that escaped her lips.

"I didn't say that I did," her husband clarified. "I said I know it hurts."

The contraction began to subside. Terra wanted to tell him she wanted to kill him for putting her through this, but she refused the impulse. As soon as they returned to Dae two days ago, Alex had ordered a cloth stretcher made and kept in the house. He and Darren had carried her on it at a sprint to the gateway arch as soon as the labor pains started.

Terra noticed that a soft, grey light bathed the area around her. "I'm here!" Hanna shouted.

"Good, let's go." Alex and Caitlyn grabbed the top and bottom of the stretcher and carried Terra through with Hanna by her side.

The woman felt a tingling suffuse her lower body, and the pain faded away. Terra looked at Hanna and said, "Oh, thank you, you perfect girl. How did you do that?"

"You won't like it," the young changeling said after they had passed onto Earth. A few balls of light bathed the room in a warm yellow glow.

Terra felt the urge to push, but it was more distant now. The pain was more a general sense of discomfort than the screaming blast it had been. "I doubt there's anything you could tell me to make me angry with you right now," Terra said.

"I disagree, but I'll tell you anyway. I've been talking to Doctor Moore, specifically about how the brain works," Hanna said as they settled Terra down on the bed.

"You've been doing WHAT?" the Nexus shouted.

"Terra, keep it down, or you'll wake the neighbors," Alex said.

She looked around. They were back in the apartment she and Alex had shared. "We'll talk about this later," she said to him. "What have you been doing talking to that bastard?" she asked Hanna.

The little girl sighed. "It's obvious that his understanding of anatomy is far beyond what we have access to on Dae. He's the one that told me how pain works, and I figured out how to make a spell that blocks it. If you don't approve of me using something I learned from him, I could always remove the spell from you," Hanna said.

"No! No. I don't approve of how you attained the knowledge, but I'm not going to complain."

Hanna smirked triumphantly. *She's been spending too much time with Alex... Wait a second...* "How did you get the idea to ask Moore about that?" Alex cleared his throat, and Terra glared at him again. "I am officially angry with you," she said.

Before Alex could say anything, Hanna lifted Terra's heels into the air and held them in place on small beds of air. "You two can argue after we get this baby out of you," she said. Terra felt herself become buoyed up into the air as Hanna wove a larger bed of force beneath her. "I need you to push on your next contraction."

"All right," Terra said. She felt her stomach grow tight, and the need to push, though faint, nudged against her mind. Terra bore down as hard as she could. The contraction faded, but she felt as if she hadn't done anything.

"That was good," Hanna said. "She moved down most of the way with that last one. I think the bubble around her is helping. Come on, Terra, one more push, and you get to hold your little girl."

Terra nodded and closed her eyes. The urge to push swelled again. She took a deep breath and pushed. There was a popping sound, and Terra saw a spiral of lights whirl up to the ceiling.

"She's beautiful," Alex said with a huge grin and tears in his eyes.

A few seconds passed, and Hanna said, "Hello, Jessica, I'm Hanna. It's nice to finally see you. I'm going to hand you to your daddy now so I can take care of your mommy." The changeling handed the baby to Alex. "She's fine. Healthy. Do you have any sterile needle and thread?"

Alex took Jessica from her and smiled down at her. "Hello, Beautiful," he cooed. Alex glanced at Hanna. "Yeah, there's a medical kit in the bathroom under the sink. Big, red bag with a yellow cross on it."

"Good. Caitlyn go get it for me." The older changeling nodded and almost ran into the bathroom.

Terra was exhausted from having endured the pain of labor up until they came through the portal to Earth. She felt lightheaded from the effort. "Can I hold her?" Terra asked.

Alex turned his grin to her. "Of course Mommy can hold the baby." He handed Jessica to her, and Terra saw her daughter for the first time. She had one green eye and one hazel one, and a matted mass of brown hair. When the light showed through only a few strands, it looked dark red.

Caitlyn ran back in from the bathroom and tossed the bag to Hanna. The little girl ripped the bag open and began tearing through it looking for the needle and thread. "What's wrong?" Alex asked.

Jessica seemed to be breathing at a normal rate, and she looked around with curiousity. Terra's eyelids started to feel heavy. "Alex," Terra whispered. "Take the baby. So tired, don't want to drop her."

Alex reached down and picked up Jessica at the same time Hanna said, "She's bleeding out! I can't stop the bleeding." As soon as Jessica left Terra's chest she started to cry.

Terra's eyes fluttered closed, and the last thing she heard was a tiny voice say, "Mommy."

Continued in Earth on Fire:
Book Three of the Nine Realms Series

Prologue of
Earth on Fire
Book Three of the Nine Realms Series

Prologue – The Fire is Lit

Max Gilroy looked at the kid he had brought on to help him five months ago. Joshua Hrynkiewicz had looked like a half-drowned sewer rat when he had tried robbing the small electronics store Max owned back in spring. The younger man had turned twenty last week, and Max had treated him to a gourmet dinner of pizza and soda. *I had the extra room in my apartment for him to stay in anyway. I'll save money with him paying half the rent.*

"Everything's done and ready for us to open, Mister Gilroy," Josh said.

Max let out a sigh. "If you call me Mister Gilroy again, I'm going to rip off your arms and beat you to death with them." The retired Marine was certainly large enough to perform the feat, but he had threatened the boy with dismemberment many times before to no avail.

Josh laughed at the statement as he always did. "Whatever you say, Boss." The kid unlocked the door and sat back behind the counter, all puffed up and proud. It was the first time Max had let him open the store by himself. The owner of the shop trusted the young man to perform all of his duties with a meticulous attention to detail, and after the recent business sale Josh landed increased their annual sales by a significant margin, Max decided to give him the combination to the floor safe where he kept the on-hand money for the day to day operations of the shop.

"It's always a bit before the first customer rolls in, Josh, let's turn on the news and see what's going on in the world." The young man picked up the television controller and pushed the power button.

A found-footage style horror movie was on. "Run!" the woman on the screen screamed. "Oh, God, what is that thing!" An eight-legged monstrosity that Max couldn't describe any better than a cross between a man and a spider leapt from the side of a building and landed on the woman. Blood and gore spattered everywhere as the thing attacked her.

That looked extremely realistic. Crazy special effects these days. "Come on, kid, put it on the news." Max looked at Josh and saw his face was white as a sheet. "What?"

"I never changed the channel yesterday. This *is* the news," he said just as the image changed to a woman and man sitting in a newsroom. The blonde woman's hands shook, and the man looked to have just vomited off camera.

"We apologize for those scenes of graphic violence," the woman said, her voice hardly louder than a whisper. A hand from off-screen tried handing her a paper, but it took her a moment to steady herself enough to reach for it. "The President has ordered an immediate evacuation of the following cities: Seattle, Washington; New York City, New York; Los Angeles, California; Houston, Texas; and Atlanta, Georgia. If you live within seventy-five miles of these cities, gather what non-perishable items you can, and evacuate to the northern central United States."

Everything began to shake as an earthquake struck the city. The power went out, dust fell from overhead, and the two men hunched down next to the wooden counter. The light from the windows was cast into shade as something enormous ran by outside. "Did you see that thing?" Josh shouted. "What the hell was that?"

Max shook his head. "I saw it, but I've got no fucking clue what it was." He reached behind the counter and pulled out his Mossberg shotgun. *I wish I had The Baby with me, but what the hell was I going to do with a .50 caliber machine gun in an electronics store.* Max set the shotgun down on the counter and grabbed the Remington Josh had tried to use to rob him. He handed the cheaper shotgun to the kid. "You know how to use that?"

Josh shook his head, his face was still white. "I've never shot it before."

"Kid, look at me," Max said. He tore his wide eyes from the window and slowly turned his head to look at Max. "I need you to keep it together, Josh. I don't know what's going on. I won't let anything happen to you, but you have to stay in the moment. Don't worry about what you don't see. Just do what I tell you, and everything will be fine. Do you understand?"

"Y-yeah," Josh stuttered out.

"Come on, Josh. I need you to do better than that. Do you understand?"

Josh took a deep breath and some color returned to his face. "I understand. How do I use this?" he said, lifting the gun a little.

Max took it from him and showed him the basics. "This is the safety, push it through to engage the trigger. There's a round in the breech already. Pump it after each shot. Other than that, it's a simple point and click interface." Max held the gun out to Josh. The younger man put his hands on the shotgun, but Max didn't release it. "Rule number one: do not point the gun at anything you do not intend to destroy."

"I got it," Josh said as he nodded. Max let go of the shotgun just as the windows shattered. The retired

Marine snatched his larger shotgun from the floor, and his left ear rang when Josh's gun fired.

Max swung his gun forward, but Josh's shot had obliterated the man/spider thing's head. "The floor safe still open in the back?" Max asked.

"Yeah."

Max glanced over his shoulder at the young man he had come to respect. "Good, get the cash, shells, and our lunches. We need to stop by the apartment and pick up a few things."

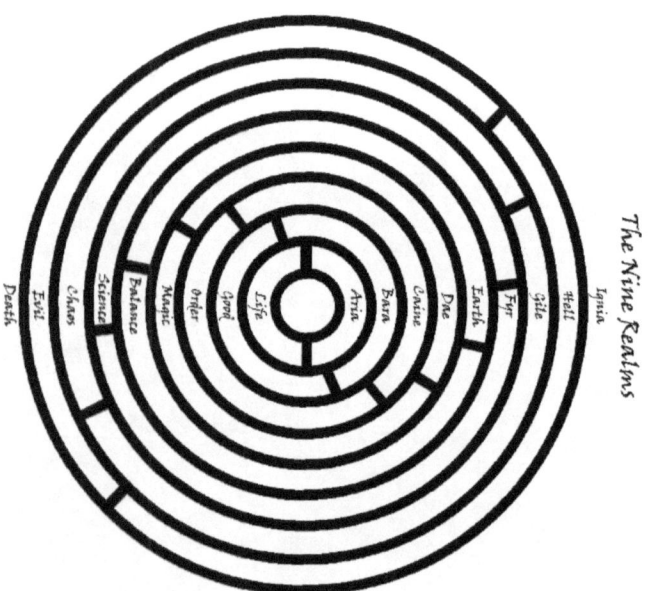

The Nine Realms

Death · Evil · Chaos · Science · Balance · Magic · Order · Good · Life · Aria · Bara · Daine · Dae · Earth · Fyr · Gile · Hell · Ignia

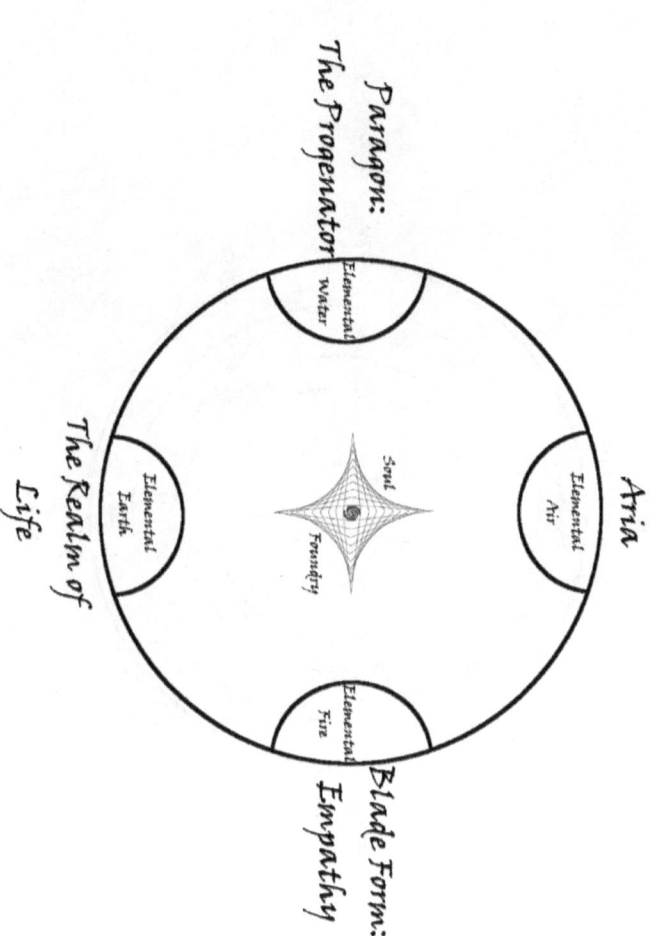

Paragon:
The Progenitor

Aria

The Realm of
Life

Blade Form:
Empathy

Elemental
Water

Elemental
Air

Soul

Foundry

Elemental
Earth

Elemental
Fire

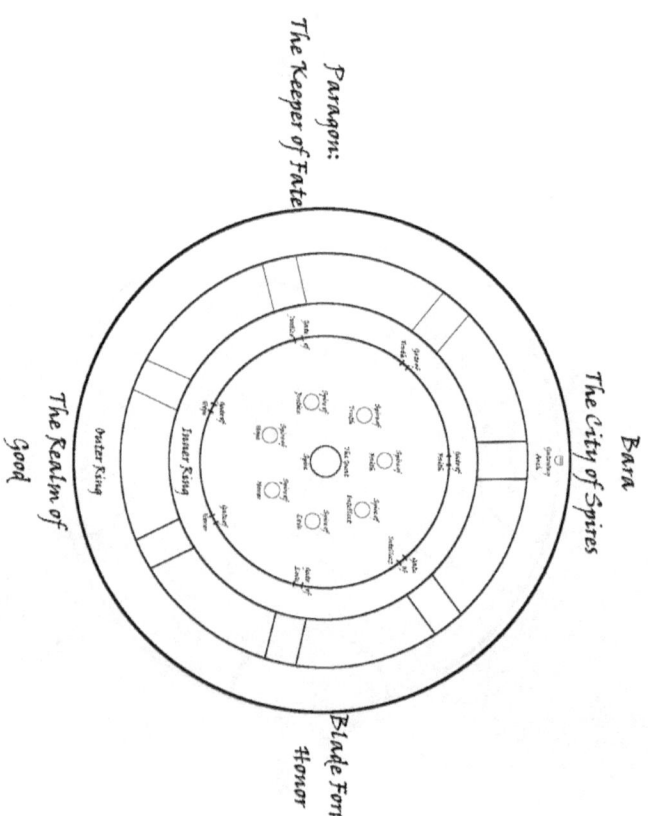

Bara

The City of Spires

Paragon:
The Keeper of Fate

The Realm of
Good

Blade Form:
Honor

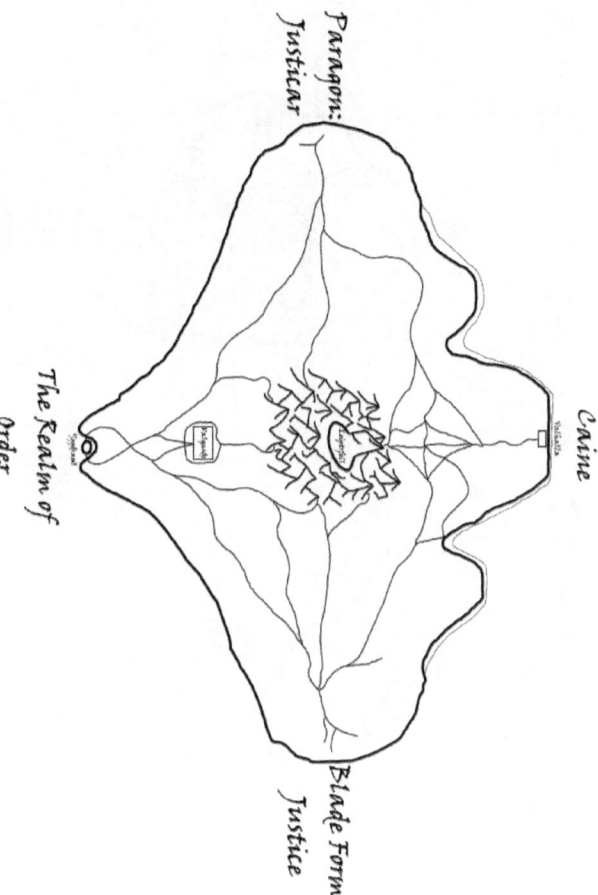

Paragon:
Justicar

Caine

The Realm of
Order

Blade Form:
Justice

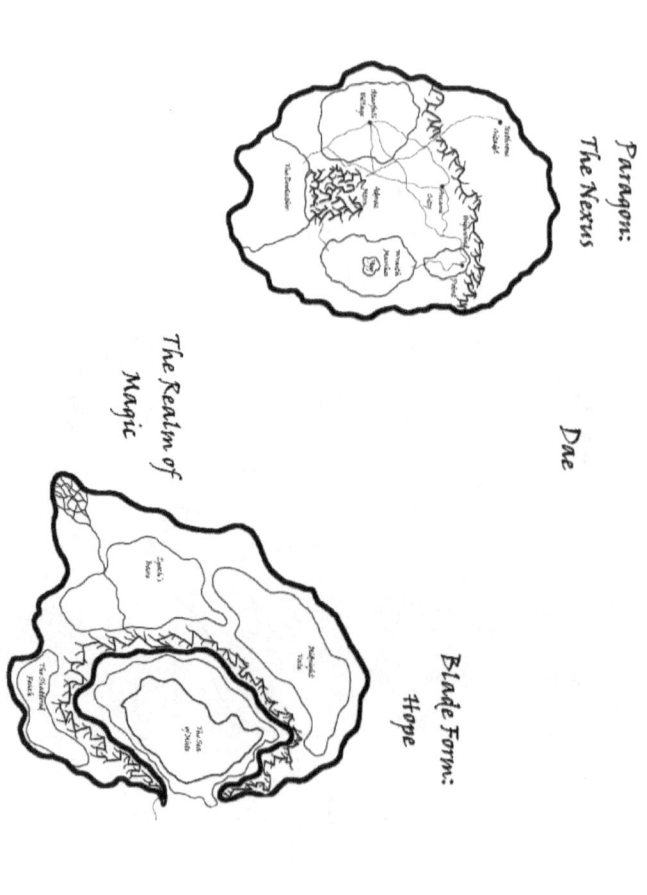

Paragon:
The Nexus

Dae

The Realm of
Magic

Blade Form:
Hope

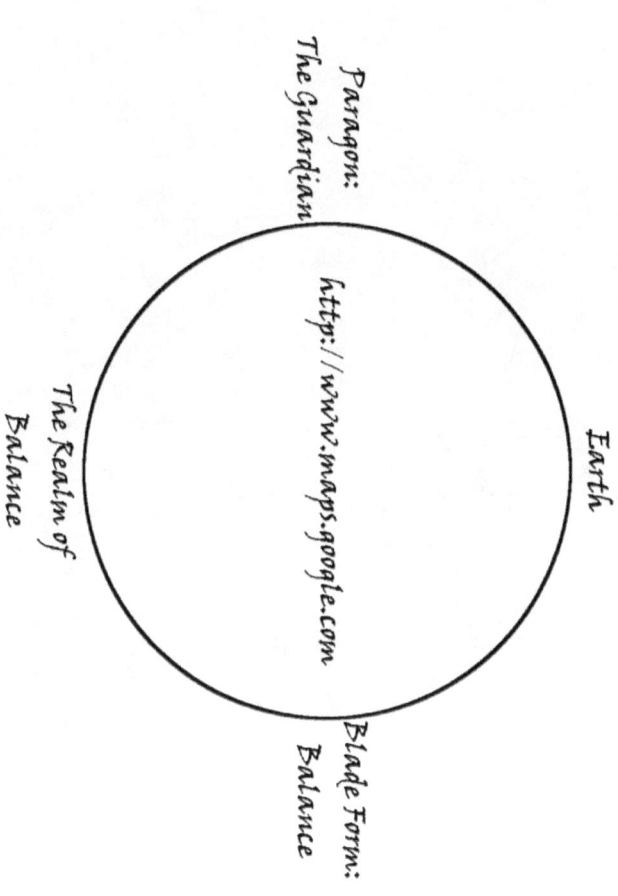

Earth

Paragon:
The Guardian

http://www.maps.google.com

The Realm of
Balance

Blade Form:
Balance

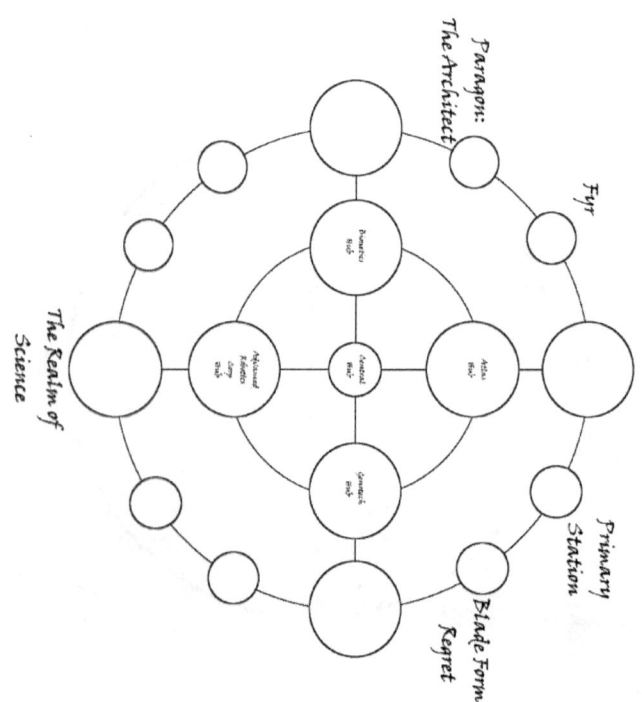

Gile

Mutable and ever-changing, the strongest
wills and minds control the landscape,
causing mountains and lakes, buildings
and cities to appear and vanish on a whim.
Little is known of Gile and the Effreet that
call it home, and the Effreet are more than
willing to share what they know,
for a fee of course.
The Realm of Chaos

Paragon:
The Voidwalker

Blade Form:
Torment

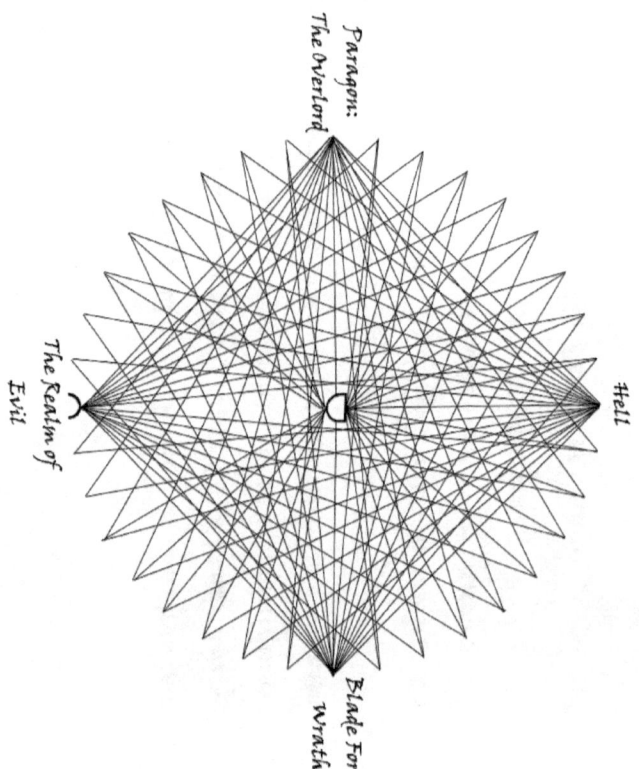

Paragon:
The Overlord

Hell

The Realm of
Evil

Blade Form:
Wrath

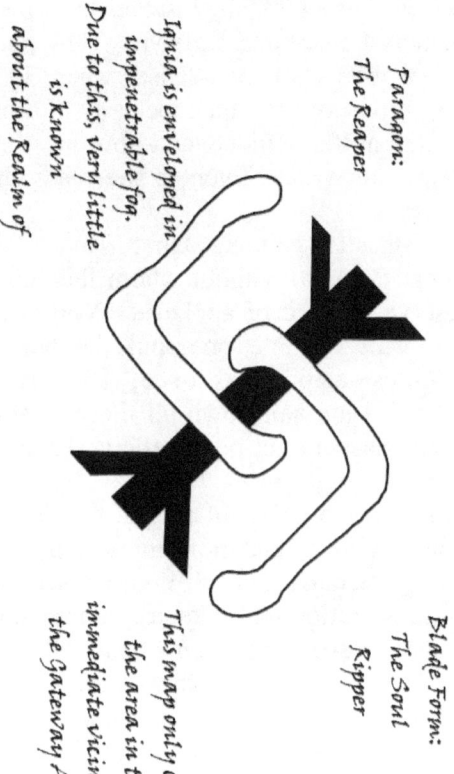

Igrisia

Paragon:
The Reaper

Igrisia is enveloped in
impenetrable fog.
Due to this, very little
is known
about the Realm of
Death.

The Realm of
Death.

Blade Form:
The Soul
Ripper

This map only covers
the area in the
immediate vicinity of
the Gateway Arch.

Acknowledgments

Once again, I find it impossible to include everyone that's helped me with this book, but I'll do my best to catch as many as possible.

The real heroes of all this are my wife Jennifer and daughters Lainey and Katelyn. They put up with my random bouts of non-sense when I suddenly become inspired to write an especially clever passage down, and Jennifer will never know how much she really helps me write. Even if she reads this. (Hi, Babe!)

My fantastic editors, Janet Taylor-Perry and Lottie Brent Boggan, without whom this my may not exist, deserve a round of applause. You can clap for them; I'll wait. Come one, put the book/e-reader down. You can clap at least once. These two miracle workers helped me nail down all those errant phrases and all that exasperating punctuation. Thank you two immensely.

Adding to the group of people that have no idea how much they've helped me commit to paper over the years are my amazing family. Your constant stream of praise and inspiration really keeps me tapping away at the keyboard. Never stop, even when I tell you to.

The 2012-13 crew of the Coast Guard Cutter Mellon deserve a shout-out here as well. They read this book when it was in its most basic form, and they always gave me the best feedback. You guys all rock.

The watch team at Coast Guard Sector Mobile Command Center, especially Christina, Hillary, and James. Ya'll's input on the first and second books have really helped give me some ideas for the third and fourth books.

And last, but not least, thank you! If it weren't

for my fantastic fans, I would never be inspired to write. Your kind words keep me going, and I look forward to us telling many more stories together.

About the Author

Mark Cole is an Operations Specialist in the United States Coast Guard and is currently stationed in Mobile, Alabama. He lives there with his wife and two daughters.

If you have any questions, comments, or just want to tell Mark how much you loved his story (Aren't you so sweet), feel free to contact him at mcthew@outlook.com or www.facebook.com/mcthew

www.ingramcontent.com/pod-product-compliance
Lightning Source LLC
Chambersburg PA
CBHW030553180626
46816CB00005B/1530